Wheel

Wolf

Wheel

Wolf

Nail-Biting Bone-Chilling Horror

January Valentine

Printed in the United States of America

ISBN- 13: 978-0615873350 (Paperback)
ISBN- 10: 0615873359

Library of Congress Control Number: 2013948825

Book Design by Victoria Valentine
Edited by: Phaedra Valentine
Cover Art by Vin Hill (https://www.facebook.com/VinHillArt)
Wheel Wolf is also available in Kindle version and audiobook on Amazon.

Water Forest Press Books
PO Box 295, Stormville, NY 12582
waterforestpress.com

January Valentine Books

Love Dreams Contemporary Romance
Michael is in a wheelchair. Sienna has been emotionally damaged. They keep having accidental run-ins, but can they find love?

Sweet Dreams in the Mind of a Serial Killer
He plants roses ... in dead women. A witness says: He doesn't look human.

Fighting For You Steamy Contemporary Romance
Jewelia wants to work for the NYPD. Indigo is a medical student with baggage. They come from two different worlds. Can they beat the odds?

Beautiful Experiment Paranormal Romance Book One of The Island of Defiance Trilogy

Six unruly teens are kidnapped, sent to an uncharted island. Caretaker, Brook, is hot. Father is mysterious. Will they find a way home before the island is overrun with demons?

All titles are available on Amazon, B & N and through other booksellers in print and ebook format.

Find all of my books on my Amazon Author page
http://www.amazon.com/January-Valentine/e/B007Q28DFE/

I think we all have to fight the werewolf within us somehow.
—William Kempe

January Valentine

Wheel Wolf

My werewolf ... my second skin ...
When the moon is on the rise,
I go naked into night.
I am never dressed to kill.
                            —January Valentine

You try to be a decent human being,
but sometimes the world is just so evil,
it's all about ... REVENGE!
                            —January Valentine

January Valentine

Wheel Wolf

Prologue

The stage lights burned out with the sun
while the moon fell into a sea of blood
a lone wolf howls to a starless sky
no night; no day
in longing desperation
hungers for his departed
stormy eyes flood eternity
separation, unbearable
soon he shall perish
body and soul into void
mind racing to the brink of insanity
screams unheard, so loud as to deafen
the ears of the one who cries out with anguish
too weak to live; too strong to die
lights faded, deserted stage
death is calm
the peace not found in living hell

January Valentine

Another Time, Another Place

The storm blew into the Pacific Northwest with fury, battering the mortuary with such force, the woman feared the plate glass windows would shatter, and the rich mahogany caskets might float down the hall with rainwater and splintered glass.

She stalked the length of the showroom, lowering polished lids, drawing velvet draperies closed.

"I can save the wood," she lost her breath to the lifeless room, "but if these plush linings get soaked they'll mildew. Who wants to foot the bill for someone to be buried in a moldy casket? Leave that to the earth they're entombed in." Her pinched nose sniffed the musty air that had scented the room for as long as she could recall.

The power clicked off and the place went dark. A gulp caught in her throat. She snapped on the flashlight she always carried in a pocket, anticipating nights like this, which came often. The batteries were practically drained. Maybe tapping the casing would buy more time.

A wolf's howl punctured the night, seeping in with icy wind through an open kitchen window. The wolf sounded close, which interrupted the woman's thoughts, and her displeasure of the power failure flew to the back of her mind. Another high-pitched wail charged the air, and the tiny hairs on the back of her neck. What flowed into her ears were solitary howls, and not followed by the usual chorus of the timber wolves' bark she had come to know all too well during her lifelong existence in the ghastly town.

Lightning scorched the air, but only for a moment while thunder rocked the house with unnerving concussions.

Her husband's heavy footsteps creaked up the stairs and paused in the archway. She knew the sound his feet made, and the pungent aroma of his skin: hearty spice mixed with sweat. In the storm's momentary silence, his calloused fingers could be heard sliding across the stippled wall as he gained his footing and leveled his bearings.

His bellow filled the stillness. "Some storm. When did we lose power?" His breath came faster as he groped his way around a corner. "Sounded like something crashed into the ..."

Her voice sped across the darkness. "We lost the power an hour ago. Where were you?"

"Working downstairs. The lights flickered, guess the emergency generator kicked on without me realizing."

"I've run out of batteries," she moaned, clutching the collar of her robe to her throat. "Why can't you connect the upstairs circuits to the generator?" Her whine resembled the pitch of the wolf's. He despised her pissing and moaning, along with a few other things, but still, she was a good cook and housekeeper.

His grim voice, indicating a scowling mouth, grew closer as his feet shuffled on the carpet. "It's a small unit. You know it can't power the entire house."

"The wolves are about." She shivered a whisper. He imagined the fear in her eyes. "I've been hearing them a lot lately."

"It's breeding season." Patience evaporated, his tone turned tart.

"But this one was different. It had a distinct tone. Warning or ..."

"Attracting a mate," the husband clucked.

"It didn't sound like any mating call I've ever heard. In fact, I've never heard anything quite like it." She pulled her robe so close, the collar met her lips. "It almost had a human edge to it."

Another howl resonated, this one low-pitched and menacing, louder than the thunder which was finally ebbing.

"I see what you mean. That doesn't sound like a mating call." He honed in on her location, and shuffled in another direction. "Perhaps it's a lone wolf crying for a lost mate."

"Or it's hunting," she croaked, and as she sought a safe corner, a lamp wobbled on a cherry wood tabletop.

"You're letting the dark get the better of you. Come down to the crypt. The lights are on."

"Please. I see enough dead bodies all day. I don't need them at night. I'm sick of touching dead bodies, talking to dead bodies, smelling dead bodies." Her sigh rattled with phlegm from a past pneumonia that had almost gotten the better of her. "I'd rather sit in the dark."

"And brood," he grumbled, stumbling into his wingback chair. He lit the last cigarette in the pack crushed into his breast pocket. The flickering flame brightened the grooves in his face. His lips puckered, his cheeks hollowed, and the glowing red tip arced as the moist end was plucked from his lips.

Something hopeful filled her otherwise sallow voice. "A nice young fellow called about the apprenticeship. Said he's new in town. Likes it here. Wants to settle into a career. Sounds like a good candidate."

"I can't believe you're bringing a stranger into the business ... our home." He puffed out annoyance with a feathering stream of smoke that circled his head like a halo. She noticed this when a rogue clip of lightning burst through the undraped window beside her.

As her eyes readjusted, her husband became a silhouette again, not a ghost. "We'll be dead and buried and the business will still be here. My back is killing me, and your daughter doesn't want any part of it. Not that I blame her. It's a dying business." A derisive laugh ripped from her throat, rattling the phlegm again. "Let someone else make the killing."

"Where *is* Lucy?" His annoyance escalated. The burning red tip of his cigarette grew brighter.

"Where does Lucy ever go? Out. That's all I know. She tells me nothing."

"A fifteen year old belongs home by nine. Ten the latest. You should keep a better eye on her."

"Like you? When you pull her into that closet down there?" She pointed to the direction he had come from, the stairs leading down to the embalming room.

"What's wrong with you? You make everything dirty. I'm trying to show her the ropes, that's all." He mumbled a curse she couldn't quite decipher, but imagined it to be one of his four letter favorites. "I've got plenty of company downstairs that never complains."

"The fat six inch rope? Is that what you're referring to?" She spat the words that had held her hostage for so long. "You're sick. You know that? I should have left you years ago."

An interruption pounded at the front of the house. "Who the hell could that be at this hour?" She fixed her robe and groped her way down the hall to peer through the glass paned entry door and straight into the headlights of a van. "For heaven sake," she cried to her husband, shielding her eyes from the blinding beams. "Did you expect a delivery tonight?" She yanked the door open and poked her head out.

Wheel Wolf

A man shifted from foot to foot, blowing on his bare hands. "Good evening."

"Good evening? It's almost midnight," she snarled. "Bring it to the back."

The man, who worked for the coroner's office, nodded and faded into a chilling mist.

The coroner's deliverymen hated coming here. They resented her nastiness, her wrath, but if they wanted jobs they had no choice. Employment didn't exactly grow on area trees, so one held his tongue and did what he was told.

As ordered, the deliveryman and his partner showed up at the back of the mortuary. On screeching gurneys they rolled two cadaver bags stuffed with mangled victims through the doorway where the husband stood smiling.

"Doubt there's much you can do with these," one warned the husband who ushered both men into receiving, an alcove adjoining the embalming room.

"Oh, I don't know about that. My skills are noteworthy." The overhead light flickered; *the generator must be running out of gas.*

The man who had stood on the front porch tried to swipe his face dry by dabbing with the edge of the sweater he pulled through his vinyl coat sleeve. Again, he shifted from foot to foot, scrubbing his hands together. "Terrible accident out on the old Cross Bridge Highway." Although the storm had dwindled, his raingear glistened.

As the husband, also known as the mortician, laid a hand on one of the thick plastic bags, the house lights sprang on with a surge of power. When the entire place glowed, they all jumped. All but the mortician, who was about to examine the corpses. "Damp, still warm though. No autopsies?" He stared at the bags as the coroner's men exchanged a concerned glance. They knew they were not supposed to use the van's heater while transporting cargo, but the night had been so raw.

The mortician didn't notice, or perhaps he didn't care. His eyes were too busy for concern.

"Nope. Coroner was at the scene. Took care of the paperwork. They're all yours." The deliverymen edged toward the door, where a brisk wind curled around the peeling wood frame.

"And you ask why I've quit my job without notice?" The wife, leaning on the door casing, not actually standing in the small room, smarted off in front of the coroner's men. Her only display of vulnerability was the way she hugged her midsection.

The following day, the young man who had responded to the help wanted advertisement arrived promptly at noon, as scheduled by phone. The wife immediately took to him; the husband had no choice but to hire him.

"He's big and strong and healthy looking," she drummed. "And since you need help hauling corpses, washing the bodies, shampooing the hair, manicuring the fingernails," she smirked, "all the odd jobs I've always done ..."

His stern jaw and narrowed eyes stopped her. "I'll still handle the emptying of the stomach and intestines, of course. Draining blood from the veins, pumping in chemicals." His chest puffed importantly. "Aspirating the bodies with the air pump for a rounded, healthy appearance."

"Yes. I know you make the dead look alive. Do you want a medal?"

He shook his head and left her standing in the kitchen, cleaning up after dinner.

"He'll have the extra room downstairs," she called after her husband. "He's awfully handsome. Our daughter will probably be spending a lot more time at home. Did you see the way he looked at her?" She scraped mashed potatoes from a pot then scrubbed it, mumbling to herself. "Love at first sight, I tell you." When the howl of a wolf all but sliced the room in half, she slammed the window over the sink shut.

"Over my dead body," the husband bellowed from the next room. "He'll not be with *my* daughter. Helpful or not, if that boy doesn't keep his lips and hands to himself, I swear by the balls I was born with, he's fired."

The wife was stunned. The husband was rarely this alpha. Maybe when they'd first married, and he'd impregnated her with Lucy, but over the years he'd mellowed into the mush he was today.

That very night, the man and woman were awakened from a dead sleep by a flashlight trained on their twitching eyelids. Bound and gagged, they were hauled downstairs, dragged into the showroom, and sealed inside caskets. Under polished mahogany and through closed windows, no one heard their blood-curdling screams.

They weren't discovered for a week. By the time the coroner's deliverymen lifted the lids of the caskets, the husband's and wife's fingernails were torn off, hands caked with blood, and they were stark raving mad. The state had the couple committed. A relative reported Lucy missing.

January Valentine

Jenny's Porch; Tonight, New York

*W*hoever said "think of life as you do the weather" needs to revise his quote. Sure, both are unpredictable. Indecisive. The weatherman isn't always on target, but at least he can tell you to stuff a poncho into your backpack, 'cos there's a sixty percent chance the sky's gonna rock with one of the meanest storms of the season. Who's around to warn you not to stop at the lake on your way home from your girlfriend's house? Avoid dusty back roads because you never know what you'll run into.

The moon is full and crimson, as though a beating heart at the core is pumping blood through its craters.

It's a warm spring night. Breezy. Smells like musty leaves and pine. Early blossoms. All kinds of good karma surrounding me, reminding me of her.

Jenny is the best thing that's ever happened to me. Since I'm standing on her front porch, I don't need to be reminded. Gazed at by a pair of dreamy violet eyes, grinned at by lips still rosy from mine, is melting me, gluing me to the two planks my boots have been planted on for the past fifteen minutes. The aroma of the dinner cooked by her mother lingers. Pot roast and potatoes.

Almost like my mom used to make ...

My fingers slip around Jenny's waist, mosey up her back, bringing her sleek black hair over one velvet shoulder. Wrapping a satin skein around my fist, I pull her into me. "Mmm." I nuzzle her throat, growl softly against her peach-scented skin. "You taste so good."

She giggles. "You want to taste something good? Try this."

She's hanging on my shoulder, draping herself around my side. One of her smooth legs is climbing mine. Her body is so toned, I feel the tension of her calf muscle beneath my jeans. That's not all I feel.

"Come on. Open up." She's taunting me with a home baked donut, gliding it back and forth inches from my nose.

Now she's on tiptoes, and the sound of her laughter washes every thought from my mind. Every thought other than how to dodge the plump, doughy thing that's being shoved at my mouth, because I've already made a pig of myself.

Arms wrapped around her, I'm trying to shove her off, pulling my head back and straining away. I'm laughing. "I can't, babe. I won't be able to button my uniform. Rule number one: spotless and wrinkle free, professionally dressed at all times. I'll be written up for insubordination before I even start my new job."

Starting with my deltoid, the fingers of her free hand squeeze their way down my arm. She shakes her head, making the cutest clicking sound with her tongue. "Never happen. You're solid muscle, Jack Bailey." Her eyes fill with a passion that elevates mine. Which doesn't take much. A glimpse, even a thought is enough to do it. "The fittest ranger that will ever roam these forests. Devoting himself to our wildlife." She's lifting a brow, warning, "And that better be all, because you know how some women around here have a tendency to jump hot guys in sexy uniforms."

"You mean like you did to me in ninth grade before I had a chance to make it to the locker room?" I shoot her a snarky grin, waiting for her reaction.

I'll never forget how she looked at me that September day. Kind of how she's looking at me now. Eyes sparkling, like there's a secret longing to spring off her tongue, and I'm the one she wants to share it with.

She punches the same arm she just complimented. Her shoulders shudder with an unrestrained bout of laughter, and her silken hair ruffles as her head dips and lifts. She squeezes her cheeks into adorable twin dimples, then tries to act flippant. "What can I say? You looked so cute in your gym shorts. I've got a thing for hairy guys." She runs her fingers through my hair, tugging on a handful. "And no cutting this. Ever. Not even if your superiors want you to, 'cos they'll have to deal with my wrath." She pushes a thick lock behind my ear, then a delicate finger brushes aside a few long strands that all but conceal my stare.

"You've got a thing for defenseless animals, you mean." I drop a kiss on her forehead. I can't believe she's mine, and feel clingy for making her confirm it every damn time I fall into one of these pathetic moods. "Tell me you'll always be here." My lips dig into the notch at the base of her neck, while I block the memory of how I lost my parents. Almost a year ago. Naturally would have been bad enough ... or to an accident. But a robbery homicide while on vacation?

The throbbing veins in my head beat with my heart as I swallow the pain. Robbed and thrown overboard tied to an anchor isn't a picture easily erased. Neither is the fact that I should have been there to protect them. I fight off a wave of nausea, then gaze into Jenny's eyes again, because she's the only thing that keeps me alive. Grounded.

"Oh Jack." Her lips sink onto mine, slowly sliding across my cheek as she whispers, "As soon as I'm finished with school, I'll be there with you." Her breath is sweet. She takes my face in her hands. Rubs her nose against mine. "I know how difficult it is, how sad it is being in that house alone. So empty, but full of memories. We'll make our own soon, baby."

"We have already, Jenny. The first day I set eyes on you the clock started ticking." I tap my forehead. "Everything's stored right in here. Forever."

Her eyes hold mine. She presses a kiss onto her index finger and with it, crosses my lips. "Forever ..."

When I sigh, my lids fall into a long blink. Even after six years, nothing has changed. We're still new. Exciting. I want to sweep her off the porch, throw her over a shoulder, hop onto my bike, take off for parts unknown. Just Jenny and me. Me and Jenny. Forever.

My eyes scroll her face, stalling on her plush lips. I pluck the full bottom, but my gaze is fixed on the cupid's bow that drives me nuts. I trace the perfect outline of my kissable favorites, then run my fingertip up her soft cheek, across an arched brow. "Yeah. You've got a way with strays." I smooth her hair back, nibble on her earlobe. Slide my palms up and down her back. Hungry. She makes me so hungry. I'll never get enough of this girl. As long as I live ... she'll be all I ever need.

The interior lights are glaring, so is her father as he peers out the picture window, attempting to zero in on us through dusk. I shoot him a lopsided grin, a respectful nod, then swing my head away, chuckling, because he should have seen us an hour ago, upstairs in her room. Her bedspread might never be the same.

"Baby, I better go." I slide the tip of my middle finger over the massacred donut before she tries to hide it behind her back.

When she grins up at me, I smear the white powdery sugar down the slope of her nose, planting my fingerprint onto the sculpted tip. "There. You're stamped and ready for delivery. Number One Bailey Way. Express mail ..."

I'm slipping into my black leather jacket that I retrieve from the porch swing, because I'm about to throw a leg over my

Kawasaki and head home. I don't want to, but it's Sunday, and Jenny has to get up early for work. During this semester of college, she's interning at a veterinary clinic, and six a.m. rolls around fast.

I'm thinking about her warm bed, the one I didn't want to vacate. No, I'd never slip under the covers with her. I wouldn't feel right doing anything with her parents sitting downstairs. But that's never stopped us from panting our way through some heavy make-out sessions, like animals. There's something about Jenny and me. We're both drawn to animals. Animals keep popping up in our conversations. My thoughts. Maybe because I feel like one when I'm around her. Which is tough, because ...

Jenny is a virgin and vows to remain one until she walks down the aisle. Or through a field of wildflowers in a flowing dress, because that's Jenny: all outdoors.

I have to give her credit. She's got a lot of willpower. Me, on the other hand. Well, let's just say, this wouldn't be the first night I've had to leave her house bundling my jacket in front of me, while fighting the urge to turn caveman, dragging her with me by the hair.

Before I have a chance to work the zipper of my jacket, Jenny's hand parts the leather, circles my abs, then her fingers drill into my ribs until my eyes water from laughing. She tugs on the bulky cross that's supported by the braided chain she's just wrapped around my neck.

"What is this, some kind of weapon?" I chuckle, holding the cross out before me to examine it. The silver edges are so finely chiseled, they're almost serrated. "It doesn't look like any cross I've ever seen."

"Wear it and like it." She pokes my chest. "It has history."

As the story goes, her grandma somehow gained possession of the relic from the Northern Crusades. Through hundreds of years, scores of hands, and fanciful folklore, it mysteriously made its way into her family, and onto my chest.

It feels like a twenty pound saw blade is hanging around my neck, but what can I say. It's from Jenny ... and her grandma. Possibly some king or warrior. Who knows?

"I'm not about to argue with royalty." I flutter my brows.

She's giggling, shoving the donut at me again. "One little bite, or I'm not stopping," she threatens, her fingertips digging harder into my gut.

I belt out a laugh. "You're relentless. Sadistic ..."

"I made them for your sweet tooth." She pouts, then tears the donut apart, shoving the largest half at me. When she bites down, a squirt of jelly dots her chin. She's like a little kid. Only sometimes.

I smile and shake my head, but don't sink my teeth into my half. Instead, I dip my tongue into the center, then lick my lips. "Hey, this is pretty good. How'd you stuff all this goo into such a little hole?"

She lets out a burst of laughter, then pops the last bite into her mouth. I watch the movement of her throat as she swallows, then giggles. "Leave it to you to analyze the innards of a donut." The way she sucks the jelly off her fingers makes me hungrier ... but not for food.

"I'd rather analyze yours," slips through my lips, followed by my tongue that swipes the glob of jelly from her chin on its way to the hollow behind her ear, which is even sweeter. I work my way down her neck, into her cleavage, stopping when the porch light flashes.

"I'll call you later," I whisper, then my lips settle onto hers for a final taste of jelly ... and Jenny.

"Drive slow." She always warns, even though she knows damn well I'm responsible. Her face is lifted, her pouty lips pursed. She pushes up for a parting kiss, then steps back and aims the cutest wave at me. "Take care of you ... for me," she sings out.

January Valentine

There's something in her smile that grips my heart. Longing? I sense she wants me to stay. God, how I want to stay.

"Take care of you, for me," I call back and wink as I turn the key and press the starter button. With the beast ignited, I strap on my helmet, and with a twist of my wrist I'm leaving her behind.

Wheel Wolf

Phantom Lake

*B*oughs of pine steeple the road, but there's so much moon, the pavement glows with ghosts far beyond the Kawasaki's headlight. Why I don't ride directly home is something I can't exactly put my finger on. Maybe it's because it's still early. I'm not tired. I hate walking into a dark, empty home. No, it's no longer a home. It's a haunted house with creaking floors, full of all kinds of memories. Happy, loving, tragic. Twenty-one years of laughter has been downgraded into perpetual sadness. All because of some scumbag, or scumbags, I'm dying to get my hands on.

Wasn't taking my parents' hard earned cash enough? Did they have to kill them too? Drown them like unwanted kittens. Trash the boat my dad waited thirty years to buy. And I'm the one who talked him into buying the cruiser ...

The wind blows tears from my eyes like raindrops from the windshield of a speeding car. But I'm not speeding. I'm doing twenty, slowing to pull onto a side road, when my headlight washes over a crude sign someone posted: *Phantom Lake. Enter if you dare.* This is the road we use when we gather at the lake for keg parties. Or for total isolation when we have a score to settle with our heads.

The actual name of this dark body of water is Hosner Lake. But because of the gnarled trees and shadows that look like the dead have risen and are about to walk the earth, we call it Phantom Lake.

Barely fifteen minutes, and I'm already missing the hell out of Jenny. I think she fired off a reminder as I was pulling away: "Don't forget to call me!" As if ... So I won't hang around the lake too long. Just long enough to decide how I'm going to ask her to marry me. Will I drop onto a knee? Or pick her up, swing her into the air, let her warm body slide slowly down my chest as my heart pounds with love. Kiss her hard. Tell her she's my everything. I want to spend the rest of my life with her. Only her. My beautiful Jenny Rudéa.

When my voice fills the night with a thunderous, "Jenny *Bailey*," my lips stretch so wide, every muscle in my face pulls into my smile. Warmth flows into my cheeks. Of course she'll say yes, dickhead. Can't you get it through your Neanderthal skull? The girl loves you. She's not about to leave you.

The lake is endless, the moon's reflection glistening. The smooth surface ripples with a gusting breeze. The breath of night ... Calming. Inviting. I get this urge to strip and dive in. Cool my emotions. Lose myself. But all I do is park the bike, hop off, un-strap my helmet, and drop onto pine-needled scrub grass near the shore. Dig my fingers through pockets of grit. Gather a handful of rocks, stand, and one by one, skip them across the glassy surface. I've been skipping rocks since I was a kid. I'm a pro.

"Jenny. How long have we known each other?" I'm actually talking out loud ... to myself.

"Since when were you stricken with amnesia?" She'd cock a brow. "Six years, silly." She'd smack me and grin, then her squint would demand an immediate explanation.

Wheel Wolf

"Jenny. I love you." I'd take her in my arms. When? Before I say this or after?

Hands on hips, her head would bob, like when she's dancing. "What's up with you, Jack? You're acting weird."

"*That's* weird," I whisper to the night, not to Jenny, because I've just heard disturbing sounds coming from the other side of the lake. I hope my senses are on the mark. Because I'm not in the mood to play crisscross-crash with a mama bear, or Lord knows what else might be lurking out here. On the other side of the lake ... I hope.

There it is again. Louder. Rustling. Something skimming through brush. Feet crushing dry fallen leaves. Something is stalking. Yeah, there's definitely something out there other than a raccoon. Something larger. Heavy-breath-noisier. Not deer. I know the sound of deer. Does whatever it is know I'm here?

Twigs snapping? Nah, too pronounced ... different ... denser. Sharp. Splitting. Cracking. Like when I break a thick branch over my thigh for firewood. Fucking snapping bones? Holy shit. Is something feasting out there? On the other side of the lake ... I hope. Is someone fucking with me? One of the guys? No one knows I'm here.

The night is suddenly darker than it was when I got here. The full moon isn't shuddering through branches, isn't reaching the ground. Or does it seem that way because my eyes are narrowing to peer through the mist that's rising now that dusk has hopped behind the clouds, cooling the air. My breath is coming faster than the breeze that's whipping my pant legs. Flooding my ears. Masking the unpleasant sounds. I can't get my bearings. I should get the hell out of here. My forehead is beaded with perspiration. I'm gulping down alarm. Inhaling damp, musty air.

Get a fucking grip, Jack. You're gonna be a ranger, for shit sake. In this forest, in a couple weeks. You're going to be faced with crap like this all the time. I am? But I'll be prepared. I'll have a flashlight. A weapon. Maybe not a .45, but a tranquilizer gun. For emergencies. Like this. Man up ... Grab a flashlight. The one that looks like a small club. Dual purpose: If you can't see it, club it. Ha, Jack. This isn't the right time for sick humor. Shit, did I ever put my club-light back into my trunk? *The Kawasaki's headlight, idiot. Now that'll blind anything.*

Eyes darting, I back-step to the bike, quietly, so I don't disturb whatever is making what has turned into shit-your-pants sounds. Snorting? ... Gorging? ... Bear? I position the bike so it faces the grunts, snapping sounds, or whatever the fuck is going on ... on the other side of the lake.

Turn the key, Jack, but don't start the engine. Fight that urge to run like a wuss. This is your chance to prove to yourself. Had you been on the boat that day, you would've found a way to save them. You'd never have punked out. You would've stood up and fought the bad guys. Like you're about to do right now.

With the flip of a switch, the Kawasaki hurls a fireball across the lake. It's bare-eyed-sunlight-bright, even on the back end. It's burning my eyes. So I imagine it's melting whatever is out there. Disintegrating it on the spot. I stare into the glaring cone, grainy as it fans out and dies. Killed by the fog that's forming all around me.

Like a fat finger, the spotlight points out trees. Tears down heavy brush. Nothing moving out there. Nope. I don't see anything. My imagination? Move the handlebars. Train the light. There. Right there is where I think the noise was coming from. Was. It's stopped. The night is silent. Not even the chirr of crickets fills the air: the breath is mine; the fog is nature's. All kinds of creepy shapes dance in the distance.

I'm standing beside the bike, leaning on it for security, I guess. I'm fucking hugging my bike, actually. Like I'm about to mount it, fuck its brains out, or in this case, fuck its engine out. I try for a laugh because I'm feeling ridiculously nervous. I'm literally sticking my neck out, straining to see what's inside the cone of light.

A hairy hump? The ass end of a bear? I swing the light a bit to the left and sonofabitch, I catch something head on.

What was a hairy bump in the middle of a thicket, rises like a demon from hell, then jerks up the most gruesome head I've ever seen. I'm being studied by glowing red eyes.

Face it, Jack. You've *never* seen anything like this before, so don't even try to compare it to something it's not. Not a bear. Deer, no way. A gargantuan wild boar? Not in this neck of the woods. Neck. This thing has no neck. A huge head grows out of massive shoulders. With pointed ears and snout, it's very canine looking but seems to be standing on two feet. I surprised it. Fucking interrupted its meal, because the light is illuminating a king-size set of angry chompers and ... holy fuck ... fangs.

Barely breathing, I'm frozen to the spot. So is the thing. We're staring. Me, through the light at it. It, into the light at me. How the fuck can it see me with this powerful beam in its eyes, through darkness and fog?

Its face is stained with blood, gooey stuff dripping from its gaping mouth. It stands its ground. Doesn't even try to hide. It's brazen, which in itself is scary as fuck. Then what makes my heart trip even more, as if to taunt me, it lifts whatever it's been eating over its head. Like the shredded animal with dangling flesh, or holy shit, I hope it's not a human, is weightless. Like a bed pillow. A ragdoll. Air. Air is the only thing between us. And the lake. Thank Christ for the lake. Unless it dives in and swims to me, it'll never get to me in time. Because the lake is huge, and I'm about ready to hop onto my own beast and split.

Take an accurate mental snapshot, Jack, so you can report this aberration. Tall. Seven feet? Broad. Broader than any player on my college football team. Refrigerator broad, in fact. Hairy as fuck. The face. Mother of God ... ugly. Snarling, elongated snout.

Holy shit. A wolf? What kind of wolf stands on two feet?

Thank Christ for cell phones. Mine is out of my pocket, trembling fingers pounding 9-1-1. As discreetly as possible, I'm hoarse-whispering, "This is Jack Bailey. I'm out at Phantom ... I mean ... Hosner Lake. Few miles south of Heathcoat. There's something weird out here."

My croaking voice is going for an audible whisper. The operator is grumbling, "What? I can't hear you, sir. Speak up."

"Fuck, lady. I can't speak up ..." I'm growling through clenched teeth. Trying to bury myself in shadows. It's bad enough I'm taunting this thing with a glaring light. I don't want it to hear me, lock me with those glowing eyes again. "Get someone out here. Send loaded guns. It's a freak of nature."

"Freak? Sure kid. Go haunt another neighborhood. And by the way, Halloween isn't for another seven months." Click.

"Bitch ..."

You can't stand your ground. Don't try to be a hero, or snap a picture with your phone. No one would believe you anyway.

There's no way you can take this thing on. Just get the fuck outta here, Jack. I'm wheeling my bike backward, edging closer to the path. Leaves, please don't crunch! Don't bother with the helmet. "Take care of you ... for me." Jenny's words are flipping through my head like pages of a book.

"I'm trying, babe." My reply is lost somewhere inside my head, battling with the blood pounding at my temples, the brain cells fighting for reason. Think. React. Move, Jack!

The instinct for survival is overwhelming, kicking a central nervous system into autopilot when your limbs feel like jelly. Can I possibly hear it breathing? Keep your head and you'll be safe. It can't possibly get around the lake this fast. Then I remember the old footbridge. The one that's almost crumbling but still spans the lake, giving whatever is out there an advantage. I stop moving, hearing only the ringing in my ears. When I move again, it moves.

Wheel Wolf

Crunch, snap, then a distinct, "Grrr."

Holy shit. It's stalking me. I don't stop to look around, or to check out the dark figure that's leaping off the bridge. When it lunges for me, I throw my body to the side, but a rush of air brushes my body. Or was that fur?

The hard seat of the bike never felt so good. Safe. Instant ignition. What a beautiful sound. I'm shifting gears, cutting through darkness. But it's okay. I could find my way outta here in a coma. I know this forest like it's the brother I never had. That's why I'm gonna be a ranger. In two weeks, I'll be in uniform, patrolling the entire area. Five-thousand-eight-hundred-fifty-two square miles of woodlands, fields, mountains, and lakes. Watching over the environment, including our four-legged, and flighty feathered friends, maybe rescuing dumbass kids who invade the place at night, like I'm doing.

The rutted path is crunching beneath my tires. Dirt's flying. So is my hair. Without a visor, wind is stinging the hell out of my eyes. Now and then a peg scrapes the ground when I navigate a turn at high speed. But my boots are solid. After a couple hasty skids, I'm breaking out of darkness, cruising into pulsing moonlight, blasting down the paved road like a maniac, heaving a sigh as my pulse normalizes. Now I'm doubting my own ears and eyes. Sanity. Did I just run from shadows and wind? Christ, I don't know anymore. I'm actually trembling.

As I downshift, I make a mental note: Contact the game warden in the morning. Find out what the hell's creeping around the lake in the dead of night. Animals don't sound like that. I don't think humans do, either. The sounds were *off*. The sight was worse. Eerie enough to throw me into a panic. That's saying something for the guy who dove off Fisher's Bridge, which stands more than fifty feet in the air. Did I mention, in the dead of winter? My boots breaking through icy water. Did I also mention, a boatful of my buddies were waiting for me below when I crash-landed?

January Valentine

They more than likely saved my life. But it was Jenny who brought me out of depression, booze, and addiction.

In my peripheral, trees whiz by like lines of wooden soldiers. Stationary troops. Alert defenders. Yeah, I'm losing it. Can't wait to get back to the house. Barricade the door. Pop open an ice cold Brooklyn Summer Ale. Hop into the shower, bottle in hand, then into bed with my cell phone. Dial my girl. Should I tell Jenny where I've been? What went down? What are you, crazy? You'll never hear the end of it. If she knew you were riding helmetless, she'd slash your tires. Or maybe glue the damn helmet to your head. You should know better, idiot.

Jenny ... My arms tighten around her. I can still feel her lips on mine. Then, out of nowhere ... something, other than my jacket, is clinging to my back. There's a thud. A guttural groan, gurgling, moaning. Silence.

Strange, I'm thinking as I'm airborne. I didn't see anything cross the road that I never took my eyes from.

Well, maybe for a second to unhook my helmet from the handlebar ...

I'm trying to figure this out in the flashing instant of bone-shattering impact, mine with the pavement, then I'm no longer thinking.

Wheel Wolf

Jenny: ICU

"Jack ..." I manage to whisper his name through the lump in my throat as I sweep my hair back with one hand. I don't want it falling on his face when I lean in close. My legs are like rubber. I don't want *me* falling on him either, so I fight to steady myself. Rephrase that, Jennifer. Yes, you want to be on top of him, but not here. Not while he's in a hospital bed, unconscious. Wired to all kinds of machines. The kiss I leave on his cheek is every bit as soft as my voice when I repeat his name, with more strength this time.

His skin is so cold beneath my lips, I actually shiver. My eyes run over him, head to toe. His neck is restrained by a stiff brace, his body hidden beneath a loose white sheet, making it impossible to judge the extent of his injuries with the naked eye. The message of the cervical brace sinks in. Please don't let his neck be broken. I know the damage a motorcycle accident can do to a body. Broken bones, internal injuries. Brain damage ... Spine.

Machines take up an entire side of his bed, registering, beeping, jarring every raw nerve that's daring my mouth to fly open with a blood-curdling scream. One machine is breathing for him. Responsible for the rise and fall of his chest. What would happen if it was disconnected? This lifesaving machine is the most difficult to comprehend. I'm standing at his free side, closest to the window. A chill shoots through me as the horror sinks in. I can't face the intubation. He was just kissing me. Now his lips are sealed shut, tubed, taped. I run a finger over my lips, still feeling his. Tasting them. I can't handle this!

I take a deep breath, and a moment, to gaze down at the parking lot. Jack is surrounded by machines. Cars are surrounded by oak trees and streetlights.

My gaze is drawn to the huge crimson moon, which is a stark contrast against the black sky. I've never seen a moon like this before. I imagine it to be shedding blood ... doom over the entire town.

Snap out of it, Jennifer!

I stare at my Jeep, because I'm not sure exactly when I'll be able to approach Jack again. Seeing him like this is otherworldly. I have to digest this nightmare. My head hurts. My heart aches. I know if I look in a mirror, a ghost will be staring back. I'm in a ghostly state of shock. That's more like it. Not a ghost. A ghost is dead. Jack's alive. I'm alive. Pinch yourself. This might be a dream. A horrible dream. Pinch again. Wake up. Wake up. Wake up!

I can't believe Jack has been involved in an accident. A serious accident. My mind's racing to comprehend exactly what has occurred. Not more than ten miles from my house. From his. What happened to the man I love? The guy who left my porch not more than two hours ago. Or was it three? Was it longer than that? What time is it? Oh my God. I can't think straight. I have no firm grasp of anything, especially reality.

No one has given me the details, but I know it wasn't Jack's fault. It couldn't be. He's a careful rider. An expert. I've been on the back of the Kawasaki so many times. He calculates. Knows every move before he makes it. He's anything but a risk-taker.

I manage to swing my body around. Turn my neck and slowly face him.

Move closer, Jen.

Second glance is easier. Not great, but at least I've conquered the instinct to run. He looks so fragile, I'm afraid to touch him. But I have to touch him. I steady my hand, carefully brush back the hair I love. The hair my fingers long to tangle in. Often do. It's matted. Not from my touch. From his helmet, no doubt. And streaked with blood. My jaw clenches. Doesn't anyone in this place know how to care for a patient?

His hands are a scary dry-cold, his forehead feverish-clammy. I rush to the bathroom sink, dampen a paper towel with cool water, return to his side controlling my pulse, and gently stroke away as much dried blood as possible without applying too much pressure.

He must have sustained a concussion, otherwise he'd be awake, right? His head isn't bandaged, though. So it can't be all that bad. Thank God he was wearing his helmet. He better have been wearing his helmet. Still, I'm worried about his neck.

"Jack," I repeat, praying his golden brown eyes will open. That mine will be the first face he sees. So he'll know he's safe. "I'm here, baby," I murmur directly into his ear, then ease back, devour his profile as if I'm seeing him for the first time. If sleeping beauty could be a man, Jack would be him. He's handsome. Stunning. Knockout perfect. Masculine jaw line, straight nose, long dark lashes that are now still, resting on his cheekbones. His scraped cheekbones. How much can a heart break before it stops beating?

I drag a chair to the bed, cautiously rest an elbow on the mattress, so I'm eye level with Jack. I sit and I stare, as if my eyes have the power to pull him from his coma. Coma. The word makes me sick to my stomach. I really think I'm about to hurl, so I carefully take back my arm, jump to my feet, race back into the bathroom. Click the door closed. Hover over the lidless toilet. But nothing rushes from my throat. Nothing but sobs. I willfully quiet myself, so I'm not tossed out on my butt for disturbing the patient. The patient who probably doesn't hear a single mechanical beep. Or my very human, trembling voice.

Jack and I live in upstate New York, in a town called Angel's Bend, where everyone knows everyone. Almost. Everyone's business. But not their secrets. My father owns the Evening Sun, a bar and grill, the local meeting place. He's a member of the town council. Volunteer fire department. Strangers passing through quickly come to know I'm dating Jack Bailey. Of course, I was the first one contacted. Of course, the first responders knew there was no one else to call. That I'm the only next of kin. Poor Jack. For more than one reason. My poor Jack.

A nurse pops in and out of the room, *like a gopher* runs through my mind. Watching her is tiring. She keeps checking the machines, IV drips, Jack's vitals. She's wearing surgical scrubs, a mask tied loosely around her neck, as though she's just detached herself from an operating room. Maybe the one Jack had been in.

"What is the extent of his injuries?" I ask each time she enters. "When do you expect him to regain consciousness?"

A tight but sympathetic half-smile follows each plea. "You'll have to speak to his doctor."

I'd love to, I want to yell at her. But yelling will only get me thrown out on my ass. And Jack needs me. I need him. "Where *is* his doctor? What's his or her name?" I control my demand. "Who's on night duty?" I'm wondering if I'd know if she told me. Veterinarians often mix with doctors. We're in the same profession, after all. Saving lives.

Her eyes drift from Jack to me. "I'll put the word out that his family is inquiring. See if I can't get someone in here ..."

His family. Jack's an only child. I am his family. The only person he can rely on. I was there for him when his parents were murdered. When he went to pieces and threw fits. Wanted to kill someone. Wanted to die. Punched holes in walls. Slammed his fists against his own head from anger, frustration, grief. Smoked too much pot, ingested illegal substances. I almost lost him several times, but love pulled him through. Pulled us through. I pray the same holds true in this case. If love could heal, Jack would be bolting from bed, and I'd be dragging him out of this room faster than a racehorse being whipped to the finish line. I want to shut down. But I can't.

I've stopped shaking, but I'm so nauseous, the room keeps threatening to spin. My heart's no longer tripping, my breath is slower. I want to climb into bed with Jack. Faint beside him. Share his coma. Wake up when he does.

"Jenny?" The deep voice startles me. My head whips around, and I'm staring into soft gray eyes.

"Doctor Sloan ... Greg." I'm relieved. I know this man. He's a skilled surgeon. My eyes want to water, but I refuse to break down. "What's his condition? Prognosis?" You're trained for this, not with humans, but animals are every bit as valuable. Healable. "Will he come out of this okay?" I can't let myself think he *won't* come out of it, so I'm thinking positive; that will make it true. He's going to be fine. After a few weeks, Jack will be back to what he was a few hours ago. He's amazing. He can do this.

Greg takes long breaths. Each time he opens his mouth, I brace myself. But he's not talking. Why isn't he talking? To keep my sanity, I start babbling. "We hiked fifty miles of the Appalachian last summer." Now I'm stuttering. "Jack's starting a new job ... next ... no, not next. In a few weeks. He's planning a mountain climbing trip next summer. Did you know he's an athlete? Could have had a football scholarship if he'd applied himself ... Do you realize what he's been through? ..." I suck in such a ragged breath, I'm sure Greg thinks I'm gearing up for a heart attack, or nervous breakdown. "Oh my God. Say something, please." I want to pat down his brain.

Now I wince. That's the beginning. I'm about to fall apart, I can feel it. Wait, I can't. My legs are numb. My stomach is rising to my throat. A fleeting thought hits my spinning head. Where are my parents? Why aren't they here? Then I remember. When Jack left earlier tonight, they disappeared into their room. Closed the door. Lights out. An officer called me on my cell phone. Jack must have given him my number at the scene. So cold. The scene. I can't imagine Jack lying in the middle of the road, or on the shoulder. Broken. Bleeding. I close my eyes. Clench my teeth. If he was unconscious, the officer must have found my number stored in Jack's phone. My photo in his wallet. Sure, that's how he knew to call me. I didn't even think to wake my parents. But I scrawled a message on the whiteboard by the kitchen door before I flew out like a rocket.

Jack. Accident. Mercy Hospital.

If they're not here by now, they must be asleep. I'll call them later. Or they'll come looking for me. Right now, I don't care. I can only worry about one thing at a time. My mind is filled with Jack.

The room spins faster. Greg's face shrinks into darkness. The next thing I know, I'm sitting in a chair, a blanket slung around my shoulders. The thermal knit fabric is hanging to the floor. What the hell? A blood pressure cuff is strapped to my arm. Greg is pumping the device up himself. Listening to my life through a stethoscope.

Will I live, doc? I don't want to if Jack can't.

Wheel Wolf

Jack: Coma

I'm so out of it. Last I remember, I was floating in the sky. Sinking in black water, like when I jumped off Fisher's Bridge. Now my body is being lifted by invisible hands. I'm rocking, swinging in a hammock. A cradle? Mom? I'm trying to gasp for air, but I can't. My lungs are tight. My neck is stiff. Am I coming off a drunk? Can't be. I haven't touched anything in months. My brain's not working right. Not working. I can't think straight. My head is pounding, the room is spinning, and my eyes aren't even open. Is it physically possible to feel this way when you're sleeping? If I were sick, wouldn't I wake up puking or something?

This isn't Jenny's room. There's no sexy perfume overpowering my senses, or scented candles making me sneeze. No body lotion or hand cream, either. Makeup. Delicious shampoo. Soft voice. Firm hands. Thinking about it isn't making it happen. Dig deeper ...

It's not my room, either. There's no TV blasting through the air. Only a sickening smell that I can't seem to identify. It's not leftover pizza or Chinese takeout. And damn, who the fuck turned off the TV? I never go to bed without noise. I can sleep through westerns and crime dramas. Shootouts and screaming people trying to escape zombies. I need the racket that helps me sleep like a baby. The blaring TV is part of my ritual. My life. Every minute I'm in the house. Day and night. Ever since ...

What the hell am I smelling? What are those sounds? Machines whirring, beeping. Alarm clock? Where am I? I hear mumbling, but I can't open my own mouth to say, "Hey. Who the fuck are you? Why are you in my head? Shit. Why am I here?" Am I tripping? Drake must have slipped me something.

I want to laugh, because it's almost comical. I feel drunk. I think I'm about to piss myself, because I can't get up to walk to the bathroom. There goes the mattress I bought to replace the one the cat sprayed.

Is anyone here? I can't move. Am I dreaming? Jenny, is that your whisper? What's with the gruff voice? Who's with you? It better not be Donnie. Some friend you turned out to be, Donnie dickface. First you try to steal my girl. Now you chain me to my bed. I'll fucking kill you ... as soon as I can move. Another laugh. Donnie, you're a freaking bastard.

My eyes have to be glued shut, because for the life of me, I can't open them. Hard as I try, my lids won't move. Neither will my hands. So I can't reach up and peel them open manually to see what's going on around me. Donnie, I want to scream. You fucking glued me to the bed so you could hit on Jenny. If you touch her, I'll fucking kill you.

This blows. I'm hearing voices, maybe Jenny's, not Donnie's. The tone isn't right. My hearing is getting better, but I still can't see, can't feel. Can't move. Will someone tell me what the fuck is going on?

Backtrack. While you backtrack, listen closely. Try to figure out what they're saying.

A man's voice. Comforting. "The police are outside, Jenny. They want to talk to you."

Wheel Wolf

Jenny? Police? Is she okay? I'm asking. For Christ sake, why aren't you answering me? My heart's pounding. The alarm clock's beeping like mad. Turn off that fucking clock. It's driving me insane. So, you're not going to answer me? Fuck you. Fuck me.

"What do the police want?" Jenny's voice hits an alarming octave.

"To talk to you about the accident."

"Can't it wait?" Jenny's voice again. Agitated.

More consoling. "They say no. Jack wasn't alone. They have questions."

"What do you mean, he wasn't alone?" Was that a screech? Jenny's?

"Jenny." Firmer male voice. "I don't know. You should speak to the detectives. Then we'll talk about Jack's condition."

"I'm not leaving him." Jenny can be stubborn. I want to smile, but my lips are sewn together. Shit.

"Humor them. Take a moment to step into the hall. I'll wait for you here."

The voices stop. Mechanical sounds fill the air. Machines and stinking odors. Bleach? Stale food?

A woman's voice; Jenny ... you're back. Why are you crying?

"I can't do this now. My legs are like jelly." Ragged breathing. A sob.

You can't do what, baby? Come here. Let me hold you. Make it all better.

"Come down to the lounge. It'll only take a few minutes. We have photos," a guy says. I know it's a guy. His voice is like gravel. Different from the other. Commanding. Don't talk to her like that! I'll break every bone in your body.

"Photos?" I know that tone of voice. Jenny is pissed off. Gearing up for an argument. "Pictures of a dead girl?"

Jenny ... don't faint! What the fuck is she talking about?

"No. I'm not leaving him." Her voice is firm. Like when she

stops me from trying to fuck her. How I want to fuck her. "There's a table in the corner. Over there. Across from Jack's bed. Next to the window. We can talk there. There's my Jeep," she mumbles under her breath. But I can hear her. Because she's mine. I love her. "Mercedes, Beamers. I didn't see those cars before. Did I park in the staff lot? Is that what you want to tell me?" She's huffy. That's Jenny. Piss her off once, she's pretty forgiving. Twice? She'll come out swinging. "Write me a damn ticket and leave me alone. Can't you see Jack's hurt?"

Jack's hurt? Staff lot? Hospital? I'm in a fucking hospital?

Jenny confirms. "Why do you have to bother me in the hospital? Can't this wait?"

A voice drops like a hammer. "A girl is dead."

A dead girl? Are they talking about me? I'm a guy, buddy ...

"What does a dead girl have to do with Jack's accident? I don't understand." From the sound of Jenny's voice, I can picture her movements. She's tearing at her hair, then tugging on the hem of her shirt. When she's finished with that, she'll ball her fists.

"Greg ... do we have to do this?" Her voice sails across the room.

"Listen, detectives. I haven't even had a chance to talk to her about Jack. Give us a few minutes. Go have a cup of coffee."

"We'll step outside," authoritative voice, "but only for a few. There's an investigation going on."

Investigation? Their footsteps are heavy. The rank cologne is fading. Cheap garbage. Doctor Sloan is my doctor, I guess. So I had an accident. I'm alive. What's wrong with me, doc?

"Jack sustained a mild concussion. I expect he'll come around within the next twenty-four hours."

I've got news for you, doc. I'm already around. Just not able to move.

Jenny blows out a sigh of relief. I can only imagine the look on her face. Something like when she's running late for class, or work, and finds her misplaced car keys before her absentmindedness causes her grief. Jenny's always misplacing her keys. I want to chuckle, but I can't seem to breathe right. There's something on my chest. The movement of my head is restricted.

"So he's going to be okay then?" It's like Jenny is belting out a happy song. From the sound of her voice, she's beaming. Those wide violet eyes flashing all kinds of signals.

"I didn't say that." He's cautious. Something tells me he's right beside me now. Jenny too. I smell her. Peaches. Cherry blossoms. Stress-strong fragrance filling the air. Powerful, like when we work out together. Yeah, that's her perfume alright. God, it smells so good. Thank you for being here for me, Jenny. You're always here. I love you, babe. And I'm gonna tell you, as soon as my damn mouth starts moving again. Christ, I hope I'm not paralyzed. Holy shit.

She sucks in a long breath. I'm counting. One, two, three, four, five ... Forty seconds? "Give it to me straight. Right now." She's forceful.

The breath he blows out is louder than the one she just let out. There's a shit load of breathing going on in this room. But no one is cluing me in.

"Jack doesn't have internal injuries. A couple of broken ribs. Fractured tibia. Contusions. Lacerations. Something took a chunk out of his chest."

Her vocal chords suck in air. "His chest?" She gulps. "Through his leather jacket?"

"The bike. The road. The heavy cross he was wearing. I'm not sure, Jenny. We sewed him up. Those injuries will all heal. What we're concerned about is ..."

Jenny jumps the gun. That's Jenny. Patience is not her virtue. "His neck. Don't tell me his neck is broken." I can see her jumping the doctor. Grabbing his collar in her fists. Shaking the truth out of him.

"Come on. Sit down." I visualize his hand on her shoulder, trying to lead her away.

"I'm fine." She touches my arm. I'm sure it's her. The pressure is gentle. It's Jenny.

Heavy sigh. "He sustained an injury to his spinal cord. He could be partially paralyzed. We won't know until he wakes up. It might take a while to assess the full extent of the injury."

Jenny's body must hit the seat of a chair, I hope not the floor, because after her hand slips away I hear a thud. A thud. A thud. Holy fucking shit. It's coming back to me.

Wheel Wolf

Jenny's Interrogation

I'm sitting in a chair beside Jack, my top half draped over the bed. Inches from his face, I'm staring. I swear one of the muscles in his cheek keeps twitching, as though he's trying to smile. Too bad Dr. Sloan isn't still here to see it. It's encouraging.

I think Jack knows I'm here. He must. "Jack ..." I whisper. "Can you hear me?" Turn up the volume, Jenny, I tell myself. But keep desperation out of your voice; you have to sound chipper. "If you can hear me, open your eyes. Move baby. Even a pinky." I grip his wrist, manipulate each finger of the hand I'm cradling manually.

I feel the two detectives before I see them. They're staring at my back, lurking in the doorway as though they're afraid to enter. Don't worry, you won't catch anything. I want to sneer at them, tell them to fuck off and leave us alone in our misery.

At the sound of their footsteps, I lift my head. I don't know these guys. They could pass for traveling salesmen. They're not local. Mink County? I'm surprised Donnie isn't here. I wonder if he knows.

"Do you recognize this girl?" A detective is suddenly hovering over me, sticking an eight-by-ten glossy under my nose. He smells like spice. Why do all detectives smell the same? Sweat, spice and tobacco. How do they get these pictures developed so quickly? Stupid thoughts. I want to close my eyes, shut down entirely. Don't look at it. If you don't see it, it can't hurt you. Jack would never cheat on you. They're lying.

I force my eyes open but don't even peek. I cringe up at the annoying man in dark slacks and pinstriped dress shirt before my glare tackles the picture. I'm not sure if I want to vomit or scream. The girl is sprawled out on the road, darkened more by blood than night, I'm sure. Her limbs are skewed, would be spread eagle if they were all attached. One leg is aimed at her shoulder; the leg and shoulder that are almost torn off, as though she was dragged. Drawn and quartered. Naked bones snapped. I shudder. She's posed in an awkward, unnatural position. She's nude. Body coated with blood, she looks skinned. The photos are color and very close up. Blown up. Oh God. What looks like blonde hair, long and coiled, soaks up most of the crimson puddle around her head. Her torn neck ...

"She a friend of yours? Of your boyfriend, maybe?" This man is heartless. Puffiness beneath his dark eyes makes his stare more penetrating. He's got a flattop cut, which is like a thick brush covering his scalp. Army flashes through my mind.

I shake my head. "Na ah." Tears roll down my cheeks. I can barely utter, "It's kinda hard to see her face with all the ... What happened to her?" The whisper crawls up my throat. This gruesome picture is inches from my nose, but I'm concentrating on the space between this man's two front teeth, breathing his coffee and hint of onion breath.

"That's what we're trying to figure out." The second guy moves to my other side. He's younger and not as brusque. Smells like ocean. Not sweat. "It appears she was riding on the back of your boyfriend's motorcycle." He clears his throat, stops chewing his gum for a moment. "That was my first thought, anyway." His manicured hands drop into the pockets of his navy blue trousers, and he slightly lowers his head. This, and his warm hazel eyes, makes him human. I want to relax, but I can't.

"Why would she be riding naked?" Stupid question. Why was she on the back of the Kawasaki would be a better question. The one that's now tearing my brain apart. And my heart. They're wrong. They're lying. They're trying to pin an unsolved case on Jack. My cheeks begin to burn. The first sign that I'm about to explode. Scratch this guy's eyes out, even though he seems human, because he's trying to pin a murder on Jack. Maybe a rape. "Jack is faithful. He'd never even look at another girl. There's no way she was riding on the bike with him." I'm adamant. I'm certain. I'm glaring.

"Which leaves us with. Why was your boyfriend pinned to a naked girl on County Route 44 after losing control of his motorcycle?" Detective number one shoves another photo at me. This one I can grip with my fingertips, hold it out before me. It's a snapshot of the bulky silver cross I draped around Jack's neck just after dinner. I told him it would protect him. How ironic. Is this my fault?

"Jack didn't lose control." I seal my lips together, then force them apart, licking them because they're so dry they feel about to crack. My tongue doesn't help at all; it's just as dehydrated and sandpaper. "And what do you mean they were pinned together?" I spit the words out. Can this get any worse? My heart is beating wildly. It's difficult to breathe. I don't want them to know I'm this nervous. That would make Jack guilty. Me too for not cooperating with them. Don't be a bitch. Be calm. Cool. You'll get through this.

I take my eyes from the picture to steal a look at Jack, wondering if he knows what's going on. What he's being accused of. What happened out there tonight, baby? What were you doing on 44? Who is this girl? Why was she with you? My eyes are drilling into his head.

"How do you know he hit her? Maybe she was there already, and he ran into her ..." Oh my God, I'm making it sound worse. Like he wasn't looking where he was going. You should have seen her Jack! Damn it. How could you have run her over?

"Because their bodies were tangled. We've got those photos too. In living color. Want to see them?" Bad cop is enjoying the bulge of my eyeballs.

I blow out a panicky, "No." Then shoot him a look of disgust.

His jaw is working hard. He's not finished with me yet. "The exact cause of death is to be determined by the coroner."

I think he's taunting me. "Wh ... what?" I choke out.

He can't wait to reply. He's angry. Accusatory. I want to shove my fist in his face. "She was almost decapitated. We're not sure if that occurred after death, or caused it." His voice is as flat as his head.

When his words slam into me, I can't help but fly off the chair. I practically leap across the room, straight to the window where all I can do is wish I was in my Jeep, home, school, work. Any place but this. Jump out, crosses my mind. Only I'm four stories high over Maple Avenue. The moon is so big and bright. A lover's moon ...

"Hey," the tone of nice cop draws my eyes to his. He's glaring at his partner. "Lighten up, Vince. This girl had nothing to do with it." He shoots him a stare I wouldn't want directed at me.

For the first time, I realize I'm wearing blue baby doll pajamas under my rose colored sweater. The belted one that reaches my hips. Regardless of my inadequate attire, I square my shoulders and face them both, my expression daring their eyes to stray from mine. That's when I find my voice. "This isn't getting us anywhere. Someone please tell me straight. What do you *think* happened?" I push my sleeves to my elbows, then drag them down to my wrists and hug myself.

"She's naked. No clothing found. No I.D. No purse. No shoes. Nothing. If she wasn't on the bike, I'm guessing she came running out of the woods at the exact ..." Nice cop is reciting to Vince. At least he's trying to make sense of it.

"Obviously. If she was naked," I throw the words at them. "She must have run right into Jack." I let out a victory breath, because now I believe I'm solving the mystery. "Someone was attacking her. She saw, maybe heard Jack coming, and it was her chance to get away. She must have rushed him. She's the reason he's lying there." I thrust my head. I can't believe I'm blaming a dead girl, but it's easier than blaming the guy I love. Trust.

A cruel, sarcastic laugh is plucked from Vince's throat, like his mouth has nothing to do with it. His vocal chords are overtaking his brain. "It's dark. Jack doesn't see her, or she darts out in front of the bike. He doesn't have time to stop, or tries to and skids, runs her over, he goes flying. Lands on top of her, because the cross he was wearing slashed her throat. Yeah, that's what probably killed her."

"We'll defer to the coroner." Nice cop's eyes meet mine. They're soft.

Jack: Am I Awake?

*W*hen my eyes spring open, everything is blinding white and dotted. I'm in a storm and the sky's full of snow. That's the ceiling, dickwad. I blink and look around, but my range of vision is limited, because my neck stops my head from moving. All I can do is rotate my eyeballs. I panic, then realize I'm wearing a brace. I can't speak, but I can swallow. And a freaking tube is scratching my throat raw, so I start choking, gagging. Hey, I'm making sounds. Progress, I hope.

"Jack." Jenny is at my side, staring down at me with wet violet eyes. Sad. Worried. Frantic actually, but relieved. Her eyes tell me all of these things with one glance. Jenny's eyes are beautiful. Along with their shocking color, their expression amazes me. The very first day we met, her eyes were what tipped me off. The girl was a goner. Yup. It was all in her eyes.

I try to speak, but can't even mouth. So I start blinking, and my cheeks dampen. I'm crying?

"How do you feel, baby?" Jenny's face pulls into an adoring look, like I'm an injured kitten or something soft and cuddly lying on a vet's exam table. I'm waiting for her to reach out and pet me.

Her fingers stroke my cheek in a very human gesture, though. She brushes my hair back. My eyes flutter for an instant, then follow hers.

This machine is working against me. I'm trying to breathe on my own, but the damn thing is actually choking me with its fucking mechanical rhythm. I'm ready to convulse. "Get it off me." I think that's what I'm grunting. "Get a doctor." She must get the message because she pats my hand then takes off. I hear her yelling. "We need help in here! Stat!"

In a matter of moments, two nurses and a doctor are standing over me. So close, I can smell their breath, even their skin and the organic odor escaping through their pores. While they check the machines, they stare at me like I'm a specimen, or a cracked china cup. Then they turn fucking boisterous. Christ, this is a hospital? It's noisy now. Yeah. That makes me feel at home. They throw everyone out of the room. Then they go to work on me. Prodding, pulling, studying. Their hands are all over me.

"Welcome back, Jack," a nurse says. She's grinning like a proud grandma. Her face looks a bit distorted, like she's in a too close camera shot at a bad angle, but I think my eyes must need to adjust to being awake and open. For her sake, I sure as hell hope so.

The doctor is serious. "I'm going to remove your breathing tube, Jack. I think you can breathe on your own. You were intubated upon arrival. Just as a precaution. We weren't sure how long you'd be out. You've surprised us." His light eyes smile, but plunge into mine. "This is a good sign. You're strong." He pats my shoulder.

Bet your ass I'm strong. "So why can't I move my legs?" That's the first thing I ask when the tube is out and I'm breathing and swallowing water through a straw. The next is, "When can you take this damn thing off my neck. It's killing me."

"Get a soft cervical collar. I read his films. He's good." He shifts his glance for a moment to address the nurse.

"I'm good?" I may be good, but I feel like crap and I'm ready to cry like a baby. "Does that mean I can get outta here?" I'm groggy, blinking like mad trying to clear my vision. "My eyes are dry."

I hear a woman's laughter. "He's on the mend." Must be another nurse, because it doesn't have a musical rhythm like Jenny's laugh. Her laughter, her voice, the way she sings when we're rocking out, could be a hit score of a Broadway show. "I'll get you some eye drops." This voice has an aging tone to it. Maybe she's just tired. Who knows. Who cares. I just want out of here.

"Not so fast, Jack," the doctor says. Serious again, he scowls. "We need to talk." He cocks his head and quirks a brow. "Are you up to it?"

"Bring in the reinforcements and you can do whatever you want to me, but I'm worried about my girl, who you threw out." I grin and try to shrug. "She's gonna be asking a million questions. Best if it all comes from you."

He nods and says, "I hear you." Then he tells a nurse to bring in Jenny.

Jenny wants to fling herself across the bed. I can tell by the way she moves, her enthusiastic voice, and I just know her. She hangs her head over mine, looking upside down weird. "Hey..."

"Hey. How are you, baby?" I'm more worried about her than me.

"I'm okay." She sounds choked up. I want to hold her, so I lift my arms.

"Hey. My arms work." I'm thrilled.

"Oh Jack." She lays her head on my chest, carefully, barely, and I'm able to run my hands up and down her back. My fingers slip under her sweater and I feel familiar silk. I'd draw back, but since I can't move, I push her forward and cock a brow. Great. My brows move too. Now if only I could get my legs to work.

Wheel Wolf

"Are you wearing pajamas?" I ask her, grinning, wanting to shake my head. She's so adorable. And the best part is, she's mine. "Forever," I whisper and pucker my lips, signaling my need for a kiss.

She lets out a laugh, then she's crying.

"I'm sorry, baby." My heart breaks for her. "I hate to put you through this." I bring her hands to my lips and maul them. The way I want to maul her. I can't figure out why, lying in a hospital bed, my libido is through the roof. I wonder if it shows through the sheet. Must be the medication I was given. But still ... my cheeks want to flush, but I'm so cold.

Jenny tries to stand up straight, but I won't let her go. I want to hold onto her when the doctor tells me what I'm not sure I want to hear. I'm bracing for the worst. Steadying Jenny.

"What's the story, doc? Am I paralyzed?" I can't believe I said what I've been thinking about, even before my eyes sprang open. And believe me, saying it has made the thoughts a million times worse.

The dragging sound must be him pulling up a chair. He introduces himself as Dr. Gary, and tells Jenny to sit. She's obedient. I'm shocked. Arms folded, he stands on the side of the bed where the ventilator stood, but was wheeled away, thank God. From there, he can get a good look at us, but unfortunately, I can't see him too clearly.

"Please stand at the foot of the bed so I can see your face, Dr. Gary." Dr. Gary. I feel like he's my pediatrician. His hair is dark, but the graying sides remind me of duck feathers. He's too young to be gray. His complexion is polished. Yep, plenty of visits to the spa keep this guy in shape.

"Of course. Sorry. So this is the story." He picks up my chart and thumbs through pages. Talk about drama. Stress. The beeps on my bedside machine grow faster, making me even more nervous. Self conscious. Damn it, there's no hiding from the machine. The cuff either. The one that's strapped to my arm and keeps inflating itself. My emotions are out of control. So is my dick. I should be thankful. At least it works. I am sure it works. I can feel it pulse. What the fuck? I want to burst out laughing.

Dr. Gary starts reading off the chart, but I having a feeling he knows what's wrong and just doesn't want to face me. "Mild concussion. Fracture ..." he repeats everything I heard Dr. Sloan tell Jenny while I was semiconscious. "Cervical strain. Nothing that won't heal in that area." Along with his professional voice, he finally targets me with his eyes. "How does your head feel?"

"I feel like I've ingested half a bottle of oxy." I smirk. "Dizzy."

He lifts a brow. "Jack. Your broken leg will heal. So will your bruises. But your spine. We're not sure. Only time will tell."

"Is it broken?" Flows out with a shocked breath.

Both of his brows arch. He tucks in his bottom lip. "A millimeter more and you wouldn't be moving your arms, either." I believe his nod is meant to convince me I should be thankful.

A "Phew," gushes through my lips. "Sounds serious." Suddenly, I'm squeamish just thinking about my damaged spine, wondering if I'll ever walk again. "What's the game plan? You can fix it, right?"

"You'll be here for at least a month. Maybe more. Then rehab." His physician tone continues. "I doubt you'd agree with me at this time, but you're fortunate. Things could have been a lot worse."

"We can deal." Jenny, who's been uncharacteristically silent, squeezes my hand. I believe she's trying to reassure herself, as well as comfort me.

"There are two detectives outside. If it were up to me, I'd have them tossed out. But ..." He sounds paternal.

"I've already spoken to them," Jenny is defensive.

"You weren't in the accident, babe. Let's get this over with. Tell them to come in." I lift my hand and finger-wave toward the door.

The thud of flat heels tells me there are two men entering my room. When they stand at the foot of my bed, I'm certain.

"I'm Detective Vincent," one says in a gruff voice. He looks and acts military. "This is Detective Sherman."

"Ed ..." The younger of the two, with a full head of dark hair, nods. "How are you feeling?" He offers a shadow of a grin.

I shrug my brows. "I'll let you know as soon as I find out."

Vincent has a manila folder clutched under his arm. When he moves to my side, I hear the rustle of papers.

"We need you to look at these." He holds glossies over my face.

"Holy shit," I mumble. "This is my accident?" I can't stop my lips from quivering. I'm talking to Vincent, but looking at Ed, who nods. He squints and tightens his jaw, like he's in pain.

"Christ. Looks more like a serial killer crime scene than an accident. This poor chick is really messed up. What the hell happened?"

"You tell us," Vincent's voice bombs my ears. "That's what we're here for."

Since I can't turn away from the pictures he's shuffling around over my head, I squeeze my eyes shut. Eyes open or closed, this is a sight I'll never forget. I think of my parents. How they were beaten. I wonder if they looked this bad. By the time they were shipped home, after twenty hours in the ocean, autopsies and freezers, bruises weren't detectable. Blood was washed away. I want to puke.

"So you never saw her?" Vincent keeps asking in his monotone for what feels like a full five minutes.

My eyes spring open. "No, no, and for the fucking fiftieth time, No! I didn't see anything. Hear anything. She came out of nowhere, I guess. Because I never saw her at all." I don't tell them I felt her. That she pounced on my back. They'd never believe me. Less is best. Especially without counsel. I learned that a long time ago. But that's another story.

"That's hard to believe." Vincent is staring down at me, shaking his head. "And what's with the giant silver cross-thing? What are you into voodoo?"

"It was a gift," my reply is sarcastic. "For your information, crosses aren't voodoo, they're Christian. It's big, so I tucked it into my jacket. Is that a problem?"

"It is if it's a murder weapon."

"Oh, Jesus. Here we go again."

Jenny's hand clamps down on mine. "I think you better leave," she directs at Vincent, then whispers to me, "Don't get upset, we'll get an attorney. He's fishing. It'll be fine."

"A girl went missing from around here not too long ago," partner Ed cuts in. "We were wondering if it could be her. That's primarily why we're here, troubling you at this time."

"I knew the missing girl," Jenny jumps in. "She used to come into the Evening Sun. It's not her." Her hand tightens around mine.

"Evening Sun?" Vincent jumps at her.

"My father's bar," she shoots back.

"How about you, Jack ... did you know the missing girl?" Vincent hammers. "You hang around the bar I imagine."

"Yeah and it's not her." As he's moved to the foot of the bed, I can give him a strong eye. "You from Mink?"

"He nods."

"You're off your turf, aren't you?"

"Lending a hand to an understaffed department. Go over it one more time." Vincent is relentless. Trying to trip me up, I bet.

"I was on my way home. Stopped at the lake." I can't see Jenny, but imagine both of her brows are elevated. When her grip loosens, I get nervous. "Trust me. It was nothing, Jen. I'll tell you about it later." My tone deepens. "If you want to do some serious investigating, detectives, head on over to Hosner Lake. There's some strange animal or whatever out there. I heard it. Saw it. Maybe it was chasing the girl, and she tried to ditch it by running into my bike."

Then it hits me. I remember the sound of crunching bone. How the thing held something over its head like a fucking trophy. Everything rushes my brain at once. I shake so hard, someone throws a warm blanket over me. Jenny leans down and shushes me. That's when I realize weird sounds are coming out of my mouth. Whimpering? Christ.

"That's enough," a nurse says. "Everybody out. Let my patient get some rest."

She's just released the threat when another nurse bursts in. "Detective Vincent. You have a phone call at the desk."

Vincent grumbles, "Never fucking left alone." He coughs, then sneezes. "Damn allergies. Finish up here, Ed. Read him his rights."

My rights? "What the fuck?" If I could launch off this bed, I would. Cop or not, I'd bounce him off the wall.

Jenny starts going off on him, telling him her uncle's a lawyer, and his department will be sued for harassing a seriously injured patient who they never read rights to in the first place. "Reading rights to a comatose person won't hold water in court." My girl's on fire.

Vincent stops her with a laugh. Some laughing matter. A girl is dead, and I'm half paralyzed.

"I'll meet you downstairs, Ed." He coughs his way out of the room.

Ed is cool. He apologizes for his partner's bad sense of humor and crappy attitude. "Vince has been on the force too long, and is sick of crime," he says.

"So he should retire," I counter, "instead of taking his frustration out on law abiding citizens."

"Yeah ... well. You can pick your accident report up in forty-eight hours. Or someone can do it for you." He clears his throat apologetically because he knows I'm not going anywhere for quite some time. "Submit it to your insurance company. Your bike is at Towners garage. I'm not an adjuster, but in my opinion, it's totaled."

"Thanks for the great news, Ed." I stick out my hand.

Vincent's voice sounds from the across the room. I'm assuming he's back and standing in the doorway. "I have to talk to Jenny," he informs us. For some reason, he's behaving like a human, which concerns me.

Jenny is still beside me. Holding my hand again.

Vincent positions himself so both Jenny and I can see him. "Jenny," he repeats her name, and I'm wondering what's on his mind. "Your parents are fine, but there was a home invasion."

"What?" she screams. "Someone broke into my house? Oh my God ..." She's rattling off phrases faster than I can process, showering me with peppermint spittle. "Are they okay? What happened? Were they touched? Who did it? Were we robbed? Were they caught?"

"Your parents are fine," Vincent assures. "So is your dog. No one required medical attention. Seems your father scared the perp away with a shotgun after the dog's barking woke them."

I can't help but chuckle. "That's so your father. Sometimes I think he'd like to do that to me, too."

Jenny jabs my arm. "Not funny, Jack."

"So did they rob them?" I begin my interrogation. "Was that the motive?" I'm thinking, thank God Jenny wasn't there. "Run this by me. Are they transients? How, when, why?" They had to be transients, because no one in this town would mess with Jenny's dad. He's a rough and tumble bartender with a shotgun *and* a bat.

Vincent gets a funny look on his face."Not exactly sure it was a they. Might've been one guy working alone. We've got people out there now, going over the scene." He turns to Ed.

Throwing an arm around him, he whispers something that makes Ed's brows crunch. The two wander farther from my bed.

The concussion must have affected my ears, because sensitive isn't a strong enough word for how they're suddenly picking up sound. I'm plugged into everything they're saying. I even hear Vincent squeeze out a fart from across the room. "The word is, the place was ransacked. Like a tornado ripped through. Or a small army. Something pounded on the bedroom door, almost tore it off the hinges. The old man fired off two shots from his ten gauge ... through the door. Said everything went quiet. He waited a few minutes before he entered the hallway, but nothing was there. When he looked out the window, he saw a figure loping away."

"Loping?" The word seems to catch in Ed's throat.

"So I was told," Vincent says. I envision his mouth gathering to one side, like an accordion. The same way he spoke to me through the side of his mouth earlier.

"What broke in, a fucking antelope?" I interject, visualizing the animal kicking down the door. I'm staring at the ceiling. Vincent and Ed are silent. Jenny doesn't respond to my comment. I hear her grabbing tissues from the nightstand, blowing her nose.

Vincent sounds cautious. "We'll know more in the morning. I wanted to break the news to Jenny so she didn't see the activity at her house when she got home, and freak out. She's been through enough."

You're just realizing that now? I want to shout. "I appreciate your thoughtfulness. Jesus, what a night." Then I really start worrying. "Jenny. I don't want you going back there. Stay at my place."

"As if," she snaps.

"Yeah. Okay. A hotel then."

"Another thing," Vincent says. "Forensics ran the dead girl's prints."

I think all eyes have fallen on him. Mine would too if they could.

"She's not from around here."

"No kidding. That's what I've been trying to tell you. I never saw her before. Who is she?"

"A fifteen year old runaway from down south." He sucks a breath. "Been missing two years."

"Makes her a seventeen year old dead girl." I verbalize the sickening thought, purposefully forcing the photos from my mind. But they keep coming back. I have the strangest feeling something is way off with this entire scenario.

"What was her name?" Jenny's voice cracks.

"Can't divulge that information. Next of kin has to be notified."

I keep wanting to shake my head. All I can do is blow out a breath. "This is whack. You've got a lot of investigating to do."

"Poor girl," Jenny mumbles. She drops a kiss on my lips, pressing this time. "I'll talk to you tomorrow, Jack. I want to get home and make sure Mom and Dad are okay."

I'm so wired, my scalp is tingling. "Jenny. I'd rather you didn't ..."

"We'll have a car outside all night, Jack." I know Ed's trying to comfort me, but it's not working. "Rest easy, buddy. She'll be fine."

~~~~~~

I'm bathed in silence, and the moonlight creeping through the window.

Jenny's gone. The detectives packed it in. The nurses gave me something to help me sleep, but it's not working. My side bothers me. My chest actually. I slip my hand under the blanket, beneath my gown, and feel the bandage. My ribs feel swollen. Or are those my abs? I'm curious. Since I can't sleep, I might as well bug the staff, so I ring for the nurse.

"What's wrong, Jack? In pain?" The one with the aging voice is beside me, snapping the light over my bed on.

"Nah. You got me high enough to ward off pain. I'm just wondering about this." I lift the blanket with one hand, and point with the other. I stare into her kind blue eyes.

"It's one of your wounds. Don't worry about it. It will heal." By the tone of her voice, she's trying to either dismiss me or ease my mind. I'm not sure which.

I squirm. "It's taking all my willpower to not scratch it."

"Itchy, huh? Let me take a look." I feel her prodding fingers. Her fine lips gather with a cryptic, "Hmm."

"What's wrong?" I'm like a baby now. Having panic attacks over horseshit.

"Nothing's wrong. It's odd, that's all." Now she's acting breezy. Is she blowing me off?

"Don't leave me hanging ... What do you mean it's odd?" I'm feeling stronger. I actually lift my head off the pillow. Strain at the foam collar to try to catch a glimpse of my side.

"You had a deep wound. Down to one of your ribs. A jagged tear."

"How'd that happen? I heard someone say a chunk was missing. I was wearing a leather jacket. How could that have happened?"

"I dunno, Jack." She shrugs her brows which are as thin and pale as her lips. "Accidents, especially motorcycle accidents, cause all kinds of injuries. But I wouldn't worry about it."

"You don't have to worry about it. You're not the one lying here. I don't understand. I can't feel pain but I'm itchy as all hell." I give her a snarky look. "You still didn't tell me the odd thing."

She clicks the light switch and the room falls dim. "Just medical stuff. Nothing for you to worry about. Now get some rest." She pats my shoulder and tucks my sheet. "You've got enough medication in you to knock out one of those three-hundred pound sumo wrestlers." She clicks her tongue. "That's the odd thing I was talking about."

Yeah, right. Good save ...

She steps in front of the window, arms crossed, the moonlight outlining her fluffy hair. Then she checks my IV and monitors.

I'm not sure if it's her movements, or the fact that her shadow looks bulky, but I get a flashback and jump. Electricity courses through my upper body.

"What is it, Jack?" She's back at my side, hanging over me with widening eyes that glisten.

My airway is raw, congested. "Nothing," I rasp. "I just thought ... I remembered that I was ..."

She has no idea what I'm babbling about. She pats my hand. "Don't you worry, dear. Dr. Sloan is an amazing surgeon. He stitched you up so good, I could barely see anything. You had a serious wound, but it's like a scratch now. You might only have a small scar."

"Praise to my surgeon. So it's itching because it's healing? Maybe it's getting infected." My bedside machine beeps faster. Here we go again.

"Nope. It's closed up nicely and already healing." She's on her way out the door. "I have other patients. I'll check in with you later."

Wheel Wolf

Jenny: The Morning After

I'm sitting in the hospital cafeteria, a raw nerve, drowning, waiting for my lifeline; the start of visiting hours. I cut out abruptly last night, but did phone the nurse's station at midnight to inquire about Jack's condition. I feel terrible about deserting him, but so many things are happening at once, I can barely think.

The tips of my fingers are drumming Formica. It's tacky. I keep wiping the tabletop with a napkin, but I think the surface is just old. Tired, like me, because I barely slept. My eyes are dry. I'm not wearing makeup, so I can run my hands freely over my face. Smooth away anxiety, or attempt to, anyway.

I keep glancing at a nearby table where a couple of Jack's friends are sipping from cups like mine. Maybe coffee. Hot chocolate? I wonder if they're waiting to visit him, and why they're not acknowledging me. Too enrapt in conversation, I guess.

I'd know Drake's faux hawk anywhere. Beside him is Steve with the freshly buzzed head. Jack's riding buddies are all unique, like Jack. I'm surprised they hang in the same circle, because they appear so opposite. Like mismatched socks. Clashing colors. They're nice guys though. I'm tempted to join them. I could use the company. Positive reinforcement, because they appear pretty cheerful, considering the circumstances. This makes me resentful. I wonder what subject matter is interesting enough to hold their attention, keep their eyes trained on each other. Cars, bikes, or girls. Take your pick, Jen.

Not only am I still freaked out over Jack's accident, but my house was nearly destroyed last night, with my parents trapped inside their bedroom. Thank God they weren't injured. But the home invasion occurring right on top of Jack's accident is like grinding salt into an open wound. Thinking about Jack, about the condition of my house, my parents, I'm trembling. It takes the strength of two unsteady hands to lift the cardboard cup to my lips.

Before the wall clock reads ten, I'm up and heading for the elevator. Dropping my empty cup in a waste receptacle positioned between the two metal doors, tapping the *up* button a few times, because patience is not my virtue. Especially at a time like this. I feel the floor beneath my feet quake and worry about my legs that still feel like caving. Then I realize it's the vibration of the elevator car sliding down the cables that's making the stone slabs shudder.

Suddenly a crowd gathers around me. It seems I'm not the only one anxiously awaiting the opportunity to cram into one of the intimate rooms upstairs. In my peripheral, I see Jack's two friends near the back of the crowd. They're still talking a mile a minute, oblivious to their surroundings ... and me.

A bunch of people squeeze into the car. I'm backed into a rear corner. When the door slides closed, I'm almost bowled over by a combination of perfume, aftershave, and deodorant. Then the air that I'm sucking in is flavored with someone else's coffee and mints. Close ... too close. Difficult to breathe, but not enough room to faint, so get a grip.

A guy standing beside the control panel calls out, "What floor?"

Wheel Wolf

"Four," I reply with a forced smile. My neck springs with an involuntary jerk, whisking me from the man's clear blue eyes to the smooth steel wall, while I wonder if he's a doctor because he's impeccably groomed and dressed in a suit that screams expensive. He has an air of indulgence about him. I'd like to be standing beside him, instead of the cold wall. Tap into his reservoir of strength.

Steve and Drake didn't make this elevator. Maybe they're not here for Jack after all. Just as well. I'd rather have him all to myself. By the time we reach Jack's floor, there are only two of us left. The professional looking button pusher and me. The door slides open. He nods and waits for me to exit.

The heart of the hospital reeks of antiseptic and breakfast. Butterflies gather in my stomach. My studded Steve Maddens skim the tiled floor soundlessly. I don't intentionally peer through open patient doors; I can't help myself. Stealing a sneak peek of misery must be a human reaction when one is making their way down the corridor of a healthcare facility. Curiosity I guess. Or perhaps assuming someone is in worse shape than your loved one offers some kind of sick comfort. I know it sounds dumb. I'm trying to occupy my mind with something other than the condition of my home. My frantic mother.

This floor houses the ICU and Step Down units, where critically ill patients are fighting for their lives. I've never minded hospitals ... until now. My pulse picks up, and it's not because I'm half jogging. I glide around a collision course of food carts filled with scraps on trays, occupied wheel chairs and stretchers, medical staff. The place is already hopping. No one notices me. We're all on our own preoccupied planets.

I slow at the nurse's station, but it looks abandoned. So I shrug and continue on to Jack's room. To the doorway that's wide open, waiting and welcoming. I put on my biggest smile as I bounce into the room, cradling a box of cookies.

"Baby!" Jack calls, stretching his arms out to me. He's not flat on his back anymore. The head of his bed is elevated. He's grinning like he does when we're able to grab a quick cup of coffee before work. There's a sparkle in his eyes, like he's been dying to see me and is thrilled I've finally arrived.

Suddenly my smile isn't pasted on, because the sight of him is like a shot of booze, a relaxing bath, the whirlpool tub surrounded by lighted candles. I don't feel myself fly to his side, but I must because I'm almost on top of him and I've only taken one light breath since entering. At least I have enough presence of mind to restrain myself from slamming him with my full weight.

"How are you feeling, honey?" I hold back tears and the urge to throw myself into his arms, but let my face burrow into his muscular shoulder while I count my blessings. "How was your night? Are you in pain?" Lips pressed against him, the warm breath I release ricochets back to my face.

Through the lightweight cotton gown he's cuddly warm and smells like hospital. Not woodsy, but sleepy sexy just the same. I push off the sides of his mattress that support my palms and me, examining him with my eyes, then my fingers. I brush back those stubborn bangs which are really too long to be called bangs. Then I drop my lips onto his and let them slide at will, savoring the softness of his mouth. His hands run up and down my back, fingers tightening. He tastes like orange juice and medicine. I think he's getting turned on, because he's pulling me closer or straining toward me. Maybe both. Leave it to Jack to get all kinds of horny in a hospital bed. The thought makes me smile, break our kiss.

He moans and cracks the cutest smile. "Better now that you're here." He pulls me closer. "I like your shirt. Along with the curves ... and the color." He grins. "That purple almost matches your eyes."

"Jack," I breathe against the side of his face, sliding my nose up his cheek, to his ear. Then I draw back and gaze into his eyes which are brighter today. The gold flecks more prominent. "You look great, baby." I can't keep my fingers out of his hair while I leave a trail of kisses across his forehead.

"All things considered, I feel pretty great, Jenny. How are you holding up?" He cups my cheeks with his palms. Stares at me intensely.

I'm standing in an awkward position, my body so twisted, my back hurts. I have no choice but to step back, pull up a chair, and drag it as close to the bed as possible. Cradle his arm to my breast. Nuzzle his hand. "I'm okay. What a crazy night, Jack. When they told me my house was broken into, they underestimated *broken.*"

His eyes widen. The arm I'm cradling readjusts so that his fingers can grip the back of my neck reassuringly, and massage. "Tell me, babe. What the hell went on? How are your folks?" His voice is urgent, like his eyes. "Dobie okay?"

"Dobie's still walking around with his tail between his legs. He hasn't stopped shaking. Neither has my mom. They're traumatized." *Traumatized* ... I've been trying to swallow the lump in my throat all morning. Since last night, actually. I let out a hoarse breath because my insides feel raw. It's the weirdest sensation. Like every nerve inside and out is overcharged and screeching.

"When I pulled up and parked the Jeep I almost fainted. It looks like a bomb went off, Jack. The front door is now a pile of splintered wood lying on the porch. The swing was thrown through the picture window. Along with exterior damage, almost every piece of furniture in the living room was overturned or ripped apart. Dining room table karate chopped in half. Broken china scattered all over the place. Even the wood railing leading upstairs was torn down. Spindles stabbed into the wall like toothpicks! Sticking out like ... Who could do that? How?" I can't hold back a sob. "I'm worried about my mom. She's taking it the worst."

"Holy shit, baby," he swipes his free hand over the stubble on his cheeks, then pulls on his chin, "what the fuck. Do the cops have any leads? I mean, why would anyone do this? Besides being destroyed, was anything of value taken?" His eyes are shifting. I know he's trying to make sense of what I'm saying, but unless he witnessed it, he couldn't even begin to imagine. There aren't any words.

I shake my head. "Nope." I find swallowing as difficult as my next words. "If I didn't know better, I'd think someone had it out for me and my family." Just the thought of someone harboring such anger toward us makes me feel frightened enough to run into the bathroom again to vomit. "I *hope* I know better Jack, because honestly," my voice is shaking, "it's like someone was motivated by rage. Unbelievable, indiscriminate, insane ..." I want to keep talking, trying to reason, but hard sobs cut off my words.

"God, baby. I want to get out of this bed. Be with you. What a time for me to be ..." he slams his fist onto the mattress, "to be stuck here without legs." His head jerks toward the window. The same window I stared out last night while seeking refuge. Is he doing the same thing? Thinking of the irony of it all. Wanting to jump out. Escape this incomprehensible fate.

I bring his face back to mine. Kiss the tip of his nose. "All you need to worry about is getting better. We'll be fine, Jack. My dad had a long talk with one of the detectives. They're checking out the possibility that it could be someone from the bar. Maybe a grudge ..."

He draws a raspy breath. "A grudge?" He runs his hand up and down my arm, then twirls the hair hanging over my shoulder around his finger.

"Maybe he refused the wrong drunk another round. Or being on the Town Council might make him a target ... maybe someone didn't get a building permit or something ..." I'm droning. Not buying my own words.

"The house is wrecked huh?" Jack's deep frown tells me he's right in there, suffering along with me. "Where are you staying? 'Cos you all can use my house, you know that, right?"

"Thanks, honey." My lips part minimally. "We're staying in Tidalfalls." My fingers are gently threading through his hair. "One of my dad's friends is already patching the place up. We're renovating while we're at it. It'll be like a new house."

Can our eyes lock any tighter? I'm so drawn to him right now. If he wasn't in this bed ... What's up with this, Jen? You're suddenly magnetized to the guy you've been with for years? Like you can't tear yourself away? Maybe it's because you almost lost him. Realized just how precious he is. Important.

"That's good, baby. Stay as far away from this town as possible, till all of this crap is sorted out." His lips are moving in slow motion. He's as lost in me as I am in him. "I love you so much, Jenny."

"I can't believe I almost lost you," catches in my throat.

"Never, baby." He's so choked up his eyes are watering.

I'm leaning against the side of the bed. Cradling his head. Rocking him. He's holding onto as much of me as he can reach, his neck brace and cheek pressing into my rib cage. This is how we are when Steve and Drake creep into the room.

"Hey," Jack is the first to greet his friends. Locked in our special moment, I didn't hear them enter. "How'd you know I was here?"

"You kidding? It's all over the news. Papers, radio, even TV. They're showing the stretch of 44 where you dumped the bike, the same video over and over," Steve says, rubbing his hands over his head. Then they drop into the pockets of the jeans wrapping his muscular thighs. "I'm sorry, man. How are you doing?"

Both Steve and Drake are visibly shaken. I guess I now know what kept their heads pinned together earlier: Jack's accident.

Trying to figure out what happened to their good buddy. Wondering if the same could possibly happen to them.

"I'm handling." Jack squeezes my hand, and I know he'd be more open with them if I wasn't standing beside him.

I step back, retreat to the foot of the bed, because I feel Drake's breath on the back of my neck. They lock hands they way guys do, all tough and macho. "Me too, Jack. I'm sorry, bro," Drake consoles. He acts and sounds as stiff as his faux hawk. "What the hell happened out there? If anyone knows how to ride it's you, man."

It suddenly occurs to me. Jack never explained why he was out on 44 when he said he was going straight home. The photos of the dead girl flash across my mind, and I can't help but wonder what went on.

"Yeah, Jack. What happened out there?" I must sound miffed, because I'm suddenly the focal point of three heads and six pairs of straining eyes. "You were going to tell me after the police left last night." For some odd reason, I find myself massaging his toes.

"Yeah, we actually never got around to it." Jack puckers the side of his mouth and scrubs his quickly sprouting beard with the palm of his hand.

Drake's and Steve's intense expressions mellow, as though they're apologizing for just acknowledging my presence. "Hey, Jenny." My name chimes with precision timing. "What's up?"

Now we're all standing at the foot of Jack's bed.

"Hey." With one word, I mock up a smile. "Want a chocolate chip cookie? Jack doesn't seem to like my cookies anymore."

"I love your cookies, babe." Jack winks. "I'm just not hungry right now. I just ate eggs." He makes a barf face.

"I thought you like eggs?" I tug on his foot, hoping for a reflex.

When he shrugs, his muscular shoulders push up his collar.

"Eh. I'd rather have sweets." He sticks out a hand. "I'll take a couple of those cookies ..."

"Listen, Jack. Maybe we'll hit the road." Steve sounds eager to leave, and I think my attitude is giving him an out. Or is he ready to hit the road because his buddy is lying in a hospital bed? Maybe both.

"Yeah. Gotta get to work," Drake agrees, then shocks me by saying, "Jenny. What happened at your place last night? Between Jack's accident and the disaster at your house, there's nothing else on TV."

"We don't know, Drake. The police are still investigating." A chill shoots up my spine, because it's reality. Having my misfortune broadcast on the news, and others watching it, makes it undeniable.

"Who was the dead girl they're talking about?" Drake's wide eyes probe Jack's. "They're not saying much other than a body ..." The tone of his voice sounds gossip hungry.

Jack shoots him a sharp look. Tightens his jaw.

"So listen. When are you getting out?" Steve, who's been standing by with his hands in his pockets, breaks the tension. I doubt his friends realize he's partially paralyzed, otherwise they wouldn't be inquiring about his discharge.

"Not sure. Maybe a month." Jack's arm is still extended, his fingers wiggling. "How about those cookies."

Steve hops around the bed to take the box from where I left it on the night table, pops a cookie into his own mouth, then sets the box down beside Jack. "Knock yourself out." I watch the way Steve chews and swallows. "Mmm. These are really good, Jenny."

"A month?" Drake's eyes widen further, then he walks around the bed to grab a cookie from the box. "Why so long? You look fine," he says, munching.

Jack's palms level a solid smack on his thighs. "I've got a little problem." When he hits his legs again, the box bounces off the bed. Steve makes the save. "These guys won't work." I know Jack. He's biting back emotion. He has to be. Jack's not one to be inactive. This has to be devastating for him. It is for me.

Both guys pale, but Steve also reacts by rubbing his buzzed head. "Christ, Jack. I hope it's not permanent?" He blurts out more of a question, than statement. I can't believe we're gathered at Jack's bedside, talking this way. My heart goes out to Jack because he has to reply to such an intrusive question.

"Nah." Jack is all false bravado. "I just need time to heal." His eyes aren't seeking out at any of us. He's staring at the ceiling.

"Listen, dude." Drake grips the back of his neck, then drops his hands into his pockets, and rocks on his heels. "If you need anything ... and I mean anything at all. Text me. Call me. Whatever. Whenever. Okay, bro?"

"Sure." Jack sounds detached. He's sobering. I have a feeling seeing Drake and Steve has helped turn his denial into reality.

"Me too," Steve adds. "Hit me up. Anything. Anytime."

Jack tries to nod, but the collar restricts his movements. He manages to jerk his head toward the ceiling. "I'll call you later." I know he means he'll call them to disclose everything he's yet to tell me ... as soon as I walk out the door.

Jack has radar. The moment their footsteps recede, his arms summon me to his side. "I didn't get to ask. Where did you stay last night, babe?" He nuzzles my hand, gripping it so tightly the bones pain.

I massage his arm, detach his hand from mine. "We stayed with a family friend last night and checked into a hotel this morning. Inn at the Falls in Tidalfalls." I chuckle. "Catchy, huh?"

He laughs. "Don't think about going tubing without me."

His laughter lifts my spirit. My lips go straight to his. "Room three-twelve. I'll store the number in your cell." I stand and straighten the waist of my yoga pants. "Where's your cell?"

"In the drawer." He reaches out to pat the nightstand. "Good.

Stay there. Don't even come to see me. We'll talk on the phone. I don't want you anywhere around this place."

"What, you don't want to see me?" I pout, then I feel my mouth tighten.

His stare deepens. Any part of his body that's able to move tenses. "I just want you safe, Jen. It's not safe here."

My one arm is braced at the head of his bed, the fingers of my other hand are curling the edges of the neck of his gown. I pull up my brows. "Why did you tell the detectives to check Hosner Lake? I thought you were delirious, but ..."

He blows out a breath, and crushes my hand again. "I saw something out there, Jenny. Surprised it is more accurate." I've never seen Jack's eyes so severe.

I'm breaking out in goose bumps just watching his expression. "Wh ... what? What did you see?" I know Hosner Lake and how creepy it is with nighttime shadows and noises, which is why we call it Phantom Lake.

Jack's brows level. "I don't know, baby. It was bloody, angry ..."

"Jack, you're scaring me."

"Don't be scared, Jenny. I don't want to ever scare you. Just be careful. Don't go anywhere near that lake, or the forest." His voice is urgent, his eyes plead.

I deadpan. "You know I'd never go there without you. I don't even like going there *with* you." I narrow my eyes at him. I have to ask the question I've been evading. "Why was that girl there at exactly the same time you were, Jack? Coincidence?" My eyes burn into his. "Why was she naked?"

Jack: Jenny I'm Innocent

*M*y stomach is doing a slow roll. Curling up into a tight ball. I haven't eaten much. The hollow walls are clawing. Jenny has this look on her face like she's doubting me. I figure Steve and Drake drilling me about the accident has gotten under her skin. We need to stop talking about it. Try to get on with our lives. Maybe that's what she's attempting to do when she escapes to the window, turning once in my direction. Her sigh cuts right through me. I can feel her frustration, pain, fear. I'm experiencing the same things.

She's leaning against the metal cabinet of the heating and cooling system that's pinned to the wall beneath the window. Her raven hair flows down her back like it's mixed with indigo ink, the ends feathering as the exchange pumps fresh air into the room. She's wearing a purple tank top and gray yoga pants. I can't quite make out the designer name stamped on the foldover part, because her hair is concealing her back and half of her ass. But her calves are sleek, satin, and bare.

"Baby," I make my voice as soft as possible, which isn't easy with a throat that's still on fire, "come back over here."

I watch her shoulders lift and pause, imagining her to be struggling with a major decision.

"I want to talk to you, Jenny. Please come here." I try to pull her in with a desperate tone. Pathetic ...

When she turns, her mouth is gathered on one side. Her thinking look. Trying to decide something look. God, don't be breaking up with me, please.

"That girl came out of nowhere, Jen. I don't know her. You can't seriously be thinking I'd be with someone else."

She spins, taking such a deep breath her breasts lift deliciously, along with her eyes that stare at the ceiling for a few seconds, then she tilts her head, sucks on her full bottom lip and drifts to my side. "What ..." She lets out the sigh she's been holding. I know this because her shoulders settle. Her breasts drop back into perfect placement.

"Jen. You know how I feel about you. How much I care. I love you, baby."

She turns her killer eyes on me, and mine burn because they want to tear and I won't let them. She's sliding her fingers up my arm, across my chest, up the side of my face and through my hair, which means she's not really pissed at me. When she runs her fingers through my hair it usually means she wants to make out. Right now I think it's because she's trying to hold onto something. And this is her way of bringing us closer. I hope.

If she's about to falter, I'm gonna catch her before it's too late. "I stopped off at Hosner Lake on the way home because ..." An explanation loosens my lips, while my gaze holds hers steady.

Her lips purse, murmur a throaty, "Why?"

I squeeze my temples, then rub my chin. "I needed to think."

She lifts a brow but doesn't say a word. I think she's waiting for me to fuck up or something. "Don't you trust me anymore?" I breathe out concern.

Her gaze begins to boil. She twists the edge of my pillow in her fist. "It's all crazy, Jack. Too much to comprehend. And that girl. Those photos. I can't get it out of my mind. And you." Her eyes brim with tears. "This shouldn't be happening. We shouldn't be here. Why didn't you just go straight home like you always do?"

While her eyes are accusing, mine are piercing, trying to tell her things difficult for me to talk about. I've turned into an introvert. I need her to haul my ass out of this hole that's devouring me, because I can't. "I was trying to make a decision, Jenny."

She raises a brow, tilts her head. Christ, she looks sly. She must be clairvoyant. Her lips start quivering, like she can't keep them sealed, can't stop the corners from springing up. My stomach, which had been stuck in my throat, falls back into place. Thank God she's responding. She's not leaving me. Don't ever leave me, Jenny. You're all I have in this world.

"Like what kind of decision?" She's pinching my cheeks. Fluffing my pillow. Playing with the loosened tie of the stupid hospital gown I'm wearing.

I run a fingertip across her chin. Press down on the center, which tugs down her bottom lip. I'm suddenly feeling incredibly inadequate. "Bring me some clothes tomorrow, will you, babe?"

Her eyes narrow and she huffs out, "That's what you were deciding? What to wear?"

My bruised ribs stifle a painful laugh. "No, honey. Not hardly." I grab her hand, pull it to my lips. Gazing up at her from the corners of my eyes, I explain between moist kisses I place on every one of her fingers. I really want to run my tongue over every inch of her body, but manage to control the urge.

I single out her ring finger, gently twist and nibble it. "I was sitting by the lake. Counting stars. Days till I'm solid at my new job. Thinking about you. About the first time we met. How much we've been through. How much I love you." My opposite hand tightens on the back of her head, wraps her hair in a fist, draws her mouth an inch from mine like I'm about to suck out her soul. "I was thinking about how to ask you to marry me." My heart thumps as I whisper my intention.

Her face melts. Literally melts like an ice cream cone in summer sun. "Oh, Jack. I ..." Tears break from her eyes, tumble down her cheeks. She looks so beautiful. Raw emotion. Smooth skin. No makeup. Thick black lashes holding back what now looks like a tidal wave about to gush from her violet eyes which have deepened. *Like gorgeous flowers in a rainstorm* runs through my mind.

Then her face is on my chest, and I'm smoothing her hair. "I love you so much, Jen, it hurts. My heart. My head. Every part of me. I love you so much, sometimes my chest feels swollen inside, and my heart feels like it could burst with emotion I can't control. Has that ever happened to you?" Every ounce of my love shoots out with one raspy breath.

Her lips press my cheek, then release for her whisper. "Only when I look at you. Think of you. Hold you. Kiss you." She brings her face around, grabs the sides of my hair in her fists, and kisses me in a way that lifts the sheet on the bottom half of the bed. Yeah, I get all kinds of horny around her anyway, but right now, the way her tongue is sliding with mine, her hands running all over my body, is turning me from vegetable to animal. I think if we were alone, she wouldn't be a virgin when she walks across that field of flowers.

Our moment is broken by a deliberate cough, someone clearing his throat. Our heads spring up at the same time. Her lips are red and swollen. I'm licking mine, because I want to relish the taste of hers for as long as possible.

"Excuse the interruption." He's businesslike but his clear blue eyes are smiling as he stands in the doorway. I manage to turn my head enough to see the guy who just barged in on our private time. Wearing this collar is teaching my eyes to swivel like a parrot's.

He must be a doctor, because he's wearing a white coat with insignia. His hands are stuffed into the deep pockets, but his thumbs are sticking out. His mahogany shoes are highly polished. Their distinct leather smell rushes into my nose. His pant legs are cut to just the right length. Meticulously tailored so they don't touch the top of those thousand dollar wingtip shoes.

"I'm Dr. Milton. Dr. Sloan's associate. He asked me to stop in to evaluate you," he explains in a smooth voice as he approaches my bed.

I shrug, wondering exactly how many medical professionals have been in and out of this room, poking and prodding, and how exorbitant the hospital bill is gonna be.

Jenny must be on cloud nine, because her voice is musical again. "Hi doctor. We rode up in the elevator together." I don't know if the man is turning her on, or the information he'll either offer, or she'll drag out of him.

"I remember." Did he just wink at her?

When he steps to my side, Jenny inches toward my feet, but remains close enough to stick her nose under the blanket he lifts. He pulls back my chest wrap. The air feels good. I've been tapping it all night, carefully trying to stop the itch without opening the wound. Sonofabitch, the air is soothing.

"Hmm," he says. "Interesting."

Here we go again with the fucking interesting crap. My fingers brush over the area that seems to have him stumped. I'm snagging long strands of ...? When I meet his eyes, he looks as puzzled as I feel. "What's that, doc? Did part of the bandage stick to me? Is that what I'm feeling? Gauze?"

He's looking at me sideways, so I turn my head as much as I can to watch his mouth form a theory. "You've been blessed with a good head of hair, Jack. And body hair goes along with it. Androgens. Genetics."

Wheel Wolf

"Androgens?" My eyes jump to Jenny, but she's also engrossed in my side. What are they seeing that I'm not?

"I'm referring to testosterone. We'll check your levels, if you like. Your chest hair is excessive, and growing back quickly, surrounding the wound."

"Chest hair?" I know I'm hairy, but I'm not a ... I'm ready to freak out. "That's not my chest, doc. Those are my ribs. I've never had hair on my rib cage." Could surging testosterone be causing my almost constant erections? I should ask him, but ... "Sure. I ... I have great hair, but I've never had this much. Could medications cause this, you think?"

"Possibly. Let me check your chart." He slips my chart from the holder on the door, flips through accumulating pages, and his heels thunk back across the tiled floor. Poker faced, he puffs out a, "Nope. You're not on steroids or any meds that could generate hair growth."

Jenny is silent. Arms folded across her chest. Lips parted, her stare is shooting from me to him, until he excuses himself. Then her eyes are all mine.

"What do you think, babe?" I ask when he marches out the door to arrange for my blood test. "Have I always been this way? Maybe I just never noticed."

She shakes her head. The side of her throat pulses. "I would have."

Jack: Shadow Lane Rehab

During the next twenty-four hours, a steady stream of doctors, nurses, even visitors, drop by to check out the miracle patient. It seems the professionals are dumbfounded. My chest wound has almost healed. Hair is sprouting where it never grew before, concealing the damaged area. The dissolvable stitches have already dissolved. I won't even have a scar. The bone in my leg has finished knitting, but I still can't walk.

Although Dr. Sloan estimated my hospital stay to be a month or more, I'm sitting in a wheelchair, being rolled through discharge and tossed onto a gurney. Taken by ambulance and admitted into a rehab, all within one week.

My arms are forklifts. I maneuver myself off the gurney, plop my ass into the waiting chair, and wave goodbye to the attendant I cracked sick jokes with on the ride over. They've got me dressed in sweats, t-shirt, and socks. I almost feel like I'm about to lounge around at home. But I'm far from homesick.

"This isn't a bad place," I remark to the redheaded chick wheeling me from the intake area. With plants, flowers, glass walls, admitting is part of the solarium. Nice touch. Even picnic tables circle a patio outside. I bob my head approvingly. "Yeah, Shadow Lane rocks."

I'm checking out the immaculate tiled floors as we head off in another direction, admiring clean paint, plenty of headroom in the hallways for tall dudes. Wide too. For wheelchairs. We pass closed doors. Open doors. A variety of residents. Cool gym. Massage rooms. Swimming pool. Excellent sauna. The redhead gives me a full tour. I think I've somehow been transported to Club Med.

"It's an awesome place." Even her voice smiles. She's nice. I like her. She's not Jenny likeable, but she's nice. "My name is Rachel Huntress. I'm your therapist, psychologist, nutritionist, all around anything you need just call on me person."

"Huntress?" I chuckle. "Jack of all trades, huh? So, have you seen my kind of injury before?" I try not to whine. Which I almost want to do, because my condition is so fucking confining. I'm used to being a guy on the run. Running. Sports. Potential forest ranger. My stomach contorts. I'm not sure how long I can remain incapacitated and cordial.

"I know what you're thinking. I don't hunt." She deadpans. "I've seen your type of injury many times. And I know what you're about to ask. No, I can't predict whether or not you'll walk again, but we're sure as heck gonna try to keep the muscles in those legs in tiptop shape. Just in case."

"In case I need to make a run for it?" When she doesn't laugh, I feel like a jerk. "You'll get used to my dry sense of humor." My chuckle fails too. Gimme a break lady. I roll my eyes, imagining the turn my relationship is destined to take with this mind reader. So much for snap judgments.

She wheels me through the double size doorway. My room isn't big, but it's neat. Jenny would call it cozy. Blinds covering the window, which is nice, as I plan on doing a lot of sleeping. A variety of aromas swirl through the air, along with dust. With the rays of sun shining through the slats, I can pinpoint the gazillions of particles my lungs must be taking in, as this is the air I'm breathing. I can almost taste the microscopic fur balls. Sour. They say, take time to smell the coffee. I say, take a minute to check out the dust. It's pretty amazing. Fluffy little critters with a life of their own. Eyes, noses, antennas. They actually squiggle.

Rachel is sweeping her arm around the room. "Here's your dresser. Nightstand. Closet. Your bed. It's a twin, but since ..."

"Yeah, since I won't be rolling around, it's fine. I know." Checking out my new residence, I'm droll.

"Double window for plenty of ventilation, but only one side opens."

I squint at her.

She's not smiling anymore. Her lips pinch together. "No sneaking in and out."

"Do I look like I'm going anywhere?" I roll my eyes, but she's not focusing on me. She's dragging something off the closet shelf.

"When I found out you were coming, I picked up some motorcycle magazines." She plops them on my lap. "Hope you like them. And here's yesterday's and today's news. Have fun. Call me if you need me."

I nudge my head at her. "So how do I do that?"

"Buzzer beside your bed." She plops down my duffle bag and gawks at me.

"No ice water in the jug on the table? What'll I chase my booze down with?"

She shoots me a slow, sarcastic blink. "You know damn well that's a urinal."

"Actually, I've never seen one up close. I guess the gooseneck should've tipped me off." I shrug. "You can take it with you. I'll never use it."

"It's for late night emergencies. So you don't have to bother the staff ... namely myself. Unless you don't think you know how to use it." She rounds both brows.

I attempt to pull off cocky. "Believe me. I know how to use it." My voice is so cool, it tries to swagger without me.

"Then we'll get along just fine." She moves to the window, opens the slats of the blinds.

I throw an arm over my face. "Close them," I snap. "The light hurts my eyes."

She shoots me a dagger stare. "Seven am until seven pm, Jack will be awake — blinds will be open."

Christ, what am I in for? "Copy that." I salute her with a head nod. "Thank you, Rachel. You're an excellent host."

"Hospitality is my middle name." Her stare is long and hard. "You think I'm kidding?"

Phew. This chick is not only at least six feet tall, but she's weird. Elvira attractive. But weird.

"I take it you don't do much kidding." I'm fucked, because joking is my way of hiding when I can't deal.

"I don't do kidding." Her green eyes are like glass.

A deep, "No shit," is buried under my breath. I wouldn't put it past this drill sergeant to wash my mouth out with soap.

Before Rachel splits, she strolls to my side, lifts and shoves the front page of today's news under my nose. Gruesome details of a murder make my head want to spin. She just watches me, like she's gauging my reaction. My shock must be satisfying. Her porcelain face cracks, and without a word, she's out the door. Her Crocs squeak as she takes the turn after her exit. I'm left in the middle of the room, my mouth dropping. Her head pops around the door. "No visitors in patient rooms."

"What? I didn't read that in the new patient handbook."

"No visitors in my rooms, Mr. Bailey. My rule." She stares, then winks. Man is she out there.

"I'll save the mags for tonight. Take my mind off Jenny. Do

January Valentine

I even want to read the news?" I'm already talking to the walls that are closing in on me. I toss the magazines onto the bed. The front page of the paper almost pulls my eyes out of my head. *Missing Angel's Bend Woman Found Dead.* Holy fuck. Not far from Jenny's house. What the hell's happening to this town? This must be the unfortunate girl the detectives were quizzing me and Jen about in the hospital.

What used to be a small, quiet berg, is bursting at the seams. Growing so fast, I can't keep up with all the new faces. I'm clueless as to the lure. Angel's Bend is nothing but a bunch of big-assed mountains — and we're the valley between them. The pollen bowl, with nothing but a bunch of sniffling, sneezing, residents. I should have left a long time ago. With Jenny, of course. I don't know why anyone would come here. Maybe the hunting? Camping? Nature? Freedom? What's freedom anymore?

Before wheeling myself to the window to draw up the blinds, I grab a pair of Esquire sunglasses from my bag. I'm on the ground floor, staring out at a garden. No wonder they call it Shadow Lane. The entire place is surrounded by a forest of willows and oaks dropping shade over everything. Flowerbeds, walkways, the guy riding a mower, another who's pulling weeds. The forest is one huge umbrella.

That's odd ... I cock my head. I don't need to reposition my ear. Through the closed window, I can hear the gardeners breathing.

Even with shades on, the sun is bright as hell. Charging through the trees. Patterning the lawn. My eyes sting. I pull off the glasses. Rubbing rough palms over closed lids isn't exactly soothing.

Enough of the great outdoors; my eyes burn and water, so I drop the blinds and go back to the newspaper that's now spread open across my thighs. Taunting me. I can't help but dive in.

I'm chewing the earpiece of the glasses that are dangling

from my teeth, while scrutinizing the small black fonts:

Story continued from front page. The mutilated body of a local woman reported missing by a family member was found ten miles north of Hosner Lake, near the scene of a deadly motorcycle accident which some authorities are connecting to a possible homicide.

Great. Now it's a homicide. Am I still a person of interest?

Due to the age of the victim and nature of the crime, identity of the deceased is being withheld, but sources indicate the wounds found on the body are not consistent with another recent area death. The still unidentified young woman found earlier this month was presumed to be a runaway struck by a motorcycle operated by local resident, Jack Bailey, who was partially paralyzed when he lost control of the bike. He is receiving care at Shadow Lane Rehabilitation Facility.

Sure, splash my name and whereabouts all over the news. Why protect a potential suspect? *Lost control* is the worst part. Liars. I know what tackled feels like. Fuck you authorities and newspaper.

Medical examiners and authorities are dismayed by the causes of death and condition of the bodies of both victims. Autopsy results are being withheld pending further analysis.

Residents are cautioned not to panic, but advised to remain in their homes after dark and avoid wooded areas. However, a curfew has not been imposed. The victims may be linked to a rash of murders police believe may be a result of a serial killer traveling across the country.

[For an expert analysis of serial killers, Article on page 26. Dr. Arnold Grass, renowned psychologist and author of *Looking Through the Eyes of a Serial Killer*.]

"Yeah, right. Thank you, not." I roll the paper into a funnel. Bring the tip to my lips, and blow bugle taps. Then let it sail across the room, where it almost knocks over a lamp.

Another girl is dead. I can't get homicide off my mind. "Just my luck to run into a crazy chick and get involved in this mess." I'm talking to walls again. Swiping perspiration from my upper lip with my pinky. *Who the fuck was she? Who the fuck is running around here killing people?*

I'm sitting here pondering why all hell is suddenly breaking loose. This town used to be dead. No pun intended.

Rachel strolls into the room, her long legs covered by baggy cotton pants, but the shapely outline of said legs is evident through the soft fabric. "You've got a visitor, Jack." She steps behind my chair. I can feel her truck driver hands swipe my shoulders, then grip the handlebars.

"Whoa. Where are you rolling me to?" I'm still wearing the foam collar for support, but can damn well turn my head. I'm indignant.

"The solarium. You need to get out of this room for a while. Have a glass of orange juice, a cup of coffee. A snack. Greet your visitor."

"No. I'm not leaving my room." I grip my wheels, pouring every ounce of my stubbornness into my fingers, until moving my chair is a physical impossibility.

She's still behind me, but her head is lowered, snaking around me. She's breached my comfort zone. I'm struck with an uncomfortable feeling, like I'm a baby, and she's peeking into my carriage. "Do you suffer from social anxiety, Jack?" This chick can't grasp the meaning of privacy. Or no.

"I don't suffer from anything other than sounds that kill my fucking eardrums." I got her attention. She stands in front of me, hands on hips, and cocks her head. She's stonewalling me. This means I have no choice but to explain.

"I can't take the noise in the solarium. In the cafeteria. Through the closed window. I heard the old man next door piss in his urinal. The grunt when the one on the other side of me," I flick my head to the back wall, "took a shit ten minutes ago. His bathroom must vent into mine. It still reeks. I can even hear the air whistling through your windpipe, Rachel. I can't stand it." I'm gearing up for an explosion, because I never knew sounds, other than a rock concert or blasting radio, could hurt this much. Make my ears ring without mercy.

When she clicks her tongue, I focus on the tip. It looks pretty damn moist. Stop it, Jack! "What you're experiencing is a classic symptom of a head injury called hyperacusis. I'll get you some Xanax."

"I don't touch that stuff." Now I'm fixating on her scarlet mouth. Dammit.

"Suit yourself." She stares, then says, "I'll bring Dr. Sloan in."

She disappears and my cell phone chimes.

HEY BABY.

HEY BACK. WHERE R U, JEN?

HANDS FULL W/WORK. MOM. CAN'T COME TONITE. :(

Shit.

HOW ARE YOU HOLDING UP, JACK? HOW IS SLR?

OTHER THAN A LUNATIC P.T. OKAY.

LOL.

Yeah, right. I hope you're getting a kick out of this.

ANY PROGRESS WITH LEGS?

NO. GUNNA START WALKING ON HANDS.

LOL. I LOVE YOU, JACK. C U TOMORROW XOXOXOXO

LOVE YOU, BABY. B SAFE. 4 U & ME :D XOXOXOXO

When Dr. Sloan walks through the door, the first thing I notice is his feet. "So what's the urgency that you're visiting me on your day off?" I roll up to stick out a hand.

His grip is light. He cocks his head.

"Yeah. You're dressed pretty casual. And you're wearing

golf shoes."

He chuckles and advances into the room. Settling into an easy chair in a corner, he crosses his leg. "How are you doing, Jack?" He digs into a pocket and comes up with two pieces of hard candy, unwraps one and hands me the other.

"I'm handling. What's the word, doctor?" I'm feeling the butterflies that usually accompany only Jenny. "Get my blood test results your associate Dr. Milton ordered?"

"Yes. They're normal." He strokes his beard.

My molars crush the cherry jawbreaker rolling around inside my mouth. "Hmm. Okay. That's good, right?" Thump. Skip. Heart, calm down.

His foot starts bobbing, which makes me nervous. "Yes. The blood tests Dr. Milton ordered are good. But ..." He sucks and blows air like the hospital ventilator. "The night you were brought in, I took tissue samples from the wound on your side. I didn't like the way it looked. It was ragged and ... suspicious ..."

"Don't stop now. I'm about to jump out of this chair, doctor. Too much has been happening. I'm not sure how much more suspense or weirdness I can handle."

"I'm sorry, Jack. It's just very unusual. I don't run into things like this on a daily basis, so I wanted to be sure. I received the pathology report this morning."

"And?" I can feel my eyes pulse as they work their way into his head. "Normal?"

"Unusual." The candy bump in his cheek shifts sides.

"Yeah. You already said that. What kind of unusual? I've seen it before unusual. Or, I have no fucking idea what's wrong with you unusual?" My teeth are grinding remnants of the jawbreaker. The feedback hits my ears. It sounds like a cement slab is being dragged back and forth inside my ear canal. "Christ. My ears. When is this sensitivity gonna stop?"

He waves off my question. "I believe you were bitten, Jack."

Wheel Wolf

He's so blunt, it takes a few seconds for his diagnosis to penetrate.

"Bitten? Do you mean to tell me, a chunk of my flesh is inside some animal's gut?" Holy fuck. I'm about to be sick. "Do I need a rabies shot?"

"You've already had the first of the series." He uncrosses one leg, and crosses the other.

"Christ. A dog bit me when I was lying on the ground unconscious?" I'm lowering my head that's moving side to side, rubbing a palm over my sandpaper cheek.

"I'm not sure what bit you." More bluntness. At least he's honest.

My head snaps up. "Come on." I grip my wheels, roll back and forth. If I could use my legs I'd be pacing. "Are you serious?"

"Traces of saliva point to a human, but the teeth marks don't. In my estimation, they resembled some type of canine."

I'm shaking my head, blinking so fast I'm feeling dizzy, wondering if I'm about to experience a fit of Epilepsy. Why not? Seems I'm developing all kinds of health problems since the fucking accident that I didn't fucking cause. Bit by an animal with human spit. So now I need rabies shots. Fucking terrific. What next?

He unfolds his hands, lifts them from his lap and straightens his shirt collar. "Are you comfortable here, Jack? Do you need anything?"

I'm at a loss for words. "A psychiatrist, maybe," I mumble.

He offers a patronizing smile. "I know this a lot to digest. You've been through hell. But things will work out." He leans forward, his hands forming a steeple, like he's praying. His eyes run over my hands on the chair wheels. I'm gripping so tightly, my fingers pain. "Would you like me to order a motorized chair? You've got good insurance. All of your bills are being taken care of."

"Believe me, doc. Money is the least of my worries.

I've got plenty."

"Your folks left you ..."

"Well off. But I'll keep the cheapest chair on the market." I pat the wheels. "These are my motors." I flex my biceps. "I have to keep something in shape. And why are you talking motorized wheelchairs? I thought this isn't really permanent?"

"That's what Rachel will be concentrating on. She's incredibly experienced. Has a great track record and designs a fantastic program. She'll put you through the paces." He nods and waits. Is he waiting for me to agree? "How are you two getting along?"

"Great, if you like female wrestlers taking you on when you have no chance of defending yourself."

He lets out a belly laugh. It seems I have the ability to make everyone around me smile and laugh. Why not me? I slap my thighs. This is why, moron.

If Dr. Sloan leans any farther out of the chair, he'll be on my lap. Or stretched across the floor, because I'm backing up. Retreating. Crawling into my shell. If there was a door behind me instead of a wall, I'd punch it open and propel myself out. If there was a door behind me, the only place I'd end up in is the old guy's bathroom. Face it. You're trapped.

"I'm going to be frank with you, Jack. Because I might need you to work with me. Something is weighing heavy on my mind. Another body was brought in this morning in the same condition as the first, or second rather. The morgue is busy. Our medical examiner is working around the clock on this."

Blood drains from my face, my arms; I'm not sure where it's going because I feel numb all over. My scalp is tingling. "You're telling me there are suddenly three mysterious deaths in this small town?" I eye him with suspicion. "What do I have to do with this?"

"Don't get alarmed." He holds up his palms.

Wheel Wolf

"Yeah, sure, right. I'm a person of interest in a possible homicide, and now you're the bearer of more bad news. How can I help but ... What does any of this have to do with me?"

His gaze sharpens. He resembles a mad scientist. "I'd like you to submit to more tests, tissue and fluid samples, because ..."

"Nope. No more tests. I'm not a pin cushion and you're not putting me in a Petrie dish." I shake my head, then squint. "What kind of tests and why? Am I being implicated?"

"I'm working independently of the authorities. I'd like to order some additional pathology. There were peculiar similarities in the saliva found on the bodies of the local women. I'm looking for a connection."

My jaw slackens. "Were there teeth marks too?"

"No. Well, yes. Similar patterns, but ..."

"You've got me going in circles."

"Tell me about it." He's suddenly on my level. "There hasn't been this much excitement or activity around here since they carried the Torch in 2004."

"Who, or what, bit me? Any idea?" Droll is a great cover up for panic.

He shakes his head. He's solemn, so I know what's coming. Nothing. Why did I even bother to ask?

He runs a palm across his forehead, then his eyes dig into mine. "I'm upset with myself."

Now I'm getting upset with him too. "Why is that?" I drum my fingertips on the armrests of my chair.

He's shaking his head, staring into space, talking as though to himself. "I should have had the bite analyzed."

I'm rethinking my refusal. "I'm right here. Analyze away."

His eyes snap into mine. They narrow. "The girl's bite."

"Something got both of us when we were lying on 44?" Misery loves company doesn't get you anywhere.

"No, Jack. Match her teeth to the bite on your side. We should have taken dental impressions for bite mark analysis." He keeps rubbing his temples. "The lab found her DNA on you. And I noticed what I thought were teeth marks, but since your bodies were tangled, there's nothing conclusive to tie two and two together."

"Back up. So now, I was bitten by the girl?"

"As I told you earlier, I can't be sure. I've never seen marks quite like that before."

"Nothing you're saying makes sense." I'm cradling my head. If I don't, it will roll off my shoulders and onto the floor. "Does anyone know who this chick was? What she was doing running naked in the woods ... biting people?"

"All I was able to find out was her prints matched those of a robbery suspect."

"The papers said she was a runaway. They didn't mention she was ..."

He shakes his head and waves me off again. "Forget the papers. They're guessing."

Now I'm guessing. "Don't tell me. She was a runaway thief and no one claimed her body so we have no clue who she was or whatever." I cock my head and stare.

His eyes are clouded with compassion. His hands are folded and he's clicking his thumbnails together. "I'm not exactly sure of what's going on, Jack. I'm just a doctor trying to do what I was taught in medical school ... detective work."

"How *about* the police? What do *they* say?"

"It's hush hush. From what I understand, there was some kind of discrepancy ... a problem positively indentifying the remains and reaching the next of kin."

"What about whoever she robbed? Couldn't they ID her?"

"They were found dead at the scene. There were no witnesses. The crime is still unsolved."

"With modern technology, no one can find out who the hell

she was?" My mouth is hanging, my shoulders shrugging, my palms spread out before me.

One side of his mouth pulls, like it wants to frown, but his facial muscles are tied up in thought. "It's confusing. Someone had to have screwed something up along the line. Nothing matches up."

I watch his neck pulse; listen to blood surge through the artery; count the rhythmic beats of his heart. Saliva backs up in my throat. I stare at the rain of spittle when I speak. "So, let me get this straight. She may or may not have bitten me. She was probably a minor, and a robbery homicide suspect who ran away from home, and no one reported her as missing, otherwise they would have claimed her by now. So there's no way to match her to anyone or anything, other than dead victims who can't ID her. Do I have it right?"

He tightens his lips, spreads his hands out, and nods.

"And in the meantime, they buried her?" My lips twitch.

"Our questions will go unanswered. Unless we have strong enough evidence to warrant exhumation of the body, there's no way. I'm sorry."

"Not as sorry as me."

Jack: Night Out With The Cows

I'm tossing and turning. My brain hurts. It feels like it's fucking bubbling inside my skull. I'm twisting in and out of bizarre stages of sleep. I'm taking colorful naps. Beneath my sealed lids I'm seeing shadows and rainbows. Shuddering. Dancing. Circles. Lines. Dots. I bolt out of a fifth dimension of symbols and strobe lights, picturing faces, hearing voices. It's enough to drive me even more insane. A sliver of moon is filtering through the crack on either side of the blinds. Other than that, my room is dark. A tomb. A sexy tomb.

I'm smelling all kinds of mouthwatering aromas. Scents. Female. I'm tasting Jenny on my lips. Inhaling her peach perfume. I'm like a dog in heat, fighting incredible urges to hump something. Someone. I wonder if Rachel's around. Holy shit. Jenny would fucking kill me if she knew what was going through my head right now.

Unaware of how I got into this position, I find myself half hanging off the bed. What the fuck? I can move? Your arms dumbass. You're having nightmares, and you're dragging yourself across the bed.

Wheel Wolf

No way. I'm awake. Which I know, because I'm sitting up wiping drool from my mouth, and about to jerk off. Then I stop myself. I've got to get this boner predicament under control. My skin is perspiring profusely and is itchy as hell. I'm scratching myself raw, delighting at the smell of my own blood that's seeping from claw marks and pores. My senses are so acute, I believe I'm about to learn the meaning of unearthly. Everything abnormal. Dark. Deadly.

Next thing I know, my legs are twitching, dangling over the side of the mattress. I'm wiging my toes. Shit. I think I can walk. I'm balancing on the balls of my feet, padding across the carpet, pushing up the unlocked side of the window with two furry things that don't look like familiar hands. Legs over, I suck in fresh air and leap onto dewy grass. Wearing boxers? The night smells beautiful, exotic, seductive, like Jenny. Jenny.

I feel absolutely fantastic. My head is clear. My eyes are like new. Like old ... the old me. Sight without pain. Thank God I'm healed. I'm sidestepping mushroom lights trimming pathways. Leaving the shaded grounds of Shadow Lane behind.

Arms cocked at my sides, I'm picking up speed, bounding down the open road. I'm beyond athletic. I'm superhuman. Scenery is flashing past me, like a sped up movie. It's psychedelic. It's fragrant. It's beyond comprehension.

The best part, I don't have a care in the world. Just fighting the hunger.

The moon is on the rise, sailing through the sky. It's night-dawn. I'm digging the moon ... all silvery, shimmering through branches of trees, sprinkling fairy dust all over creation: all over me. I'm darting in and out of darkness, having no problem seeing, feeling no pain.

I'm on my way to Tidalfalls, to Jenny, when it hits me. I'm splashing through streams, cutting deeper into the forest. Running like a demon, with ease, with the wind, covering territory like wildlife. Cruising on two powerful legs. It feels amazing. Exhilarating. Free! I'm scenting everything the world has to offer. The woodlands. The night. The butcher shop on Ninth. Christ, I'm so hungry I could eat a cow. Brilliant idea.

I'm going ballistic, like the madman I am. But I'm a creature of the night. A raging beast. I'm the bullet whistling down the barrel of a .45, whizzing through the air, powerful. Deadly. Precise.

I'm like a kid with new kicks, a spring in my step. I've got a mind like a steel trap, the physical strength of a dozen men. I don't want to hurt anyone, but I have to know if I'm the badass I think I am. 'Cos I feel like I own the world.

I'm loping down 44, in the direction of my house, wondering if I left any steaks in the freezer. The place is dark, looks deserted. It is, asshole. Jack doesn't live here anymore. He's in rehab. Remember?

For the hell of it, I'm sniffing around my windows. Mentally staging a break-in. I even take a piss on my front lawn. That's when I notice I'm naked. Not covered with clothes or skin. Fur baby. Nice soft fur. I run my hands up and down my body digging the feel. I'm a beast, yet I can reason. And reason tells me, I'm no longer Jack Bailey. I was bitten by something that turned me into an animal. An animal craving flesh. Raw, bloody flesh. I need to get me some.

I'm angry, hungry, all kinds of emotional, but most of all, I'm out for blood. Dying to tear some poor bastard's throat out. Home invasion pops into my head.

I pad down a driveway at the end of a cul de sac where the night is murky. Lonely. I creep around the backyard. The entire downstairs seems unoccupied. Dark. Nice and inviting. The best part, a second floor light is glowing, attracting me like a moth.

Pause paws. Think. Do I break the back door down and go charging up the stairs? Burst through the bedroom door while he's on top of her? Or climb up that ivy trellis. Crash through the window. The element of surprise makes my heart beat like a drum. Pump my boiling blood more furiously through my arteries. I feed off fear. It makes me stronger. Bolder. I want to suck up every ounce of terror flowing from their human pores. Yeah. That's what it's all about.

I'm calculating, climbing, panting, teetering on a ledge, gaping jaws dripping excitement. I still have this fucking erection. I'm about to surrender to castration. I'm peering through the bedroom window, salivating. In soft pink light, they're putting on an interesting show. Sure enough, he's fucking her. Only she's on top of him, meaning, she's fucking him. I'm getting hotter by the minute. Excess saliva is dripping down my throat, so now I'm wheezing.

Here I go. Hurl my body through the window. Feet first. Shattered glass is tinkling, sprinkling, falling on white carpet like snow. Her head spins. Her blue eyes bulge. I inhale her wine breath, her passion, her terror. An amazing blend. Arousal never felt this sensational. She's on her feet, a scream lodged in her throat. Deserting the guy, she's breaking for the door.

Nah ah, sweetie. You ain't goin' nowhere. Before she can blink, I'm on her, sweeping her off her feet, holding her high over my head, so her feet are dangling off the floor. My nose is in her crotch. I'm inhaling deeply. Losing myself. She's kicking up a hell of a fuss, but I love it. I'm licking my chops. Sniffing her taste.

Her old man's still spread eagle on the bed, wearing a blindfold. Cuffed to the headboard. I have to laugh. He's out of commission, so I drop the girl, beat my chest, and let out a blood-curdling howl. I need him awake and wide-eyed to fully enjoy what's about to go down. It's showtime, folks!

Her screams are driving me wild. I want to fuck her brains out. Literally. Crack her skull like the shell of a nut and eat her brains while I'm doing her. Then sink my fangs so deep into her throbbing throat they enter one side and exit the other side. Feed the leftovers to her old man.

He knows something's off 'cos he stopped grinding, moaning. He hears me snarling. His girl is screaming her lungs out. The cops are gonna be here any minute, because the neighbors would have to be dead or unconscious not to hear the racket I'm making. We're making. She's screeching as loud as I'm howling.

Home invasion hits me hard; is this what he would have done to Jenny if she was at home the night he broke in? Only I wouldn't have been there to fight for her. Like this guy's trying to do. Struggling to free himself. It's ironic though. Both of us chained to our beds when our ladies need us. Him cuffed. Me lying in a hospital bed. Shit is swirling through my head like crap flushing down a toilet.

She throws her head back, lets out a raspy scream, then hops off him, disappearing into what I assume is the bathroom. Must have been one hell of an orgasm, is what I'm thinking when he snaps off the light. The show's over.

So it was all in my imagination. I'm out for thrills, not kills. I needed to know what it might feel like. That's all. To smell the terror. Maybe take a lick. Convince myself I *am* the badass.

I have every instinct of a wild animal, but fight it off. I know I can't break in. Just wanna watch normal people. The way I used to be. Enjoying life. Like I used to.

I need to feed or I'll die. That's what my body's telling me. Deranged thoughts are eating my brain. Kill. Kill. Kill. Holy fuck, I'm a lethal raw nerve. Raw. I'm licking my lips, foaming at the mouth. Instinct tells me to kill a human, but the thing beating double time in my chest won't let me. Okay, an animal then. No. It's your job to protect wildlife. Not eat it. I'm caught between shit and the tide. What the fuck am I gonna do? I pound my head with my fists. For some reason this clears it.

I stumble upon a farm. A tall white fence surrounds it. I know this place. They have a dog. Be careful. Quiet. Skulk. At the thought of what's in the barn, saliva nearly chokes me. I run a clawed finger across the lips tightly drawn over canines and needle sharp incisors. Then I touch my hairy face. Am I what killed those three girls? Holy fuck. I'm a murderer.

I scale the fence with ease, creep across the field, hunker before the barn. Ready to spring, I drink in sounds: Cows lowing. Breathing. Farting. I hesitate, then consider the situation. What the hell? I shrug. Why not? They'll be slaughtered and eaten anyway. Might as well make it quick and easy for my pick of the stock.

I rip the lock off the door, fling it at the sky, peer through dimness. Sniff the air then step inside. Tantalizing. Big selection. I choose the easiest. The Hereford closest to the double door. The restless one with the white head and brown body. All the while, I'm thinking quick getaway. 'Cos there's a house not far away. I'm on its back. It should be mooing, but it's squealing like a pig, trying to throw me off. Then it lets out a warning growl. Fuck you, cow. I'm on top.

I grab its horns, pull up the head, stretch my jaws, and sink my teeth into the big fat neck. Warm blood flows down my throat, sweeter than fresh squeezed fruit juice. This is what it's all about. And then some. I throw the dead animal over a shoulder, the hump on my back actually, and I'm out the door, heading for the field. Dropping to the ground, I feast.

They say the first is the hardest. This wasn't hard at all. It was fabulous. I savor the flesh like I savor Jenny's lips. I shouldn't bring her into this. She's innocent. Pure. I'm a bastard. Worthless. Loser. My grunts, crunching bones, jar my memory of the night at the lake when something turned me into what I am now.

A dog starts yapping. A flashlight shoots an arch of light. The farmer comes running toward me with his shotgun. Like Jenny's dad, circles my head. I can't control myself. I'm almost on him. Ready to pounce. He blasts a round that sounds like it could take the side of the barn down. I dodge it. He's shaking too badly for a proper aim.

Even with the wide range of a close-up blast, he misses his target, pumps another shell into the chamber. I'm faster. I can have him. No I can't. Sinking my teeth into him would be like cheating on my faithful girlfriend. Sliding into something brand new might seem awesome at the moment, but think of how you'd feel the next morning. Like shit. Like I'm starting to feel right now. Weak and queasy. The moon is sailing behind clouds. Dipping. Diving. Got to make it back to Shadow Lane.

I'm crawling over the dew-logged grounds. Dragging my throbbing body. Pulling myself up, inch by inch, scraping my naked belly over bricks. With the strength of my arms, propelling myself through the window I left open. Crashing into a pathetic heap on the floor.

I can't feel my legs. But I do feel a stream of tears shooting from my eyes. I drag myself to the bathroom, work my fingers up the front of the cabinet, pull myself up to the sink. When I get a glimpse of myself in the mirror, I almost have a heart attack.

My face is smeared with gel-like blood. Thick, coarse hair is receding from every square inch of skin as I watch in disbelief. Panic stricken, I look down at the floor and my feet that aren't standing. They look broken, lying kind of sideways, balancing on ankle bones. Caked with mud. Floor and feet. That's not even the worst part. My eyes. What the hell happened to my eyes? Last time I checked they were brown. Now they're bright yellow and bloodshot, like deviled eggs sprinkled with paprika.

My pupils don't look normal. They're jet back disks. I can't look at myself anymore. Fuck you, Jack. I drop to the floor, drag myself to the walk-in shower. Reach for the grab bars, pull myself up. Plop my bare ass on the cold plastic seat. Slam the half-door closed and turn on the hand held shower. A cold stream spits, stinging my pores. Doesn't matter how I adjust the temperature. This water is like acid, burning my skin. The craziest thing is, I'm enjoying the pain. But my joyful moment ends abruptly when my mind starts grinding out pictures.

Head in hands I'm thinking. My memory is crystal clear. Regardless of hideous thoughts, I still had a lot of humanity in me last night. Does this werewolf thing come on gradually? Or hit you like a sledgehammer. Did I transition one hundred percent? I'm not quite certain. I didn't feel every joint in my body pop, my skin stretch, or my bones crack into another shape. I didn't walk on all fours.

Did my jaws extend into a snout? By the time I reached the mirror, I was me. Definitely me. Just beat and bloody, with dissolving facial hair. I did have a hell of an overbite though. My jaws bulged with teeth, big, strong teeth. I know this because I nicked my own hand when I gnawed on tendons belonging to the cow. I felt the stab. But there's not a mark on me now.

This is how Rachel finds me when she bursts into the bathroom. Slumped in the shower, head hanging, palms holding up my face.

"Do you ever consider knocking?" When I lift my gaze, I'm livid. "Suppose I was taking a dump?"

"I've seen it all. Smelled it all. What are you doing in here, Jack?"

"What does it look like, Rachel?"

"What's all over the floor?"

"Ask housekeeping. They're the ones who don't vacuum."

She pitches a hip, then throws her hands on both. "If you think I'm gonna clean up after you, you're out of your ever-lovin' mind." She stalks out and slams the door behind her.

"Thanks for the towel," begins my round of cursing.

The door flies open. Palms on the frame, Rachel is filling up the doorway again. "Get ready for your workout." Her voice is flat. Then she's gone again. No good morning. How are you. How did you get into the shower by yourself? Can I do anything for you?

I have the worst taste in my mouth. Foul. Wretched. Who's gonna hire a guy with bad breath and broken legs? Toiletries line a wire shelf positioned just within my reach. Rachel thinks of everything. I scrub the hell out of my teeth, brush so hard my gums bleed. I spit out a hunk of hide, almost losing the contents of my stomach: cattle.

I used to admire cavemen. Their endurance. Perseverance. Thinking of their hygiene, I'm grossed out, wondering how they managed to swallow two thousand times a day without the use of mouthwash. There's no way they had Listerine back then. Thank Christ for Listerine. After a few mouthfuls, my palate does feel cleaner.

I drag myself out of the shower. Then I'm like an inchworm trying to cross the floor. Crawling to the towel rack, I snatch the low-hanging terry cloth hem and slap the bath sheet over every reachable body part. Being a misfit blows. I hate myself. My demented, sadistic, blackened soul included.

Hours later I'm in my chair. Palms sliding over thighs, massaging the assault and battery inflicted by Rachel. I have no muscular strength in my lower extremities, but whatever the hell she did to me for the past two hours is making my legs ... tingle?

I'm thinking about my midnight run. Blowing out breath instead of steam. I can't believe what I am. As if things weren't bad enough, I'm some kind of animal-vegetable. Not even. Half man, half animal, doesn't fit into any species of plant life or animal breed I know of.

And I might be the serial killer the cops are looking for. Should I turn myself in? Should I confide in Dr. Sloan? Let him do the tests he bugged me about for thirty minutes before he up and left? No fucking way. In either case, I'll be locked in a cage:

criminal or guinea pig. Christ, what am I'm gonna do?

Since my hospital stay, I haven't thought much about my appearance. Not that I really give a shit at this stage of the game. I'm wearing dove gray sweats, and even though I'm not about to get up and jog to the laundromat, or diner, or deli across the street, two neon blue Nike Airs are the only things stopping my feet and toes from curling into balls of taffy. My hair is growing like weeds. I know Jenny likes it long, but I'm starting to look Biblical. I haven't shaved. My scruff is full-blown beard. Bushy. Wild. Caveman.

Jenny: Territorial Females

*T*he Jeep purrs down Maple Street. I love my Jeep. It's comfortable and reliable, just like Jack, I muse. My driver's window is wide open, the sweet breeze ruffling my hair. My bare left arm is hanging out the window, and I'm listening to Maroon 5, singing my heart out. My fingers start tapping the exterior door trim as I take a right at the traffic light, proceeding down the winding road at a steady fifteen. Mine isn't the only car around. There's a white BMW up ahead of me, a black Escalade following close behind.

My eyes are flicking all around. Left, right, up, down. Lovely grounds is my initial observation. Lush lawns, like those rolling up to a southern mansion, are Ireland green. Shrubbery. Perennials. Azaleas: red and purple and flowering, alternate with beds of tulips and tiger lilies. In the distance, a thickening forest completes the picture of serenity.

For as captivating as the grounds are, I can't take my eyes off the building, especially the tall, smoky windows, wondering which room my Jack is in. I'm about to surprise him. He doesn't expect me this early. Can he see the Jeep? Me behind the wheel?

Wheel Wolf

I can't wait to see the look on his face when I walk through the door. I peek at myself in the rearview mirror. I'm wearing mascara today, and rosy lipstick. I don't need blush; I'm flushed.

Sunlight shoots through the Austrian crystal sword on the silver chain dangling from the mirror. The Jeep rides so smoothly on fresh black asphalt, it's motionless. The workmanship is beautiful. Thank you, ancestors, for bringing this gift to America. With the tip of my finger, I nudge the heirloom. Now it's swinging like a pendulum. The rainbows of sparkling colors are brilliant, mesmerizing, especially when the sword is moving. Moving. Maybe I should give it to Jack for good luck. When he wears it he'll think of me. I laugh. The last thing either of us need are reminders. We're embedded into each other's souls.

A security gate lifts automatically, interrupting my visual inspection of the gardens. I grab the first space in the visitor's parking lot and cut the engine. Without much thought, I carefully un-loop the silver chain, bring the crystal sword to my lips for extra good luck, then work the necklace over my head. The sun-heated sword drops between my cleavage.

The sun is shining, warming the crown of my head. I reposition my lavender lens sunglasses higher up my nose. As I walk, I watch the building expand before me, feeling as though I'm involved in a movie as well as reality, because I'm a bit lightheaded, trying to shake off a dreamy feeling of being drunk without liquor. I pop a piece of gum into my mouth and start chewing away anxiety.

I haven't been sleeping well. Between the break-in at my house and Jack's accident, my well-planned world suffered a hairline crack straight through the center. Nothing that won't mend. I smile to myself, because there's no one here but me. The two other vehicles went straight. Didn't bear right with the road that turns into this facility. There's a big complex down the road. A medical center, I believe. Maybe they're doctors, patients. Who knows. Who cares. It's early. I hope I got the right visiting hour information when I phoned.

As I walk, I'm examining the exterior of the red brick building which is three stories high, with wings. I can't stop admiring the lovely grounds, picking out a spot under a willow tree bordering the forest, where Jack and I can have a picnic lunch some day. Yes, I'm thinking long term, possibly summer, because Jack was pretty banged up. He'll be here for a while. I'm already bracing myself for the medical assessment Jack received upon his arrival here, praying for a stellar progress report. Four months, perhaps? Hopefully less.

Shadow Lane Rehab is a classy place. Like a resort, actually. A brass plaque is mounted at the peak of the portico, with the initials *SLR* engraved in the center. I'm happy Jack is receiving the best possible care in such a well-equipped facility. State of the art. Clean. Tranquil.

I'm beyond excited. I'm giddy. I know it's only been a couple days, but butterflies are munching on my stomach. I push through the revolving doors, fluffing my hair. Shoving my glasses up like a headband, blotting my lips, adjusting my happy face. I'm smiling at everyone and nothing. I love everything about life. Especially the day. I'm on my way to see Jack. The man who makes the earth spin.

Once inside the stylish building, the first thing I notice is the tiled floor. It's spotless. With each step, my high heels click on granite. I stop at the L-shaped desk which looks like the front desk in a classy hotel. Pamphlets are stacked neatly on the polished mahogany surface. Bookends holding folders, binders, and papers occupy a small section of the desktop, along with silver mesh pen and pencil caddies. Two computers are positioned at each end. Two uniformed attendants wearing adorable visors make me think: golf. Nice setup.

I smile at the first person my feet select, a graying woman

arranging the potted plant she's placing on the counter. Before her gaze meets mine, while she's still fussing with whether or not to swing the fullest, shiniest leaves to the front, or keep the best on her side, I sing out, "Jack Bailey?" No other words are necessary. I'm sure my eyes are saying, "What room is he in?"

"Just a moment, dear, and I'll look him up." Removing her eyes from the plant, she's smiling too. I'm surprised she's not familiar with Jack. His face, personality, name. Jack normally leaves a big impression. He's one of those remarkable, memorable, charming, unforgettable guys, especially where women are concerned.

Regardless of their ages, everyone checks Jack out. But this lady must not have been present when Jack was admitted. She adjusts her monitor screen, blows off something that apparently looks like dust. Then she picks up a microfiber cloth and proceeds to clean the screen.

Now I'm getting stressed. Annoyed. I've never seen anyone move so slow. She folds the cloth, stows it under the desk, then touches a few computer keys gingerly, smacks her lips and says, "Okie dokie. Let's see. Jack Bailey." Pause. "Jack Bailey." I watch her pearl colored eyes scroll beneath the lenses of black rimmed glasses. If she says Jack Bailey one more time, I'm hopping over the counter and locating *Jack Bailey* myself. Tension broken. Thank goodness. "One-Seventeen, dear."

The last thing I want to do is appear perturbed with someone who could be my own grandmother. Heaving a sigh, I tilt my head. "Thank you. Which way, please?"

Before the woman can reply, more than likely because she speaks as slowly as she moves, an Amazonian girl comes swooping out from behind knee high planters lining a glass wall to my left. The planters hold bushy ferns and stalks with splashy broad leaves. Nothing fancy. Just greenery. Spiky and full. When her large hand parts the foliage, she looks like she's working her way out of a jungle, armed with a misting bottle.

"You're looking for my patient?" Is she possessive or dedicated?

"I'm visiting my boyfriend." Before I can alter my tone, conceal aggravation, "Jack Bailey is my boyfriend," fires through my lips like a threat. I don't care if I sound rude, or stare. My eyes fix on her name tag: Rachel Huntress. I almost gag. Jack's therapist's name is huntress? The name fits her appearance. I'm not sure how I pictured his caretakers, or even if I thought about it, but in my wildest dreams I'd never have expected to run into someone like her.

We start sizing each other up. She reminds me of Wonder Woman, but not brunette. She's a striking redhead who looks like a model. But I feel she could use some sun. She's gorgeous, in a natural way. Unusually tall, but elegant. Her black scrubs are a striking contrast against her coloring, but I find black scrubs odd. I've never seen heath care providers wear black.

"That's an interesting piece," she says, reaching for my crystal. "May I?"

I grasp the sword, pull it as far away from my body as possible, because I don't want her fingers anywhere near my skin. Her focus on my neck gives me free reign to study her as closely as she's studying my crystal. She twirls it in her fingers, then lets it drop. The moment has ended.

I'm trying to figure out if she's a true redhead. Those long, wavy locks are an amazing color. Carrots? No, strawberries. With golden highlights. Yup, amazing. My eyes make their way to hers, bright green and inquisitive. Although I've stopped blatantly assessing her, she's still giving me the once over, which makes me kind of uncomfortable. The side of my mouth I've been chewing on automatically tightens. So does my stomach. Something about this woman caring for Jack makes me uncomfortable. Intimate. They have an intimate relationship. In a way, she's the other woman in his life who is replacing me. Temporarily. Still, she's putting her hands on my man. I wonder if she gives him sponge baths. My happy butterflies are smothered inside my grinding stomach.

She lifts her chin. "I'll show you to Jack's room ..."

I lift mine. "Just point me in the general direction. I'm sure I'll find him." I don't like the way she says, Jack. It sounds too familiar. Shouldn't she be calling him, Mr. Bailey?

"Patients normally receive visitors in the solarium." Is she testing me?

Annoyance escalating, I gawk at her. "If that's the case, can someone let him know his girlfriend is here?" I stress, *girlfriend*.

My attitude doesn't seem to faze her. "Jack's having issues. I'm making an exception for him. You can see him in his room."

She's *letting* me visit my own boyfriend in his room? Issues? "Is his condition worsening?" She's suddenly above me. I'm looking up to her due to more than her height.

"I think he's becoming depressed."

"Oh." I let out a breath. "Is that all ..." She had me thinking he suffered a physical setback. This girl has no idea of what we've been through. I've nursed him through tragedy, depression, recovery. I'm sure I can help him handle this bout of depression.

She frowns disapprovingly. Is it something I said?

She points. "See that elevator at the end of the corridor?" Her arm is slender for such a full figured person. Come on, Jen. All that's full is her chest. Jack's a T & A man. I stop my eyes from rolling, or staring at her boobs. I wonder if he's noticed her rack? He's human, Jennifer.

I can't help but inhale her amber scent. Appealing. Expensive. With a job like hers, why not soap and water? "I see it." I'm short.

"Take a left and Jack's door is the third on the right." She spreads her full, cranberry lips into a devious grin. "I just got finished with him." Her brows are a deeper shade of cranberry, which I assume is natural. Their arch makes her look even more sarcastic. Malevolent. She knows he's my property. She just touched what belongs to me — God knows where — and she wants me to know.

Two territorial females. She wants me to know this too. I can tell.

I shoot her my *don't fuck with me bitch* warning grin. She could be ten feet tall. When it comes to Jack, I'd fight the devil himself. He's mine. And I'm going to let her know it. "I'm sure I'll find him just fine. We've got radar. That's how it works when you've been together for almost seven years." Okay, I pushed it a bit. It was six years six months ago. So we're halfway there. Same thing.

Jack's room is easy to find. I wouldn't have had to ask had he told me he was on the first floor. I bounce through the door wearing one of my broadest smiles, although I'm still feeling scathed by the confrontation with his caretaker. "Jack ... How's my favorite caveman?" After pausing for impact, I'm ready for my dramatic entry.

Jack: Jenny's First Visit To Rehab

"**J**ack," she belts out my name like a rock star warming up a stage, hugging a bakery box tied with blue ribbon. More cookies. I can smell them from the doorway. She looks killer in a short skirt and knit top, calling me her caveman while pinning me with an analytical stare. She's got something on her mind. I can tell.

She should know how accurate her pet handle for me has become. Shit. Should I tell her what I am, is my first thought. It's difficult to face her. How do you look your girlfriend in the eye after the despicable act you committed less than twenty-four hours ago? Or kiss her with the same lips that sucked flesh off a cow's ass last night? My easy out is gaping at her ... from head to toe. Admiringly. Hungrily. I almost blurt out, *You're wearing sex shoes.* Black leather with pencil thin heels. And her legs. Holy shit, what's she trying to do to me?

Words are stuck in my throat, but I have to say something, because she's standing there, staring at me like she's waiting for me to invite her in. She looks so uncomfortable. As much as me? Why is it so difficult for us? I know my problem. What's hers? "Jenny! How'd you get in? No visitors in patient rooms." Christ,

I sound like Rachel. Then I palm my forehead. What a way to welcome the woman I love.

Jenny smirks. "Nurse Huntress?" She scrunches her face into a questioning expression further enhanced by her brow that gathers half of her forehead to her hairline. A deliberate tug tenses her jaw sarcastically. Her face is expanding and contracting faster than my eyes can track. I can imagine her emotions. "You've got yourself a witch, I see. Or a warden," she says with animosity.

"Welcome to the house of horrors." I sigh, shrug, and mouth a kiss. "It's so good to see you, babe. I missed you." I want to kiss her so bad, but cringe at the thought of inflicting my fermenting cow breath on her. Or bovine bacteria would be even worse. Raw beef. Mad cow disease. Who the hell knows what I ingested last night.

"What are you talking about?" She breezes to my side, drops a kiss on my head. Great. I can't even hold her in my arms standing on two feet anymore. Press our bodies together. *Talk about torture.*

I stretch my chest and arms as high as they'll go, aiming my lips for hers. After a peck I explain, "Me being with a witch is better than a stripper." I force a grin. "Right, baby?" My chuckle, or explanation, doesn't get me anywhere.

Jenny's face continues to prune. Insensitive stripper comment, Jack. I suspect she's thinking about the naked chick I might or might not have run over. Murdered in cold blood. Was I an animal then? Did I bite myself? Did I bite her? Was what Sloan hinted at correct? Did the dead girl really sink her teeth into me? Before or after she stopped breathing. That's the question I'm dying to have answered. I wish he would have bagged her teeth.

"How are you feeling, Jack?" She says, then does a double-take and smiles. "Wow, they removed your neck brace. You must be making progress."

"Yeah. Feels good to stretch." I rotate my neck and rub it.

"Awesome." She drops the box of cookies in my lap, bends

at the waist, looks in my eyes, and runs her fingers over my beard. "This is going a bit overboard, isn't it? Don't you have a razor? I can bring ..." Her jaw drops. "Your eyes ..."

"I know. They're yellow. I read anesthesia can change your eye color."

"Fade it. Not change it entirely. Your eyes aren't brown anymore. They're yellow." While her voice hits a pitch, she keeps tilting her head from side to side. I watch her pupils grow and shrink. I'm sick of being examined. Being a specimen. I just want to be Jack again. The guy who's gonna be a forest ranger. The guy with a future. The guy who wanted to ask Jenny to marry him. What's gonna happen now? I can't have her tied to someone like me. I have to give her an out. Not just yet, though. I can't bear the thought of being without her.

"You brought me goodies." I grip the box with one hand, sliding the palm of my other up and down Jenny's arched spine. She feels so good. My exploring fingers have sensors implanted in the tips. My touch is as acute as my hearing, my taste, my vision. I can feel cells cluster beneath her skin, blood flow through her veins. Warm spinal fluid lubricate her backbone and intricate nerve endings. Feel the pulse of her heart as it throbs throughout her entire being. Identify each vertebrae I'm touching. L4, L5, L6 and so on.

I've lost my taste for sweets. All I want now is meat. Nice and bloody. My eyes fall on the food tray on the table by the window. The steak is gone, but I must have missed some of the juice that is now beginning to congeal around a sliver of remaining T-bone. I thought I had licked the plate clean.

Jenny breaks free to stand and make a crisp, visual sweep of my room. She smoothes her skirt and tucks in the hem of her top that, with the help of my fingers, slipped from the back of her waistband. "Are you hungry? How are the meals? I was going to bring you a sandwich ..." She focuses on the table holding my tray, then swings her head around. "Lunch? Already?" Her gaze runs over the walls, as though searching for a clock.

"Breakfast actually. And I was surprised. Thanks babe." My folded hands rest in my lap.

She tips up my face with a finger. "What do you mean, thanks?"

"For sending me the steak." My blinking eyes thank her again.

Her entire face crunches with confusion. "I didn't send you anything."

"You sure?" My eye starts twitching.

"Like I'd forget something like sending you a steak for breakfast?" She cocks a brow. "Did they bring you eggs with it? That's good protein." It's like she's got dietician radar. "They've got some menu here, huh?"

"Not really."

"So it's take out?"

"I guess. I assumed you sent it as a gift or ..." My voice trails off because, come to think of it, why would Jenny send me a steak?

She shakes her head, shrugs her brows, and opens the lid of the box which is resting on my knees. "Dessert." She shoves a cookie at me.

"I'm not hungry." I draw my lips tight and shrug. I'm a connoisseur with a limited appetite. She should know ... No she shouldn't.

"Aww, poor baby. You miss my home cooking." She's leaning over me, smothering my face with her luscious breasts as she hugs the hell out of my head. She's expending all of her energy, showering every bit of affection on my head. Nothing else. Not my shoulders, my arms, my chest. Just my damn head. And not even with her lips. Just her tits. Which I wouldn't ordinarily mind, but I haven't seen her face in days. And I want more.

I lean forward, lock both arms around her butt, then let my

hands slide to the front of her thighs, easing her a few inches away. I want to reach up and take her face in my hands, but since I can't reach, I just stare into those violet eyes I miss so much. "How are you, Jenny? How are things going, baby? How are your folks?" I feel pain contort my face when I talk about her parents, knowing what they've been through, and how it's all affecting Jenny. "How's Dobie doing?"

"Everyone's okay. My mom's better. Dad's been fine all along. You know how strong he is. Dobie is coming out of it, but he won't go outside alone. I have to walk beside him." She shakes her head, coils her lips. She showers me with her tropical gum breath. "I don't know what he saw that night, but whatever it was scared the heck out of him, Jack. He's always been a watchdog, now he's a lapdog."

"Hmm. Crazy." Is all I can say, because I'm thinking. If Jenny's Doberman ran into me the way I looked last night, what would he do? Rip my throat out? Or cower. The thought is unnerving. "When are you gonna be able to move back home?" Not that I want her to. I feel a hell of a lot better with her out of this damn town.

"The house is pretty much patched up. Not entirely renovated, but they can do that when we're back, which will be tomorrow." Her eyes light up. "Living out of a suitcase is such an inconvenience. I can't wait to get home. Plus traveling back and forth to work is costing a fortune in gas."

"I bet," I say absently, because I'm already worrying about tomorrow. "How'd you bake cookies? I didn't know they had ovens in hotel rooms."

She looks smug. Cute smug. "I had access to a kitchen."

"You chummed up with the cook, huh?" I narrow my eyes at her.

She giggles and takes another look around. Maybe looking for a chair, as it's awkward with her standing and me sitting. "My dad hated the hotel, so we moved to a bed and breakfast, and yes, I helped the owners out, promised to cook dinner tonight." She winks. "So they let me bake these cookies for you. Why don't you try one? I added extra chips. Under-baked them, so they're just the way you like them ... chewy."

I don't know if it's the way she says, chewy. The view of her abdomen from my seated position. Or her scent that's wafting into my twitching nose. I'm not sure what comes over me, but I blurt out, "I don't want cookies from a box, Jen. I want your cookies." She must not fully comprehend what I'm saying. She appears confused, then gives me a phony grin and scruffs my hair.

"All I wanna do is eat you, Jen." I'm dead serious. I'm so serious my face is stiff. Like my dick.

She steps back, beyond my reach. "Yeah, babe. I miss you too." Jenny is compassionate. I think she's giving me the benefit of the doubt. Or she thinks I'm over-medicated. Deranged is more like it.

"Are you on medication?" She quirks a brow.

Sure enough. I'm a mind reader too.

"Jenny. I have an insatiable appetite. But not for food." I reach out to her, beckoning with my jittery fingers.

She cocks her head so dramatically it's actually sideways, and studies me. "Your therapist says you're depressed. Is it true?"

"Not when you're with me. Come here." I pat my lap. "I want you on top of me." I want to fuck her, and am about to tell her so. I can't hold anything back lately. I'm painfully honest. I think if she'd mount me, I'd be able to move my hips. If she was on top of me, I'd bounce her through the ceiling. I feel that strong.

"I want to fuck you, Jenny." I shrug my brows. Lick my lips. Almost tumble from the chair as I reach for her arms, yanking her close so I'm eye level with her tummy again. Nose inches from her privates. "You smell so good, baby. Every part of you. Fruity breath, coconut hair, your skin smells like, mmm, cherry blossoms and anxiety." I'm working up a sweat just thinking about what I want to do to her. My clammy hands are braced on her hips, fingers digging in. Through closed eyelids I'm seeing her, just by touching her. Smelling her with my fingertips. "And then there's your strongest scent ... you woman scent. The desire ..."

"Jack," she sounds flustered. Maybe I'm turning her on. "Stop it, Jack."

"What? I'm just calling a spade a spade." I lift a brow. "That's a pretty weak *stop.*"

"I'm not a deck of cards." Her escalating breath makes my eardrums flutter.

My breath is getting heavy, too. "Don't I know it. You're soft, you smell delicious, and I'm horny."

She's staring down at me, her eyes bulging. "That's enough, Jack. You're acting like a damn animal. Stop sniffing my crotch!" At the sound of her indignation, I snap to attention.

"You're right." I bury my face in her firm but feminine stomach where her essence is so strong I start salivating. I'm caught between a rock and a hard place. My nose and Jenny's crotch. I can't raise my head, because I'm barely able to look at her, or pull myself away from her womanhood. I *am* like an animal. I have these uncontrollable thoughts, urges, fucking desires.

I start whispering every thought that's banging around inside my head. "I smelled you before you set foot in the room. Your scent drives me berserk. I want to throw you on that bed over there," I hitch my head toward the wall, because that's what my bed is pushed against, "rip your panties off. Spread your legs and ..." I stop myself from disclosing the rest of my raunchy thoughts. I want to run my tongue up and down your body, outside, inside. Lick, suck, bite. I wanna fucking bite Jenny. What's wrong with me?

"C'mere." I'm demanding. "Let me hold you." I try to drag

her onto my lap, but she's backing away. Her lips are tight. She's got fear in her eyes. Like I'm a rabid dog cornering her in some dark alley. My Jenny is afraid of me. This snaps me out of it. Holy fuck. My own girl is looking at me as though I'm something from hell that's about to attack her.

"I'd never hurt you, Jenny," I say. The words catch in my throat because I'm holding back a sob. But she's not buying any of it. She probably thinks I'm a back-peddling monster. She's right.

"Something happened to you, Jack. More than broken bones. You're broken inside. Twisted. I don't know if I can help you with this one. Sometimes you just have to find your own way." She's picking up her shoulder bag that she flung on a chair when she first entered the room. When she came to me with love in her eyes. Now she's leaving with despair.

"Jen, don't go. Please, baby. I'm so sorry." Tears roll down my cheeks, soaking my beard.

My pathetic voice stops her dead in her tracks. She turns, her face melting with love. "Jack ..." In two strides she's on me. Literally on me. A leg braced on either side of the chair, she's straddling me. Running her mouth up my neck, across a cheek, until it finally finds mine.

In less than a minute we're panting. Although Jenny's lips are firmly pressed against mine, she's talking. So basically, she's talking into my mouth. I'm tasting her lips, her breath, the omelet she ate for breakfast.

"Jack," she's hoarse, "I spoke to the guys who are renovating my house. They stopped by your place. You can come home baby. I'm moving in. I'll take care of you. They're fitting the house with ramps and equipment for ..."

This turns me right off. As I pull back, my erection shrinks. The fingers that were massaging her back move to her shoulders and squeeze. "For cripples."

"No, Jack." She's not giving up. Jenny never gives up. "Handicapped," she corrects. "In my heart I know this isn't permanent. You're going to walk again, baby. And I'm going to take care of you until you do. And after." She kisses my neck again, nibbles on my earlobe. "Even if you never walked again, I'd still be here. You're not getting rid of me, so get used to it. And stop trying to push me away. I know that's what you're trying to do." Her tongue is enticingly moist as it plays with my ear. "It's not working."

"Oh, it's working," I rasp.

Her lips come down on mine so fiercely our teeth clash. I know she means well, but I can't help but feel inferior. I know what she's planning. She'll have low counters installed in the kitchen and bath. Ramps. Maybe even an elevator for my staircase so I can inhabit my old room. Jenny's so good. She's got a heart of gold. I don't deserve her. I can't help but compare myself to a helpless kid. A two-year-old can climb onto a chair to get what they want from a cabinet. I can't lift a leg.

I'm serious; my eyes pour into hers as I bring her face to mine. "Jenny. You know how much I love you. I'd do anything for you. But if that anything was going to hurt you, even if I wanted it with all my heart, and it upset you ... What I'm trying to say so clumsily is, if you had your own reasons, and you truly wanted me to walk away from you and never come back, I'd respect your wishes."

She looks like I rolled up a fist and hit her. "What the hell are you talking about?" she sputters. Before I can explain, she starts sobbing. "You're breaking up with me?"

"No, baby. Just giving you an out. I don't want you to be saddled with me. God knows how long I'll be this way, or if I'll ever be anything else. I never expected our life together to start out this way. This isn't how I want it. You can take the out. No hard feelings. If you know what's good for you, you'll take it,

Jennifer." She has no idea of the real reason I'm giving her an out. And I don't have the balls to fess up.

"Jennifer?" She flares. "You haven't called me that since ninth grade. When we were strangers." The pain on her face makes me wince. Take the hint, Jennifer, I'm thinking. We're strangers again. You don't know me anymore.

She hops off my lap and starts pacing around the room. Her face is turning all kinds of colors. She's breathing heavy, like she's got a thousand pound weight on her chest. I feel like I have one that's crushing more than my chest. My heart is breaking.

Jenny stops walking and stares out the window. When she turns, her arms are cradling her stomach. "I know what you're trying to do, Jack. And it's not working. I don't give a shit what you say. How many times you turn your back on me, I'm gonna keep getting up in your face." She leaps across the room and literally sticks her face an inch from mine. "See Jack? I'm not afraid of you. Not of your attitude. Your depression. Your physical limitations. You know why?" Her lips are pursed. Her eyes are like violet fireflies. "Because I love you. And love is stronger than broken bones and inhibitions. Ransacked houses. Naked girls. Pushy physical therapists."

We both start laughing, because Rachel is a laughing matter. She's in a world of her own. You don't try to understand or question Rachel. She's flying her own craft, and it's on autopilot. "I know you're referring to Rachel. She's a trip, isn't she?"

"She sure is. She gave me a hard time when I got here." Jenny is hunched at my side, hovering over me. A sparkly thing dislodges from her cleavage, swings from her body, and smacks me square in the nose.

"But you held your own with Rachel, of course. What's this?" I snatch what looks like a glittering miniature dildo. Roll it in my fingers. Sniff it.

"It's a good luck charm." She slips it off her neck and tries to work it over my head. But the chain is too small, so it's lying across my forehead, the dangling crystal caught by the curve of my top lip. "I'll get you a longer chain," she says, still trying to work it over my face. "It will keep you safe." Her breath is flowing over me. I love her so much. At this moment, not even for sex. Even if she didn't have a pussy, I'd love the hell out of her anyway.

I'm thinking, if this crystal is anything like the killer cross she hung around my neck, I better watch my ass. This thing might have magical powers. Like turning into a deadly weapon. Maybe help me slash another throat unintentionally. I cringe. "You keep it babe. Being around me, you need the luck."

She resists, but finally let's me slip the chain over her head. After careful examination, I bring the crystal to my lips. I'm sure it's not a dick, so I kiss it, and tuck it between her breasts which I nuzzle for a sweet moment.

Then my arms tighten around her. I'm pulling her deep into my lap. Kissing her until my lips hurt. I know my beard is scratching her delicate skin, because I notice the crimson burn on her cheeks when I slide my mouth from hers to go for her throat. But I can't stop my lips from working. This girl is incredible. She obviously loves me more than life, and I should be thrilled. I'm gonna treat her like the treasure she is. I'm gonna fight this thing. Kick it. Walk her across that field of flowers, recite my vows, and take care of her for the rest of my fucking life.

While I restrain myself from chewing on her neck, and enjoy careful nibbles, she says, "I can't imagine who would have sent you a steak. Drake ... maybe Steve?"

"You kidding? Those two wouldn't spring for a burger." I munch on her chin then return to her neck.

She puts on a shrewd-thinking face. "Donnie?" The word sounds distasteful. At least that's the way I'm hearing his name. "It would be a nice gesture," she whispers, "Not like him though ..."

"Bastard Donnie?" My chuckle is sour. I draw back to stare at the silver dollar size hickey I implanted on her throbbing jugular. "Highly doubtful. I haven't seen him since ... since he expedited the shipment of my parents' bodies and took care of the funeral arrangements."

Apparently realizing we need to change the subject, she does a one-eighty. "So, this is your room. Nice TV. Plants. That's your bed. Looks comfy. It's a nice room, Jack. Clean. Cheerful."

"Oh yeah?" I give her a breath-stealing squeeze. "You think my bed looks good? Wanna try it out?"

Jenny surprises me by hopping off my lap, removing her purple sunglasses from her head and throwing them into her bag, kicking off her heels, padding to door, and pressing the silver lock button until it clicks. She makes a slow turn. Hands locked behind her back she leans against the door, one knee bent in this sexy pose. She tosses her hair and raises a brow. Her smile is sly. My heart is pounding.

Jenny: Doing Jack

I just locked Jack's door, rattling the knob a few times to make sure it's secure. I'm plastering myself against the painted wood, trying to keep my lips from quivering. I'm not simply striking a sexy pose, the door is supporting my body, bolstering my courage.

We've been together over six years. Maybe it's about time I let go of an unrealistic dream I've had since I was a little girl. Being a virgin bride. Make your wedding night something so special, you both climb walls, shoot for the moon.

Maybe making love will help boost Jack's morale.

That's not the right reason to have sex, Jen.

But if it will help him.

Make sure, Jennifer. Don't do it out of pity.

I don't pity him. I love him. What's the point of waiting? He needs something, right now, to bring back that spark of life. To make him feel good about himself. Satisfying me will do that. Lift him out of depression.

Open the gate and let the estrogens flow. What am I saving myself for? Maybe it's time I grew up. Stopped living in a fairy tale world.

Nothing is perfect, Jennifer. This is just one of the many hurdles you and Jack will have to leap.

Jack looks stoned. His eyes are heavy, his jaw loose. I imagine he's wondering what's going on. Maybe he can't believe I'm acting this way. That we're about to do something he's been wanting to do for months. Years, actually. Jack's always been bursting with testosterone, but he's managed to keep his urges in check. For me. He's okay with our heavy make-out sessions. And he's faithful.

Jack's hands are tightly folded in his lap. His watery eyes are taking me in from head to toe. He's chewing on the side of his mouth. "I don't want to force you into anything, baby." His voice is raspy.

I'm about to do a cat crawl across the floor. That's what Jack's voice and eyes are doing to me. Watching arousal overtake his gorgeous features is making me moist. I know in my heart I'm doing the right thing. I want him, now more than ever. I almost lost this man.

My eyes are talking to his as I slink across the room, lean into him, run a finger across his jaw line, over his lips. I start backing his chair up. He nips at my finger, but doesn't make a move to touch the wheels of the chair. Just sits here, watching me. Love hungry. Sucking on the finger of my one hand, while I turn the wheels with the strength of my knees and thighs.

I maneuver him beside the bed. His strong arms manage to pull his body out of the chair and onto the mattress. I stand before him, urging him to lie down. I'm barefoot, bare-legged, and horny as hell. The look on his face, the rapid rise and fall of his chest, are bringing me close to an orgasm. I can't believe what he can do to me without the use of his hands. Just his eyes, his voice.

"Baby," he whispers, holding out his arms. "Come here." He's so throaty, it's almost a growl.

As I lift my skirt and straddle him, a chill runs down my spine. I lower myself, my panties colliding with his sweats. His passion is so big. He's so hot. I immediately start grinding, staring deep into his yellow eyes.

"Jenny. Don't take anything I say seriously. I'm not myself lately." His breath is his voice. "But I want you so bad. I almost taste you. Let me taste you." His tongue runs across his lower lip.

"In a minute, baby ..." The harder I grind, the faster his tongue licks. I shoot him a sexy look, because that's how I'm feeling at this moment. Like the sexiest woman alive. I grasp my top by the hem, and cross-armed, pull it over my head and let it fall to the floor. I'm wearing a black pushup bra. Did I have a feeling I'd be disrobing when I dressed this morning? I don't know. But I'm happy I'm wearing this bra, showing off the cleavage Jack can't take his eyes off.

He reaches for me. When I lean forward, he catches me with both palms, cups my breasts. This is nothing he hasn't done before, but today something is different. He's all alpha. And I'm his submissive. He's handling me carefully, but I have a feeling, in a moment, that's going to change.

Reaching behind me, he unclasps my bra. The crystal falls along with my breasts and bounces off the side of his face. He catches a nipple between his teeth, and I suck in a breath. When he bites down, I scream.

"Ssh, baby. I don't want Rachel bursting in, thinking something's ..." That's all he says, because he's pulled me completely onto him. His mouth is covering mine, his tongue doing incredible things to my lips, the inside of my mouth.

Although his lower body is still, my hips keep on rocking. Harder, faster, working for both of us. I don't mind. It feels so good. Empowering. Now I'm the alpha. I lift my shoulders, throw my head back and let out a moan. With each movement my hair flies wild, like the beat of my heart.

I want to slide my flesh against his. With a sweep of my hand I pull his t-shirt up and over his head. Rub my breasts across his bare chest until my hardened nipples are sore. He's clutching my ass, massaging my back, groaning in my ear.

His fingers begin working between us until I gasp. Then he lifts me. "Get on my face," he pants.

"In a minute, babe," I whisper, as I bring a hand behind me, caressing the bulge between his legs. My other hand runs over my breasts, cupping and squeezing. He looks frantic. I think he's about ready to jump off the bed. He starts tossing his head side to side, making animal sounds.

His passion keeps growing. I can't believe his size. "Are you still mine?" he growls. "Tell me you belong to me. Only me." He reaches out, gripping my arms, jolting me.

"Always ..." I'm caught up in such a state of bliss, I toss my head, moaning. "Only yours, baby. Forever."

"Prove it," he growls, while I'm tossed into the air, coming down forcefully, my back slamming the mattress. Jack is on top of me, bracing himself with his muscular arms. He staring down at me like he's ready to take a bite out of me. It's an incredible feeling. I possess the power to turn him into an animal.

"Take me, Jack. I want you so bad, baby. Make love to me." I squirm into position, then thrust my hips so hard my back feels the strain.

Jack has one arm on either side of my head, boxing me into a circle of ecstasy. He's panting so hard, I'm afraid he'll keel over. A sliver of drool runs down his chin, onto my chest. His breath is so hot, it's scalding my face. I'm getting so turned on, I reach a hand between us to pull my panties aside.

I want to lower his sweats, guide him into me. I'm so wet ... I can't wait. The only problem is, the lower part of his body is crushing me. I can barely breathe, no less undress him. And since I'm the only one moving, trying to lift his pelvis with mine is becoming exhausting.

"What's wrong, baby?" He draws back, his tortured expression hanging inches above me. "Am I hurting you?" His words are slurred, like he's having trouble controlling the movement of his tongue, or it's too big for his mouth.

"It's hard to breathe, that's all." I hesitate to admit my discomfort, but I can't help it. I'm being flattened like a pancake and unable to draw in air. I feel faint, wondering if it's a result of overexertion, or lack of oxygen.

I need to reposition, because I'm fighting off dizziness, but the last thing I want to do is completely destroy his ego. We're walking on shaky ground as it is. My libido has died. I can feel Jack's deflate, as well.

Defeat tugs down the corners of his mouth. "This is your out. You can leave, Jen. No hard feelings." He rolls off me and into the wall. I draw a deep breath, then another, staring up at the ceiling when I hear the clunk. I'm not sure if Jack hit his head or if his shoulder connected with the wall. Maybe a fist. It's not that I can't turn my head to look; I don't want to.

The next thing I know, I'm edged off the bed and my ass thumps on the floor. Jack drops heavily beside me. He doesn't want to look at me, either. I sneak a peek. His face is red, perspiration coating the skin not covered by hair. Sweat drips from his temples. I want to reach out and wipe it away. I want to take him in my arms, tell him it's okay. I understand. Next time, we'll make it work. But I'm afraid to move. To confront him. I initiated this. I believe I've caused enough damage for one day.

His full beard makes him look hotter. Uncomfortable. His breath is a series of strangled, wheezing sounds. The man sprawled out beside me doesn't look like my Jack anymore. I choke back tears. As a cover, maybe to break the ice ... I have no true idea what possesses me to do this ... but the next words to leave my mouth are, "Want me to shave you?" Why did I just say that? My stomach is churning so badly I feel like I'm about to lose it. Lose myself. Lose my Jack.

After I blurt out my ridiculous, inconsiderate thought, Jack immediately glares at me. But only for a second. I feel like I'm with a stranger. My reaction is to cover my bare chest with my arms.

He pulls himself to a sit, the muscles of his arms straining. They're beautifully toned. Thicker than I remember. He appears so strong, it's difficult to comprehend his limitations.

He works his body up into his chair and drops his face into his hands. "I can't do this, Jenny. Find someone you can have a life with, 'cos it's not gonna be me." He's blunt. His words are final. "I wouldn't hang out with an asshole like me, either."

Modesty out the window, I'm on my knees, crawling to his side. "I'm sorry, Jack. It's okay, baby. We'll get through this. We can't consider this a setback, because we haven't started moving forward yet. We're still adjusting."

"I'm not adjusting." He reaches down, runs his fingers through my tousled hair, curls strands around his fingers. I love his touch. I miss his touch. His eyes are soft. God help us.

"You will, baby." I'm pressed into the side of his chair, rubbing his thigh. Then I realize he can't feel my fingers, so I stroke his arm. "Give it time. Give us time ... a chance." I'm up on my knees, urging him toward me, burying my face in his shoulder. "Don't give up on us."

I lift my face, but he's not looking at me. He's contemplative. Stiff. Pale. Then words start tumbling from his lips in a pained, secretive tone. A confession? "Jenny. Last night I ..."

I must look shocked, but I'm actually hurt. After everything that's transpired, nothing would shock me. My eyes release a flood of tears he dries with his thumb, reciting, "Baby ..." again and again.

I shake my head fervently. "I don't want to hear it. I don't care what you did. I understand you're not yourself." Naturally I'm considering he's about to tell me he and Rachel got it on. I'm not sure how, but I'm ready to overlook anything at this point. I just can't lose him. "You belong to me, Jack. Forever."

Jack: Rival Don Delgado

*M*y arms are like iron. It's easy for me to mount her, but my ass is dragging, so are my legs. I'm an asshole. I'm half lying on top of a girl half my size, crushing the air from her lungs. I can hear her gasp for a breath. I'm putting so much weight on her, emotionally and physically, I can see the stress on her face. Not the desire I'd hoped for. This kills me. A knife in the chest would be less painful. This isn't how I want it. Damn sure not how she envisioned our first time to be. This I know by the look in her eyes. This isn't working. This isn't right. Why am I even trying to fuck her? That part of my life is over. Over? I almost laugh. It never started.

That's when I roll off. I'm so disgusted I slam my fist into the wall. Fucking mattress is too small. That's what I tell myself was wrong. If I had more room, I'd have been able to function better, maybe move. I have to tell myself this or I'll lose it entirely. And the last thing I want is to go to pieces in front of Jenny. It's bad enough I can't make love to her. I can't let her see me cry. I'm so choked up, I can't talk yet. Can't look at her. So I pull my dead ass into my chair ... after I clumsily knock both of us onto the floor, that is. Bury my face in my hands. Try to think about something else. Try to forget. How can I forget? Head in hands I break down. Leave, I want to say to her. Well, not exactly in those words, but what I manage to say means just the same.

"Get outta here Jenny. Get a life. It's hard enough for me to deal with this. I can't expect you to. I can't do anything for you anymore." The speech I want to make is poisoning my brain, but I can't hurt her. Not like this. I have to be gentle. Like Jenny.

"You should leave, Jen." I run my palms over my face, shocked at the amount of hair covering my cheeks and chin. No wonder she offered to shave me. I must look like hell. A drifter. A bum.

"First you're attacking me. Now you're throwing me out?" She's shooting me an uncertain smile. Trying to make light of it. Like we're playing some kind of game. A sick game.

"Bastard Donnie is coming. I don't want you around him." Him around you is more like it.

She tips her head. "You never mentioned Donnie got in touch with you."

Pulling my t-shirt over my head, I'm gruff. "He didn't."

"How do you know he's coming?" She swallows what could be a sob or surprise. I'm not sure.

"I could smell that bastard a mile away. He's walking down the corridor as we speak."

"Jack. You're scaring me." She picks herself up off the floor. Tiptoes to the window and stares. She's still topless. I lick saliva off my lips just watching her bend over, pick up her clothes, slip into her bra and fasten it.

I hear Donnie's voice before the tap at the door. I don't have to wonder who he's talking to, because Rachel's voice is also drumming my ears.

When Jen opens the door she's fully clothed, all smoothed out and neat looking. Like nothing ever happened between us.

Every trace of romance has been washed away by failure. Both of us know this. It's all over our faces. I hope Donnie doesn't pick up on it.

Donnie is standing there in all his glory. Arms pressed to either side of the molding, he's half hanging through the doorway, looking from Jen to me, a dumb grin on his face. "The door was locked ..."

No kidding, asshole.

"Your therapist is hot, man." His lips pucker with a "Phew" and he rolls his eyes.

His remark snaps Jenny's head around. Her eyes dart from him to me. She tries to act inconspicuous while swiveling her head around the doorway, then back in. Rachel is obviously not out there, or she'd take Jenny's obvious interest as an open invitation and be in here, too. Joining the fun.

I blow out aggravation and shake my head. "Stay away from Rachel."

Jenny narrows her eyes at me, like she's wondering if I'm being protective of another woman. It's not that at all. I don't want Donnie anywhere around me, or anyone I'm associated with.

"Hope I didn't interrupt anything." His grin widens at Jen as his eyes sweep over her, then he saunters into the room wearing tapered jeans and cowboy boots. His plaid shirt is unbuttoned, and a blue t-shirt is tucked in at the waist. I know this from one quick glance. The only asset I've got over him right now is my hair. His is cropped and blah brown. Mine is brown too, but shiny, thick, streaked with natural highlights Jen says any girl would kill for.

"Who invited you?" I want to say, but don't.

My stomach starts to churn. "Well, if it isn't my high school rival," I mutter beneath my breath, because I don't want him to know I considered him a rival back then. I don't want him to know I considered him anything other than a thorn in my side.

"Come to gloat, Delgado?" I run a hand over my beard, parting it from my lips so he can catch an unobstructed view of my smirk. My slam is followed by the slap of my palms on my thighs. Then a blank stare.

Jenny screws up the corner of her mouth and scrunches her brows. Her arms are folded over her chest. They're standing close together, but she's looking at me.

Donnie belts out a laugh and shakes his head. "Life hasn't changed you, I see." I have a strong feeling he's referring to my accident as life.

Then he turns to Jenny. "What's he on?"

"Love." My voice snaps across the room like a rubber band. "What brings *you* here?"

"I just got back from a hunting trip. Would've stopped by sooner, while you were still in the hospital, but ..." The way he chews on the toothpick stuck between his teeth is annoying. The sliver of wood is shifting north and south as he speaks. He licks it into the corner of his mouth where he anchors it.

"We haven't seen each other in months. What's the sudden interest?" Leaning back in my chair, I'm acting cool. My distain for him is obvious. "But then, I wondered how long it would take you to drag your dead ass out here to stare at the cripple."

He ignores my sarcasm. Maybe our past altercations are deeply imbedded in his memory.

"Sup, bro ..." He takes a few strides, extends a hand. "Good to see you, buddy. Like I said, I would've been here sooner but I was upstate hunting." He cocks a brow and tips his head, like he's agreeing with himself. "You're not the only nature lover."

"True, but I don't kill it." I deadpan. Well, except for that cow ...

"Yeah, I know. Give the deer a gun and all that cavalier bullshit. Hunting is in my blood. What can I say? And since I'm on their turf, I need a gun."

Wheel Wolf

"Leave nature alone," I mumble. "Leave us alone ..."

His skin hasn't changed color yet, so I'm assuming his immunity to my hatred toward him is still in effect. I've never known anyone to take constant beatings and keep coming back for more. But then, Donnie's always been a big question mark.

"It's human nature, Jack. Mine. Not everyone's got the admirable qualities of an environmentalist." He shrugs. "He's still the nature boy, huh Jenny?"

"Why don't you give wildlife a break and play video games?" I snarl.

"Truce, buddy. I heard about what happened. You're big news. Even upstate." He shakes his head and frowns. "Thought you could use some backup. So here I am."

Before I have a chance to reply, he hones in on Jenny. "Hey, girl. How are ya?" He has the balls to draw her to him with one of his muscular arms. Press her against his rib cage. My blood starts to boil. My skin prickles. Next I'll be sprouting a full coat of body hair, because this is the lead-up to how my transition began last night. Stop it, Jack! Control yourself. It.

Jen shoots me an appeasing look and squirms away. "Hey, Don." Her voice is stiff. "This is a surprise. How have you been? How's the job?"

"Awesome, Jenny. I'm in Mink full time now."

"Ah. A Trooper, right?"

Don't look impressed, Jen, I'm thinking. She must catch my vibes. She shoots me a quick look, then her expressionless eyes are back on his.

"Made detective." This he says directly to me. His dark eyes burn into mine. Yep. He's gloating. "You didn't answer me." His gaze works over my chair, then gravitates back to Jenny. "How are you holding up? This has got to be stressful for you, Jen. If there's anything I can do ..."

Stressful for her? How's she holding up? Who's in the

wheelchair?

"She's got me, Donnie." My bark brings his eyes to mine. "I can take care of her needs."

He freezes for a minute, but makes a quick recovery. With his tongue he flicks the toothpick out of his mouth and into the trashcan beside the table where I eat my meals. "I'm not trying to steal your woman." He chuckles. "Just concerned. You should know better, Jack. We go way back. You still don't trust me, do you."

Why the hell should I? This wouldn't be the first time Donnie tried to outscore me in front of Jenny. Our competitions were a daily event ranging from who could spit further, to who could haul ass to the other side of Hosner Lake before the girls counted to ten. Then we had our shit-throwing contests. Who could run faster. Handle a bike better. Who was wittier. Smarter. Who had the probability of a better future. Whose father had more money. I always won that one. But that was my father's doing. Not mine. He was the stockbroker who accrued a small fortune, decided to move us from the city, bought twenty acres of prime property off 44, and built the mini mansion I no longer inhabit.

"Yeah, Donnie. We go way back to high school. I didn't trust you then and I don't trust you now. Why should I?"

"I knew Jenny before you did. If I'd wanted her ..."

"She was never yours. She's mine."

"I know she's yours ..."

"Hold up guys. What am I, dinner?"

"Sorry Jenny. I'm just trying to convince your thick-skulled thin-skinned boyfriend he's too possessive. He should loosen the leash."

She's burning. I can tell. Her cheeks are too rosy, her lips too white.

"Yeah, and guys like you will pop up right behind her." I slap my palms together, making a popping sound that almost shatters my eardrums. "Trying to slip through the collar." My fingers crawl across the air. I'm fucking dramatic. Fucking angry. Fucking hating Donnie more at this moment than when he graduated with honors, and I barely graduated.

"That's enough," Jenny yells. I've never seen her so pissed before. Guess she doesn't like being referred to as meat, or a dog.

She strides to the table, slipping her feet into her shoes along the way. She proceeds to pack up my uneaten salad. "You don't want this? It's good for you, Jack." She frowns. "It's wilted now. Okay. Don't like bread anymore, I see." She starts bundling up the remains in a plastic bag she pulls from her purse, not tossing the inedible food into the trash. She'll take it with her, drop the bag into the first outdoor receptacle she encounters. She's a neat freak. I'm just a freak.

I might be way off, but I sense Jen and Don have this thing happening between them. This eye contact, because I could swear she keeps stealing glances while she's bagging. What's passing between them? Heat? Private communication?

"Can I be in on it? Or is it private?" I ask her bluntly.

Her head whips around and she scrunches her mouth. "What is *wrong* with you?" She shakes her head and frowns. Her scarlet cheeks clash with her flaring violet eyes.

Donnie actually recoils. I know they're thinking I should be locked up. Maybe they're right. Ah. But then they'd be together. There's no way I'm letting that happen.

"I admit I'm possessive." I shrug and mouth a kiss. She's on her way over to me. I'm hoping to bring her lips to mine. Not slap me.

You're mine, Jenny. I don't want him anywhere near you, my eyes are telling her. Stay away from him. When I glare, she takes a quick step back, and says something quite unexpected.

"Whoa. What's with the alpha-ness? You're kinda scary sexy." She moves behind me, maybe it seems safer back there, and proceeds to massage my shoulders. Is she trying to prove something to me *and* Donnie?

When Donnie's head snaps up, I'm so happy Jenny just said that. She's standing up for me, is what I'm thinking. But ...

"I'm outta here." She slips around my chair, slides a soft kiss over my lips, then stalks to the door, purse strapped over shoulder, litter bag in hand. "I won't be able to see you for a couple of days, Jack. With moving back and all, I need time to get settled. The semester is ending soon, and Dr. Brantley asked if I'd be interested in working full-time this summer. I'll actually be getting paid a good salary."

"And?" I stare, wondering if Brantley has his eye on her.

"Of course I said yes."

"Does he offer all of his interns full-time jobs?" My brows are so high, I believe they've become part of my hairline. Either that, or my hairline has grown a lot lower.

"That's great, Jenny." Donnie beats me to the punch by civilly congratulating her. My mouth hangs loose. Jenny never mentioned this job thing to me before. Secrets?

"Jenny." I hold my arms out. "C'mere ... please."

She tilts her head and smiles. She knows me so well. Comes to my side. Leans in close so I can wrap my arms around her to say a proper goodbye. "I love you, honey." Gripping the back of her head, I bring her lips down to mine.

"I love you too, baby." She lifts her face. Works gentle fingers through my hair. "Don't you worry about anything. I know ..." Her eyes are glistening. "We're going to be fine," she whispers directly into my ear.

I can't bear to let her go.

"Bye, Don," she calls out as she slips through the doorway. I have a feeling she's hurrying because she's becoming emotional. I worry about her driving in this condition. Upset. Frustrated. Worried. Confused ... What's happening to her is breaking my heart. The void in my gut starts growing. I miss the hell out of her already, and she's been gone all of three minutes.

Donnie is silent, cocking his head, shoving another toothpick into his mouth. I believe he's waiting for the click of Jenny's heels to fade. I'll hear her shoes cross the solarium floor, hurry through the parking lot. I'll be listening for the key to click into the Jeep's ignition, the engine turn over.

Donnie must assume the coast is clear. He jumps at the opportunity. "What went on that night at the lake?" His eyes are wide. "Seriously, dude. You can level with me." He's staring at me with mounting curiosity, his toothpick stuck to his bottom lip. "What's up with your eyes?"

"It's the medication." I'm so sick of explaining my appearance.

"No shit." Doubt pulls down his facial muscles. "Strange. So what about the lake?"

I give him a sour look. "I'm sure you know all about it, being a detective and all."

"Yeah, but I'd like to hear it from you." He appears genuinely concerned. "Your name has been coming up in the same sentence with suspect."

"What the fuck are you talking about? It was an accident."

"Sure it was, Jack. But the other deaths weren't. Like those hikers last month. The hookers. Do you have an alibi?"

"Do you?" He looks shocked that I'd even consider it. "The grisly murder upstate. Did they ever catch the guy?"

"No."

"So basically, you could be a suspect ..."

"I'm a cop."

"All the more reason you'd be overlooked. Get away with a perfect crime."

"I wouldn't go shooting your mouth off to that effect, Jack. If you think the authorities are breathing down your throat now ..."

"I never said that. You did."

"I'm just passing on information."

"Christ," I mumble before covering my face with my palms. "Will this shit never stop?"

"Hopefully soon, Jack. What can I do for you? I want to help." He flops into the same chair Dr. Sloan sentenced me in.

"What can you do for me?" I'm stiff in my chair, deadpanning. "There's nothing you can do for me, Donnie ... On second thought, you can send over some more of those steaks."

He squints. Pulls another toothpick from his shirt pocket. So now he's got two sticking out of his mouth. I wonder if he even realizes.

"Like you did this morning." I gesture to the tray. "What was it? A peace offering? You send me a prime cut, barely cooked. Nice and rare. And you suddenly think all is forgiven?"

"Sorry, Jack. I'm not that thoughtful." He looks from the table to me. "Hmm. Must have been a good one, because you mutilated the hell out of it. And before you start your shit again, I'm not trying to steal Jenny. Especially not now. I'm not a schmuck."

"That's a matter of opinion."

"All I've ever done is try to steer you in the right direction, Jack. You always took it as a threat to your ego." He sinks back, levels a leg over a knee and rocks it.

"Why don't you just leave." Watching his leg move is as irritating as the damn toothpicks between his lips.

He hammers. "You should have used your brain in school, instead of your brawn. Not fuck around playing stud horse jock. You would have learned something. At least you'd be able to walk into a job now. Excuse the pun. Now that you can't walk, and your brain doesn't work. What the fuck are you going to do?"

"Look who's talking."

"Who got the scholarship?"

I shoot him a disinterested smirk. "Who dropped out of college to be a cop? Who stayed and got their degree?"

"Who made detective in less than a year?"

"So you're great and I'm shit."

"Jack. We were practically brothers in high school. Ran down the middle of town drunk and naked, for shit sake. We were close, dude. Why do you hate me?"

I shake my head and lower it. "Don't take it personal. I hate everyone."

"I never hit on Jenny. I wanted to, but I was loyal to you."

My eyes fill up. "Listen, man. Don't take anything I say to heart. I don't know ... I'm not myself anymore."

He spits both toothpicks into the air, and jumps out of the chair. Then he makes a lunge for me, trying to give me a bear hug. Without dropping to his knees he's unable to, so after strangling my shoulders with a vice-like grip, he stands in front of me. "Remember the fight we had outside the diner the night I really did buy you a steak?" He laughs.

"A fucking grizzly cube steak." I laugh back. "Yeah. Yeah. Don't try to make me feel any worse than I do." My head feels heavy. Like my shoulders can't support it. So it's tilted sideways. Drooping near my shoulder. My grin evaporates. "I'm not on a self-pity trip on my way to self-destruction if that's what you're thinking."

"No one ever said ..."

My raised hand stops him. "I just want you to know, I'm fucking miserable, but I don't feel sorry for myself. I hate myself."

He looks honestly concerned, then bends to pat my shoulder. "I'm gonna take off, Jack. Here's my number, if you need me. Need to talk. Need anything."

"Yeah," I grunt. "I'll be sure to call you." I'm not surprised his visit was short. I figure people can only take me in small doses, which I can't blame them for.

He hands me a business card he pulls from his pocket. "I mean it, Jack. I'll kick your ass if you don't keep in touch."

"There is something." My eyes are darting all over the place, finally settling on his face. I can't believe I'm about to say this. "Keep an eye on Jenny for me, will you?"

He evaluates my face.

"I don't have to tell you how worried I am about her." My eyes water.

"You know it, bro. Hands off. Just eyes." He winks, then gives me a two-finger salute.

"I'm serious. Watch out for her, Donnie. Make believe she's yours. Shadow her like she's part of you." I hate the thought, but since that's what I'd do right now if I could, which I can't, Donnie is the next best thing. Best? I cringe.

Wheel Wolf

Jenny: At The Clinic

"**A**re you seeing Jack today?" Mom asks as I drape myself over the breakfast table, sipping orange juice, thinking about the day ahead. One hand is supporting my chin, but my eyes are following the movements of my parents. Dobie is rolled up in a corner of the kitchen. Not underfoot. He's subdued now. His eyes are like mine, following my parents, but he's waiting for scraps. I'm waiting for nothing. I'm not hungry. I suppose I should be setting the table, but I'm tired, paying the price of another night of twilight sleep and bad dreams.

Mom is cooking scrambled eggs, filling the six slice toaster with wheat bread, reaching into the cabinet for dishes. She's like an octopus. Dad is beside her, making his famous home fries. They're bumping hips and belting out an oldies duet. I'm waiting for them to break into dance. This is a celebration. We're home. I have a feeling part of the show they're putting on is for my benefit. Cheerfulness is contagious and all. But it's not working.

"I won't be able to see Jack today. There's just too much to do here. I want to unpack, do some cleaning. And I have to work the evening shift." I feel guilty about wallowing, so I pick myself up and grab some utensils from a drawer. "Once I get with Jack, I lose track of time." I sigh as I set our places. "I hate leaving him," I mumble.

"Seeing him this way has to be very difficult," Dad jumps in. It's as though he's trying to save me the misery of talking about the accident and Jack's condition. His back is to me, but from the sound of his voice, I visualize his frown. My folks are very fond of Jack. In their own way, they're suffering along with us.

"Send him our best," Mom says as she heaps perfectly golden eggs onto a plate. "And our love. It must be awful for him cooped up in that place. What a tragedy. I still can't get over it."

"Neither can we, Mom." I want to confide in her, tell her about the change in Jack, but feel awkward and ridiculous. Of course he's going to behave differently, considering the circumstances. Get over yourself, Jenny.

"It's good to be home," Dad says, dumping more salt and paprika into the steaming pan than necessary. "Hopefully Jack will be home soon, as well." From the excessive number of shakes he's giving the glass jars, I get the feeling he's not concentrating on the potatoes.

"I almost felt more comfortable in Tidalfalls." Mom turns to Dad with big eyes, and shrugs. "Don't get me wrong. I'm thrilled to be back in the house. But this entire incident has left its mark." I hope she's not gearing up for a menopausal panic attack. Not when she's just beginning to show signs of emotional recovery.

Dad slings an arm around her shoulders, bringing her cheek to his. "It's okay to talk about it, hon. It was traumatic. Home invasions aren't something anyone takes with a grain of salt. You have every right to feel the way you do." He steals a look at me and nods. "Jen feels it, too. Even though she wasn't here. Right Jen?"

"Yes, and if you keep salting the potatoes, we'll be holding five pounds of excess water after we eat them, Dad." Now that makes me laugh. Mom and Dad are adorable. I'm fortunate. I wouldn't have believed it, but joking about Dad's cooking has managed to jumpstart my endorphins. "I'm still feeling the aftermath, too, Mom." They have no idea just how bad. There's no way to explain. I wouldn't want to inflict this distress on them anyway. "Let me get you a cup of raspberry tea instead of coffee, Mom." I'm on my feet again, filling the kettle with water. Sticking my arm between them as I reach for the burner my mother just surrendered and relight it.

"I hear Donnie stopped by the rehab yesterday," Dad says, piling potatoes beside the eggs.

I put out two mugs, add teabags, and steep them in boiling water. "Yup." I'm evasive.

Dad brings the food to the table, then settles himself in the bay area of the kitchen, sinking onto a new chair right beside the window. "How is he?"

"He's still Donnie. Maybe more so now that he's been promoted to detective."

"So he's working down county? Or just visiting," Dad prods as he pushes breakfast around on his plate.

"I'm not sure. I never thought to ask." I scrunch my brows, shake my head. "Why would authorities from Mink be brought down here? Jack's accident was just that. An accident. We have our own police department conducting investigations." I'm becoming agitated just thinking about the two detectives who grilled me while Jack was still unconscious. How insensitive. Insensitive also applies to Don Delgado. He proved that yesterday in Jack's room.

"From what I understand, this is ballooning into a federal matter." Mom massages her temples. "Kidnappings. Murders. Cross-country chaos." When her voice pitches, Dad and I exchange looks. We know a change of subject is in order.

"Time to get moving," I say, draining the tea in my cup. I

stuff the remaining piece of toast into my mouth and head for the stairs." While I turn to my mother, I swallow. "I'm going to start with my room. Then I'll come down and help you out down here."

"Okay, honey. Thanks."

As I head up the stairs, I hear her say, "She's such a good girl. I worry about her. I think she should carry a gun."

~~~~~~~~

After hours of organizing I'm finally satisfied. The entire house looks better than the one we left behind. Much better, considering the place is no longer ransacked. A chill runs down my spine just thinking about that night. I wish they would catch the perpetrator. Our still under construction home is secure, however, with solid oak doors, casement windows, and especially with the new alarm system Dad had installed.

It's been almost ten minutes since I pulled off 44, finally making my way down the driveway of the clinic, ready to begin my four to eight p.m. shift. The ride isn't really long, it just requires traveling a lot of back roads.

The strong rays of sun stayed behind on the main, open road. We rarely see sun at the clinic. It would take laser beams to penetrate the protective canopy of foliage surrounding the place. It feels like sunset is just around the corner. I shiver because there must be a ten degree difference in temperature out here in the middle of nowhere. I bring my arm in and roll up my window before I even begin to park.

The front of the small building I work in is sided with faded blue shingles. I'm wondering why the only cars in the lot are Chickie's, Barry's and Ben's. At this hour, there should still be patients here. The clinic doesn't normally close until six. I stay until eight to tend to the animals in the kennel, which is a low cement block building out back.

My eyes travel across the face of the clinic, stalling on the pitch of the roof. The wind chimes hanging from the peak give the only indication of welcome today. It's quiet. It's freaky. Where is everyone?

I'm noticing for the first time how creepy this place is. The thought that I've spent late nights here alone makes my skin crawl with goose bumps. A place that I used to feel comfortable in, now makes me nervous as hell. I don't want to be here. Maybe I'll quit when summer ends. After I've earned enough to help ease the burden on my folks. The Evening Sun is a good source of income, but expenses are high. The last thing I want to do is cut into my parents' retirement fund. I'd give notice tonight, but the summer money will come in handy filling the gap between tuition and what my student loan doesn't cover.

The clinic itself is old, but comfortable. Compassionate. No neighbors around to hear barking dogs. And we get plenty of them. Barking dogs. Not neighbors.

Before I cut the engine, the musical tone of my cell phone sounds from my red pleather bag which is lying open on the passenger's seat where I tossed it when I left home. I recognize the number immediately, as well as the name lighting up across my screen. Why not? This is his fourth call today. He made me store his cell phone number yesterday, during the first of his half dozen calls.

"Hey Don. What's up?" I'm exhausted. I'm disinterested in what he has to say. My voice can't be any flatter. The phone is locked between my ear and shoulder as I climb out of the Jeep. Does he not believe in the convenience of texting?

"Hi beautiful. How are you?" His voice is smoother today. Hmm. Does he think we're still seniors in high school? Flirting his butt off, trying to wiggle his way between Jack and me again? No wonder Jack feels the way he does.

"The same as I was two hours ago," I huff. If he thinks I'm about to cheat on Jack, he's in for the surprise of his life.

His chuckle in the phone is throaty. Making me think of Jack. I miss him. He doesn't call me half as much as Donnie has been calling me. I know he's busy with rehab. Rachel ...

With my bag strapped over my other shoulder, I head down the dirt path lined with weeds. We don't do frills here. No cement sidewalks. No manicured gardens like the ones beneath Jack's first floor window. Everything is natural here. Droppings disintegrate much more quickly that way. No shoveling poop. Just let the earth take care of it. The kennel out back has a cement floor. We hose that one down several times a day. Still, droppings flow into the forest, blending with nature.

Donnie's voice reminds me we're still connected, but only by the cell phone tower, which today gives pretty bad reception. "What are you doing later?" His voice is crackling.

"Crashing. I'm exhausted from cleaning and unpacking."

"How about breakfast tomorrow?"

I grip the phone and sigh. "No Don."

"Lunch?"

"Don ..." my tired tone warns.

"I'm just doing what I promised Jack. Attaching myself to you. Shadowing you is what the man told me to do."

Jack ... My sweet Jack. This has to be killing him, in more ways than one.

Before I reach the clinic door I gaze through the picture window, realizing the office looks more like a modest country home than a veterinary clinic. I wonder if anyone ever lived here. Nah. It's buried too far off the beaten path, down back roads. Side streets. Darkness. Seclusion.

No one would want to live back here, alone, practically in the heart of the forest. Which does make it great for animals. Not humans, though. I get a chill down my spine just thinking about being here alone tonight. The spotlights on the side of the building are somewhat comforting, but ... nope. Would never want to call this my permanent residence.

"So Jack talked you into being my guardian angel, huh?" I'm smiling as I open the door and step over the mat and into the waiting room. If I step on the mat, I might be stepping on pee or poo. Although we hose it daily, the rubber mat holds the scent. Pups and kits love emptying their bladders and bowels upon entering, usually from the stress of their surroundings, and upon exiting because they can't hold it. I've come to learn they do this because they're so well-trained they won't make it in a cage, or on the table, and after their ordeal is over they can't possibly make it outside. So the mat is the next best place to make.

"Hey Jenny," Chickie says. I nod, because Donnie is chewing my ear off, in one breath telling me how much Jack loves me. In another getting his point across that the road to recovery is going to be long and difficult.

"I have to go. I'm just getting into work." I'm whispering, because Chickie is a busybody.

"Hit me up when you leave, before you pull out of the driveway. That way, I can time you. Make sure you get home safely."

"For Pete's sake, Don!" My whisper takes flight. Chickie stares and lifts both brows. I believe she heard me say, "Don." I turn my back to Chickie so I can freely hiss at Don. "Listen. I'm not going to do this every day. I'm fine. And I'm in love with Jack. Do you hear what I'm saying?"

I listen to his deep inhale and wonder if he's smoking pot, because he sounds like he's holding in a breath. "Better yet ..." slow exhale "... I'll be parked at the end of the road waiting for you to wave to me when you pass by on your way to 44." He chuckles, then turns serious. "Jenny, don't take my concern for interest. I know how I'd feel if I were in Jack's position."

I don't believe him ... He's not listening to a word I'm saying. Did he just slam me? I cut him off. "You're not." Click, I disconnect the call.

"Why's it so dead in here?" I ask Chickie, a thirty-something year old divorcee who wishes she had two men care about her. Maybe not. She's the victim of domestic violence. Hiding out in this job, in her apartment, from her ex, I believe, and from life. I feel so bad for her. Maybe that's why she's so interested in mine. Not only did her ex give her a broken arm and grief. He gave her an STD. I should hook her up with Donnie. He's not the greatest, but he'd never abuse her. I don't think so, anyway. Now I've got myself thinking about Don Delgado and how he treats women? No way.

"We cancelled all afternoon appointments. There was an emergency. A shepherd pup was brought in with a hole in his heart. He would've died if Dr. Brantley didn't perform emergency surgery." Although Dr. Brantley told us to call him Ben when patients aren't around, Chickie insists upon calling him doctor.

"Did the surgery go okay?" My heart trips with concern. "Will the pup be alright?"

"I think so." Barry's in there with him. He'll need follow-up care during the night. I hope Barry knows he's staying. That I'm not about to spend another creepy night in this place. I'm just a clerk. Not a tech. Or a vet in training." She gives me a sour look.

I feel for her. She's been traumatized. It takes a long time to recover physically from being beaten and left for dead. Even longer to recover emotionally. If it's ever possible, that is.

I stow my shoulder bag in the metal cabinet drawer in the spare exam room where we store bandages and tape, and slip into my lab coat. I'm buttoning the coat over my jeans and t-shirt, bending to fasten the loosened tie on my sneaker, when I hear the gurney being pushed down the corridor. I fly out the door.

"Hey, Barry. How'd surgery go? Will the little guy make it?"

Barry gives me a hard look. "We're talking about Ben Brantley's expertise here."

Wheel Wolf

I nod and tighten my ponytail, hoping he's not seriously reprimanding me. "Of course. Dr. Brantley is the best." Barry isn't anyone you want to play around with. He's in his fifties. Ears gauged. All tatted up. Big, balding and scary. Where animals are concerned, Barry is all business. So am I, especially when he catches these attitudes.

He surprises me with a grin. "Of course pup will be just fine. I'm pulling yer puddin', kid."

I let out a gush of air, first because pup will be okay. Second because Barry is just about to leave for the day. I think I'd rather be here alone than be stuck here with Barry for my entire shift. He's too unpredictable. Anxiety-inducing. Downright weird.

Dr. Brantley is on his way out of the O.R. He looks like the surgeon he is, in green scrubs, gloved and capped.

"Hi Ben. I understand your amazing talents saved another life."

I run my palm over the head and neck of the shepherd that is still sedated. He's adorable. Caramel and black in just the right places. "Will he be out long?"

"A few hours, give or take. He's sleeping naturally."

~~~~~~~~

Everyone's gone. I check my watch. It's eight fifteen. Barry was supposed to be back by eight to check on the pup. I phone Ben.

"Hi. No everything's fine. Pup was awake. Yup. I managed to get some pablum down his throat. He lapped it up." I giggle. "Barry didn't show. And he's not answering his phone."

"He must be asleep. With Syd on vacation, Barry's been working almost around the clock this entire week. Listen. If you're sure the shepherd is fine, and the kennel is quiet you said?" I didn't, but it is. "Yes, all is calm. The shepherd is fine. After I fed him I went out to the kennel, fed and watered the brood. Yes, I hosed down the floor. The guys should all be set for the night." I stifle a yawn. I'm ready to be set for the night, too. "I also cleaned up the mess Barry left in the break room. Since when does he bring T-bone steak for lunch? I've seen him bring sushi, leftover Chinese, pizza. So I guess a steak isn't any big deal, huh?" Even though Ben's on the other end of the phone and can't see me, I shrug.

"You took care of everything. Perfect. I'll have a talk with Barry about the break room. You're a dream, Jenny. Lock up. Go home and relax. I'll keep ringing him. He should be back over there within an hour. Either way, I'll take care of things. One of us will get over there. Don't you worry. You're doing a great job. Did I ever tell you that? If not, I'm telling you now. I don't know what I'd do without you." So much for giving him my notice. "I'll stop by later and hang with Barry and pup, after the game. If I'm still conscious. That surgery was over five hours. Took everything out of me."

Stifling another yawn, I agree. "I can imagine."

"Thanks for going the extra mile, Jenny. I'll make this up to you." I'm not sure what he means, but a bonus would come in handy.

I lock up, take another walk to the back of the building, through the yard that is practically pitch black, making sure the kennel night lights are on. The kennel is resting in the center of the soft glow oozing from every window. The automatic flood lights snap on, reminding me the sun has set long ago on 44, and the moon is on the rise. I'm peeking through a hole in the forest ceiling. It's not a full moon. Half maybe, but not nearly enough to light my way back to the Jeep.

A mini flashlight dangles on the end of the keychain Jack gave me. I use it to count my steps, relieved when I reach my car. The night is alive with eerie forest sounds: crackling leaves, snapping twigs, my heart in my ears. Why do I feel like someone's watching me? I let the feeling of a creepy presence get the better of me and do a three-sixty, then mumble, "What's wrong with you? You practically live out here. Knock it off."

The breeze that suddenly blows my hair feels like fingers. I actually jump, my hand trembles, and I drop the keys ... under the damn car. The sounds keep moving, circling. I wonder if Donnie is playing a joke, pretending to stalk me. Nah, frightening the hell out of a woman alone would be too evil, even for him.

Dangerous too, as I'm a pro at roundhouse kicks. Besides giving me a mini flashlight for nights like this, Jack has taught me how to fight like a dude.

My knees are weak when I drop to the ground, flatten my body and slide halfway under the chassis of the Jeep, thanking God it sits high off the ground. My fingernails cake with dirt as I scratch around for the keys.

"Where are you, keys?" I whisper, on the verge of tears. My fumbling fingers finally clutch the chain and I'm up on my feet again, pressing the unlock button on the key fob. The instant the lock chirps, I rip the door open, hop in, hit the auto door locks, snap the interior lights on, crane my neck to make sure nothing, no one is in here but me, and let out a huge, shuddering sigh.

"Where are you now, guardian angel?" I say, and laugh. I can laugh because I'm safe inside my car.

I ease down the driveway, avoiding the ruts, when something slams the side of the Jeep. I suck in a breath, jam my foot on the break and put the car in park. Straining through the windows to see if anyone is around is futile through darkness and trees. "Is anyone there?" I call through the closed window as butterflies build.

Did I hit an animal? Oh my God! Could one of the pups have gotten out of the kennel? I shake my head, whispering, "Na ah. I locked it myself." I pull the keys from the ignition and switch on my flashlight. I don't want to, but I have to get out of the car to see if I hit something. Otherwise I'll never rest. Before my fingers grip the door lever, I consider backing the car up, shining my headlights, but suppose I run something over again?

Come on, Jenny. You're being ridiculous. But I did hear a definite thump. Or did I feel it? An animal might need help, so I'm out the door breathing heavily as I begin to search. I walk around my car, casting nervous glances over my shoulder. My pulse is racing. I don't see anything other than forest and my feet. I flash the light around the tires, under the frame. Dirt, stones and sneakers ... mine.

The air is crisp and fragrant. If it were daylight, the sight around me would be beautiful, instead of occupied by ominous shadows. You're being so silly, I scold myself. My heart rate slows and I heave a sigh. "Thank God I didn't hit anything."

So what *was* that thud? I'm running my hand over the back fender, feeling for a dent, when I hear a rustle of brush, more snapping twigs. Footsteps? Blood drains from my limbs. On my way to the open door I trip over my feet, fall into the car and aim the key with almost uncontrollable hands until the engine miraculously starts. "Holy shit," I'm moaning. "Is something out there?" The Jeep jerks into gear. As I speed away, I slam the door.

The headlights cut through air thickened by darkness as I follow the desolate back road, finally pulling out onto 44. CR 44 isn't the most well-traveled road, but at least it has some street lights. Not like the inky back roads I've just fled. My pulse is finally slowing.

By the time I pull into my driveway, my dash clock reads nine-forty-five. What a fiasco of a night. The unexpected. Always be prepared for the unexpected, I remind myself. All the while, Jack has been in the back of my mind. Now he's all that's inside my head. As I walk to my door, I'm hitting auto dial on my cell.

When I hear his "Hello," my face breaks into a huge smile. My worries are over. I'm talking to Jack. Even if I can't be with him, at least I can talk to him. "Hey baby. How are you?" I'm upbeat, experiencing a natural high. That's what Jack does to me.

He sounds sleepy. I picture him with bed-hair, wishing I was with him. "Did Wonder Woman give you a good workout today?"

He chuckles. "She did. But nothing half as wonderful as your workouts."

Just thinking about yesterday, and how close we came, I blush. It's said everything happens for a reason. What is the reason I'm still a virgin? It's beyond me.

"How are you, Jen? How was work? You're late. I was just gonna call you. I was worried."

"Don't worry about me. I'm fine. Worry about you." I smack my lips together, sending a squeaky kiss through the line and wait for his.

"A pup needed emergency surgery," I whisper as I unlock my front door and punch the code to disarm the alarm. The moment I'm inside, I punch it back on.

Jack gasps. "Oh no, is he okay?"

"Yeah, he's fine. Not sure about me."

"What do you mean?"

I sigh. "The boogeyman I guess ..." Then I belt out a laugh. "My mother wants me to get a gun."

"I've never agreed with your mother more. We're gonna have to talk about these late nights ..." I hear a woman's faint voice in the background. Faint but gruff. "Listen, babe. I have to run. Shower and all that good stuff. I'll call you before lights out, okay?"

"Sure. I'm about to fall into a nice warm bath followed by bed."

"Go on. Rub it in." His groan makes my legs weak. Even though it didn't work, I can't get yesterday and Jack's bed out of my mind.

"I love you, Jack." My whisper is seductive. Considering

phone sex, I almost giggle.

"Love you, Jenny. More than you can imagine. Take care of you for me, baby." He lets out a heavy sigh.

Jack hasn't said that to me in a while. Not since right before his accident. I wonder what prompted it. He's hopefully returning to normal. That would be wonderful. Miraculous. "Take care of you. For me." I blow another kiss into the phone before we disconnect. We hate to disconnect, so we end up doing the, one, two, three ... don't dare say another word and just hang up, click.

I pad down the hallway, listening to the sounds coming from my parents' bedroom. TV and whispers. I pop my head through the doorway. "Hey, I'm home."

"Hi, Jen." It's Dad. "Glad you're home. Now we can go to sleep." He chuckles.

"How was your night, honey?" Mom's voice is accompanied by the rustle of sheets as she fluffs her pillow and slides under the covers.

"The usual. I'm gonna take a bath and hit the sack. I'm exhausted. See you in the morning."

As I head to my room calling back, "Sleep good," their light snaps off behind me. So does the TV. They always wait up for me. I shake my head and smile.

My bath was delightful. I'm refreshed. Relaxed. Ready for a good night's sleep because I have myself believing Jack is on the mend: physically and emotionally.

When my cell phone chimes, the clinic is the farthest thing from my mind. My first thought is Jack. Not Jack's voice, though. In my sleepy state, I'm thinking ... "Don?" But it's Ben. Oh crap. Not tonight, please.

"Jenny. I'm sorry to disturb you, but I got a call from the police department. The pups in the kennel are kicking up a hell of a fuss. Someone called it in."

"Who? There's no one around there for miles." I fight to

clear my groggy head.

"I know. I have no idea. Anywho, I can't reach Barry. He must be sleeping it off. I'm already dressed and ready to head out the door, but ... Jenny. I'm concerned."

"And you want me to take a ride out there because it takes you a half hour to drive to the clinic and I can be there in half that time if I leave right now."

He lets out a breath of relief. "I'll make it up to you. If it wasn't for the shepherd I wouldn't be as worried. The other pups might have picked up something in the air. You know, sixth sense and supersonic ears."

"Ben, I heard noises earlier. I'm a little concerned ..."

He cuts me off. I imagine him waving a hand. "Don't worry. A patrolman is out there waiting for you. I made sure of it. The dispatcher promised me he'd stay." A moment of silence, then Mrs. Brantley is in the background muttering something inaudible. "Meet you there soon, Jenny. I owe you one."

"No problem." I hold back a sigh and a scream, not sure which I'd like to hit him with first. "I'm on my way."

On with the jeans and t-shirt, freshly laundered ones of course. Socks, sneakers, hoodie over head, and I'm out my bedroom door. I pass by my parents' room. Silent. Dobie's new habit is sleeping at the bottom of their bed, so he's probably dead to the world, as well. The house is eerily silent. I scribble a note on the whiteboard by the kitchen door. Had to check a new pup at the clinic. Back soon. Love you. :-) J.

I'm in such a rush, I almost forget to disarm the security system. I tap the code into the panel so I can leave without setting off the warning signal; a brash screech that can break your eardrums if you happen to be standing close enough to the panel, which I was when the installer tested the system. All I have to do is set off the alarm. Dad will come flying down the stairs with his shotgun. No thank you. Before slipping out the door, I make sure to key in the night code. I hear the speaker echo, *night stay*, know they're safe, and I'm on my way back to work.

The town of Angels' Bend is built around County Route 44. Busy in the center of town, deserted as it stretches north, every other road connects to 44 on one end or the other.

It's a Wednesday night. Heading out of town, the road is barren. I check the Jeep's fuel gauge. Phew. Just enough gas to get there and back. Have to remember to gas up first thing tomorrow morning, before I visit Jack. I can't wait to visit Jack. Maybe we'll even fool around. Finish what we started. The prelude to making love to him was beautiful, before things went wrong. Maybe it will work this time. Should I call him back and tell him? Nah. He must be snuggly and sound asleep by now. This gives me something to think about as I drive. I start running my fingers through Jack's gorgeous hair. Tasting his lips, his tongue. My hands are sliding over Jack's chest as I pull off 44.

When I edge down Wild Berry Road, before my tires have a chance to crunch on the clinic's pebbled driveway, I see the red flash of bubble lights. I'm immediately relaxed. Sure enough, the dogs are howling. I hear the racket they're making through closed windows. They sound frightened. A shiver runs through me. I want to grow eyes in the back of my head, better yet, be accompanied by a bodyguard. Where's Donnie when you need him? The patrol car door is open. The officer must be walking around the building, which stops my stomach from rolling into a knot.

Thank goodness I don't have to face this alone. I park and hop out of the car, bypassing the clinic's front door, as everything looks locked up tight. Just as I left it. "Hello?" I call as I proceed around the building, following a path that isn't really a path, but rather beaten down scrub grass snaking through the backyard, which is in total darkness, because the flood lights are not shining. Neither is the moon I left behind on 44. Odd, I think. But the police car's lights are bright, so ... before looking in on the post op pup in the quiet clinic, I check out the surrounding area.

"Hello?" I call again, louder this time. My voice fills my ears as alarm builds.

Hmm. I figure the officer must be down at the kennel, where the dogs are in fact howling more urgently. Belting out mournful wails. Sounding scared out of their minds. Creating such a ruckus, my stomach *is* tying itself into that knot. I'm relying on my keychain flashlight, which is brightening everything around me, for all of three or four feet. Why didn't I grab one of Dad's? I could kick myself.

I belt out another, "Hello?" but the officer still does not reply. I'm really getting the creeps now.

I tip my head to listen to the sound of crunching leaves and snapping twigs, while a sudden gust of wind steals my gulp of air. *The devil's breath*, shoots through my mind.

Against my better judgment, because I feel like turning right around and heading home, I tiptoe down the incline and up to the kennel. The door is locked. Everything is intact. I peek through the window because I don't have the keys that open the door. They're inside the clinic in Chickie's desk drawer. Through the soft glow of interior night lights, everything inside the cement block building appears to be in order. Stainless steel table. Enamel desk. Wooden chair. Supply cabinets tacked to the side wall. Neat rows of cages, like jail cells, but still larger than pet shop crates. I'm stumped. Not only because I can't imagine why the dogs are going ballistic, but where is the officer who drove that patrol car almost through the front door?

I decide to head back. Let myself into the office and call the station. Even with my trusty little light, the night is almost pitch black. My pulse is picking up. I'm walking faster, almost turning an ankle in a rut. "Damn," I cry out to the crickets and branch-rustling breeze.

I gain my footing and find my way back to the path, testing each step. Hmm. What is that? My groping sneaker slides through something soft. Great. I've stepped in dog poop. I huff. Barry should *not* let them crap out here. That's what cement floors are for. Not pathways where my new sneakers are now ruined.

I don't smell poop, but a repugnant odor wafts into my nose, so I shine the light, drop my gaze, and scream. I'm standing in the middle of something that looks like it should be in a butcher shop. Entrails? Organs? My stomach lurches. My temples pound. What the hell? My mind isn't processing. I follow the bloody trail, and what I find almost drops me to my knees. But I can't let that happen. I'd be kneeling on someone's flesh and bones. *Human sacrifice* slams my brain. What the hell went on out here? My head swings around, followed by my body, while I try to determine if anyone else is around. A witness. A murderer? I can't fall into shock ...

I'm crouching in tall grass, just a few feet from the kennel, trying to blend with the scenery. Not far from where I made a first pass down the path. I force myself to return my eyes to the puddle of remains at my feet. I know it's the police officer, because my light shines over scraps of blood-soaked uniform edged with blue. A badge. Part of a leather belt. Empty holster.

I know I shouldn't, but I flash my light up and down what should be his body. What body? He's been torn apart. The only thing somewhat intact is the chest, which has been carved up the center, cracked ribs laid open like cage doors. I've done my share of anatomizations, and know what lungs look like. This chest cavity has only one. At the sight and thought of: Where is the other lung? Where is the rest of the body? The contents of my stomach rise to my throat. Am I standing on a kidney? I gag and lift my foot, but can't determine where to set it down, because the entire area is a carpeted with bits and pieces of what was once a human being.

Wheel Wolf

What did this? My heart starts pumping. I'm struggling to decide which way to run. Something's out here with me. Not only a dead cop, something alive, because it's breathing ... heavily. Snorting, like a sneezing dog. And it's getting closer. A bolt of panic travels up my back and hits my head. Blood pounds my ears where it must be trapped, because I think every ounce of my blood has left the rest of my body. My hollow veins have collapsed. I'm numb. Tingly. A fist in my chest is choking my windpipe. I'm about to have heart failure, I'm certain.

The howl that cuts through the air is different from the yapping dogs'. Deeper. Menacing. Blood-curdling. Everything on me freezes, other than my heart which is pounding through my chest. Tech found dead behind Angel's Bend clinic. Cause of death: coronary. The morning news. My face plastered all over the TV. The officer no longer has a face. After tonight, will I? I have the ability to consider every aspect of my situation as my mind is going a mile a minute. Whirling, spinning out of control. I'm about to faint.

My ears are buzzing like they're filled with bees, making it difficult to concentrate ... to hear. I know I have to get out of here, but I can't move. Something is out here, with me, in the dark. The moon isn't shedding enough light on the grounds because it's moved from the one crack in the forest ceiling.

Coursing blood floods my optic nerve, strengthening my vision. Maybe it's a defense mechanism from our ancestor days. Like scent or ... I smell it. Rank. Foul. An outline in the distance grows larger, and it's moving toward me, slowly, but still advancing. I can't decide if it's a man or an ... Dear God. Save me, please. It's big and furry? And it has pointed ears. Is it the devil?

My tone is guttural. "Who's there?" I'll use my voice as a weapon. Frighten it off. "The police are on the way."

It's not about to make friends with me, and since there's a

dead body ... this approach is obviously not going to work.

My limbs spring to life and I run like my life depends on it, because it does. Whatever killed the officer is stalking me. Closing in on me. Almost breathing down my throat, because now a disgusting odor is entering my nostrils. Animal odor. Dirty, damp, rancid animal.

I'm sobbing. Running. Stumbling. My trembling fingers fish inside my bag for the keys to the front door of the clinic. I have a decision to make. A life or death decision. Clinic. Patrol car. Jeep.

I'm standing beneath a weak spray of porch light, in full view. Not good. Decide what to do. Get your ass inside, Jennifer. Wait. If I lock myself inside the clinic, I'll be trapped.

Another reverberating howl breaks through the night. This one sounds almost on top of me. I spin a three-sixty.

Should I make a run for the patrol car with bubble lights that are still orbiting? Without much deliberation, I start then stop. My cautious side, the one separating itself from the terrified side, tells me to weigh my odds first.

The patrol car is close to the clinic's front door. Not more than five feet from where I'm standing. Shaking. The driver's door is flung wide open, but the problem is, the closed passenger door is facing me. So close. So close. The car has been hastily parked on what would be the lawn, had someone planted grass seed. Nothing grows around here but weeds and prickly wild berry bushes. Scraggly shrubs. Gigantic trees. Shadows. Monsters. Brain start working!

I want to try for the cop car. Although it's been abandoned, siren not whooping, it offers protection, hope, salvation, humanity. Everything I need right now. Keys? Suppose the keys aren't in the cop car? Of course, he didn't leave the keys dangling in the ignition. Just left the flashers on. Why didn't I go to the car first? Before stomping off to the kennel? Who would have ever thought they'd stumble over a dead policeman? Meet a monster. I guess that's why I didn't bother to look inside the patrol car. Hindsight

... I have to do something fast. Get away from here.

My eyes scoot to the Jeep ... Like my feet want to do. I'm strangling the keys in my hand. I can see my car, sitting in the first parking space. Waiting for me, but it's still too far away. Whatever has been stalking me is circling me now. In my frenzied state, I'm not sure exactly where it is. The wheezing snorts seem to be coming from everywhere. The thing could be hiding behind my bumper for all I know. I don't know! I'll never make it to the Jeep, anyway. It's too far away. Major decision has been made for me.

Shaking as though I'm burning with fever and chills, my fumbling fingers manage to fit the key into the door lock on the first try. The tumbler clicks. The nightmare is just starting. I'm alone. Oh my God. The breathing is heavier, closer. So are the snapping twigs, the moving shadows. Closing in on me.

Hinges squeak as I swing the door open, leap through the opening, slam the oak door behind me and bolt it. Slide the heavy duty security chain through the guard latch as well. All while I'm panting. Shaking. Ready to vomit. Wondering if I'm going to die. Asking God, "Is this my time?" Am I going to die tonight? Please not yet. Not like this.

My back literally slams the door. My body tries to sink to the floor, along with my bag. I'm so dizzy I have to brace myself with something, like the back of the wooden chair beside me. Fight to gain my bearings and strength. Pray my heart doesn't burst in my chest, because I'm incapacitated by terror. I have to think straight. Keep a clear head and you'll survive this. Think Jenny! Think!

Why didn't you try to find the pistol on the officer's mutilated body? Because it wasn't really a body anymore. You panicked. You ran. Dammit ... Who wouldn't? Jack wouldn't. He'd stand there and fight. Jack's a guy. A big guy. I'm five-four. One hundred-fifteen pounds of raw, shattered, shuddering nerves. At the moment, my limbs feel like jelly. No, heavy as lead. Crazy.

I slip my cell from the pocket of my jeans, pound 9-1-1. Wait endless moments while the phone rings and rings. Maybe three times. The office is silent. The air dark, gradient, thanks to the soft glow of nightlights plugged into the electrical outlets low to the floor. The only sound is the petrified screech of life in my ears. My heart crying out for help. I can't help you heart. I'm lightheaded again ... motionless. About to faint this time for real, but I can't. I might not wake up again. Whatever is out there might break in. Find me. Kill me. Tear me to pieces like it did to the cop, lying in a puddle out in the backyard. I start heaving. Gagging. On the rubber mat. Adding vomit to the scent of pee and poo.

An operator finally answers, "9-1-1. State your emergency."

"This is Jenny Rudéa. I'm night tech at the Brantley Veterinary Clinic on Wild Berry Road. An officer was murdered." Pant. Gag. Cough. Sob.

Instead of trying to calm me, she's asking for details. Her voice is hard. Cold. "I don't have time for details lady! Just send the police. Fast. Because whatever killed him is after me. I hear it outside." I pause to listen. "Oh my God. I think it's walking around the building. Rattling the windows."

"Did you lock the doors?"

"Of course. That was the first thing I did." Oh no. I didn't lock the back. So as I talk, I lose more breath as I run past Ben's office, the exam room, recovery room. To the back door. It's closed. Thank goodness. Already locked. Bolted. Thank you OCD Barry.

"Windows secure?"

"I don't know ..."

"Check the windows. Be calm. The police are on the way. They'll be there soon. Check the windows. But stay away from them. Pull the shades. But don't be visible. Find a safe place to hide." She must do this a lot, gives me hope, faith in the system, because she's got this down pat. Rational and controlling. Her.

Wheel Wolf

Not me.

"I'm hanging up," I whisper as I tiptoe around, following her orders. "I have to call someone."

The next call I make is to Donnie. Hoping to God he's really shadowing me. Please be right down the road, Don. Please answer your phone. No! Not voicemail! I can't accept that! I burst into tears, trying to sob as quietly as possible, while I wait for whatever it is that's circling the clinic to gain access. I know it's circling outside because I'm following the noises it's making, from inside.

"Shit, Don," I'm breathing so heavy, I'm rasping. Whimpering. Will he hear my weak voice? My teeth are chattering. Hands are useless. Legs barely holding up my weight. "Don. As soon as you get this message ... I need help. I'm at the clinic. Something is trying to kill me. It's outside. It just killed an officer."

My next call is to Jack.

"Hey baby. I was just gonna ... Jenny what's wrong?" He immediately sounds as panicked as I do.

I'm sobbing. I don't think he understands me, because he keeps telling me to calm down. He can't hear me. Is it static on the line? Or does he mean he can't understand me? Am I talking too fast?

"Jack," deep breath, slower, "I'm - at - the - clinic." Gulp.

"What are you doing there? Why are you all upset? Did the puppy die?"

"A cop ... outside ... dead." Lump in throat is constricting.

"Jenny? Holy fuck. What the fuck is going on? Who's with you? Donnie?"

"Never mind," I snap out a harsh whisper, then groan. "Just listen. Something - is - outside. It killed a patrolman."

Why does Jack keep saying "What?" Can't he tell me what to do?

"Jack. What should I do? I'm scared."

"I'm on my way baby." Now he's panting too. Breathing so hard into the phone, his voice is garbled. Or is it the cell phone connection?

"Hurry, Jack. How will you get here?"

"I'm ringing for Rachel as we speak. Hang up and hide. I'm calling 9-1-1."

"Nooo. Don't hang up. Don't leave me. I already called them. I called Donnie, too, but he didn't answer. I left him a message." I'm fighting to hold back sobs so he understands me. So the thing doesn't peg my location in the clinic. So Jack doesn't freak out too much more, because he sounds like he's about to die of a coronary. Am I going to die?

"He didn't answer? Bastard. Typical cop. Never around when you need him." Ragged breath. "I told the bastard to shadow you."

"Jack ... There's a shadow outside the window. It's moving. Creeping around. I'm so scared, Jack. It's scratching at the glass." I whip my head around. "It's on the other wall now. Rattling a window."

"Jenny. Listen to me." He's desperate. "You have to stay calm. Quiet."

I hear Rachel's raspy voice in the background. "This better be good Jack. It's midnight."

"You have to drive me. Jenny's in trouble."

"I'm in my pajamas, Jack." She's so emotionless, cold actually, but her voice never sounded so good. At this very moment, I love Rachel Huntress. I'd throw myself into her arms if I could.

He's not talking to me. He's mumbling to Rachel. "Don't hang up Jack."

"I won't baby. I'll talk you through this. You'll be fine. Just do as I say.

I'm on my way. 9-1-1 will be there in a matter of minutes. It's important to remain calm. Keep your head on. Remember. Take care of you ... for me." His voice cracks. I think he's covering the phone. Sobbing.

Stay calm? He's not calm. How can I be calm? I'm about to

be ... God knows what that thing is about to do me. I'm gasping, fighting for air. Hyperventilating?

"Can you get your hands on a weapon?" Jack's voice is urgent.

"There aren't any weapons here." I manage to croak out between my struggle for air and speech.

"How about a knife?"

"Scalpel, I guess. In the operating room." I'm whimpering.

"Get it. Get anything else you can find and barricade yourself in a closet. And for Christ sake. Be quiet."

"The closets don't have locks."

"The freezer, Jenny. Get inside that big old freezer in the back room."

"I can't. It's full of euthanized animals. Pickup isn't till Friday."

A desperate, "Christ," is blown into my ear.

"Are you in the car yet?"

When I hear the wheels of his chair bite into gritty pavement, I believe I've answered my own question. His heavy breath is blowing through the line. A sliding door squeals and slams, thank God. Then come the sounds of clinking metal, huffing, jostling. The engine starts. He's in the van. The tires screech. Thank God, again, Jenny. It won't be long now. He's on his way. He'll be here soon.

Just knowing Jack is on his way helps slow my heart. Balances the erratic beats. I don't hear the thing anymore. Just my blood. Bees. Maybe it's gone.

"I don't hear it now, Jack. I'm gonna check the window."

"No Jenny. Don't go near the window. Stay put. Hide till the cops get there. Till I get there."

Rachel has actually turned on the radio? It's blaring. I can't hear Jack anymore. Not even his breathing.

"Jack!" My panicked whisper peaks. I've been trying to hold my voice low, but now I'm almost confident the thing is gone. Maybe it knows help is on the way.

"I went around checking every window, Jack. The recovery room. Ben's office. The surgical suite has high windows. I have the scalpel. I'm checking the waiting room ... looking for headlights. Oh my God, Jack. The picture window. No shades on it. It's still here." Shock fills my being, because this is the first time I'm able to get a look at what wants me. "It's outside. I can see the shadow. It's tall. Big. Moving back and forth. Watching me? It's taller than the window, Jack!"

The fleeting thought flashes; I should call my parents to say goodbye. But I don't want to leave Jack. He's my security. I need him with me. Right here. Right now. "Jack ..." I let out a scream, because the thing's outside looking in. It knows I'm here, so why bother to be soundless.

Jack is crying. "Jenny hide. We're turning off 44 now. We'll be there in a few minutes."

"I hear breathing Jack. I think it's in here. With me."

"It can't be. Everything's locked, Jen. Right, babe?" He's drawing in sobs with gasps for air. "Please clean out the freezer, baby." Jack keeps crying. "And hop inside. Close the door. You'll be safe."

"I'll be locked in." I'm not thinking. I'm on autopilot, but I'm crashing. I think I'm shutting down.

"That's the point. I'll let you out as soon as I get there. Soon, baby."

He'll take me in his arms. That's what I need. To be in Jack's arms. The thing outside the window is hideous.

"Who's out there?" Jack keeps demanding.

"I don't know what it is." I want to hide my eyes, but I can't. It's punching a clawed fist through the window. A thick, hairy arm stretches through the shattered glass. Followed by a massive head, broad shoulders. With terrifying, muscular ease, it leaps through the opening it's made with its body that has not only crashed through the plate glass window, but the wall as well. Wood is splintering, shooting across the room. The thing lands heavily, but gracefully, on two feet. It's standing here, staring at me.

"It's hairy! Jaws! Drool! Oh my God. It's a huge animal!" I tighten my hold on my cell phone, on Jack, and bolt from the waiting room, into the operating room, because that's where I have access to a variety of instruments. Sharp ones.

I'm pitching forward, running on an angle because my feet can't keep up with what's going on inside my head. When I reach the doorway, I don't stop running, so I body slam into the door, fall into the room. Fling the door closed. Fight to catch my breath. "Jack. Are you still here?" Please be here.

My fingers run over the wall, feeling for the light switch. No! No bright light! Then my eyes adjust. A row of emergency lights near the ceiling shower the operating room with diffused light. I'm standing in the strong spray. The generator must have kicked on when the power was cut. Great. There's no way to hide in darkness. My eyes dart around the room, looking for a cabinet big enough to hold me. Hold me, Jack ... "Jack?"

"I'm here. The cops just passed us, Jen. They went flying by. Ambulances too. You're gonna make it through this."

I'm frantic, scanning the room for a weapon. Plural. Weapons. Because I'm going to need something big, powerful, like a machine gun, to mow that thing down. All I know is it's not getting its hands on me. No way.

"Where is it now, Jen?"

"I can hear it coming down the corridor." Thudding of padded feet. Clicking of clawed toes.

"Is the door bolted?"

"Yes."

"What did you find in there?"

"Scalpels. Scissors. Choral Hydrate! If I can get close enough, I can jam a bottle of anesthesia down its throat. It's fast acting."

Jack's voice is fading in and out. It's either my brain shorting out or the phone line. "Remember your roundhouse kicks. Surprise it by fighting back. Crouch. Spring. Kick. Kick it in the balls. It must have balls."

I'm so paralyzed by fear I can't reply.

The doorknob turns back and forth, slowly, nerve wracking. My heart's thumping. The knob rattles urgently, only for a split-second. Something on the other side slams the wood with a sold thud. A shoulder? The oak planks creak. Another body slam and the door bulges, like in an animation. Surreal. The wood cracks down the center. I catch my first good look through the slice in the door. It's not possible!

My eyes burn from straining. All I can make out is matted fur as I try to pinpoint exactly what is breaking into the room. It's mangy looking, with a long, pointed snout. Black lips curl into a snarl, baring huge, razor-like teeth. A hand, just as mangy and surreal, slips through the crack in the door, fingers snapping off a larger chunk of wood as though it's peanut brittle. Now I get an even better look and my heart wants to stop, because there's no way I'm escaping this thing. I'd rather die before it touches me. I grab a scalpel from a drawer, hold to my wrist, ready to slice. Death by my own hands would be easier ...

"Jack!" I can't hear Jack anymore.

It's not playing anymore. The operating room door is blasted from the frame that instantly disintegrates, shooting shards of molding across the room like sharpened spears. *Weapons*, flashes through my mind, but the spears are beyond my reach.

Now there's a gaping hole where a locked door stood moments earlier.

This gargantuan abomination fills the room, yellow eyes gleaming. *Strangely familiar* is a fleeting thought that shares part of my brain with *terror*.

Sounds. Unbelievable sounds. Slow motion. Blurred vision. Splintering oak, like gigantic toothpicks, still settling on the floor like someone knocked over a canister full. Something created by a mad scientist, or hell, is growling at me. Snarling. Arms extended, it's approaching on clawed feet. Slowly, but it's coming.

Each step filled with purpose. It seems to be toying with me. Maybe it will let me go ... after a few thrills seeing me collapse on the floor brings, it will disappear. Halloween costume? This cannot be real.

It has the body of a man, but it's not a man. It has bulging deltoids and trapezius muscles, forming a hunched back that keeps it from standing up entirely straight. I'm backed into the row of cabinets, the sharp edge of the counter slicing into my back. I'm trying not to look at it, but not squeezing my eyelids closed. I'm shifty-eyed, gauging the distance between it and the hole in the wall. I think I'd be better off taking my chances with the window, hurl myself through the small glass opening, rather than confront, no less try to fight this thing. My best laid plan would be like putting out a fire with a water pistol. My eyes fly to the scalpel I'm clutching, then the blue veins in my wrist. Should I? Then I hear Jack's voice.

"Jenny. Jenny," Jack keeps screaming, breaking my concentration.

I can't drop my phone, so I let go of the scalpel and reach for the bottle of Choral Hydrate. I take aim, and the moment it opens its jaws to bite me, I hurl the bottle at its head. The bottle smashes. Fluid runs down its face. Into its mouth. Yes, mouth. Please fluid, run into its mouth. That's my only chance.

The thing shrieks. Growls. With a furious shake of its disgusting head it repels the sedating fluid that's supposed to be knocking it out.

"I pissed it off more. Shit."

"Use the scalpel, Jenny!"

Obediently, I snatch another scalpel from the drawer, sobbing, "I'd have to get too close to do any ..."

It's on me. Foul breath pours over my face. I lose my bladder. Frantically stabbing at the head to get at the throat, I manage to sink the scalpel into the thing's tongue. I think. It shrieks. When it lifts its head, the sleek steel handle is sticking out of its mouth.

January Valentine

Blood is flowing. Is it mine? Oh God. It's furious. Yellow eyes pin me with hatred. It's spreading its jaws. Dislodging the scalpel. Spitting it to the floor, along with bloody saliva. And it's making guttural sounds.

Reaching behind me, my fingers wildly search the countertop, slipping over cold metal. A pair of surgical scissors are a perfect fit for the palm of my hand. When I attempt a stab I'm so numb with fear, the instrument flies from my trembling fingers. Drops onto the stainless steel operating table, along with me, because that's what I've been thrown onto. My knees hit first, then my back, followed by my head. I'm not knocked senseless. I'm already senseless. I never felt myself being hurled through the air.

I'm not sure exactly when my cell phone flew out of my hand — maybe at the same time something hit the foot pedal that controls the operating table spotlight — but I'm still screaming for Jack, hoping we're still connected. Selfish of me, making him listen to my murder, but I don't want to be alone. I can't be alone. "Jack ... I love you," I sob.

I'm covering my face with my hands, blocking out the harsh overhead light, the thing about to sink its teeth into me. I'm ready to surrender when I feel the crystal pressing on my chest, praying it's filled with old Gypsy magic and not just glass when I ram the sharp tip through the thing's yellow eyeball and straight into its brain.

I rip the chain from my neck, wrap it around my hand, grip the sword in my fist so that the pointed tip is jutting through my fingers like an icy sharp rod.

The thing rears up, jerks its head, lets out an ear-shattering howl. I gasp. Draw my arm back. I'm ready, set, miss the eye ... my hand slides down its throat instead.

Wheel Wolf

Jack: Before Jenny Calls & After

"**Y**ou need to start thinking about getting a job, Jack." Rachel is blunt, as usual.

"I don't have to work. I'm rich." I'm dead inside.

"That's fortunate," she quips, "since you have no incentive. You can't rely on me and Shadow Lane forever."

"Fortunate," I spit the word out. "Why is fortune part of fortunate? Fortune doesn't always mean fortunate." I continue the rant building inside me. "I'm not fortunate. And my parents certainly weren't fortunate. Some fortune. More like a curse," I mumble. "Do you have any idea how you're teased in school because the street you live on was named after you?"

"I should have been so lucky. What brought that up?"

"Nothing."

"Do you want to hear my point?"

"I'm gonna anyway, I suppose."

She takes a step back to gape at me.

"Shoot." I lift my head and smirk.

"So you can't use your legs. There are worse things. You've got a brain. Two hands. A girl that loves you. Use this to your advantage. Don't wallow, Jack. Man up. You need to be useful. Occupy your mind so you don't go ..."

"Insane?"

She brings her head down to the table to my level and stares.

"I'm already there. The only thing I was gearing up for was marrying Jenny and being a forest ranger. No chance for either now." I laugh wryly.

"I don't think your girlfriend likes me, Jack."

"How could anyone not like you, Rachel?"

"I ask myself the same question all the time." She shrugs and examines her fingernails. They're painted black. "I get the feeling she thinks I'm too rough on you."

"Ouch!"

"No pain. No gain."

~~~~~~

I just finished my therapy session. Rachel seems to get a rise out of kicking my ass. Three times a day. Each round working a different group of muscles. Body parts. She works me till I feel like I'm on the verge of sweating blood. I'm just about ready to strip and plop my butt cheeks onto the shower seat when my cell phone rings. It's got to be Jenny. She's the only one who calls me this late. I guess this means the two of us are insomniacs in tune. I smile.

I like to be showered and in bed for the night when she calls. Her voice is soft and comforting. If there's such a thing as an angel, Jenny is one. Her appearance. Her temperament. She relaxes me. When I talk to Jenny late at night, I get drowsy. Fall asleep clutching the phone ... lulled by Jenny's sweet voice.

I shouldn't have been so pigheaded when she offered to move into the house with me. She went through the trouble of getting estimates on equipping the place for the handicapped: Me. The least I could have done was thank her. I'll do it now. Something's happening to my stomach. I'm suddenly ... happy? Butterflies are gnawing because Jenny's on the phone. And we'll be moving in together. Life will be good again.

I wheel to the table, pick up my phone and check the lighted screen. Yep. It's my angel babe. Her grinning face. Her number.

"Hey, baby. I was just gonna ..."

She's screaming in my ear. What the fuck? "Jenny! What's wrong?"

She's sobbing, her voice shaking so badly, I can just about understand what she's saying. I must not be hearing her right. This damn connection is full of static. Between her crying, and the crackling on the line, she sounds like she's calling from the other side of the world.

"Jenny. You need to calm down. Tell me what happened. Where are you, baby? What's going down?"

My initial thought is, there's been another home invasion. What? Who? Why?

I switch ears so I can hear her better. But she still sounds the same. Distant. Hysterical. Filled with terror. She's telling me some crazy story about a dead cop. What the fuck is she doing out at the clinic at this time of night, anyway? She should be in bed now. Sleeping. Having phone sex with me. Shit.

She's breathing so hard, poor baby. I'm trying to calm her but it's not working. She's either snapping at me or whimpering. What the fuck? I'm fighting to comprehend. My hands are shaking; the one holding the phone, which I'm afraid I'm about to drop, and the one that's pumping the fucking buzzer on the wall. Where the fuck are you Rachel? We only finished up about an hour ago. Rachel and her fucking night massages. Saunas so I sleep better. Lava rocks. Fuck. I don't sleep anyway! Leave me the fuck alone! Don't be in the shower, Rachel, please.

"I need a ride. Jenny's in trouble." I jump down my therapist's throat the minute she bursts into my room, cursing like an old man losing a game of poker. She's in her pajamas, shooting me dagger looks, freeing her hair from what looks like a bungee cord. But when I try to explain something I'm not even sure of, she immediately agrees to drive me to the clinic.

I need to take a piss. Two minutes later Rachel is pushing me out of my room and down the corridor. I'm talking to Jenny the entire time. She's scaring the shit out of me. Is someone really trying to break into the clinic? Why? Because she's alone? Holy fuck. She could be ... I'll fucking kill him. Whoever it is. He's dead meat.

"Jack. I'm scared. Someone's trying to get in. They're rattling the doorknob. Pounding on the siding. The walls are cracking! Whatever it is is growling, Jack." Her voice drops to a frantic whisper. She sounds insane. I imagine her huddled in a corner, swatting away spiders and webs ... shadows. "I think it's in here with me. Something not human. Oh my God. What is it?" She sounds petrified. So much for whispering. She belts out a scream that blows out my eardrum, then she blends with the barking dogs I'm hearing in the background. More growling. Yelping. What the fuck is going on out there?

"I'm going to take a quick peek. I have to know what I'm up against."

"Jenny! Stay away from the window!"

"There's a shadow outside," she whispers, her tone sending a chill through me. "I'm peeking through the window. There it is ..."

"No window, Jenny!"

"It sees me, Jack. It's staring at me. Oh God!"

It must punch a fist through the glass, or throw a rock, because I hear the window shatter. It sounds like a bomb is going off: furniture is overturned, bottles thrown against the walls. This is what I'm envisioning. Between the animal yelping, human screams, guttural growls, my sensitive ears are ringing like a bitch.

"Jenny, where are you?" A heavy clunk slams into my ear,

along with muffled breathing. Another scream. Jenny's. Then silence.

"We're in the van, baby. Heading out to 44. Listen to me and you'll be safe. Grab a weapon and hide. I'll be there in three shakes."

When I tell her to hang up, that I'm calling 9-1-1, she has a fit. She sounds like she's battling an asthma attack: wheezing, coughing, gagging. Why can't I be there with her? Instead of her?

"Get into the freezer, baby." This whole thing is crazy. Even more macabre when she tells me the freezer is full of dead pets waiting to be delivered to a crematorium.

"Find a closet. A scalpel? Good. And remember how I taught you to fight? Go for the balls. He must have balls." I'll slice them off myself in about ten minutes. If he's still there. "Balls first, then the eyes. When he's down, run to your car." Maybe I should have told her to stay there, slam him in the head with something, knock him out before making a run for it. I envision her taking a step and a hand reaching out, grabbing her ankle, bringing her down beside him. Then she's fucked. "Jenny ... make sure he's unconscious before you turn to run."

Sirens pierce the night, then headlights, followed by red strobes on top of the patrol cars. Rachel yanks the wheel and we're off the road, riding on the shoulder, yielding so the fleet on a rescue mission can pass. I let out a breath. "The troops are on the way, honey. Hang in there."

"Looks like a convoy of army tanks," I say to Rachel, ready to cheer because for the first time since we left SLR, I'm hopeful.

I've never been so happy to see cops. One, three, five cars whiz by. Our van bumps back onto the road. I'm trying to convince Jenny everything will be okay. Hopefully the sirens will scare him away. Ruts in the road cause the van tires to thud. I envision a flat tire. Drag both hands through my hair and pull. Pray harder. Watch Rachel's profile for signs of stress. We're hitting the ruts pretty hard. At high speed. I'm wondering if she notices.

She breaks the silence between us. "Don't worry, Jack. We're not gonna have a blowout."

I sink back into the seat. "Just get us there, Rachel. I'll make you a rich woman for this."

"Money can't buy me."

I'm not about to argue. Whatever can or can't buy her is her business.

After the patrol cars pass, there's darkness again. Nothing but the morbid trail of our taillights. Morbid, because that's my gut feeling. I wouldn't wish this crisis on anyone. Not even a worst enemy.

"Damn, Rachel. Turn down the fucking radio. I can't hear a fucking thing."

"Sorry. Just wanted to see if we could pick up some news. Find out what's going on."

"The cops aren't even there yet. How the hell's a news crew gonna be there?"

"Don't be so cocky, Jack. The news hounds often show up before the cops. They all have police scanners. Sometimes they even turn out to be heroes."

"God, I hope you're right. Even though I know you're trying to make me feel better." The moon has passed through a gathering of clouds. The road has opened up into two lanes. It's brighter out. Eerie. I watch trees flash by. The outlines are still trees, not blurs. "Drive faster, will you?"

If I could move my feet, I'd be stomping through the floorboards. The hell with the floor. The gas pedal. I can't blame Rachel. She's driving as fast as the engine will haul the vehicle. Speeding, as she's insisting. But it's not fast enough. I keep checking the dashboard clock. We're taking too long. I've got to get to Jenny.

My throat is tight. My gut is churning. I'm trying to hold it together, to keep Jenny calm. Safe. Alive. Christ. I don't usually pray, but please God. Keep my baby safe. I start making the same dumbass promises desperate people make when fate is torn out of their hands. I can't believe myself. I can't believe Jenny's being attacked. By what? I have no fucking idea. One thing for sure, the clinic sounds like a war zone, and Jenny is in the middle of it.

Jenny is breathless now. Lifeless. The fight's out of her. "Jenny. Hold on. I'm like ten minutes away. The cops passed a while ago. They should be almost there ... Donnie, too." Fucking bastard Donnie. When I get my hands on you ... Thanks for treating her like your own, man. Thanks for nothing. Fucking bastard. I'm taking my emotions out on the van, pounding my fists on the door. The window. My fucking wheelchair. Anything within my reach. Rachel would be next if she wasn't driving.

Jenny sounds winded, running on empty. "I'm on my way down the corridor, Jack. Locking myself in the operating room. Knives. Scissors. Anesthesia!"

"Yeah, baby. Now you're talking. Smoke the bastard with acid if you have to. Go through the cabinets. Chloral Hydrate? Whatever works. If it gets through the door, shove the bottle down its throat."

The way she's screaming would be sending shivers down my spine, if I could feel my spine. Still, the rest of my body is taking the beating. My head is pounding, my veins bulging. My fists are cocked so tight, my fingernails are cutting into my palms.

"Jenny!" My voice is exploding, because all I can hear is something like a bomb going off on the other end of the phone.

The door? It got through the door? Christ. She's got no place to run.

"Baby ... baby," I sob, gasping for air. What help are you, Jack? Bawling, praying, ready to throw up. I think she's gone. Sounds like the phone just hit the floor. "Jenny! Jenny! I love you! I love you!"

January Valentine

The phone must have dropped at her feet. All kinds of sickening noises are flowing into my ear, along with static. It's as though there's a camera in my ear, sending me a clear picture. A gruesome picture. The Chloral Hydrate didn't work. Neither did the scalpel, or the scissors. Jenny's been emitting such agonizing screams, she's rasping now.

Jenny can't scream anymore, but the thing that's been growling its guts out this entire time is still hitting vicious notes with ease. Following an ear piercing howl and more heaving panting, Jenny calls my name one more time. "Jack ... I love you."

Now there's gurgling. A bubbly moan. Christ. Jenny is gurgling. Her throat ... her blood? She's trying to tell me something. All I can make out is one word. "Wolf."

The next sounds come from me, slamming my skull against the headrest, then the window. I don't stop my fit of self-destruction until my blurry eyes spot flashing lights in the distance. My pulse picks up again. Even though I haven't heard a sound since, "Wolf," there could still be hope. She might be unconscious. Or ... the phone battery died. That's more like it.

By the time we reach the scene, I'm tasting blood from grinding my teeth so hard. My head is splitting. My temples are exploding. My heart is twisting in my chest. I strain out the window, trying to make sense of what's going on.

Squad cars are pulled every which way, hogging the entire parking lot. Rachel backs the van up. There's no room for us. It wouldn't matter anyway, because a car with flashing bubble lights is parked across the driveway, blocking the entrance. My eyes are cloudy. I keep blinking, trying to see beyond the roofs and hoods, moving heads. Arcs of flashlights circling the clinic. The kennel in the distance.

The next thing that comes into focus is Jenny's Jeep. I've got a lump in my throat, bigger than my fist. God. Make this all go away. Make Jenny be okay. I let out a nervous laugh and palm my forehead. This has all been a big joke. Of course, idiot! A ploy to make you walk, Jack. I palm my forehead again, then glare at Rachel, who was probably in on it. Great acting, Rachel. Well it didn't work! My ass is still in this chair that's waiting to roll down the fucking ramp.

Rachel parks the van on the side of the road and cuts the engine. For the past ten minutes we've ridden in silence. Ever since Jenny's screaming stopped.

The place is noisy, and so lit up with headlights and floodlights, it looks like the clinic is on fire. Half of the front of the building is demolished. What the fuck could have done that? Donnie is half sitting on the fender of a squad car that's pulled up almost to where the front door used to be. One of his lanky legs is dangling over the metal, rhythmically kicking the rim of the tire. He's not chewing on a toothpick. He's just staring. Not at the pandemonium taking place around him. His head is turned toward the dark forest.

Did he find Jenny? Is she okay? Is Donnie waiting for me? Crying for me? My chest pains. If Jenny's not here ... I'll welcome the heart attack.

The night smells of pine and rubber. Burnt rubber and overheated oil, coming from Rachel's van. A breeze blows over me. Now the van smells are gone, but I sense another odor. Foul. More than fermenting leaves. Something lingers in the air, and it reeks. Intentionally or not, whatever it is has left its mark.

The center of attention are the two ambulances with open doors. Two attendants are sliding a gurney into the back of one. A sheet, dotted with blood, is covering ... not much, I'm thinking. Can't be Jenny. It's too small. Too flat. A kid? Christ. No. Must be the mangled cop Jenny was crying about. Or what's left of him.

Just one gurney. Thank God. Then I spot the van, with CORONER lettered on the side, which stops my breath. Chills me so bad, my teeth start chattering.

Without waiting for Rachel, I'm on my way. My wheels crunching across the poorly paved road. I work my way around the car that's blocking access. My breath has returned, but is erratic as I weave through the gathering of officers, detectives and reporters. I'm waiting to be stopped. Just let them try to stop me.

The cops are holding reporters at bay, but cameras are clicking, video rolling. Anchors with microphones are leading, getting the best angle for their station. They're immovable objects looking for headlines. "No pictures!" I flag them, my hands swatting the air. "Stop taking pictures! Get the fuck out of here." I want to plow into them, but break down instead. Donnie must hear the racket I'm creating. He hops off the fender and jogs toward me. I watch his legs bend and spring, long and strong.

"Let him through," he growls. "Jack's family." So everyone parts for the guy in the wheelchair. I roll by without looking at faces. I don't want to look up. They all know what's going on, and I don't. I don't want to see pity. All I can bear to see right now is their feet.

Once I've passed them all, I lift my face. Narrow my eyes at Donnie. "When did you get here?"

"A few minutes before they did." He hitches his head to a group of cops mulling around a couple cars.

I wipe my face with my shirt sleeve, clearing sweat from my eyes. And tears. "Where's Jenny? Did you go inside?" I hate the fact that Donnie is the last person I want to hear my weak voice crack.

He shakes his head. He's pale. Hands trembling when he lights up a cigarette.

Why am I standing here talking to Donnie? Not barging into the clinic to find Jenny. I can't bring myself to face the inevitable.

"She called you, Donnie. Before she even called me. You didn't answer." I'm gaining strength. Accusing him not only with my voice, but with my stare, my balled fists.

He takes a drag of his cigarette, then hangs his head.

"Where the fuck were you? Humping a deer?" My voice is no longer cracking. I'm shouting.

"The one time I forget to switch my phone off vibrate ..." He offers a pathetic look.

"Yeah, sure." I shoot back an expression that says I'm fucking suspicious. "How is it you showed up before the cops? Where's your ride?"

"The minute I got Jenny's message ... I rode my bike out here."

"Where is it?" I'm about to start my interrogation.

"Over there." He gestures to shadows. "Near the trees."

"What trees? There are fucking trees all around us. I don't see any bike."

Cops are stringing up crime scene tape. Leisurely walking in and out of the clinic. That in itself should tell me something. But denial is easier than acceptance.

I'm so broken up, I can't even fight with Donnie. I want to kill him, but don't have the strength. "I thought you were gonna shadow her." My voice is lifeless. Like Jenny's after she lost her fight. "Did you see anything?"

When he nods, my jaw works hard. "Who was it?"

"What was it, you mean." Smoke curls from his nose, streams from his lips. "I've never seen anything like it before. Maybe in horror flicks, but never in real fucking life."

"Stop talking shit. Give me a description. I'm gonna find the bastard." It still hasn't sunk in that Jenny was attacked by an animal. A human animal ... not an animal animal. She works with animals every day. She's great with animals. Animals love her, for Christ sake.

"How come there was a dead body out back. Jenny inside. You see the ... thing ... whatever it is you say you saw, and you're still alive. It strikes me as odd that this thing is so massively vicious and you're the only one who survived? Why did it let you go?"

"I don't think it would have if the sirens hadn't scared it away. It took off through the woods."

"Did you follow it?"

"Of course I followed it. Emptied a clip at it."

"Did you hit it?"

He shakes his head. "Dunno."

"Did you look for a body?"

He shakes his head, hangs it again.

"Hear a car, or bike start up?"

"Na ah."

"So basically, you have no fucking idea."

"It bolted into the forest and disappeared." He sucks up a lungful of smoke and flips the cigarette butt onto the dirt. "It happened so fast. It was so dark."

This makes me feel worse. God, how Jenny must have suffered.

When a car turns in the lot, headlights flash over him. I notice his face is scratched, the arm of his shirt torn. "What happened to you?"

"Branches." He hitches his head toward the forest again. "I want you to know, I chased it as far as I could. So deep, I barely found my way back."

I know the answer, but ask anyway. I want him to squirm. "Where's Jenny?"

He avoids my eyes when he says, "You know she's inside, Jack."

Admitting to myself I'm a coward isn't easy. I start wheeling by him.

"No Jack. You can't go in there."

"Like hell ..."

I'm wheeling through the front door, which is now a gaping

hole. Surprised no one tries to stop me. The place is ransacked. Ransacked isn't a strong enough word. There's hatred and rage all over the place. Everything's broken. I'm broken. In the back of my mind, I know Jenny's not gonna come bouncing down the hall. I wheel into a corner and sob my heart out. Man up, Jack. You couldn't wait to get here, so go find her. You've been hiding long enough. Find your girl, big shot.

The place is jammed. Flash bulbs are going off all around me as two guys snap crime scene photos. A figure cloaked in white is tiptoeing around, steadying a video camera. I wheel past a circle of official looking men, a couple of uniformed women. No one's dusting for prints. How do you dust a demolished building for prints? I roll a bit farther, to where two guys are leaning against what's left of the corridor wall. They're not talking. They're texting. Who they fuck are they? Press? No cameras! Get the fuck out of here. Turns out they're detectives. I know this because Donnie pops up behind me. He's shadowing me. My guardian angel.

As I'm about to enter what had been an operating room, I'm hit with the immensity of it. The day I received the phone call from the Florida Keys police, I thought I knew the meaning of shock. Now I know what shock really is. No. Not shock. I'm fucking hallucinating. Nothing could ever come close to this. I'm in a dream. I'm in a slaughterhouse. This is a blood-splattered mortuary. This is my Jenny. I slam my fists on the wheels of the chair, then on the nearest wall.

As I roll through the splintered hole that used to be a doorway, I can't believe this was ever an operating room. A bomb shelter that took a hell of a beating, maybe. After an earthquake hit. But Christ, in the center of the room, under a spotlight ... a stainless steel table, bolted to the floor. The only thing that hasn't been overturned. Shattered.

Lying on the table is ... I pull to a stop. Jenny, I gag the word.

It's no longer Jenny. I can see that from five feet away. Bits of clothing, soaked with blood. Sneakers, a foot still tied into one that looks like it's been placed on a blood-splattered chair. Pieces of life on the floor, a congealing puddle in a corner. My gag reflex won't quit.

Where's the rest of her, I'm wondering. So I roll into the room through the trail of body parts. An arm here. A leg there. Hatred all around the place.

"Why?" I turn to Donnie, who is white-faced beside me. Holding one hand on his stomach. The other over his mouth.

I make it to the table, because that's what seems to be holding her torso. I want to throw my head into my lap. Literally rip my head off my shoulders and bury it in my lap, beside Jenny's. When I reach out a hand to brush her tangled hair back, her head comes loose from her neck. She's in pieces.

I'm sobbing, screaming obscenities. Lifting her off the table. Into my arms. Jenny's head is in my lap. That's when I completely lose it. "I'm gonna kill you Donnie." I whisper with malice, like I'm possessed by the devil himself. "I talked to her on the phone for at least twenty fucking minutes. The last twenty minutes of her suffering, her life. You could have saved her."

Then it dawns on me, and while I cradle her head, I stare at him. "If you couldn't have her, no one could. Is that it?"

"Are you insane? Are you blaming me for this?" He throws up his hands. Rings of perspiration stain the underarms of his shirt. "You're calling me a murderer?"

"You weren't here when she needed you." Bile rises to my throat. "What does that make you."

Donnie lowers his face. Sticks it right under my nose. His chin brushes the top of Jenny's head. "Hit me, Jack."

My stare is blank.

"Hit me, so I can live with myself."

Two guys with white booties are watching us. Looking at

me sympathetically.

The coroners approach me. They've both got disbelieving expressions plastered on their faces. They're sickened by the massacre, too. Then I realize they're staring at Jenny's head, still in my lap. I've been holding it with one hand, smoothing her hair with the other. They're at my side, speaking softly. Gently removing all that's left of my life from my lap. God help me. Help Jenny.

I don't want to let go, but am sane enough to realize I have to.

"Careful," I say as they lift her.

"I'm so sorry," one says, while the other assures me, "We'll be careful."

I can't stop watching them, thinking about where they're about to take her. Their broad backs are to me, but I know they're bagging her head, like others are doing with the rest of her body parts.

She walked in ... is carried out in bags. The last shot of vomit tears from my gut and hits the back of their already stained booties.

Donnie has disappeared. I'm sitting here alone. Full of puke and blood. Listening, not seeing, because my head is back in my hands again. I can't look at this anymore. I hear two cops talking about, "Next of kin."

Shit. I'm her next of kin, so I start rolling up to them. Then it dawns on me.

"Have her parents been notified?"

~~~~~~

I find my way outside, and somehow locate Rachel. Arms crossed over her chest, leaning against Jenny's Jeep, she's waiting for me. She's not grim, just serious. "I know it's difficult for you to understand right now. She's at peace. With loved ones. You'll be with her again one day. Not yet. So don't start thinking about ways to end your life."

"What are you some kind of fucking fortuneteller?"

"No, Jack. A believer."

"I should be the one to tell her parents."

"Let the police do their job. You've been through enough."

"So you tell me what to do now?"

"I told you when you were admitted. I'm your physical therapist and psychiatrist. I'm not going to let you go to hell with yourself."

"We should arrange to have her car towed."

"I'll take care of it."

"I admire your strength."

"Faith, not strength."

"A holy roller."

"I never said I was holy, Jack."

"Okay. We're going in circles. How do we get Jenny's car home?" I'm beside the driver's door. Stroking it. Laying my cheek on it. "I can't go back yet. I want to sleep here tonight. In this." I pat the door handle, Jenny's fingerprints. Wrapping my fingers around the chrome, I squeeze, trying to feel her. Rachel seems to know a lot about death. "Is she still here?"

She nods.

My guts twist. "But she's at peace?"

"She will be, if you are. Her love is strong. Stronger than anything. Even death. She won't leave until you let her."

"I'll never let her go ... I'm a selfish bastard." I squeeze harder. Lean my forehead on the cold metal. "Jenny," I can't stop the sob that rises with her name, "I love you ... so much. I'm sorry, baby. For everything. Being a shit, not being here when you needed me. If you're here, give me a sign." I sit and wait. Nothing happens.

"I think you're full of shit, Rachel. Open the door. I'm sleeping here tonight." I've never believed in ghosts. But tonight, I'm hoping something will change my mind.

Through my daze, I thought I recognized the red purse slung

over Rachel's shoulder, but never put two and two together. When the strap slips down her arm, I snatch it from her wrist; I know it's Jenny's purse. I grip the smooth fabric and cradle it to my chest like I would Jenny. "Where'd you get this?" I growl.

She shrugs her head toward the scene of carnage. "Donnie ..." Even in shadows, Rachel is pale as a ghost. She pulls the door open and slings her arms around me. "Come on, Jack. Get in." With one yank, I'm lifted and tossed into the Jeep. "You need to calm down," she says in a husky voice.

I'm sprawled across the back seat, my cheek and shoulder clutching Jenny's purse. Eyes closed, I smell peaches. Jenny's scent fills the air, drenching me with memories, remorse. Breathing deeply, I suck in as much fragrance as my lungs will hold. I don't want to let out a breath. I want Jenny inside me ... forever.

Rachel is sitting in the front. In the passenger seat. I wouldn't let her sit in the driver's seat. No one will ever sit there but Jenny. And me when I drive the Jeep out of here. Yup. This car is not moving unless I'm behind the wheel.

I watch Rachel's head roll from side to side. Feeling the need for comfort of conversation, I start throwing out random thoughts. "You asleep?"

"No."

I need to talk or I'll explode. "Where are you from?"

"The love of my parents."

"Are they still alive?"

"No."

"What brought you into this line of work?"

"A calling, I guess you could say."

"How'd you make it to my room so fast?"

"I live on the grounds. In the Residence Hall, in the wing facing your room."

That's weird. She can probably see me from her window. The thought gives me the creeps.

January Valentine

Each time I begin to doze, I start and jump. Hear myself say a throaty, "Uuh." One of those stupid sleep sounds that pop out of your mouth involuntarily when you're halfway in and out of it.

Why didn't I put two and two together? I saw something at the lake. Something bit me. Made me what I am. There have been murders. Why did I let Jenny work out here in no man's land? What the fuck was I thinking? About my own misery.

Jenny's frantic cries will haunt me forever. I let her down, just like I let my parents down. I've always been worthless. Now I'm useless. I want to die.

Wheel Wolf

Detective Work

*R*achel bursts into my room, displaying her usual charm. Her black scrubs are replaced by a black sundress. The neck and upper back are cut in low scoops, revealing a lot more of her than I've ever seen. Ever want to see. There's a lot of skin showing. On her upper right shoulder is a black tattoo depicting a pair of hands in prayer, wings sprouting from each side. They look muscular. I wonder if they're Rachel's hands.

Her eyes are wide, brows arched. "Look at you."

"Look at me? Look at you, all dolled up. Where are you off to?"

"A funeral. Your girlfriend's. You're not dressed?"

"Do I look naked to you?"

"No. But you look sloppy. Get ready or we'll be late."

I jerk my head, hurl my gaze out the window. "I'm not going."

Her body blocks my view of the towering weeping willow I imagine turning into.

"It's been two days and you haven't eaten or left this room, Jack. Not showered, either. You smell." Her stare washes over me. "You're shedding like mad. Look at the hair all over the floor.

Looks like fur balls," she huffs and points around the room.

"It's called stress-balding," I reply without lifting my gaze.

"It's called you better start cleaning up your act. I'm not your maid, and housekeeping is complaining you're clogging their vacuums. So we're stopping off after the funeral to pick up a SmartSweeper. Bring cash or a credit card."

"As seen on TV ... hmph." My mouth is dry, my breath so foul it reaches my nose when I talk my shit. Try to swallow it. My throat's constricted with a damn lump again.

"Displayed on a sale rack in Walmart," Rachel is saying, her long arms unfolding from her chest. She drops her hands onto her hips. "You have to start getting your life back. For your physical health if nothing else."

"I'm out of bottled water."

"They have that at Walmart too."

Now I lift my eyes, staring with sarcasm. "Don't they supply anything around this place that's draining my bank account?"

"Consider yourself blessed to be here, Mr. Bailey."

"Mr. Bailey?" Sour laugh. Sour breath. "Just go away. I want to die."

She gives me the first ever look of compassion, which I had no idea those sharp features were capable of. "You have to come to the funeral, Jack. You can't run from Jenny's death. You need to accept it. Seeing the casket lowered into the earth will give you closure."

She thinks seeing Jenny buried under the cold hard ground will be good for me? I almost lose my eyeballs. "I have closure." I slam my chest with my palms. "Right here. It's closed. Forever."

Donnie comes bounding through the door. *The same as Rachel did a few minutes ago,* hits me. "Doesn't anyone believe in knocking? Suppose I was jerking off?"

"He's coming back to life." Donnie chuckles.

"No. I'm not." I stare out the window at clouds rolling across the sky, adjusting my sunglasses. Yeah. I even wear them indoors now. My eyes are that sensitive. "What are you doing here, Donnie?"

"Rachel called me." His eyes stalk across my untidy room. "Said you're in bad shape. This I believe. The place is a mess. So are you." He's wearing a dark suit and actually looks pretty good. He frowns, slipping his hands under the sides of his jacket and into his trouser pockets. "You're not dressed, dude ..."

"How did Rachel get your number?" I glare at her, then at him.

"I gave it to him." She shoots me one of her *I dare you to fuck with me* looks and stands at his side. With the shoes she's wearing, they're shoulder to shoulder. Her amber blends with his spice, tingling up my nose.

"I told you to stay away from her." With monocular vision, I'm now glaring at both of them simultaneously.

Donnie slings his arm around Rachel's waist and pulls her close. "You don't run my life."

"You ruined mine." I clench my jaw.

"What Don and I do is our business," Rachel defies.

I hmph and nod. I can see it coming. He's either nailed her already, or will be humping her soon. I shake my head with disgust.

"You two won't be a couple, Rachel. He's hit and run."

Donnie's jaw slackens. "How do you know what I am?"

I sigh. "Whatever."

"Enough of this crap. We've got to get going, Jack. If nothing else, you have to pay your respects to Jenny's parents." Donnie clomps across the room and swings my closet door open. "What kind of gear do you have stashed in here, bro?" He rifles through the rack and huffs out a breath. "Shit I see."

"I already spoke to Jenny's parents on the phone. They know I'm not attending. They understand." My arms fold, followed by my lips.

"Let's get a beer first." Donnie's voice drops into a tone he'd use on a chick he wants to hop in the sack with. I've heard the tone many times before. I look at Rachel and roll my eyes, wondering if she'd fall for it. Why am I wondering this? Donnie's a bastard. Maybe I like Rachel and don't want to see her hurt.

"Loosen you up, bro." Donnie keeps schmoozing. "We need to go out drinking together. Maybe hunting ..."

"Let's not."

"Why?"

"'Cos I don't fucking feel like it."

"Christ, you're nastier than usual."

"Can you blame me?"

"Stop feeling sorry for yourself."

"Yeah. Well. You didn't just lose the love of your life in a fucking grisly tragedy ..."

"I knew Jenny since grade school." He's trying to one-up me.

"I loved Jenny since high school." I'm smug. "You always hated me. Been jealous of me."

By now, Rachel has moved to the window. Back to us, she's got to be closing her eyes to us, maybe her ears too.

"It's not jealousy ..." Donnie drums each syllable. "It's *stupidity*. Mine for trying to help you. Yours for ... Look at what you've been sitting on, Jack. All your life and you never seemed to appreciate it. The spread your parents left you. Money in the bank. Jenny. Never had to use your brain in school. You used your brawn instead. In a variety of ways. Maybe if you'd have paid attention, studied substantive courses in college other than useless electives, you'd be able to pick up a desk job someplace. Face it, you're not ranger material anymore." His cheeks are pink, his neck red. He shakes his head and snarls, "Maybe you never were."

I'm too astounded to anger. "Fuck you," spits from my mouth

with saliva. There has to be a method to his insults. Shock therapy? I believe I've had enough of that. "Maybe you should go take a shit, Detective Delgado. I didn't invite you here for a lecture. I didn't invite you here at all. What the fuck do you want?"

"You might not realize it, but I'm your friend, Jack. I always have been." His face shades, and his tone drops. "I have information about the murders. I thought we could maybe put our heads together and do something. In memory of Jenny."

"Don't even think about her. Don't say her name. Don't ..." My fists are curled into two iron balls that start beating my thighs.

"Jenny's murder was a setup." Donnie's statement makes my head snap up. My hair flies with the jerking motion.

"What are you saying? Someone wanted to kill her? Plotted this?" I growl.

Donnie runs a hand over his face. The other is still plugged into his pocket. "The veterinarian she worked for got a call to go out to the clinic. That the dogs were going berserk. When he walked into his garage, all four tires on his car were slashed." His eyes narrow. He chews on the side of his mouth.

I slide my fingers over my beard, through my hair, fighting to urge to tear it out. "How do you know this?"

He rolls his eyes and throws his palms up. "I'm on the force."

My ears are singing, my brain trying to digest why someone, something, would plot to kill my Jenny. "So go on." By now, I *am* coming back to life. I'm trembling.

"Between the time Dr. Brantley arrived home that evening, and attempted to leave. Four flats. His car is hauled away on a flatbed. Oddly enough, his wife's car wouldn't start. Wires were cut. That's why he didn't show that night like he told Jenny he would."

"You know he spoke to Jenny?"

"I interviewed him myself."

"So, he was the last person to talk to Jenny, other than the nine-eleven operator, and me. Because you didn't answer your phone." My stomach twists with my mouth.

He sighs. "Are you ever gonna forgive me for that?"

"No. Did you save her voice message?"

"Yeah."

"I want it. Send it to my phone."

"Here." He throws the cell into my lap. "Take the phone. Anticipating your request, I bought a new one. There's no way to transfer messages."

I can't believe my eyes, or ears.

"You're welcome," he says wryly. "Anyway, back to the details. The tech who was supposed to be covering night duty was in the E.R. puking his guts out. Someone sent a T-bone to the clinic with his name on it. Barry thought it was a thank you from the family of a patient he went out of his way for. The steak couldn't have come from a friend because it turns out it was laced with arsenic." His stare is cryptic.

I gulp. "Someone poisoned him?"

He lifts his brows and nods. "That's what the contents of his stomach said. And the girl who works the front desk at the clinic was seeing a movie with her sister. They all check out."

"Who called it into the cops?"

"No one knows. Number was blocked and they refused to give a name. Leading me to believe ..."

"Whoever called it in slashed the doc's tires first." My eyes burn. "Disabled Mrs. Brantley's car. But why Jenny? She never hurt anyone." The pleading sound of my voice must motivate Rachel to turn to me. Her eyes look watery.

"Let me finish my theory," Donnie says. "They disable the Brantley vehicles. Barry can't be reached. Chickie isn't a tech. So, Jenny is the only one left to cover. He kills the responding officer before she even arrives. He wanted Jenny out there, alone."

His words bring on more than a shiver. I shake violently.

Wheel Wolf

"Who the fuck and why?"

"I only wish I knew," he says as Rachel throws a blanket around me, then stands behind, massaging my shoulders and neck.

"Are they connecting Jenny's murder with the others?" Her voice seeps into my ears.

Donnie frowns. "Yes. Same type of ... injuries."

"Injuries?" Offended, I choke on the word. "Call a spade a spade, dude. They were all torn to shreds."

Donnie nods. "Yes, they were ..."

The room is still, then the three of us break into sobs.

The Funeral

*I*t's spring. The fresh air I'm breathing feels good. I feel guilty. I shouldn't feel good. I shouldn't be breathing.

The three of us drive in Rachel's van to the small resting place for the dead. Intimate: creepy intimate. The thought of leaving Jenny here tears my heart out. The single road leading up to the fenced in grassy plots is filled with cars lined up behind the white hearse.

As Rachel parks the van, I stare out the window. "I should have gone to the church service." I hang my head.

"I told you," she says.

I force my head up, my eyes to creep across headstones to view Jenny's casket, bracing myself for the shock before Rachel wheels me into the circle of mourners. I should be wheeling myself, but, I'm barely here. My mind is all over the place. I'm not capable of much right now. One hand is in my lap, cradling my cell phone and the last picture Jenny and I took together. Elbow on armrest, I'm bracing my head with my other hand, thinking of how much this cell phone has been through. Words of love. Murder. Oh, God, Jen ...

Wheel Wolf

Jenny's parents are sitting on folding chairs, directly across from the casket which is draped with a blanket of pink roses. Jenny loved roses. I love orchids, lavender ones like her eyes.

Orchids are a symbol of love, beauty, innocence. Everything Jenny. I see the arrangement I ordered has been set at the head ... her head.

The immensity slams me and I shake. When I think of what's inside the attractive, expensive, polished box, I want to run. Run from the cemetery, the mourners, myself. I can't stand myself. When I examine the way her parents are sitting here, I feel worse. They look like statues. Stoned. How are they dealing with the loss? Does having each other to hold onto make it easier? Or are they medicated. They're not holding hands. Must be the latter.

I manage to permit Rachel to bring us closer, so that we're all gathered around Jenny. The minister recites his sermon, which makes even those not expecting to cry, break down. I can barely hear his prayers over the sobbing. Everyone loved Jenny. The entire town must have turned out, because there are hips and legs all over the place. One thing about being in a wheelchair, you come to learn who's who by their feet. Their shoes. The way they walk.

My blurry eyes don't see him coming, but Dr. Sloan appears at my side, which makes Donnie shift stations. He and Rachel have been holding me up so to speak. One on either side of my chair. But Dr. Sloan displaces Donnie. He's outspoken. Brusque.

"Hey, Dr. Sloan," I say without looking at him.

His voice trickles down. "How are you holding up?"

"Same as them." I motion to Jenny's parents and out of state family and friends, then finally lift my face. "I didn't expect to see you here."

"I came to pay my respects to the family. To you." He leans near my ear. He doesn't have to. I can hear him perfectly well from where he's standing, at least three feet over me. "Let's step over there. By the trees, where there's privacy. There's something I want to talk to you about." Without my approval, he starts wheeling me. Another thing about being in a wheelchair. Just about anyone can push you around.

"How are you feeling, Jack?"

"You already asked me that." I smirk at him, my hand blocking sun that's penetrating through my black shades.

"You never answered specifically."

"Just dandy. Is that specific enough?"

"I'm sorry, Jack. You've been through a lot. Rachel says you haven't been partaking in therapy. Haven't been eating." Oh, God. Someone else she's complaining to?

"What does she expect? I'm in mourning."

"I understand that. But you can't run yourself into the ground."

I want to. I want to be in the ground beside Jenny. I don't say this. These are my private feelings. Mine and Jenny's. Because if Rachel is right, and Jenny is hanging around me, then she knows how I feel. I love her. I want to be with her.

"We have to talk." His tone is so clandestine, he sounds like Donnie did earlier in my room.

"I'm all ears." In sunlight, Sloan looks different. Fragile lines frame his eyes. Salt pours through his pepper colored hair. His perfectly trimmed hairline glistens as he begins to speak.

"The murders ... mutilations. They're all connected. Tissue samples show similarities, certain characteristics found in the bites. How's your side?" His eyes are like steel beads looking through me for answers.

I pull up my brows. I've almost forgotten about what started all this crap. "My side is fine." I squint up at him. "What do you mean connected? The same person?"

He ignores my question and continues the spiel I interrupted. "Savage attacks on cattle at the Walton Farm, too." Does he mean more? Besides the one I committed? Why is he staring at me like that? "Are you familiar with those?" he grills, dabbing his forehead with a handkerchief.

"I'm only interested in people murders, Dr. Sloan. Sorry." The silver in his hair reminds me of the fine threads in Jenny's; I wonder how someone with coal black hair can have beautiful, natural platinum threads at her age. Had, that is.

"I apologize, Jack. I don't want to appear insensitive. I just thought you'd like to know everything could be linked. Everett Walton came in to see me. He hasn't been sleeping. Requested sedatives." He shakes his head. Gathers his mouth. "He told me he saw something in his field the night his first cow was mutilated."

My ears perk up. I remember being out at the Walton's. Vividly. "What did he say?"

"Something that didn't look human was eating his two thousand dollar Hereford." He pauses. Tilts his head. "We'd like you to submit some DNA samples."

"We? and *What*?"

"The coroner, Doug Fisher, is a neighbor of mine, and good friend. We golf together."

That explains it. I'm the topic of conversation over golf.

"We need more to work with. We think we might be able to narrow down ..."

"I'm not submitting to anything." I know they'd find my saliva on the Walton cow remains. But the others? Suppose I don't know what I'm doing? Lose consciousness or fall into a trance. Become the animal I was *once* ... every night?

Holy fuck. I know I often taste blood, but my gums have been bleeding lately. Tooth grinding, I bet, which I seem to be doing even when I sleep. And I do eat my share of rare steaks. I found a place that under-cooks, delivers them almost raw, cold and purple in the center. I'd like to get them entirely raw from the butcher shop, but they refuse to deliver to patient rooms. Something about health code.

Sloan's breath touches my cheek. *Caramel macchiato latte?* "Will you agree, or do I need to get a court order ..."

"Get whatever you like, doc. I'm not submitting spit, semen, or anything else to you and your crony." I can't be a suspect. Donnie would have told me. Wouldn't he have?

My eyes are shifting as I try to fathom what he's alluding to. I know shifty eyes are a sign of guilt, but since I can't pace, my only alternative is to use my eyes to release tension. My gaze falls upon Rachel, standing in the distance. I've never seen her outside in daylight before. She looks like a vampire. I feel like a creep thinking it, but hell, she looks the part. The daylight is doing something to her skin. It's paler than pale, translucent. Her hair is too red, shimmering in the sun, so are her lips, and they're too dark for that chalky skin.

Underneath the tough exterior, she's a nice girl. I realize that now. I feel like shit for thinking these thoughts. But the new me is the don't hold anything back me. What do you have to lose? You've fucking lost it all. What the hell difference does it make anymore if you're liked, hated, dead or alive? If you're stuck in a wheelchair for the rest of your life. So what?

My eyes return to his with a deliberate blink. "I have an alibi, Dr. Sloan."

His head jerks then resets.

I pat my wheels. "Not only am I unable to get around on my own two feet, but I was on the phone with Jenny right before she was murdered. And I was with my therapist."

He lifts a brow. Looks smug. "I probably should not be mentioning this, but revealing impressions were found near some of the remains."

"Footprints?" Hooves ... paws?

"Wheels. Slender. Like these." He reaches down and has the

gall to knock his knuckles against the wheel of my chair he's leaning into. "I'm sure the authorities would like to take a look at yours. Compare treads."

I can't stand being here anymore. Talking to Dr. Sloan about cattle mutilations. Fending off accusations. Watching mourners. I'm hard now. I haven't shed a tear since I saw Jenny lying on a steel table in the operating room that looked like a freaking morgue. What was left of her. I closed up like a shell even a nutcracker won't open.

"Don't try to freak me out with threats. These chairs, and wheels, are mass produced. Three quarters of the residents of Shadow Lane Rehab could be considered suspects."

"I'm sure there's something unique ..." His temple pulses.

"Possibly, but since our chairs are serviced on a regular basis, sometimes rotated, who knows who'll end up with whose chair?" He's pissed me off immensely. But I'm acting smug. Sly. Enjoying the upper hand.

He glances around, lowers his voice. "You've been bitten. By what I'm not certain. I just want to follow you. Keep tabs on your health. I didn't intend to make you uncomfortable or accuse ..."

"My health is fine. It's just my life that's screwed up." I feel every muscle in my face contort. "I'm outta here, Dr. Sloan. Catch you another time." Planning on taking myself home, to my own house, I tug on my urethane tires.

Hell bent on doing this one thing for myself, I wheel away hastily, so Rachel, and Donnie who's now brushing arms with her, don't see me trying to make a run for it.

Don't ask how, but one of my wheels hits a rut, then slippery mud from last night's storm. *No fucking way*, I'm thinking as the chair tips and gravity takes hold, throwing me onto the ground. I'm shouting out obscenities. Lying face down on soggy grass like the ass I am. Surrounded by feet, because everyone has heard my Irish temper mouth and is rushing to my aid. I've managed to fuck up Jenny's funeral. I can't believe it.

I'm able to turn on my side, and am flapping like a fish. Helpless. Fuck me. I can't pull myself into the chair, because it's lying, also on its side, two feet away from me.

I'm looking around. Not up. I'm surrounded by voices, feet, legs. Rachel's. I know it's her, because I remember her black sandals and coordinating toenail polish. Everything that girl owns is black. My eyes run unintentionally up and down her legs. Not intentionally, Jenny, I swear, babe. I'll never look at another woman as long as I live. Which I hope isn't very long. 'Cos I miss you like crazy.

My gaze stalls on the tattoo on Rachel's left leg. Black rosary beads are wrapping her calf, finished off with a perfectly amazing silver crucifix, which rules out vampirism. A ridiculous thought hits me. *Who does her tattoos?* I'm considering one. A sweeping Jenny tatted across my chest. Over my heart. You and me forever, babe, scrawled beneath it.

Two sets of feet push through the rest. I'm looking at their shoes. Up their pant legs. Hairy. Black socks brown shoes. Not so stylish buddy. It can only be Steve. Drake with the neon Nikes right beside him. "Jack. What the fuck happened, bro." Yep. It's gutter mouth Drake.

"Come on, man. I've got you, Jack." Steve and Drake begin alternating, arguing over who's going to help me up.

Rachel's feet shove all of the others aside. "Jack!" She's freaking out. I've never heard her this emotional before. "Are you okay? I'll take you home."

"No you will not. I'm fine. Just help me get my ass back in the chair and I'll be on my way." Beneath my beard, and the sun, my cheeks are generating their own heat. I'm helpless. Fucking totally helpless. Worse than a baby. At least babies are cute. I'm angry. Mean. Big and hairy. I'm aggressive. I want to kill someone.

Wheel Wolf

Donnie's beside Rachel again. I remember his feet, and his words when he first saw her. "She's hot." This makes me angrier. He's about to fall in love and I've lost mine. Everything about Donnie irks me.

What possesses me to lift my face and shout ... "She may look hot, but she's cold, Donnie. Stay the fuck away from her. You manage to fuck up everything you come in contact with." ... is beyond me, but I belt it out to the congregation. This brings me satisfaction. I'm miserable. He should be too.

Donnie breaks down. Starts crying like a baby in front of everyone, which takes the heat, and attention, off me, the original sideshow.

"Don't blame me, Jack. I feel bad enough."

"You should. You're the first one she called. Even before me."

I've managed to turn Jenny's funeral into a fiasco. Would she be laughing or throwing a fist?

"We're gonna catch the mother fucker," Donnie sobs. "I promise."

This is my turning point. My moment of soul cleansing. The beginning of my trip back from hell.

"Why the fuck didn't you get there sooner? Yeah, you were probably out humping some deer, alright."

"I'm sorry, man. That's the one call I should have answered. How was I to know?" Rachel hands him a wad of tissues and he blows his nose continuously.

In the middle of the chaos, I notice another pair of feet. A stranger. He slips his hands under my armpits and lifts me like I'm a baby. Plops me into my chair Drake and Steve have righted and delivered to my side. Once I'm settled, the guy sticks out a hand. "I'm Cage Galloway." He smiles, but there's something beneath his lips, besides teeth. A sadness. He feels my sorrow. I'm touched by this stranger.

"Hey." I grasp his hand. Suddenly there's no one else but me and Cage. Sounds like a love story, I know, but there's something about this guy. He strikes me as charismatic. Helpful. In as much pain as I am.

"I kinda know how you feel. I recently lost someone close to me, too." My eyes travel from the third button of his pinstriped suit jacket, to his neatly styled coal black hair, settle on his mirrored aviators, then slide down his chest, landing on his slim-fitting trousers.

"You're not from around here." No one around here wears suits that stylish and expensive looking.

His head hitches skyward. "Upstate. Transferred down here for a job."

My head rocks. "Oh."

Cage and Donnie exchange glances. Upstate, rings a bell. I wonder if they know each other. Hunting buddies? They're eyeballing one another. Something's fishy. My imagination? Maybe.

"Rachel?" I reach behind me, because Rachel is massaging my shoulders again. "I'm ready to go home. Let's roll."

"Home?" she echoes.

"You know what I mean." Does she always have to give me a hard time?

I find myself studying faces, rather than feet. Wondering about him, even her. Where were you on the night in question? Lately, I'm suspicious about everything. Everyone.

Wheel Wolf

The Final Turning

My veins pulse, my bones ache. My ribs feel like they're cracking, splitting apart. I'm slipping in and out of restless sleep. Mumbling incoherently. Who am I talking to? I'm hearing screams. Howling. Distant, yet the damn racket is blasting in one ear and out the other. Fucking up my brain as it rips through. It's like I have a cochlear implant that's cranked up too high. These fucking supersonic ears. I may never sleep again.

I hear bat wings flap at what must be a hundred feet over the yard. Scratching noises. Wind scraping branches against the brick building. Mice in the walls? Christ. Peace. I need peace ... and quiet. Get away from here. From everything. Past ... present ... That's where it ends. I can't see a future.

Staring at the ceiling, arms crossing chest, I'm lying here like a mummy. I want to toss and turn at will. Get up and pace. Throw myself around the room. Use my fists. Break things. Everything is stuck inside me. Fermenting. Rotting. And I don't know how to get it out. I don't know if I'll ever get through this.

Everyone says dealing with loss takes time. No shit. I've gotten this advice before. I worked my way through my parents' deaths. But I had Jenny then, beside me. Being without Jenny is something I never thought I'd have to face. This is fucked up hell.

Time might dull the events, jumble them, rewire your brain, forcing your gray matter into acceptance, but trauma is always there. Like worms under dirt. When it rains they surface. Slimy. Undulating.

Trauma. Shit word. Even when you think it's gone. It's only buried. Right now I'm so raw, there's no way to release this energy, anger, torment.

My brain feels metallic. Is it possible to feel this way? Like there are metal rods holding your head together? My mind is like a claw, scraping through a junkyard. And I'm trapped, flat on my back, trying to salvage some of the beauty that has been lost.

They say when you die, your life flashes in front of you, like a movie. That's what's happening to me now, only I don't think I'm dying. That would be too easy.

I close my eyes, dredging up memories. Snow angels. Jenny and me last winter. All cozy, bundled up at my place. Snuggling on the rug in front of a crackling fire. Blizzard on the way, but we're safe, rolling around inside, on the floor. Sipping wine. Kissing. My arms bundled around Jenny. I can actually feel her. Like I did then. Soft. Warm. Smelling so damn delicious. That was one of the best nights of my life. Jenny slept over.

I swear I can smell her now. Fruit and flowers. Even the honey she drizzles in her tea. Crazy, I still think of her in present tense. I sniff the air, drawing in as much of her scent as possible. She's the breath in my lungs. My heart trips. I feel like she's lying beside me.

"Jenny," I whisper, "is it you?"

Rachel said to talk to her. Eventually I may get an answer. And Rachel is full of shit, because no matter how much I try, I'm not reaching anything but the conclusion that I'm an asshole.

Wheel Wolf

"Come back ..." I panic, because the sweet scent is gone. "Baby. Did I piss you off? I didn't mean to, honey. Please forgive me."

I drag my pillow from beneath my head. Punch it again and again, like it's filled with all the shit I'm trying to dispose of. Compact it. Swallow it. Crap it out. Flush it down the toilet. Into the sewer. There, it's gone. Your colon has been thoroughly cleansed. Which would be great if my colon and brain were interchangeable.

I remove the arm I threw over my face and lift my head. Peer through the room filled with shadows. No one. Nothing. Even though her fragrance is gone, I'm still waiting for Jenny to appear. "Jenny?" My whisper is desperate. "If you're here, show me. Do something physically impossible for someone who's not solid matter anymore. Turn on a light. Knock something over. Make my cell phone chime. Anything baby. You, better than anyone, know I've never been a believer. Give me proof. Appear. Appear."

I'm gritting my teeth. Balling my fists. Demanding. Actually pissed at Jenny because she can't hear me. Won't come to me. Is she angry with me? Jenny, I tried. If I could've hopped on my bike, I would've been there. Saved your life. You'd be with me right now. Not in this room. Not in your house or mine. On an island, maybe. Lying in warm sand instead of a casket. Making love. Babies. The two you wanted.

Perspiration runs from my hairline and neck, soaking my sheets. Am I having a heart attack? I sure as hell hope it's fatal. What happens when you die? Is there really a hereafter? Is that where Jenny is? Not here, but somewhere out there? Outside the single window in my one room existence. Twinkling with the stars in the sky? I concentrate until my brain hurts, trying to feel my way to the other side. If she's there, I'll find her.

Rachel says I have to open my heart, my head. It's not easy.

"Your heart's bleeding, Jack. It will heal. Jenny's soul needs time to heal, too. A traumatic death isn't easy to cope with. She's probably as confused as you are, Jack. She'll come around. She needs to find acceptance, too. You need to help each other through this."

Rachel says Jenny has a choice. Pass over or stay here with me. That's a hell of a decision to have to make. Who the fuck in their right mind would choose a basket case like me over eternal rest?

I haven't been this uncomfortable since I had the flu, ten years ago. Am I sick? My body is rippling with pain. Muscles kinking. My skin is crawling, burning. The backs of my calves feel like they're being assaulted by invisible fingers. Strong fingers. But Rachel isn't here.

I'm getting feeling back? Should I buzz for her? Holy shit. Is that you, Jenny? Crawling under the covers, tickling me?

I feel so sick, I barely make it to the chair and into the bathroom where I hang my head over the bowl, belching up something that looks like lime Jell-O. Yeah, I'm exploding with gas that's gurgling up my throat from my empty drum stomach. All the while, my body is shaking. After what feels like an eruption of a volcano, I struggle to lift my head, which is stuffed with cement. No, it's metal, remember?

Blood slams my temples, forcing my eyeballs out of their sockets. My pulse increases. I'm burning up. I must have a fever. Why the fuck is a mirror mounted on a medicine cabinet I can't reach? I'm staring up at the sparkling rectangle. Trying to make my neck long enough to see myself.

For a rehab, this place sure isn't that well equipped. Mirrors should be mounted three feet up the wall. Like the grab bars running around the entire room. I spot my shower, thinking how good it would feel to let icy cold water drown my overheated body. I drag myself up until a hip hits the sink, trying to catch a glimpse of myself in the mirror. My eyes burn, so I blink a lot.

Wheel Wolf

They're dry, still yellow, the centers ... can black get any blacker? My eyes are almost entirely pupil. I push a knob and water is rushing from the spout tacked to the back of the sink. I flush my eyes until they're not yellow anymore, just blood red.

I wheel from the bathroom, stop in the center of my everything else room, doing what I always do. Stare out the window. Slivers of moonlight pulse through the blinds. The quivering shafts are bleeding like my heart. If the moon was full tonight, instead of a cheesy slice, it would look like a sun that had burst into flame.

Amazing; it's communicating with me. Luring me closer. When I glimpse my reflection in the window, I bay. Quietly. The last thing I want right now is to be disturbed.

I like the moon. It's mysterious. Captivating. I crank up the blinds as far as they'll fold, slide the window up until my body fits through the opening, tumbles out, and I fall on my ass with a thud. Spring to my feet like a gymnast.

My bare feet sink into damp grass and pansies. I pad across the grounds with rhythm, humping the earth, my toes gripped by moist soil. Insects. I'm digging it. I can't ditch the moon, so there's no way I'll free myself from its spell. I don't want to. It makes me strong. My legs work.

As I break into a trot, shadows follow me, moon filtering through branches. My ears are so sensitive, they ring with tunes of nature, man and machine. Night sounds are wild. Howling. Whining. Flapping wings. Muffled voices. Car engines, horns. Is that the cattle in Walton's farm lowing? I hear it all. Smell it too. Weeds, fungus. Ashy. Masculine. Nothing sweet like Jenny. She's not here.

The night is misty, drizzle dampening my hair that's now draping my eyes. Not my fur though. Dry as a bone. Water repellent. I imagine my sweats are lying on the floor, maybe torn to shreds leaving a trail on the grounds. Rolled into a ball beneath a tree. Who knows. Who gives a shit.

I'm loping down the right side of 44, in the bike lane, up the incline and down again. Smooth sailing. My lungs are powerful bellows. Huff. Huff. Working with ease. Once in a while headlights crest the hill. A car now and then. Sometimes a truck. That's when I hide like a cat burglar from the law. Dodging oncoming vehicles. Zigzagging around trees. Crouching behind bushes.

Running through the forest, my senses are hyped. Nature smells amazing. Exhilarating. I keep filling my lungs with night, my eyes shifting like the breeze. I'm counting gnats through darkness, watching worker ants bury larvae and eggs deep into nests. It's uncanny. I'm scenting the food trails they're laying down for their colony.

The forest is our home, but something keeps drawing me back to the road. Instinct, I imagine, because the human in me is accustomed to traveling 44 by pavement, not tree. The musty scent of soil and pungent pine linger in my airway. Heaven. An owl hoots and breaks for a higher branch. I must be a monster. Life is running away from me.

I'm pacing along Foster Road, skulking down alleyways, past dumpsters, drawn to something familiar. Enticing. The butcher shop. It's locked up tight. There's no way I'm breaking in. Especially when I pick up the scent, and voices, distant, but approaching. Kids hanging out at this hour? Hookers, sure, but teens? I can gauge their age by their tone, smell the pot they're enjoying. Barbeque potato chips. Beer.

I'm back on the shoulder of 44. Picking up steam, automatically veering down a side road, to where the balls of my feet clap to a halt. I scale a few shrubs, hop over a fence. There it is. My house. Vacant. It's been so long. The emptiness doesn't begin to equal that in my gut. Burn it down, a voice inside my head screams. Give the freaking twenty acres back to nature. There's nothing for me here anymore. Not anywhere, actually. I roam around aimlessly, until it strikes me. Why didn't I think of this before?

Jenny's house is nestled in a cul de sac, shadowed by tall oak trees with spreading branches. Bad location. Prime target. Nothing else around. No wonder it was vandalized. I creep around the perimeter, ready to make a run for it, thinking Dobie's bound to hear me, scent me.

As I crouch behind a wall of blooming lilac bushes, I'm mesmerized by a flickering light in the upstairs hallway. The one that leads to Jenny's room. I wonder if the bulb is burning out. Of course, I'd rather believe Jenny is controlling the light. Ghosts are attracted to electricity. Everyone knows this.

It's after midnight. I know this because when I passed through town the watchtower clock struck twelve. The fact that Jenny's parents are sleeping, and Dobie could give a shit something is circling his property, is tempting. I smell the scent he laid down a few hours earlier. Sly. He thinks that's going to keep something like me away? A stray, maybe. Me? He's got another think coming.

I'm dying to climb up the side of the clapboard house, slip through Jenny's bedroom window that's now closed, locked I'm sure, crawl into her bed. Lay my head on the pillow where her head rested last week. Curl up beneath the covers that must still smell like her. Oh God. This is so hard.

I'm lonely. I'm roaming. I'm envisioning night with Jenny, last summer at the lake. There's a shift in the wind. My nose shoots up, along with my ears. A sweet fragrance flows into my nostrils. Deep inhale. Hold it. Hold it. Jenny ... I break into a sprint, scaling brambles, breezing through thickets. Until I come to a sign. My heart sinks. Old Oak Campgrounds. The wind shifts again, and I'm inhaling charcoal, not the honeysuckle bushes surrounding the camp.

I can't fight the urge any longer. I need Jenny, and I need her now. A shovel. You have claws, use your paws. I want to be close to her. I have to be. So with a swift leap into the air, I'm springing in the direction of the cemetery. Leaving the aroma of steaks and roasting chicken behind me.

Once I leave the forest's shelter, drizzle turns into rain. I aim my muzzle to the sky, with slackened jowls drink it in, let out such a howl, I can't believe it's coming from the depths of my own throat. I creep around headstones, cleverly, surefooted. Dipping in and out of moonlight trailing through flimsy clouds. I'm hiding myself. From what? The dead?

I need no eyes, the fragrance of flowers brings me to the graveside of my beloved, where I crouch beside the mound of soil still freshly turned. Heaped with a haphazard collection of flowers. With a swipe of my arm I brush them aside, drop to my knees, then fall flat on my face, sobbing her name.

"I'm here, Jen," I whisper, curling up on her grave. Then it hits me: man and beast in a tug of war. I don't want Jenny stalked, slept on, by the same thing that killed her. I should leave. I can't.

I'm just dozing off, lulling in good times, when the scuffle of leaves around me disrupts all thought. Creak. Snap. Crackle. Warm eyes. Interested. I'm being watched by something. The rain has dwindled, taking with it the freshness, leaving an unmistakable stench to flood the air. I spring to my feet, position my nose, and gauge it. I sample the scent. Hmm. Animal. I'm not alone. Neither is Jenny. Something still wants her. I can feel it. I grunt, snarl, bellow. This is my territory.

Wheel Wolf

Mutual Confessions

My lungs leak my last breath of air. I spring to life with a start, gasping, sprawled on the floor. Other than a death rattle, and wheezing bout of hyperventilation, my room is silent. Dim, because my eyes are slits. I drag my fingers through my tangled hair, my palms down my face. How the fuck did I get here? I'm naked, muddy, my ass part of a puddle of rainwater. Holy fuck.

Rachel barges into my room at the most inopportune times. I'm up on elbows, twisting my head around, looking for something to throw over myself. She's seen it all, I know, but ...

"God damn it, Jack." She slams a tray onto the table, inches from my feet. Stands over me, gawking. The aroma of my bloody steak shoots up my nose, flooding my dry mouth with saliva that pooled in my throat as I slept like the dead. "If you think I'm about to mop up a flood, because you don't have the common decency to close the window during a storm ..."

I'm stunned. Doesn't she notice I'm lying here, muck-coated, in the raw?

"You're going to learn to clean up after yourself. Along with sweepers, Walmart has a great selection of floor mops and rug shampooers. Get dressed. We're going shopping." She stalks to the door, but obviously hasn't finished with me yet. Hands on hips she spins. Her lips pinch into an odd shape. "Where were you last night?" She tilts her heart-shaped face.

"None of your business," I grumble, stretching my neck to realign what feels like a bunch of herniated disks. My body has been taking a brutal beating lately.

"How'd you get out? And before you try to bulldoze me, don't try the 'Donnie picked me up,' line. It won't work." She lifts her pointed chin, wanders to the center of the room, her green eyes inspecting every corner. "He was with *me* last night." Arms folded, she's on patrol.

I gag. Picturing Rachel and Donnie getting it on is not what I want to do, especially first thing in the morning when I feel like I have the hangover from Hades.

"Steve and Drake took me out for a few drinks." I've managed to drag myself to the foot of my bed, pull down a lightweight blanket and cover myself. "So you and Donnie are romantically involved." I'm somehow capable of laughter. Sarcastic, but at least I can still find humor in something. "He's bagging you." Balancing on my elbows again, I shake my head. "He's a slut. Don't say I didn't warn you." I look down at my feet, trying to wiggle my toes. They worked last night. This intermittent paralysis is fucking freaky.

"Did you ever think I might be bagging him? Why does it always have to be the guy who initiates a sexual encounter?" She tosses her hands, slides up one sleeve of the black sweater covering her black tank top. "Regardless, it's none of *your* business."

I squint up at her. "So where'd he take you? McDonalds?"

"We went to a drive-in movie." She hits the side of my leg with the wheel of my chair. "Get in."

"What'd you see?" I scramble to pull myself to a sit, and she hauls me onto the padded seat.

"A remake of Ghost In The Cellar."

She's aimed me toward the bathroom, so I crane my aching neck to continue our mood-lifting conversation. "Was it good? Did you share popcorn? Did he try to do you in the back seat? Or were you on his Harley?"

"He picked me up in his BMW. And before you ask, the car is extravagant, like he is." She's bending, mopping up rainwater with my bath towel, running short of breath. "The movie was unrealistic. I could've done a better job scripting the plot than their writers." She pops up in front of me, flings the bathroom door open, shattering the ceramic tiled wall with the doorknob. Then she tosses the wet towel into the sink like a shortstop.

"Listen to you." I swing my face up to hers, ready to propel myself toward the shower. She's smug. My mouth gathers at one corner. "The authority on ghosts, I see. And men."

She cocks a brow, narrows her eyes. "Jack." Deliberating silence, then a blow-off, her voice normalizes. "We should talk sometime."

She's captured my interest. Rachel is an intriguing individual. Like the moon, you can easily fall victim to her spell. "What's wrong with right now? My personal hygiene can wait."

She purses her lips. Lifts her other brow and studies me. I've stoked the flame. Intuition tells me she wants to unload ... or probe. "Come over here." She tips her head.

I follow her to the easy chair in the far corner, which she collapses into. I roll up close, leaving enough space so my morning breath doesn't hit her full blast.

Just when I think she's about to tell me she's part of the spirit world, she stuns me. "There were another two murders last night."

I hold my breath. "Where?"

"Old Oak Campground. A couple was found slashed to pieces. Same as the others."

"Holy shit. Any leads? How'd you find out so fast?" My

head is spinning.

"No leads, other than prints. I spoke to a detective this morning."

My ears perk up. Wheel prints? "What kind of prints? Why did a detective call you? Who was it? Donnie?"

"I'll get to that. Something heavy left footprints in the mud. An animal."

I was an animal last night. Could I have ...?

I haul in a breath, shake my head, drop it onto my hand that's braced on the arm leaning on my chair. "What the fuck is going on?" I'm almost pleading, because Angel's Bend is quickly becoming the murder capital of the world. "Could it be a grizzly?" I mumble the answer to my question. "Not in these parts ..." I scratch my head, my beard, my thigh that feels like it has bugs crawling on it.

"You tell me." I don't like the way she's staring at me.

"How the fuck should I know? I'm still reeling over Jenny ..."

She cuts me off. "I know, Jack. You're grieving." She wets her lips with her moist tongue, as though she's about to dig into a hearty meal. "I've seen my share of odd occurrences in this life, but I think it's time to talk about you ... and yours."

"I don't want to discuss what happened to Jenny." Hell. Just thinking about her murder is disabling. Talking about it makes it all too real. Remaining a coward is so much easier.

She digs both elbows into the upholstered arms of the chair and leans forward. "I have to ask you something, and I want you to be honest."

Honest? I want to become the incredible shrinking man. "I always am." My gaze shifts to the window, then back to hers that's shooting suspicious green beams at me.

"How many times have you been out since you arrived here?" I believe a full minute has passed and she hasn't blinked once.

Wheel Wolf

Her stare wouldn't permit me to lie, even if I tried to. And believe me, I'm seriously considering it.

There's something about Rachel, though. Along with being the most eccentric person I've ever met, I feel she's trustworthy. "A couple times." My brows shrug in time with my shoulders.

Her voice falls into a disconcerting monotone. Her eyes grow as narrow as mine. "A detective called my office this morning. To question me ... about you. And it wasn't Donnie."

My heart skips a beat that alters the rhythm of my breathing. I cough, because something inside my chest is fluttering. "If they're gonna try to pin murders on me ..." My eyes leave the wall I've been staring at and slam into hers. Now I'm leaning forward too, fingers strangling my armrests.

I'm trying to remain composed, but my voice cracks. I hate when I sound pathetic. The pathetic me is reserved for Jenny. "It's crazy, Rachel. I can't move from this chair. How the hell ..." Would this be the right time to tell her I've been experiencing sensations in my lower extremities, and they seem to be working late at night, as long as the moon is out. It doesn't need to be full, might I add. Just a sliver seems to be sufficient to get me up and out of this chair.

She holds up a hand. "Don't worry. I covered for you."

"Covered what? I haven't done anything illegal." Other than eating the Walton Hereford, that I recall.

"The fact that you are somehow managing to get your ass out of that chair, out the window," she jerks her head in the direction of a steady breeze, "because you sure as hell haven't been seen wandering the corridors on two feet — and everyone knows you're a recluse anyway — and you're somehow sneaking back in again, through said window. Look at you. You look like you were just raised from the dead. You even smell like a graveyard."

My mouth drops. I cover my guilt by throwing shit against

the wall to see if anything sticks. "Have you been drinking, Rachel? By any chance ... using? Believe me, I can spot the signs a mile away ..." How the hell does she know I was at the cemetery?

She scowls. Then with a shake of her head, she draws a short breath. "Jack. I'm not even going to ask how you do it, because if I knew, I might be forced to form a different opinion of you."

I can't take it anymore. I have to spill my guts. "Rachel ... I need someone to talk to. Share what's been going on."

Her jaw works like a guy's. I'm waiting for her to grow a beard and stroke it, like I'm doing as I prepare for my confession.

After ear-buzzing silence and eye-watering staring, she nods. "Go on, Jack."

I heave a sigh. "I don't remember much of the accident. But I do know it wasn't my fault. I had nothing to do with that girl's death. As a matter of fact, I think she caused this." I run my palms over the skin on my thighs, because the blanket is merely slung across my hips. I pause for her reaction, but she's silent. Emotionless. So I continue. "I just want you to know I've never hurt anyone. Intentionally, anyway. What I do when I'm unconscious is out of my hands ... and scaring the shit out of me."

Again and again, she nods. "Explain unconscious."

"I've been going through changes ... hearing voices ... having attacks or whatever you want to call it."

She doesn't seem impressed. "I can't call *it* anything until you describe the symptoms."

"I'm hearing people inside my head. Maybe blacking out sometimes. I'm not entirely sure, but I have a strong feeling I might be turning into some kind of animal that craves raw meat. Aren't you going to suggest I retain an attorney?"

She shakes her head.

"Psychiatrist?"

"No. I'd have to see one as well."

"Don't tell me you transition too ..."

"No, I don't transition, but ..."

"You hear voices?"

"All the time."

"How long? When did it start? What caused it?" Misery loves company isn't merely an overused cliché.

Her stare is intense. "For as long as I can remember."

"Can you give me some examples?" Sinking into my chair, I sigh relief. Someone understands me, doesn't want to lock me up in a cell or psych ward.

Rachel isn't an animated person, but talking about the occult seems to be enlivening her. There's a gleam in her eyes. Movement of facial muscles I never realized she had.

"I've been one with the spirits for as long as I can recall. The first time I heard them whisper, I barricaded myself in my bedroom. Crawled under my bed. I used to stuff my ears with cotton. But nothing stopped them. I'm a receiver. There aren't many of us who are truly in tune, and when you consider the multitude of souls trapped between the physical and spiritual worlds, you can imagine our popularity."

Her sigh sounds like mine did a moment ago. Maybe she's relieved to get it off her chest, as well.

"People think I'm a bitch, Jack." Her brows shrug. "I'm solemn because I absorb the problems of the dead, and can't rest until they're solved. Their desperation becomes our depression, until we learn to deal. You feel it too, don't you ..."

I nod, but I'm so confused. "Deal?" My sore eyes attempt to bulge. "How do you deal? Because all this shit is driving me insane." I'm not sure we're talking about the same voices. I'm gearing up to fess up to everything. From the sound of it, Rachel is a helper. She's pure. Like Jenny. If it's possible to feel a color, my soul feels black, the absence of color, of everything.

"How do I deal ..." She sinks deeper into the chair, crosses her legs, and pushes the sleeves of her sweater up to both elbows. "At one point, they were screaming. I thought I was losing it too. When I stopped fighting them and started listening, it became easier. Quieter. I acknowledged them, cried with them, consoled them. Visited the objects of their emotional upheaval. The dead retain emotion. Did you know that?"

She's lost me, but has scared the life out of me. I'm like a piece of ice. Shivering. Twitching. Bugs are crawling over more than my thighs now. They're all over my body. I keep rubbing my arms. Pull the blanket up around my neck. "I ... I had no idea. About any of this. Until ..."

"I barely hear them now." I don't believe she's listening to me, or even sees me. She's fallen into a trance. "Only the ones I want to hear come through loud and clear. The relentless voices, like Jenny's." Even her tone has changed. Soulful. Distant.

"Jenny? Oh my God. She's been talking to you? I've been scenting her."

Rachel's head snaps up. She's facing me, her features melting before my eyes. This girl is suddenly gripped by intense emotion. "Scenting?" The word is like a gust of wind. I look around the room, because I'm not sure who's talking.

"Yeah. I get whiffs of Jenny now and then." There's a lump in my throat, my whisper is hoarse. I'm slipping into Rachel's world. Jenny's. "I smell her perfume. Her entire essence. Sometimes she's all around me. I almost feel her. In my arms. Lying beside me in bed. I talk to her, but I can't get through to her." A sob tears from my gut.

"She's here. And as I said. She's cries because she's gone and you can't accept it."

Rachel just drove a stake through my heart. "She's crying because of me?"

She doesn't have to nod. Her facial expression is all the confirmation I need. "Perceptive of you, Jack. Now stop being so insensitive and help her move on." Her eyes harden, like jade beads. "Make her happy or let her go, Jack. What you're doing to her isn't fair. Sleeping on her grave, like you did last night." She hisses. "It frightens her. Reminds her. You have to fight it. Conquer the beast. You can make a difference. Come to a meeting. You'll get strong. You'll see where I'm coming from."

"Holy Christ, you've thrown me for a loop. Give me a minute to digest this." I cover my face with my hands, thinking, what meeting? AA? Is she an alcoholic who's killed every brain cell? Is that why she's talking crazy?

Rachel remains patiently silent. I hear nothing more than the soft brush of her breath. My world has stopped. There's nothing outside my window. No traffic. No birds. I'm in limbo. Nothing inside my chest. I'm empty. I can't even feel the beat of my heart. After a few purging moments, I surface for air, and unload the rest of my confession.

"Rachel. It's not only voices and sounds. What you originally asked. How many times have I gotten out. Don't you want to know how I get out and why?"

"I have a general idea." She looks around the room, taps a fur ball the wind has blown against the side of the chair with the tip of her shoe.

"I transform into a monster. A wolf. Even when the moon's not full. It's nothing like in the movies. I don't understand it."

"Then do some research." Graceful as a gazelle, her body springs off the chair and floats across the room to the closet. She removes a case from the highest shelf and turns to me. Arms extended.

"I'm surprised you haven't found this already." She lays a laptop on my thighs. I feel the cold case touch my skin.

"Find it up there? You're kidding right? I'm lucky I can reach the lowest trouser bar in that closet. Putting stuff up there is like hiding candy from a kid who's too short to reach the top shelf and too dumb to use a ladder." I lift the cover and the device turns on automatically. "Awesome. A Chromebook."

We're both coming from, or heading to, the loony bin. Either approach is appropriate. "You don't appear surprised by anything I've said."

"I told you. I'm a believer." She cocks a brow. "I sense I haven't surprised you, either ..."

Wheel Wolf

Silver Burns

*B*y the time Rachel returns to my room, I've showered, devoured every ounce of flesh clinging to my breakfast steak, and licked the bone clean. I'm wheeling around in my chair, pushing my SmartSweeper across the oval rug and hardwood corners, wearing a pair of the darkest sunglasses Walmart's Optical Department had on display the day Rachel dragged me shopping.

Leaving an amber trail, she's bringing up the rear as the vacuum sucks in the last long strands of my shedding body hair. "What are you going to do with yourself today? It's lovely out. You should get some fresh air." She takes the sweeper, unplugs it and shoves it into the closet. "It's a perfect day for job hunting." She shoots me the eye. "You can use the van. It's equipped."

"As you see, the window's wide open." I draw an exaggerated breath. "There's my fresh air. And I plan on doing the same thing I do every other day. Let you beat me to a pulp, stare outside ... but this afternoon, I'm surfing the net, too." I gesture to the Chromebook sitting on my bed. "I've got a lot of homework to do before tonight."

"You need to get your mind off yourself. I suggest

finding employment."

"While you're suggesting, what would I be? Shadow Lane night watchman?"

"You may not have the ability to be a forest ranger, but your love is the forest. Why not get a desk job in the ranger's office? Work on maps, Jack. You know every acre of Angel's Bend and then some. You can man the office. The radio. Help the other rangers stay on track. I'm sure they could use someone like you on their team."

She tosses her head, then runs her fingers through her hair, fluffing her strawberry waves until she looks attractively wild; Sheena, queen of the jungle, comes to mind. I've never seen her perform a feminine action before. Impressive. I zero in on the sooty streaks she's added to her hair: zebra stripes, total jungle.

She dabs the corners of her mouth with her pinkies and smacks her lips together. "I'm having lunch with Donnie and you're invited."

"I'll pass." I feel Rachel and I have reached a new understanding, but we're not best buds. I consider Rachel, Donnie, and me, the unlikely triangle — which is likely to split apart under pressure.

Rachel has neglected to close my door. Donnie glides through like the sun streaming through clouds.

"So much for privacy," I growl. "Come on in, Donnie." I swing an arm through the air.

"Hey, Rach. Figured I'd find you here." He plants a kiss on her cheek. "You look amazing." He's referring to her slinky black skirt with thigh-high slit and matching top. Her waist is tightly belted, emphasizing her hourglass figure. "Mmm. Smell good too. What is that?"

"Fantasy." She smiles and strokes the side of her face. Go for it Rachel, I'm thinking. Yeah, that'a girl, play it cool, coy. Sock it to him and then dump him.

Her nails are polished ebony. Her brows are auburn now,

matching her lips. Without the white of her uniform name tag, she's one hundred percent gothic.

When Donnie finally pulls his eyes from her, he turns them on me. I'm ready for one of our classic shit throwing contests, but he's different. Subdued? "How are you, Jack?"

"I'm handling. You?" My elbow is propped on the chair. I rest my chin on my knuckled fist, taking the two of them in. My stomach drops with memories.

"Things are looking up." His eyes dart to Rachel. I know that expression all too well.

The strap of a brown leather satchel grips his shoulder. He taps the bag resting on the hip of his jeans, and shoots me a look like when we were in high school and he had a pocketful of firecrackers to set off under the principal's window. "I've got something for you." His mischievous grin stretches. I'm getting the impression he almost likes me.

If my eyes were capable, they would widen. He dips his hand into the bag and pulls out the cross Jenny gave me. I suck in a breath and blink furiously.

He's standing at my feet, dangling the gleaming silver under my nose.

With a slack jaw, all I can do is stare. Then my eyes mist because I fall into reverie, thinking about the night Jenny hung the cumbersome relic around my neck. The words she said: Take care of you ... for me. I haven't been taking care of me. For her. That's what Rachel ... Jenny has been trying to tell me. Oh shit. I'm about to go to pieces. A second later, I'm wracked with sobs.

I feel hands on my shoulders. Rachel is on one side. Donnie on the other. The feminine is squeezing. The masculine is patting. "Hey, bro," he says. "Hang in there. I know how tough it's been on you."

You have no fucking idea how tough it is ... "I thought this was part of the evidence?" I look up at him, questioningly, swiping my runny nose by pulling up the neck of my shirt.

Rachel retrieves her hand, seconds later, tosses a box of tissues into my lap.

Hands removed, they both stand before me, like sentinels. When Donnie looks at Rachel his face goes soft, then tightens when he turns back to me. He hitches his head to the beaming redhead. "Your therapist has convinced me you're not a danger to anyone, other than yourself. You're exonerated. Here." He loosens his grip on the chain and the weighty cross drops an inch and swings in my direction. I feel a field of electricity and flinch. "Don't prove us wrong, Jack."

A wave of nausea sweeps me. I'm almost afraid to touch the cross. The silver glow stings my eyes, like smoke does when you're near a fire. I feel the heat from inches away.

Donnie is literally shoving the heirloom at me. "Here ... take it. I thought you'd be happy to have it back." He's gruff. Losing patience. Eyes shifting to Rachel for advice. I sense his discomfort. She simply shrugs.

I squint up at him. "It'll take a lot more than this to give me a boner." I reach for the cross, but the moment I touch the silver my fingertips burn. I hear the sizzle and wonder if they do. "Holy shit," I mumble under my breath and jerk away. "Leave it on the table." I turn my face, not only because I'm hiding my beastly secret, but because I'm feeling Jenny's fingers on my cheek. I want everyone out of my sight. Out of my room. Everyone other than Jenny.

I sense Donnie feels I'm not handling the loss very well. He's right. Rachel however, does a double take when she sees my reaction to silver, and when her eyes land on mine, her arched brows level dramatically.

"We'll talk later, Jack. Let's go Donnie."

She shoots me a warning look. "If I'm not back before dark, make sure you close the window. I'm not mopping up after you again if it rains."

I can hear them in the hallway. Walking. Whispering. Donnie asking what she was talking about.

"Nothing to worry about," she tells him. "Everything's under control."

Wheel Wolf

Legends, Folklore, Myths

I've planted myself before the window, open Chromebook heating my lap, indicating sensation is really returning to my legs. It's been happening more and more. It's not my imagination. I don't know if I should ring for Rachel, call 9-1-1, or grab a beer. One thing for sure, I'm elated.

I'm trying to pin down exactly how this wolf thing comes over me. And at what point I return to normal. Is there a way to control my condition? Nothing I have read until now has been helpful. The Net is swarming with goblin and ghoul gibberish. So far, I'm a shapeshifter. A human with the ability to transform into an animal. In my case, a wolf. Tell me something I don't already know, Google. Like how did I come down with this affliction in the first place? It says here, you have to be bitten by a wolf, or cursed by an angry Bohemian with a vendetta. On the other hand, you're labeled completely insane when you're a pseudo ... a Lycanthrope. Which am I? Animal or head-case?

The crap I'm reading is mind-bending. Disturbing. My stomach is churning. Delusional? If it's all in my mind, as this page suggests, I'm suffering from a psychosis. Did I sustain brain damage when my skull hit the pavement and my unstrapped helmet flew off?

It can't be drugs. I'm not on anything, yet I'm hallucinating. My wolf-self. Jenny's touch, smell, presence which at this moment is raising the hair on the back of my neck. My entire body actually, because when I touch my skin, it's sprinkled with electrically charged fur. I drag my fingernails over my scalp which is tingling. As are the sides of my face, my lips. I'm imagining Jenny to be running her fingers through my hair. Massaging my shoulders like she always did to calm me. Christ, get a grip!

I'm back to focusing on the twelve-inch screen, clicking the blue text which appears to be linked to an interesting source. As the cursor spins, annoying me because this Internet connection is so damn slow, the grainy top of a man's head appears when the page decides to load. Bit by bit the pixels generate a face. Pitch black hair and full beard, bushy but well-trimmed. Average looking. Ethnic. European, perhaps. Distinguished. Eighteen hundreds? Nah, early twentieth century. He looks like he could have been a passenger on the Titanic. Could he still be alive?

I can't wait to dive into this article. Something in my gut tells me this dude knows exactly what he's talking about. My eyes quickly scan the blocks of text written by Heinrich Rudéa, PHD ... Rudéa? If not for the name I wouldn't think twice and just continue perusing. But the rate of my pulse increases when I make the immediate connection. My thoughts are diverted. It can't be. Can it? Jenny never mentioned anything about a writer in her family. Especially a PHD who's an expert on werewolves. And judging from my experience, Rudéa is not a common name.

My eyes jump to the date of publication. Seventy-five years ago. Hmm. Back to the title: *Roots of the Werewolf.* Heinrich opens the article as though he's writing a script for Hollywood, with eyewitness accounts, going into gruesome detail about legends, folklore and myths. About curse versus medical conditions and mental illness.

The way this guy expresses himself, makes me feel like I'm there. I mean, I'm watching this young girl, in the backwoods of Maine, confront a two-hundred pound wolf she believes to be her missing boyfriend who disappeared on his way into town one day. Holy shit. I swipe away goose bumps. Some of this stuff is fascinating, as well as chilling. Especially when you're in love with someone who suffered the terror, the agony ... the fate. And you're trying to determine if you've been infected, or just crazy with grief.

The author goes as far as defining the difference between legends, myths, and folklore. I never realized there was a difference.

Robin Hood is a legend. Hmm. Interesting information. All this time, I thought the stories about the dude were based on fact. Yeah, I chuckle. That's a legend numbskull, which I guess makes me a mythological creature. Definitely a rogue.

Rudéa goes on to explain, while scientific evidence points to neurosis and psychosis - blood and glandular disorders - the phenomenon of a flesh and blood man-beast cannot be dismissed. Unsubstantiated accounts date back thousands of years in almost every culture, but pockets of werewolves are believed to exist to this day in regions of Northern Europe, and have migrated to other remote areas of the world.

Lob Ombre.(Spain) Loup Garou. (France) Shapeshifters, Skinwalkers, Witchcraft. (Universal). A column of illustrations sets the stage. I stare at the artist's renderings of artifacts and rock carvings depicting humans with wolf-like heads and tails. Locations of sightings hit me: Wisconsin, Michigan, Canada, Maine, New York State ... Not so remote, my friend.

Rudéa himself claims to have been stricken with Lycanthropy after returning from an expedition in Romania. He agreed to be the subject of extensive physical and psychological testing, results proving inconclusive. Holy fuck! No wonder Jenny and her parents kept him under wraps. She had a loon in her family.

They shy away from silver. Wear amulets.

Rudéa was a wolf-charmer? Never heard that one before. In present day culture, the werewolf is a symbol of romance. The Alpha is a cunning creature, when in human form, utilizing the irresistible lure of blue in his eyes to charm prey. The Alpha has the ability to mask his scent, making him a formidable opponent, undetectable adversary to challenging counterparts. In other forms, and during metamorphosis, the consistent yellowing of the iris represents various stages of transition, with unusually large black pupils and bright yellow iris being a *gifted* who has cycled less than a half dozen times in as many full moons. Gifted? Is this guy glorifying black magic? Potential murderers? In which case, one could commit a heinous crime and plead insanity: I was under the moon's spell.

Rudéa claims to have gathered data disproving the myth that a full moon is necessary for transition. Those in transition have no control, and may shift during any phase, while under the influence of moonlight. Conversely, pack leaders, or confirmed Alphas, possess the ability to transform at will, night or day.

The first indication of change is eye color, increase in temperature and respiration. Right now my heart is pounding, and I'm sweating my balls off.

Complete metamorphosis is achieved following the realignment of facial features and structure of bones in spine and limbs. Rudéa goes on to explain scientific jargon about the moon and its power over the earth and all organisms. Odd he doesn't mention: living organisms. I'm trying to absorb it, dispute it, because who the fuck wants to believe the world they live in is also inhabited by blood-thirsty creatures?

If not for my affliction, I'd be considering this guy to be some unknown horror fanatic, trying to take the literary world by storm, make a name for himself.

Name ...

Wheel Wolf

The Chase: The Kill

The sun is setting. So is my stomach. I'm exhausted, but not looking forward to sacking out, or anything, for that matter. My life is gloom and doom without Jenny. I'm not sure how I'm going to go on without her. Maybe when I'm on my feet again, out of this town, things will be different.

I know Rachel is right. I need to get my life back together. I'll call McCabe first thing in the morning. Better yet, I'll drop by the office and surprise him. He's a cool guy. We immediately bonded, which is probably why he hired me on the spot. All I needed to do was attend orientation ... which thanks to ... let's just say I never made it to the class.

I'll hop in the van and drive myself. I'm sick of having others do everything for me. This is my first step toward regaining independence.

I flick through TV stations. Nothing interests me. But I stumble upon a sports channel and next thing I don't know, I'm snoring in my chair. The parched throat, pain in my neck from bending unnaturally, combined with the obnoxious noise blasting from the speakers, wakes me. Crackling tendons grit inside my ears. Revving engines and screeching tires block my canals. The cars seem to be racing the beat of my heart. I flick the TV off. Aim the remote, but it misses the bed, landing with a thump on the floor.

My throat is constricted. I yank on the collar of my t-shirt, which feels like it's choking me. A suffocating feeling continues to overwhelm me, so I wheel to the window for fresh air, experiencing the familiar tingling and twitching of muscles, nerve endings firing off signals throughout my body. Only this time, my left foot jumps off the footrest, slamming my leg into the side of the table, rocking a lamp, then sending it crashing to the floor before it can balance, or I can grab it.

Holy shit. I start pounding on said leg, testing for reflexes. I gather the skin on the inside of my thigh and pinch. Yeah, it hurts. I laugh. I cry. I'm in such a state of surprise and emotion, I feel like collapsing.

Can I walk? Might as well try. Resting all of my weight on the arms of the chair, I attempt to lift my body. My lower half is cumbersome, incredibly weak, but I am able to partially stand on legs that are bent, not sturdy, but attempting to regenerate with life.

I detach the screen, hang my head out the window, gasping, scenting, drinking in twilight, noticing the rising moon appears to be waxing. It's calling my name. It's beautiful. Bright yellow and sculpted. A glowing work of art. I want to reach out and touch it. To hell with touching it. I want to live on it.

I can't confirm what overtakes me, but I discover myself naked and leaping out the window, leaving it wide open, the broken lamp and all my worries, behind. I feel amazing. I'm muscular and invincible. Every part of me is stellar. Observing the area, I crouch. Sample the air through flicking nostrils. There's nothing around but me and dusk. I'm something other than human, but this beast is on a mission of peace.

Wheel Wolf

I gaze at the moon filtering through wispy clouds. Inhale the night. Voice my approval with a passionate howl. I'm running in and out of mist, the wind blowing through my hair. Vision sharp, senses keen, my brain is pulsing with clarity.

There's no question in my mind, I know exactly where I'm going. I'm about to tell Jenny I'm healing, and I won't be coming back. I want her to rest in peace, and won't be interrupting her eternal sleep anymore. I'm a big boy who's about to begin pulling up his own fly, taking care of himself. Before my nightly visits become too habit-forming, I've got to let her go.

"Jenny, I love you, baby." My mournful wail chills the night. "You'll always be in my heart, but you're free. We'll meet again someday, my one and only love."

Bypassing 44, I head straight for the forest, ripping through a shortcut that leads me out of town. The cemetery is just up ahead, on the other side of the ridge. I'm pounding turf, hurdling streams, lungs pumping air that's singing in my ears. My eyes hone in on moonlight glinting like sparks off the gates.

I break through the brush, approaching the finish line, peering over headstones, around muted statues cast in yellow from the glow of my eyes and the moon.

The moon is everywhere, splashing eeriness. Different from the day Jenny was interred. I was in shock then. Now I'm in hell. The fact that I feel glazed by this freaky luster is intimidating. I skulk like a thief.

Accepting of what I'm about to do, my spirit is struggling for liftoff, but unfortunately, I'm grounded. The moon drizzles indiscriminate shadows over the field of the dead, where the living have left their mark: flowers, flags, framed photos. Memories, love, heartbreak, stages of grief ... the inescapable is being absorbed by the hallowed ground. Topside and under.

I'm padding sadly, each step deliberate, remembering the past, wondering if there will be a future. Head lowered, I drag my pawed feet through rows of the departed, focusing on one specific grave, when a burly figure springs out of nowhere, and proceeds to crouch over ... Jenny's headstone? What the fuck? I freeze in step, claws digging into soft soil. I'm sleek, I'm lithe, I dip behind a monument, with every intention of creeping up on him, the scumbag who's ... pissing on Jenny's grave? Mother fucker! He's desecrating Jenny. I bounce back onto the illuminated path. I'm dashing. I'm leaping. About to level the douche in a snarling flash, "Get the fuck away from her!" I want to shriek, even before attacking, but I also want to benefit from the element of surprise.

I couldn't save her in life, but I'll be damned if I'm going to let the same beast that killed Jenny, denigrate her final resting place.

As I lock on my target, I know he senses my glare, not only because I'm shooting hateful daggers, but because he breaks his pause to spin, warning me with a defiant look that says something like, this is my property, dude. Don't take another step.

In my fury, I miscalculate, fall short, recover my strength and make another pass. With a powerful blow, he flicks me into granite that connects with my skull. I shake off the pain, spring to my feet, and bounce off the ground. I'm pumped, ready to outperform, but he's disappeared so fast, I slam into a shadow instead of his side. I land on my ass, sinking into damp soil. "Sonofabitch!"

Balancing on hind legs, I'm enraged but I'm handling. I let out a guttural growl. Ears perked, I poise, jerk my head, sniff the air. His scent scorches my nostrils, drifting from a clearing where ... he's waiting for me?

Moonlight rains down like glitter, coating his outline with an eerie fluorescence. That's when it hits me. This sucker is freaking huge. I'm stunned, contemplating his strength, his identity. He's Jenny's killer. I'm sure of it. Not exactly returning to the crime scene. But marking his territory over her dead body.

Wheel Wolf

My blood is about to evaporate.

Nothing's going to stop me. I launch like a snorting bull. He has a head start, and he's lightning. He knows the forest well. I realize this, because he's able to lose me where foliage blackens and coils. I'm prowling, about to double back, when I spot him in a field, wide open and blustery. His fur is fluttering as his barrel chest rises and falls. His jaws are snapping, his red eyes radiating.

He's playing games. I know he's not about to let me get the jump on him, so I calculate. Do I draw back, circle and surprise him from behind? He's lurking not far from a lonely hiking trail. Glaring, baying, he's baiting me. Each time I inch within a hair of his foul odor, he hauls ass. I follow him at a steady pace, scaling rocks, hurdling streams. I'm panting, drooling, imagining he's doing the same. My heart is exploding against my rib cage, but I'm gonna catch this scumbag and make him regret he ever walked the face of this earth. Animal, or whatever the hell he is, he's about to settle up.

We're moving in the direction of the campgrounds, where the aroma of roasting meat floods the air. I'm salivating, but he's the stalker. The one who's left a bloody trail. No ... don't tell me. He's not about to ... He's up to something, because we're doing donuts, then heading back to the main road. Veering off the smoky trail, darting down a thicketed path only Rangers know. He's trying to lose me again, or is he still luring me? Into town? What the fuck?

I have no choice but to track him. We're skulking down the alley between Floyd's butcher shop and the municipal park's outdoor bathhouse. It clicks. Another one of his hunting grounds. Teens. Drifters. Hookers. Shit. I'm going to be a hero werewolf.

Imagining my picture in the news I slow my step, then realize, if I don't destroy this monster, it's unlikely anyone else will. Because this animal is not about to show himself to anyone but me. I doubt the cops would take my anonymous phone call seriously: Hey ... there's a werewolf on the loose on Foster Road. He's the serial killer you've been looking for.

The shadow of the wolf vaporizes around a corner, where the odor of stale tobacco wafts through the air. Seconds later, I hear a scream. Arms and claws extended, I'm five feet off the ground, launching my body through the air. I round the corner in a skid to be hit with a gruesome sight that makes my heart pound faster. I can feel my jaws, but I can see his. Maybe if I looked in a mirror right now, I wouldn't feel so outmatched, as I watch a nightmare unfold before my amber eyes. A girl is locked in this thing's embrace. Instead of bending her back to kiss her, he's about to sink his fangs into her throat.

He snarls, baring his full set of needle-like teeth. Razors glisten with drool. My poor Jenny. She had to face this thing alone. Fluid boils beneath the corneas of my eyes. My anger turns to rage. I let out a blood-curdling wail of pain, because my heart feels like it's being torn from my chest. My lungs are on fire. Every rib is cracked. My body is going through a meat grinder. I don't know if he has some kind of power, other than wolf, because I'm suddenly losing steam.

Still, I lunge at him, going straight for the jugular. With my bulk weighing down his shoulders, his neck caves, his arms release like a clamshell, dropping the girl like a payload. Disoriented, blood pouring from wounds, she crawls into a dark corner and cowers. Whimpers. Jenny's agony flashes through my mind. My teeth sink deeper, and with a growl, I shake my head to tenderize his muscle. I'm sure this poor girl can't believe her eyes. In the company of not one, but two beasts. I can smell the terror paralyzing her. Sobbing, she's attempting to drag herself away. Clutching her throat, she's trapped in her own pool of body fluids.

He throws me off with one swipe of a massive arm. I sail though the air, drop onto my back. His strength is admirable, fueling mine. I'm up on my feet with a bound, connecting with his side. Clamping my fangs down into his neck. Whatever I bite through is hard. Tendons? He lets out a shriek, and with a couple of shakes, swats me off like I'm an insect disrupting his picnic. Only his picnic is still convulsing in the corner. More than likely bleeding to death. He brought me here. Why? To watch him commit murder? To taunt me? What's his game?

We're snarling, growling, our jaws snapping. The girl starts belting out gurgling pleas that are sure to bring an audience. What happens next is beyond comprehension. He's only been fucking with us. This I know because he lifts me over his head with something clawed that resembles a hand, and tosses me across the alley like I'm a toy. Into darkness. There's no moon above me, only an awning. I shake my head trying to clear it, because my skull has been smashed against the side of a brick building.

I'm seeing double. Dancing figures. Flailing outlines. He recovers the girl from her hiding place and throws her over a shoulder. With one powerful leap, they have both disappeared into what is quickly becoming dawn. Holy fuck. He's about to feast on her, while I lie here helpless. I can't help you, girl. I'm sorry. I couldn't help you, Jenny. I'm sorry.

I witnessed Jenny's suffering while I listened through a phone line and static, but this ... this is blinding, wake-up-and-rip-your-heart out, reality of what must have happened to Jenny. And what this girl is about to face.

There's no way I can hunt him down in my condition. My body hair is receding, my tongue licking blood from my human teeth. I'm quickly turning back into myself, and the contents of my stomach are bubbling up into my mouth.

Breaking dawn scatters pink and gold light between buildings and trees. The moon is fading into what is shaping into a scorching horizon while I shift back into me. Fuck. My legs are weak. My head's pounding. I spit blood, his. Pull his fur from my teeth. Gross. I took a good chunk out of him, which he probably never felt through layers of muscle. I can't stop thinking about the girl. Her fate. When and where her remains, if any, will be found. Scattered across the forest? Digested by coyotes?

Christ. I'm naked in the alley. Dragging myself behind a dumpster, hoping I'm not on the trash collector's morning route. I have no idea of how I'm going to get back to rehab. Foggy as to how I actually got here. I have no phone, no money, no clothing. I'm seriously ready to sob with frustration. Walking at night, losing mobility every morning, is wearing me down. Not to mention the murders I've witnessed. Jenny's. The girl. If the police find me, ask me to identify the missing person, I wouldn't be able to. I didn't see her face. Will she have one when they find her? This animal has to be stopped, before he kills again.

Worry about how you're going to trap him later, Jack. Right now, you better figure out what to do. Hell, I have no idea what to do. I had a front row seat, watching a slaughter. I'm a prime witness. Fuck that. A prime suspect. Somehow, I have to get out of here. Not only the alley, fucking Angel's Bend. There's nothing here for me now. I'm abnormal. Part creature, part man. There are murders. Nowhere to hide, because I have a feeling the forests will soon be teeming with cops, especially once they realize what they're dealing with. I can't come forward with information ... I can't be locked up behind bars.

I'm not sure exactly how long I've been lying here, but the sudden thud of footsteps throws me into panic. My first instinct is to curl into a ball. A voice in my head says, *You can't make yourself invisible, Jack.* So I drag my unresponsive body farther behind the Foster Road dumpster, lay my face on my folded arms, and wait to be arrested. I let out a breath when I spot the Crocs. Black and familiar. My head snaps up to find Rachel staring down at me, her face twisted in a perturbed expression.

I scramble to sit, while I cover my junk. "How'd you know where to find me?" I could really give a shit. I'm babbling because

Wheel Wolf

I'm thrilled she's here.

She drops a blanket on me. Next a pair of sweats. "I hear voices, remember?"

As I drag the sweats up my legs and over my ass, my breath is settling.

"Next time you decide to take a midnight excursion through the forest and town, make sure you can get yourself back before moonset. I don't run a taxi service. I do enough for you, Jack."

She's so serious, I want to laugh. Puke. Shake. She doesn't even ask how I managed to get here. Why I was about to make a naked, public spectacle of myself. Just don't put her out again. Holy fuck. Things are getting weirder and weirder.

My Forest Ranger Competition

I'm still working my way through the stages of grief, only mine are hitting simultaneously: Depression. Isolation. Anger. Denial. Strike acceptance from the list. I don't see that happening.

I'm mulling things around, weighing pros and cons. After the incident last night, I'm climbing walls. Do I want to get out of here because I'm restless and about to tear my excess hair out? Or do I want to canvas the streets day and night looking for a suspicious stranger, the animal I chased from Jenny's grave and through the forest. The one I helplessly watched slaughter an innocent young girl before Rachel picked me up off the sidewalk. A wave of teeth-chattering terror washes over me, followed by intense determination.

I don't remove my finger from the buzzer until Rachel crashes into the room, literally snarling. I've never seen her this way.

"What the hell is your problem, Jack? In the event no one has already clued you in, I do have other patients. I can't spend all of my time posing as your nurse maid."

Regardless of the circumstances, I've managed to retain a shred of dignity. I'm about to object to being spoken to this way, when Rachel's features strain. She tosses her head to the left, then the right, as though she's looking at something, listening to someone, then she stumbles backward and into the wall, like she's been shoved. What the hell? Is she suffering loss of balance? Having some kind of fit? Is this why she's abnormally cranky? She starts mumbling into empty air, then stiffens, swings her face to mine and frowns. "I didn't mean to snap at you, Jack. I'm very busy, and needed to be reminded that your emotional state is delicate at this time, and that I should handle you with kid gloves."

"Oh ... kay." I stroke my beard. What the fuck is she talking about? If I didn't know better, I'd swear she'd just been reprimanded. Oh my God. Jenny? No way. I want to belt out a laugh, but say, "Can you hang out for a few minutes while I get dressed?"

"Sure, Jack, but why?"

I'm working through a definite mood change. "I'm taking you up on your generous offer to use the van." Waiting for her to object, I add, "I can handle it."

But she doesn't object. She flops on my bed and gestures to the bathroom door with a sweep of her arm.

I'm in and out like in a flash. Showered. Shaved. Hair combed and bound with a band at the nape of my neck. Clean blue t-shirt. Jeans ... not yet. Sweats are easier to jerk on and rip off. Rachel slips my Nikes onto my feet and I'm ready to roll.

She walks beside me as I wheel from my room, stops me in the hall and drops the van keys into my lap. "I'll escort you to the garage."

I settle my butt behind the wheel of the specially equipped van, which feels fantastic. I lean forward, practically embracing it. Rachel reaches through the open window and pats my arm. "I'm proud of your progress. You're going to be okay." During the past forty-five minutes, she's also done a one-eighty.

Driving into town is a memorable experience. Memorable,

but difficult. Passing the high school, bike shop, Evening Sun, works a number on me. Three places that played a big part in my life drive a stake through my chest. I'm tempted to do a drive-by of Jenny's place, followed by mine, but fight off temptation. Next, I struggle with the urge to double back, swing into the Evening Sun's parking lot, grab a beer, bullshit with the guys, but I don't want to interview for a job with alcohol on my breath.

Instead, I crank some tunes and head down 44, leaving the heart of town behind, slowing at the isolated one-story brick office building. I cut the ignition, reach behind the seat of the van, grab my portable chair, and when I hurl it out the door and onto the pavement, it springs open like a hooker mechanically spreading her legs. A gross assessment, I realize, but at the moment, having gross thoughts is the least of my worries. I've witnessed gross. Bloody gross. Hookers aren't even in the ballpark. I slide off the seat and plop my ass down like a pro.

The day is warm, spring-blossom-sweet, bone-easing sunny. I'm wearing my shades, feeling pretty decent as I wheel up the ramp, through the entrance and down the hall on my way to Fish and Game. My non-boss is Warden McCabe Guthrie. The man with two last names. I pause in the doorway as he finishes with a phone call, taking in the fragrance of fresh air and pine streaming through his open windows. There he is, head down, desk piled with papers, coffee cups, pushing his nameplate to the forefront of the mess, clearing a space for the phone he's balancing with one hand.

"What were your folks thinking when they tagged you?" I laugh as I roll through the door, wearing a huge smile, my sunglasses pulled up on top of my head. This is my first real laugh since Jenny's death. Maybe Rachel's been right all along. About everything. Getting out and into a job is the right move. "Looks like you need some clerical help."

"Jack," he calls out, genuinely pleased to see me. He lifts his lean mass, strides to my side and pats my shoulder while reaching for my hand. "It's great," he emphasizes, *great*, "to see you. How are you, buddy?" His green eyes burn into mine. McCabe has the kind of eyes that look right through your soul. He can't hide emotion, either. They're watering.

"I'm doing pretty good, McCabe. And yourself?" My eyes take in the room. The rosters and lists on the wall, names of rangers and delegated duties.

"Eh. Busy. The herds are flowing in for hunting licenses. Campers already set an acre or two on fire. Nothing the fire department and I can't handle." He scowls. "But these murders and animal attacks at the campground are a different story. They're leaving me shorthanded. I've got every free man on patrol." He crosses his arms. Rests his butt cheeks against his desk, striking his eager-to-swap stories stance. McCabe also likes to gossip. "Yeah, it's sure good to see you. What's been going on?"

We're shooting the breeze when I hear the shuffle of footsteps behind me. The first thing I notice, before a face, is the odor. Familiar? Not really. Odd, yes. Shit. I whip around to find him standing in the doorway, full mouth spreading in a grin.

"Jack Bailey, right?" He's on me in a heartbeat, sticking out a big hand. He might take my stunned look for confusion, or paramnesia. "Remember me?" The flash of his teeth makes me blink.

"Yep. Response number one: Jack Bailey in the flesh. And yes I remember you. I never forget a face or a handshake." And neither seem the same as the day Cage Galloway introduced himself to me not more than ten feet from Jenny's gravesite. His hand is ice cold today, he's growing a beard, and he's wearing ... a forest ranger uniform?

I should have expected this, still, a lump forms in my chest. This one feels like an iron ball with spikes. The corpse isn't cold, and his position has been filled. McCabe could have had the decency to tip me off ahead of time. Before I wheeled in and made a fool of myself. Of course, at the same time Cage walks through the door, like he's got radar. Or he's tailing me. Is he 5-0? No fucking way.

You could have spared me the embarrassing letdown, the glare I cut McCabe says. He fumbles around his desk busying himself, barely looking at me when he coughs and attempts an introduction. "Jack Bailey. This is Cage Galloway. He's covering the sectors you were ..."

"My territory," I blurt out. He hits me with a sheepish glance, then focuses on Galloway.

McCabe mumbles something inaudible, and shifts more stuff around his desk.

I'm evaluating Galloway's scent. The instant animosity between us. When we snarl at each other, McCabe's head jerks, his eyes widen, but he shakes it off, thinking it's employment-related, I'm sure. But what's going on between Galloway and me cuts far deeper.

Cage Galloway looks like he should be caged. He's tall and broad and even hairier than I am, because I'm clean shaven today. But I'm better looking. At least I've got that over him. His hands are like two iron skillets. I know this because one just came down on my shoulder.

"How are you, soldier?" He shoves his face inches from mine to stare deep into my eyes. His are piercing blue. Mesmerizing. His voice drops into a secretive tone. "Did you get that T-bone I sent you? It's my favorite cut." His grin is wide. "I've got plenty more at my place. I've been meaning to invite you over for a barbecue."

T-bone. "You sent me that steak?" My mind is whirling, trying to figure out this guy's deal. "Why would ...?"

Towering over me, he stops me with a raised hand. "Just a gesture ... man to man." He winks. "Know what I'm talking about?"

Wheel Wolf

"Actually ... no ..." But I'm going to find out. My gaze flows over him, stalling on his hands which are now at his sides, imagining the impact of his right hook. I look down at mine, lying kind of limp in my lap. My stomach drops.

Off my feet or not, I'm up for an ego-boosting animated cockfight. I grip the armrests of my chair, crane my neck, and shoot him one of my most sarcastic once-overs. I do believe he's smirking, like he's got the upper hand. Of course he has the upper hand. He has my job.

"I didn't expect you, Cage," McCabe says as he walks to the wall map and shoves pushpins into cork. "Are you feeling better?"

"Matter of fact ... " he drawls, and hooks his thumbs in the waistband of his pants, rocking back on his heels with pride. "Better than better." He swats his midsection like someone who has just devoured a good meal and topped it off with a scrumptious dessert. I'm waiting for him to belch.

Apparently McCabe feels he owes me some kind of explanation, so he angles his body, then his head, throwing his voice across the room, because he's now moved as far from us as humanly possible. He's edged into a corner, scribbling on a chalkboard. "Cage had emergency surgery the other night."

"Same-day laparoscopic surgery," Cage corrects with a nod and wink. Where he appeared Wall Street suave at the cemetery, he has now taken on a western flair. It's in his movements, the tone of his voice. His boots. They aren't standard dress, they're down-home cowboy. Cowhide brown with sharp brass tips. I'm wondering how he's going to cover the swampy sectors off 44 wearing those on his feet.

My stare leaves his boots to bob back and forth between him and McCabe, as McCabe's interest appears to have peaked at the mention of laparoscopic surgery.

"That so?" He runs his fingers through his neatly combed hair. "They removed my wife's gallbladder that way. She was off her feet for days. I thought for sure you'd be having conventional abdominal surgery, on sick leave at least a month, with those symptoms and all."

"It's amazing what modern medicine can do for a body," Cage replies to McCabe, but smirks at me as he fills me in. "Something got lodged in my esophagus. Caused me a lot of *heart*-burn before the docs removed it."

"What was wrong?" I'm trying to piece this together.

"I wolfed down dinner. Something got stuck — hurt like a bitch. Was a real surprise. I've always had an iron stomach." He punches his abs. "Everything's usually downwind in an hour ... but this meal was different. Yeah. She was a bitch."

"A bone got stuck?" Imagining his digestive system, I'm getting sicker by the minute.

"Nah. A piece of glass."

"God knows what you're swallowing when you eat out," McCabe chimes in. "Gotta watch these restaurants."

"And the hot waitresses," Galloway guffaws. He's grinning. I'm seething. "Especially those hot brunettes." He pats his pocket. "Got the culprit right here," he licks his lips, "my souvenir."

"I'll take the desk job we discussed on the phone, McCabe," I blurt out. My cheeks are burning. I've got to find out more about this douche, and what better way than pawing through personnel files on the office computer.

"Good to see you're out and about, Jack," Cage says with an air of familiarity. "When I saw you at the funeral, damn, guy, I didn't think you'd make it this far ... this fast."

"Did you know Jenny?"

"Vaguely. I guess you could say momentarily, as I only had the pleasure once."

"Ah huh." I can't seem to place him anywhere in our history. Or this town.

"So where'd you transfer from?"

"Buffalo."

"Ah huh. When?"

"I was passing through a while back. Caught wind of the opportunity. This being a friendly town and all, I decided to hang around. Environmental is right up my alley."

McCabe turns back to his pincushion wall map. From the color of the back of his neck, I believe he's flushing.

My leg twitches, then jumps. "Fucking shit!" I yell, mainly because my lower extremities are springing to life at the speed of light. It feels like my right leg is filled with boiling water, and I'm peeing acid down my left.

McCabe spins, his neck dotted crimson. He's pulling on his perfectly starched uniform collar. One thing he doesn't stand for is foul language. Another is sloppy dress. Galloway is also impeccably uniformed.

"What the ..." McCabe's voice picks up steam.

"Tourette's?" Galloway seems to think his reply is hilarious, but my non-boss must take him seriously, because his attitude takes a sudden shift.

"Sorry, McCabe," Galloway apologizes. "Maybe it's something I said that ticked it off." McCabe's angry face lightens. They're best friends and I'm shit on the side of the road.

"So, how do you two know each other?" McCabe asks.

"Met recently, but I could tell right away, we'll get on fine." Galloway's blue stare tries to cut through me. "You're here to pick up a desk job, are ya, guy?"

Galloway moves like liquid. Without warning, he's on top of me, cupping a hand at the side of his mouth, chuckling in my ear. "Wasn't ordinary glass. It was Swarovski crystal, dangling on a chain."

"You fucking douche bag." I shout at the door he's just whisper-closed on his way out of the office. McCabe whirls around glaring. I must look like shit, pale face, sagging jaw, because he softens.

"Tourettes?" He sits on the edge of his desk, leg dangling, arms crossed. "Jack, I understand your accident left you with certain ..." his eyes sweep the chair, then my head, "injuries, disabilities. But if you're going to work here, you have to try to control yourself. Is there a medication you can take for Tourettes?"

I'm reaching for my cell phone, ready to pound 9-1-1, to tell them I can point them to their killer. How will I get them to believe me? My hands are tied. I envision climbing out of this chair, tackling Galloway, pummeling his face until his brains leak out his ears. Bide your time, Jack. His days are numbered. You'll make sure of it.

Wheel Wolf

Next Stop The Rudeas

I can't believe I just came face to face with Jenny's killer and couldn't do anything about it. God dammit! I pound my fists on the chair, cursing my way down the ramp and into the parking lot. As I roll to the van I'm plotting how I'm gonna make Cage Galloway suffer, but I have to keep my head straight, plan for it so I don't fuck this one up. That piece of shit even came to her funeral. My stomach is tied in knots.

Wheeling down the ramp, I'm furious. I'm curious. I have to know more about Cage Galloway so I can nail his ass, but I also need to talk to Jenny's parents about Heinrich Rudéa. I check my watch. There's still plenty of afternoon left.

I hate to bother them at a time like this but, I'm going to call them. Better yet — pay them a visit. I aim the van for Old Sleepy Oak Road, which is beautifully picturesque, serene. Everything opposite of my mind.

Jenny's mom's car is parked in the driveway, so I figure she's home. The problem is, I can't walk up the steps to the porch. The new, freshly painted porch brings back old memories. Good and bad. The good part was holding Jenny in my arms each night before leaving. The bad, the night the place was vandalized. The night I lost my ...

I park the van, hoping she's heard me deliberately rev the engine before I cut it, and looks out a window. When she doesn't, I open and slam the door a few times. Still don't have her attention. She must be locked up tight with closed windows. Closed heart. Like mine.

I feel like a rude creep, but have no choice other than to start blowing the van's foghorn. In a minute or two, Mila Rudéa's face pops through the gap in the cautiously opened door, and when I stick my head out of the window, she comes onto the porch. Wrapped in a sweater, wearing baggy trousers, I can't pinpoint whether or not she's actually lost weight, but something tells me she's thinner. Certainly, worn. Battered. Suffering heartbreak. I know the symptoms pretty well myself. Lately, I can count my ribs.

"Sorry," I call to her. "Can't navigate the steps."

Curiosity replaces caution as she heads down the driveway.

"Sorry to beep," I repeat, grinning sheepishly. "My mobility is limited these days." I falter.

She doesn't reply but comes around to my side of the van, pausing about a foot away.

"Hi Jack. How are you doing?" She's lifeless. A walking, talking corpse.

"Eh, handling. How are you and Georges doing?" I have a good idea, but politely ask.

Riding with the open window has loosened my hair, ripped the elastic band out and deposited it somewhere between McCabe's office and here. She frowns. Reaches in and pushes strands from eyes. Is this where Jenny got it from? Nah. Jenny didn't care what I looked like. She just loved to touch me. In any way. Reason or not, her hands were always part of me.

"I have to be honest." When Mila's frown exaggerates, I

notice every line creasing her face cuts deeper. The circles beneath her eyes are like sooty thumbprints. "It isn't easy. We're putting the house up for sale."

"Too many memories, huh?" I shake my head, knowingly.

She nods, eyes glistening. Jenny will never be forgotten. If I live a thousand years, as many miles away, her face, her voice, her essence, will be fresh in my mind. "Me too, Mila." I touch her hand that's resting on the inch of window jutting from the door channel. "I'm dumping everything. House. Land. Maybe donate it as a preserve." I blow out a frustrated breath in another direction.

Fingertips of both hands clipped to the slice of window, she looks like a kid gripping the side of a candy case. But the look on Mila's face couldn't strike a joyful note if someone held a gun to her head. I know this because ... well, misery is a sign of our grief. That's all we share in common now. "Will you be staying in Angel's Bend or leaving, Jack?"

"Getting as far away from this place as possible." I feel like a traitor, leaving Jenny's remains behind, but with luck, her spirit will always be with me. Maybe someday she'll hear my whisper.

"Mila, I don't know exactly how to ask ..."

"You can ask me anything, Jack." She pats my hand. "Look at what we've been through together."

"Your bloodline is Romanian, right?" An odd look passes over her face when the question is aired.

"Your heritage." The tone of my voice apologizes for my bluntness.

"I understand." She nods. "And Georges is French."

"Thought so." I scratch my head.

"What's wrong?"

"What isn't?" I give her a crooked piece of smile. My eyes pleading for her to be Jenny. "Do you know a Heinrich Rudéa?"

She squints, as though closing her eyes will nudge her memory.

"A writer?" I prompt. "Among other things."

"I don't ..." Her hazel eyes are dull. "Rudéa yes, but I don't recall the first name as being anyone in Georges' ancestry. Why do you ask?"

"I read an article he wrote seventy-five years ago ... and the name and all ... it's nothing. Just figured I'd inquire. And it gave me an excuse to come visit you." My lips pull into a tight smile.

"You don't need an excuse. You're still part of the family."

"Mila ... the cross Jenny gave me has a history?"

A genuine chuckle escapes her lips, so much like Jenny's. "Legends grow with time. I have no idea ... it could have come from a jewelry store down the road, for all I know." She smiles with memory. "Jenny was into genealogy. She liked to think the cross was handed down from royalty, with mystical powers. She was a dreamer."

"She was a lot of things." I draw a breath and hold it, otherwise a sob will ambush my poker face.

"I know." Her chuckle is like soft bells. We're loosening up. Talking is good. "She was tracking our lineage on one of those Internet websites."

"So, what's the story with the cross, though? Is there a legend? Was it worn for protection?" I'm starting to wonder if Jenny had premonitions, then rethink the way I phrased the question, and cringe.

Mila catches on and giggles, then sobers. "She loved you deeply, and since the cross was said to have certain powers." She dabs at a tear. "You know how legends can stretch with the years, if there's truth at all. Does it have magical powers? I don't know." She shakes her head. "When Jenny decided she wanted to give it to you, she asked if it was okay with me, as it did belong to someone in the family, somewhere along the line. She wanted you to have it before you started working as a ranger. The thought of you being miles deep in the forest and alone concerned her."

Something inside my chest starts swelling, fluttering again. Gas, or my heart. Who knows. "It makes sense now." I nod.

She tilts her head so far, it's almost sideways. "What makes sense?"

"Jenny is the most thoughtful, kindest ..." I feel worse. Knowing Jenny wanted to take care of me, wear the cross, and now I can't touch it because it burns my skin. I feel like shit.

"You still speak of her as if she's here." She lifts a brow.

"She is." I tap the void in my chest posing as a heart.

"Are you making progress?" Her eyes move from my chest to my face. "Emotionally and physically?" Her sigh shudders. I know she's holding back a sob. "Both, I hope ..."

"I think so, Mila. Time will tell."

"It will never heal." She's adamant.

"I know." We're starting to cross the line between a casual visit and grief counseling. I'm feeling quite uncomfortable.

"Whoever would have thought such a thing could happen, Jack?" Insurmountable pain fills her eyes. The woman is nothing but a shell of the emotional Mila I used to know. "And the fact that they never found the killer makes it worse. If there's any way to say something could make it worse."

"I know, Mila. It's a nightmare. Surreal. Almost impossible to live with."

She looks at me almost sideways through the window again. "Have you heard anything about the investigation?"

My jaw tightens. I huff out air. Tap the steering wheel, hoping my voice doesn't give me away, disclose the fact that I was a suspect. Does Jenny's mother have any idea of this? "No news. And as they say ... scratch that. Either way it wouldn't be good news. Nothing is good. Bodies piling up. No leads. I don't know." I run a hand over my face, practically dragging my head down with guilt. "What about the crystal Jenny wore? Was it blessed or anything?"

"It was old. I don't know. Jenny believed in it ... in things. The cross and crystal being two of them."

My stomach churns just thinking where the crystal ended up. It has to have had powers. It led me to the killer. I wonder if Jenny knows. I'm going to destroy that piece of shit.

She squeezes my shoulder. "I have to get dinner into the oven. Take care of yourself, Jack." For a minute I see Jenny, in Mila's face, saying: Take care of you, for me.

Tears stream from my eyes, but they're caught by the furry scruff that is already carpeting my cheeks. In my gut, I doubt I'll be seeing Mila again. I want to hop out of the van, put my arms around her, comfort her. But all I can do is reach out, sling an arm around her neck, pull her face through the window, kiss her cheek, and mutter, "Goodbye."

I don't watch her walk back into the house. Swatting at tears, I start the engine and coast out of the driveway, pausing at the side of the road for a few minutes before I turn my head, see that she's gone, and the door is closed.

I'm not quite ready to return to Shadow Lane. Events of the past few days have been whirling through my head, spurring the idea I'm toying with. Seeing Mila, pulling up Jenny's driveway, is reinforcing the idea.

Wheel Wolf

Yamaha

I cruise into town to make a quick stop at the bank. As I guide the van into the lot, I spot the yellow town truck pulling up to the curb in front of Madison's deli. Drake and Steve hop out, wearing jeans and tees. They toss their hardhats into the truck, like they're unloading bags of trash. Joking and laughing, they disappear through a circle of guys hanging out on the sidewalk.

It's lunchtime. Life is moving along. On my way into the bank, I run into my teller friend, Shane. He's happy to see me. We shoot the breeze while he completes my transaction. He almost makes me feel like old times. Occupy your mind, Rachel says. I plan on occupying more than my mind.

Banking done, I'm wheeling down the ramp with a pocketful of cash when I notice Steve and Drake exiting Madison's, lunch bags in hand. I never planned on a meet-up, but they spot me right away and jog across the street.

"Jack! What's up? How are you, bro?" Drake's voice booms.

Steve is apologetic. "Sorry we haven't stopped by to see you, Jack. We've been working overtime ..."

"And riding." I grin and hold up my fist for a bump. "Don't

worry about it. No need to make excuses. I know how busy life gets." I forgot actually.

My eyes drop to their worn work boots, and spring right back up again. They're both cocking their heads. From the angle I'm at, it looks comical.

"Where are you off to?" Their brows level. I'm wearing my shades, but still shield my eyes as I lift my face, feeling like I'm staring up at two giant redwoods.

I hitch my head. "Right over there ... the Yamaha dealer." I grin.

They almost lose their eyeballs, swipe a hand over their hair. They look like two puppets, except Drake's faux hawk is not styled today. His hair is flat, exaggerating his funky razor cut.

"You buying a bike?" Steve sounds as if his breath was just knocked out of his throat.

"Holy shitballs, dude. Seriously?" Drake's jaw drops.

"You getting your legs back?" Steve, the more compassionate of the two, asks with caution.

"Yeah. I've been getting some sensation back. I have a gut it won't be long now." I check my watch. Time is slipping by quickly. I'm ready for Rachel to send out a search and rescue team. "Listen. I'd like to hang and bullshit, but I gotta haul ass. It was great running into you." My head rocks.

"I'll give you a call," Steve says, throwing up an arm. "Maybe we'll meet up."

"See you soon, Jack." Drake's head bobs. "Yeah, let's meet up. Maybe on the road ... Who knows, right?" His head continues to bob enthusiastically, but his eyes wander.

"Back on the road together. That's cool, Jack. Can't wait." They're talking simultaneously. Both with the same doubtful tone, stiffening lips.

"Yeah, who knows." I slap a leg and the muscle responds. "See ya."

Wheel Wolf

As I drive across the road, I'm thinking ahead. How the fuck am I gonna track Cage Galloway down. Destroy him like he did Jenny, our lives. There's a knife in my gut, a voice inside my head screaming: He's a maniac. The murderer the cops have been looking for. Turn him in? Sure. Get laughed out of town. That's not the way I plan on leaving Angel's Bend. With the roar of an engine, yes. In a cloud of smoke and dust, for sure. Definitely not laughter.

As I shop for the most killer Yamaha, the salesman keeps giving me a dumb look, finally offering in a weak voice, "We have three wheelers that operate just as smooth and efficiently as ..."

I smirk. "It's for a friend."

"A good one I imagine." Cash deal. Big commission. He's smiling like a carved pumpkin.

"Deliver it to One Bailey Way."

"Bailey?"

"Yep. Like my name." After I throw down an overstuffed bank envelope, I reach into my other pocket. "It's a long driveway, wooded, easy to miss. Here's the key to the garage behind the house. Lock my bike up and leave the key under the mat on the front porch."

Hard Cold Silver Cross

*R*achel beats the crap out of me, double time, because I missed my noon session. I shower, then lie in bed staring at the ceiling. I'm thinking about Jenny, of course, but Galloway's face keeps haunting me.

I go in and out of restless sleep, seeing Jenny's face clear as day. Hearing her voice. Touching her skin. Nothing new, because it happens every night. Sometimes during the day her voice sneaks into my head. I have a feeling she's trying to tell me something. It's crazy. I have to blow it off or I'll take Rachel up on her offer for me to attend one of her spiritual meetings. I never considered myself one for the occult, but I'm coming close.

Sunshine streaming through the window wakes me. My eyes crack open and I wince. Someone neglected to pull the blinds down ... Rachel must have been in my room last night, bolting my window shut. I feel something on my chest. A weight. I bring up a hand and freeze, because I'm feeling hard, cold, silver. The same silver that burned my fingers when Donnie returned Jenny's cross to me. I pull my hand away and suck in a breath. *What the shit?* Using only the tips of two fingers, I lift the heavy braided chain that's hanging around my neck, scrambling to remember. Did I put this on last night? Positively not.

I'm stretching my arm, dangling the cross over my nose, while trying figure out: *How the hell did this get here?* Last I looked, it was on the table, exactly where Donnie left it. Where I sit and stare at it, but never touch it. Stranger things have been happening, I guess, which brings me to ... Rachel? But why? I let the cross fall back onto my chest, roll myself into my chair, wheel into the bathroom, and pull myself up to the mirror.

I give the silver a quick tap with one finger, then quickly pull my hand away. I'm shocked because it doesn't burn or sting, and there's no charred imprint on my chest. Without another thought, I bring the cross to my lips for a kiss. The metal is smooth and cool. "Oh God, Jenny. I miss you so much, baby." Tears roll down my cheeks.

Wearing the cross, I shower and dress. I'm never removing my silver charm.

I'm sitting in my chair, staring out the window, when Rachel eventually pops her head through the door, asking, "Ready for your workout?"

"Yeah. Sure. Rachel ... hold up. Come on in for a minute."

She's yawning when she enters the room, squinting when her eyes wash over me. But when her languid gaze hits the cross lying on my chest, her eyes widen. Her mouth twitches, then folds. "You're wearing ..."

I cut her off and narrow my eyes, holding my breath for the right answer. "You slip this on me last night?"

"Nope." She shakes her head, lifts her chin, then beams with reverence.

I let my breath flow. "You're sure?"

"Of course I'm sure," she snips. "You didn't ...?"

"No."

For a moment, we stare in silence.

January Valentine

Although I'm wearing the cross, I'm hesitant to wrap my fingers around it for too long. I have a fear that I'm dreaming, and the cross will heat, or I'll wake up and it will be gone.

Paranoia rushes from my throat. "Did you lock my window last night? Leave the blinds up?"

"No, I didn't." Rachel is radiant, as if she's just witnessed a miracle. "Jack, come with me to a meeting. There are quite of few of us ... and a variety. No matter who you are, no one's an outsider. No one asks questions. We share our gifts. There's always something to learn, someone to teach ..."

Wheel Wolf

Ready To Walk Outta Here

I lie in bed and pray. Beg. Please help me get out of this mess. I must be sleeping, dreaming, in heaven? Jenny is standing in front of me, clear as day. She's not transparent: She's solid. She's whispering, smiling, brushing my lips with hers. Her violet eyes are flashing with love. Jenny ... When I wake up I'm standing, my arms wrapped around her.

Wait ... I'm hugging myself? But she was here. I know she was. Holy Fuck, I'm standing. The minute I realize this, my legs crumble and I crash to the floor. I'm crying. Crying because I can't be with Jenny. Crying because I thought I could walk again and I can't. A phenomenon? Can the disabled walk in their sleep and not when they're conscious? Am I conscious? Or is this another dream ... I'm not dead, because I'm breathing. Shallow, yes, but my chest is rising and falling. Shuddering.

I'm still lying here when Rachel bursts in with a flighty attitude. She scrunches her mouth and shakes her head. "I'm starting to think you like the floor better than your bed, Mr. Bailey."

"What, are you and Donnie having problems?" I haven't heard from him since the funeral. Misery loves company. I have to know. "Is that why you're back to bitchy again?"

Rachel is smug. She pushes up her sleeves and heads for my chair. "Not at all, and I'm not bitchy. I'm busy. Donnie and I have been seeing a lot of each other. Things are progressing beautifully. As a matter of fact ..."

With an elbow on the floor, my head is resting on my palm. I'm staring up at her at a narrow angle. "Rachel, you don't have to explain. I was fucking with you." I cut in, because she's starting to go off on me, and I have more important things to say.

She crouches beside me, head lowering, tips of hair reaching the floor. Her eyes are flashing. "You're fucking with me? What else is new ..."

I'm staring at her knees. Her big hands are gripping me under the armpits. "We've got work to do. Get up."

"Rachel ... wait. I think my legs worked, only for a minute though. I never mentioned it to you, but you know that broken lamp?"

She drops down beside me. Her nose is almost pressed to mine. "The last thing I'm ever going to clean up for you? You mean *that* lamp?"

"Yeah." I nod. "My leg kicked the table and knocked it off. I've been feeling things, sensations ... tingling, thumping, the heat of the Chromebook on my lap." My voice starts pitching. "After the accident, I didn't feel anything. But lately I feel numbness, and my legs prickle like when you're coming back from sitting on them and you have pins and needles. Can I be ..."

"Paresthesia? Why didn't you tell me?" Her eyes bulge, then she squeezes my shoulders.

"I didn't want to jinx myself." I shrug my brows, because my one shoulder is bracing me, and Rachel is controlling the other.

"Understandable," she mumbles, then jerks away, pounding the keypad on the cell she just whipped out of her pocket. "Doctor Sloan, this is Rachel Huntress, Jack Bailey's physical therapist."

As she speaks, she keeps patting my head. "I think you should pay him a visit."

Great. Sloan's going to start bugging me again about testing. Before I can complain, Rachel's got me up and in a chair, and she's wheeling me down the corridor to the elevator. To the basement housing X-Ray, MRI, and LAB. All the stuff I shy away from these days.

We're greeted by a tech who rolls me onto a table, and slides me into the MRI tunnel. All the while the machine is clanking, my eyes are closed. I'm doing my damndest to slip back into the dream that brought me out of bed, onto my feet, into Jenny's arms.

I lose track of time and place, until the guy slides me out and helps me off the table. "You're finished, Jack."

Rachel scoots from behind the glass partition and into the room where I sit, feeling disoriented. Things are happening so fast, my mind is having a hard time keeping up. "Dr. Sloan needs the results, stat," she orders the young guy around much like she does me.

"Give me ten. I'll burn a CD and you can hand it to him yourself." He winks and nods.

So for the next ten minutes, Rachel and I sit in the lounge, staring at each other over cups of coffee she carries back from a dispensing machine. We're waiting for the CD. Waiting for Dr. Sloan. She's texting Donnie, while I sweat it out.

"I'm glad we had this opportunity to meet again," Sloan belts out before he's even entered the lounge. He stands in the doorway, slipping into a lab coat. "I've been meaning to get in touch with you."

Here comes the nagging. I need your DNA, Jack. Go fuck yourself, Sloan.

He shrugs his way toward us. Rachel hands him the CD, and before he says another word, he disappears into the office marked: MRI.

Nothing like leaving me hanging, on edge, praying I slip through this without any hitches. Rachel is quiet as well. I have a feeling she's afraid to get my hopes up. She's no longer texting. Maybe she's even afraid to think.

A few minutes later, Dr. Sloan strolls out of MRI. He shocks me by shaking my hand and saying, "I've wanted to apologize." He pulls a chair up beside me, so I'm trapped between my doctor and my therapist. "Your recovery is extraordinary. I want to applaud you for your strength of character as well as physical endurance. You've taken some blows, Jack, and handled it all with dignity."

That's news to me, doc, I'm thinking, but of course would never admit, especially to the man who treated me like a suspicious specimen. He has no idea of how close he came to discovering who I am. What I am. And I plan on keeping him clueless.

"I've never seen anything like this before. Can I submit your files for inclusion in a medical journal? It will certainly help others."

I shrug. "If you want to…" Then I squint. "What's so special about me?"

He pulls his chair out so that he's facing both of us. And as he begins to explain in medical terms, Rachel beams. Then he translates for me.

"The inoperable disk that had been compressing the nerves has snapped back into place." His face is blank. So is my brain until I realize. Snapped? Holy shit. I felt a snap, assumed it was inside my head, or my dream. It never dawned on me it could be my back realigning. Is it a result of my transitioning? Or did Jenny squeeze me back into shape. She's an angel. It's a miracle.

"I don't know what you've done to him, Rachel." She's smug, devouring the credit for my miraculous recovery. Who gives a shit? From what Sloan is saying, I'm going to be walking out of here soon. I can't believe it. I'm about to burst into tears. "Whatever it was you've done to Jack has moved that disk, naturally." He shakes his head in wonderment.

At this point, I don't really need specifics. I just want to know ... when. "How much longer until I can walk, Dr. Sloan?"

He lifts both brows. "From what I can see, it's just a matter of regaining strength in your muscles. Could be several weeks, or one. We'll add TENS to your sessions." He focuses on Rachel. "I'll leave detailed orders."

"Perfect." She shoots him a professional nod.

This is all so sudden, it's difficult to comprehend. I'm speechless, taking it all in. Sloan doesn't mention anything further about the tests he had wanted, other than to offer another off the cuff apology. "Sometimes doctors chase rainbows, and the mysteries we're trying to solve turn out to be Mother Nature stepping out of the shadows. There's something wild running around our forests. It's out of the hands of the medical community, and up to Fish and Game and State Police." He shakes his head, then turns to Rachel, as though deciding to include her in the conversation again.

He looks from me to Rachel as he explains, but I'm his primary focus. "The original tissue samples I took from the wound on your chest must have been contaminated. Same as with the Walton cow samples. Inconclusive." His mouth is drawn, but he appears satisfied with his explanation. So am I, and I'm completely lost, wondering why he's even bringing it up. It's dead and buried. I'm going to walk again. That's all that matters.

"These things happen, so we normally collect fresh DNA, run more labs." He shrugs. "But that's neither here nor there anymore. The human victims," he shakes his head, lifts himself off the chair, and shoves a hand into the pocket of his jacket, "they were killed by an animal. They have canine DNA all over them. Crazy though," he rubs the back of his neck, "I'm not sure

I've ever seen bite marks like those, or a species like that around here before."

Thank goodness Rachel breaks into the conversation, because I'm about ready to keel over with a coronary. "Maybe whatever it is will find its way out the same as it walked in," she says, then shoots me a side glance.

Sloan leans in and pats my thigh. "Keep up the good work. I'll check you in a few days."

On his way through the doorway, he stops and turns. "Sometimes there just aren't any answers, Jack. We just have to take our licks and chalk it up to experience."

I know I must appear confused, because I am.

Wheel Wolf

Leaps And Bounds

I'm gaining strength by leaps and bounds, pardon the pun. Within a week, my legs are strong enough to lose the wheelchair. In two, my sessions are about to end. I'm moving back to the house, seeing Rachel for a couple of outpatient visits, or as needed.

Rachel insists I have to concentrate on healing my psyche, by gathering my thoughts. The only thing I plan on gathering right now is my bike, with my legs. What else is there to gather? I'll never get over losing Jenny, which is a good indicator that my emotional state will remain as it is today, the day of my discharge from Shadow Lane Rehab.

Checking out is a hell of a lot different from checking in. Standing in the glass enclosed solarium, I let my mind drift, reminisce, then quickly pull back to the present. Christ, so much has happened I could fill a thousand page book with love, stress, and horror.

Rachel and I exchange a tearful farewell, during which time I promise to keep in touch. "If you miss the two visits I've scheduled for you next week, Jack, I'm coming gunning for you ... in the van. Just remember that." On top of tearing up, she actually winks. The girl is human, after all.

"The van," I snort. "I just might miss that old relic ... and you, too, Rachel." I shrug my brows and grin, then throw my arms around her. "Thank you for everything."

With my backpack slung over my shoulder, my helmet under my arm, I head for the door, turning only once to look back. Rachel waves. I salute. We're both grinning like fools. There's something in her eyes though. I can tell she's gonna miss me. I have to admit, something will be missing from *my* life as well.

As requested, Drake dropped my bike off last night, and it's sitting in the visitor lot, right here in front of me, waiting for my ass to hit the seat. This is the first chance I get to check out my new ride. It's sleek and looks rough. Like me. I've put on about ten pounds of muscle, thanks to Rachel. But it's not just about looks. The bike, anyway. It's comfort. Ride. Power.

I circle the impressive machine, inspecting. Straddle the seat. "Yeah," I whisper in a smooth voice I'd use with a woman. Correction: not just any woman. Jenny.

When the grips fill my hands, something washes over me. Something that tries to alter my outlook. Hope? No. Excitement? Not really. Freedom. Yeah, that's the word. I'm free. And I'm alive. I can walk. I have my life back. My independence. Then my gut wrenches, because I don't have Jenny. If she was sitting behind me, my world would be perfect.

My brain starts reminding me how to ride. Not to fear. Don't worry, brain. My legs are back and nothing, no one, is going to take them away again.

The thought of roaming silent rooms makes me feel desperate . I'm not ready for wall climbing at home. I need to unwind. Bolster my courage with a few drinks.

After lighting up the bike, my first thought, my first stop, is the Evening Sun. Why am I torturing myself? God knows. When

Wheel Wolf

I walk through the door, my temporary high dissipates. With one hard look, I take in every inch of the place, from every angle: the scattering of tables, the dart board on the far wall, the pool table set beside the L shaped bar.

My stomach sinks. George Rudéa isn't standing behind the bar. Smiling. Cracking jokes. Doing shots with patrons. Some guy with bushy gray hair, a towel slung over a shoulder, is wiping the nicked oak surface with one hand, dipping glasses in a sudsy tub with the other.

The interior hasn't changed, but I don't notice any familiar faces. Have I been gone that long? Heads turn in my direction for a momentary once-over, then the four guys and two women on barstools return to tipping their glasses and chatting.

I'm ignored, which I'm thankful for. I'd be bad company for any normal person. Bad company, period. I don't take a seat, just make my way to the deserted end of the bar and order a shot of tequila, which I immediately pour down my throat. "Keep em coming," I tell the gray haired guy , pushing the empty glass toward him. "So, you're the new owner?" I ask, after downing a second.

He shakes his head. "Nope. She is." He hitches his head to a middle aged blonde leaning against the office doorway, observing. "That's Maggie."

"I've never seen you around," I say, "or Maggie." I shoot her a respectful nod , then lift both brows at him.

There's a knot in the pit of my stomach. Of course I should have expected this. I knew Jenny's folks were selling the house and leaving town. Of course that included transferring ownership of the Evening Sun. Did I not expect to feel so terminal?

Jenny's parents were the last shred of reality I could hold onto, the fantasy glue holding me and Jenny together. Now that the cord's been cut by cruelty, I'm falling flat on my face. And there's not a damn thing I can do about it but drink myself into a stupor. Only it's not working. My brain is in overdrive. My nerves are shot. My head is spinning, but not from booze.

I blow out a breath and flush another tequila down my throat, which is trying to close. So I close my eyes instead. Tormenting myself even more by dwelling on the days and nights I spent here with Jenny and her folks.

The bartender's voice pulls me back into misery. "My name's Hank. Just started working here." He sticks out a hand. "You a regular?"

"Was." My head bobs a few times, but my face is like stone.

He nods. Although sharing your problems in a bar can be therapeutic, my attitude must tip this guy off that I'm not in the mood for personal, or friendly, because he lines up five more shot glasses, fills them to the brim, and moseys down to the other end of the bar where people communicate and laugh. Look alive.

Drinking myself into oblivion isn't working. I shake my head and smirk. I don't know why I've bothered to consume all this tequila. Alcohol has no effect on me anymore. I throw a fifty on the bar, then my gaze drifts around the room. For the last time. This I know because things have changed. I've changed. And Jenny won't come walking through the doorway the blonde's just vacated on her way over to where I'm standing. I shoot her a nod, lift a halfhearted wave to Hank, and leave before curious-looking Maggie reaches my side.

At least I've got my bike. Crazy how one can form an instant bond with something soulless, like a machine. But oh, such a beautiful machine she is. With the sleeve of my shirt, I brush off specks of road dust, mount my new baby, and sit in the parking lot, watching empty spaces fill up with cars. Bikes. None like mine though.

"Smells like rain," I mumble as I press the starter. "Time to roll. You think? Yeah, I do. Let's hit the road, Jack. You've got a mission to complete."

Wheel Wolf

I cruise out of town, grateful for the way the bike handles. Then I light her up, testing the powerful engine. She's just what I need to track down a beast.

Destination: Hosner Lake. Not just for the hell of it. I have a debt to settle with Cage Galloway. When I find him, I'm gonna rip his heart out.

Dusk is falling and a pale moon is on the rise. As I breeze down the highway, along with wind I draw in dampness. I turn down a side road, eager to scout the trails, revisit the site of our first encounter.

Prepared to become bait, I take a leisurely ride through back roads, hang beside the lake, move with diligence, picking the most isolated locations to pause. But the bastard doesn't show. I'm tempted to canvass every street in Angel's Bend to sniff him out. I've waited a long time for this day to arrive and my adrenaline is pumping. Where does Galloway live? I'm clueless. Where would a werewolf hide out? I rack my brain. My gut churns with disappointment. But, I'll plot like a human. Trap him like an animal.

The moon isn't red and full, like it was that first night. A voice inside my head tells me I'm wasting my time, to head straight home. Or is it the wind brushing past my ears? Planting thoughts in my mind.

Body Parts

After tucking my bike into the garage, I circle the house. Looks fine to me. But still I'm uneasy. Since the accident, I have a habit of looking over my shoulder, which is what I do as I slip the key into the lock and shove the front door open. Inside the foyer, I drop my gear. Peer down the hallway into the dining room. The rec room on the other side. The place is just as I left it. But it's cold. Filled with furniture, but emptier than I remember.

I force myself into the living room. Every place I stand, everything I see, reminds me of Jenny: her size six hiking boots are planted in a corner, the soles still caked with dirt from our last outing. A pair of designer sunglasses I bought her rest on the mantle of the fireplace that is loaded with half burned wood. I sniff the air, scratch my head. I don't remember the last time I lit a fire in here . Wait. Yes I do. On a passion filled evening last winter, when Jenny slept over. On the sofa, right over there, wrapped in my arms.

My neck snaps my head around for a different view, because I'm overwhelmed with memories. I glance at a plush easy chair. Jenny's red scarf dangles over the back. Damn it to hell! I can't escape it . Not that I'd ever want to escape Jenny, but Christ, I can't take much more.

I stare at the framed photo on an end table, at the snapshot of Jenny and me standing beside my bike. Arms wound around each other. Smiling. Laughing actually. I remember laughing while she struggled to take the selfie, because I was tickle-torturing her. Because she was so damn huggable. So damn cute.

The house smells like Jenny. Sweet and bakery scented. I run my hands through my hair, my fingers pulling so hard I'm sure the coarse strands will detach from my scalp. "Bald werewolf." I let out a loud, sarcastic laugh, then tears flood my eyes.

"Jenny," I sob, falling into the chair, pulling her scarf over my face, sucking her scent in so deeply, the fabric almost throttles me. Head in hands, scarf pressed to lips, I let my mind drift. Pretend Jenny is in the kitchen, baking cookies. I can see her. I can feel her. I can almost hear her moving around, humming the way she did when she was happy. Jenny was always happy.

I force myself to stop breathing. If Jenny can't breathe, then I won't either. But the involuntary reaction of my body provides my lungs with a gulp of air, and I believe I do smell cookies. Glimpse Jenny standing in the doorway, arms wide open, beckoning me. Mouthing kisses I still taste. Again and again I blink, because although I feel I could reach out and touch her, there's no way Jenny can be here.

My head falls against the back of the chair, rolling from side to side. I lift it, drop it. Each time with more force, until I'm literally banging my head against the chair back. "Jenny, I'm losing my mind." Or what's left of it.

A sugary breeze crosses my face. I swear it ruffles my hair, strokes my head like loving fingertips. I bolt upright, eyes searching the room. "Jenny? Baby, if you're here, please ... I need you. Touch me, Jen. Even with one little finger."

My shoulders slump and my body shudders . "It's so freaking cold in here," I grumble , rising from the chair to check   the windows. None are open, still, the breeze is persistent ... aromatic.

Arms crossing chest, I shuffle around the house aimlessly, until I'm faced with a decision. So I contemplate.

One: Get the hell out of here.

Two: Call Rachel. Maybe get a massage.

Three: Grow a pair and face your fate .

I pick door number three, and force myself to kick off my boots , drop my arms to my sides, and move my feet in the direction of the kitchen.

A pile of mail sits on the counter, where Drake has left it. Idly, I sort through envelopes and flyers, not comprehending, because I'm totally disinterested in what the postman has delivered. My mind wanders.

Mental note to Jack: Ask Drake and Steve if they've been squatting here, using the fireplace. The kitchen. The refrigerator. It's not that the house looks lived in, it's just a weird feeling I have.

When I open the refrigerator I'm hit with a rank odor. "Christ," I mumble, backing away. "Smells like something died in here."

The milk is sour. Eggs are rotten. Produce is fermenting mush. Nope, Drake and Steve couldn't have been squatting here. T hey'd have eaten everything in sight. Plus, the beer is still sitting on the same shelf I placed it on.

Grabbing a tall trash bag from a cabinet, I make a clean sweep of the contents of the fridge and by the time I'm finished, night has fallen. I carry the bag out the back door and drag it to the large receptacle behind the house.

The first thing I do is scope out the area, because I have a strange sensation I'm not alone. The hair on the back of my neck bristles. I feel a sudden urge to pee, and do so, all around the garbage can. Then I lift the lid and drop the bag inside.

Wheel Wolf

I stare up at the sky, hoping to see Jenny floating above my head. With beautiful snow white wings . "Asshole. Leave the poor girl alone for Christsake. Let her rest in peace."

The sky is black and low, and a few stars sparkle. Clouds part for the moon, but I can barely see five feet ahead of me. The yard is congested with darkness and trees and gathering mist. If it were October thirty-first, it would be a perfect night for Halloween. "Creepy. What are *you* talking about, Jack? *You're* creepy."

The cadence of crickets and buzzing insects invade my eardrums. They pain. Reverberate. The damn crickets zap every raw nerve in my body with their annoying screech. A few feet away, the sharp snap of a branch replaces the bugs.

My mind shifts from longing thoughts of Jenny's house, and the fact that this is the time of night I'd usually hop on my bike and barge in for dinner. For Jenny. Tonight I'm taking out the garbage instead.

Another snap. This time it sounds like twigs, then the distinct crunch of fallen leaves. Raspy breathing, like phlegm caught in a throat. Something is out there, disturbing the grounds , stirring the air. Increasing my heart rate.

"Branches scraping in the breeze, dumbass." I lick a finger and hold it high, but the only breeze is the one my breath is creating , and it's growing heavier than the air my nostrils are examining.

Something darts across the yard . I freeze on the spot, rooted like the trunks of trees surrounding the house, straining to see through inky darkness. Galloway?

"Here we go again," I mumble, struggling to reason. Deer? No. Too tall. Moving on two legs. Now it's crouching. My mind spins out an instant replay of the night at Hosner Lake.

For a moment I hold my breath, slow the beat of my heart so I can halt the pulse in my eyes, accurately track the movements with precision. Determine whether or not this bulky mass is humpbacked.

Or maybe it's just a shadow. My mind playing tricks. Maybe it's Galloway.

Soundless, I cock an ear and sniff harder. The odor I inhale is definitely animal, mixing with stagnant air. And it's familiar. I grit my teeth, restraining a growl and the urge to rush him.

I have the figure in my sights, and it's stationary , targeting me. I sense I'm holding its interest. "Do this right, Jack. Don't spook him."

The insects stop chirping, clearing my ears for the sound of a greedy swallow, followed by drip ... drip ... saliva dripping from jowls.

Holy fuck. Did he follow me home from the lake? Or was he out here ... waiting for me ... while I was out there hunting him. Has he been inside my house? Did he light a fire? My skin coats with goose bumps. Then I reason: If he wanted me dead, he would've attacked. The bastard is fucking with me.

"Play his game, Jack," the night wind sighs. "Outsmart him at his own game."

I'm poised, ready to transition, when I hear a scream echo through the forest. Chilling. Hair raising. My skin prickles: transition number one. I'm amped with adrenaline, my senses in high gear. My eyes have adjusted to darkness. My nose is at peak performance, alerting that I'm standing beside a pile of dried shit. Odorless to humans. Fragrant to wolf.

"Galloway is sending you a message, Jack. You're a pile of shit." I'm not sure what he's got planned, but I know he's trying to confuse me. Taunt me. If he's trying to piss me off, he's doing a fucktabulous job.

The cautious steps I take bring me closer. Ideal timing. I launch myself at the mass I'm hoping is Galloway, but the damn thing sinks to the ground and evaporates before my eyes. What the fuck?

A flashlight isn't necessary: my eyes illuminate the surroundings for miles: the second sign of transition. I can see through the trees, through the darkness, through the mist which is so thick, so pungent, I can taste it: fear, aggression, hatred. Murder.

Another scream hits my ears, this time, coming from somewhere behind me. So I hurl myself in the direction of what is now a whimper, followed by the baying of a wolf.

Running at top speed, I'm chasing down pure evil. About to encounter the same thing I ran into at Hosner Lake. The alley on Foster Road. But I wasn't half the wolf that I am now.

I'm hauling ass until the forest opens into what might be considered a pleasant meadow in daylight. In moonlight, it's a field of futility. A war zone. Because there's nothing in sight but ghostly weeds that I'm wading through, that are scratching my face as I stalk.

From the corner of my eye, something billows. Flutters gracefully, like a winged creature. This isn't an animal. What I'm viewing takes the shape of a woman. Slender. I can't judge the height, because the vacillating apparition is floating toward me.

My howl is reduced to a pitiful bleat.

"Jenny?" I cry out. "Baby, is that you?"

She's a mistress of illusion, appearing and disappearing before I can catch a glimpse of her face. I'm stumped, stunned. My mind is spinning.

This is either a fog bank, or a girl wrapped with long dark hair. "Stop!" The word escapes with desperation. I press my fists to my temples. "Stop driving me crazy."

Arms outstretched, I lunge for her, but my hands clutch only moist air. "You're grabbing at weeds, dumbass, blowing in the wind. It's nothing but weeds."

The night is a wizard, and I'm a fool.

~~~~~~

When I enter the house, I pace from room to room. Grab my backpack from the foyer and dig out some clothes. My feet are caked with dirt. "Just throw on your jeans and shirt, Jack," something tells me. "You can shower later. You might be heading out again."

The silence is suffocating, so I blast the stereo, turn on the TV, stuffing the downstairs full of chaos. I flop on the sofa, move to a chair, but I'm too restless to settle in any one place. The sugar is gone. The house smells gross, like dirty socks, so I run around like a madman, opening windows. Shutting down music, the news.

I'm sorting through scenarios, trying to decide whether or not I'm dreaming, when a series of guttural growls floods the room. I fly through the door, spring from the porch, and fade into no man's land.

"Fuck this shit," I snarl, sprinting across the lawn. "I'm gonna hunt you down, Galloway, and destroy you."

I race down a trail leading me deeper into the forest. Breaking through branches as the woodlands grow dense. The only things I smell are pine needles and decaying animal carcasses.

"You're chasing shadows, Jack," my mind screams. "Stop running in circles. He's got you right where he wants you. Stupidly helpless. He's cunning. You're an ass. Turn around. Backtrack to the house where you can gather your wits, devise a plan."

As I tear through brush, something sticky swipes my cheek. My head jerks up, my nose fills with a foul odor.

Body parts dangle from limbs sprouting from a black walnut tree, reminding me of a meat rack in a butcher shop. Dripping blood, the flesh must be freshly cut, torn, slaughtered is a better word.

A gust of wind hits my face. Strange ... Everything is strange. I'm here. I'm there. I'm not really anywhere. To clear my head, I shake it, realize I'm crouching in a puddle of blood.

"Butchered human on my property," I groan.

Ready to hit 9-1-1, I reach into a pocket for my phone, but my fingers slide down my furry side. "No pants, Jack. No pockets.

No phone." Saved by nudity, reality. "Sure, call in the troops. You've already been a murder suspect, Jack. What would the cops do if they found body parts hanging in your backyard?" My fur recedes into my pores. I swipe my brow. "Vincent and Sherman would be out here in a heartbeat. Cuffing me."

"Naked for the second time in an hour," I grunt. "Welcome home, Jack. Thanks Galloway." I curse my way into the house, panting, pouring sweat. I inspect every room, locking windows, testing doors. Taking the steps two at a time, I charge up the stairs. Slide to a stop on the landing. I pad around the second floor, flicking on lights, checking for intruders.

What I find inside my bedroom can only be described as carnage: the scene of a massacre. Splashed across my king sized bed are human remains. Blood still oozing from puncture wounds and shredded skin. Grotesque. I want to vomit. Chunks of flesh have been ripped from a thigh, exposing bone. My stomach lurches. Only part of a person soaks my bedspread, and without a head, I can't determine if it's male or female.

"Holy Christ. The head is missing," I choke, covering my face with my hands. In the darkness of my mind, the sight of Jenny's head in my lap the night of her murder is unbearable.

My room is trashed. Nightstands overturned, lamps shattered across the hardwood floor. A row of picture frames, strategically placed on my dresser, have been snapped like kindling ready to be tossed into a fire.

Bolts of electricity shoot down my spine: an onset of transition ... not to discount rage. Control yourself! You need to think like a human. *Then* behave like an animal.

Revenge! I can taste it. In due time, circles my mind. "Oh yeah. In due time," I vow, bobbing my head.

Galloway's left me no choice but to contact Don Delgado. *Detective* Don Delgado. Convince him I had nothing to do with this slaughter. Ask him to help me dispose of the remains. Cover up for a crime I didn't commit.

"You've been fucked all night, Jack Bailey. The party's starting, so you might as well get dressed," I grumble, pawing through my closet where I slide into another pair of jeans, slip a t-shirt over my matted head.

The screech of brakes alerts me before headlights appear, then my high school rival's mob car skids into my driveway, slamming to an abrupt stop. I watch through the window as Donnie flings his door open, leaps out, and in a few strides, lands with a thud on my front porch. Before his fist pounds, I open the door and stare.

"What the fuck, Jack?" he growls, brushing past me. "What happened?" He's scrubbing his face. Adjusting his fly.

I poke my head outside, curious if he was followed, then slam the door behind him. "I told you on the phone." My tone is low, harsh.

"Tell me again."

"Stop being a dick!"

He's squinting, shaking his head, rubbing his temples. "Where is it?" he rasps.

"Did you tell anyone?" I ask, every muscle in my body tightening. I don't know what to expect next from Donnie. Brotherly love, I hope. "This is just between us, I assume?"

"Depends on what I find."

Leading him up the staircase, for the second time, I brief him on everything that's transpired since I set foot in the door. Even the fireplace logs, mysterious odors, my fears. But I don't mention Galloway, or the fact that he's a werewolf. Donnie would be ordering a straight jacket, maybe tearing through the woods with a rifle.

If anyone is going to avenge Jenny's death. It's me.

"When's the last time you ate?" I toss over my shoulder, listening to Donnie's heels click down the hallway.

He shoots me a look of confusion. "Why? You offering me dinner?" If nothing else, Don Delgado can pull off sarcasm, but not as good as I can.

I smirk. "Dude. You better fill your lungs with air out *here*, because you're not gonna want to breathe when you see what's in *there*." I grip the doorknob.

Pulling the door open, I wait for Donnie's reaction. His jaw drops, then he gags. "What the fuck?" With a hand covering his mouth, he turns to me, accusingly.

"Listen, bro. I wouldn't have called you if I'd had anything to do with this. Get me? I had *nothing* to do with this!" Hands on hips, I'm backing into a corner, crunching on picture frame glass.

"I dunno, bro," he says, edging around the bed, "this looks all too familiar."

"The clinic ..." I squeeze my eyes shut, trying to block out the horror.

"Son of a bitch," Donnie mumbles, his face pale. "What the fuck is going on, Jack? Who ... what did you piss off? Why is this happening?"

"You tell me," I flare, gritting my teeth, controlling my fangs.

As I watch him survey the scene, mechanical comes to mind. He's regained composure. He's nothing but seasoned cop. "What a mess. You didn't hear anything in the house?"

"I told you, I heard something in the woods. Something ... someone was creeping around out there." I go to the window, pull the drape aside. Drawn to the moon, I fight the urge to turn. "So I followed it. Through the woods." I envision my fangs gnawing on Galloway's jugular. "Trying to get my ... hands on it."

"What *was* it?"

"I don't know," I growl the lie through a tight jaw.

Donnie's voice pitches. "What do you mean you don't know? You followed it, right?"

I nod. Look grim. Pull off innocent. But inside, my blood is boiling.

"Where did you go?" he spits out questions faster than my mind can process.

"For the third freaking time, I ran around the house, across the street. Down the street. All over the fucking place." I pause for a gulp of air. "I must have covered over twenty acres of forestland, dude. When I got back, I found *this* ..." I spread my hands out in a helpless gesture, then drag my fingers through my hair.

Donnie whips his cell phone from a pocket. I think he's calling for backup, and consider going wolf on him. But he starts snapping pictures, so I back off.

"Can we wrap it up," I swallow hard, "dump it someplace someone, other than me, will find it and report it?"

"You want me to be an accessory?" He jerks his head, shock in his eyes.

"Accessory to what? I didn't do anything!"

"Someone was murdered in your house, Jack, on your grounds ..."

"Dude. You know damn well I had nothing to do with this. I'm being framed."

"By who? Why would someone want to frame you?"

"Why was Jenny murdered? Why did you chase something into the forest that night at the clinic? Shoot at it. Why? Why? Why? What was it, Donnie?! You have no fucking idea! We could talk shit all night and never come up with an answer."

Donnie stares at me so long, so hard, I feel like I'm a fish on his line and he's ready to gut me. "You're about to owe me your life, Jack." He smirks. "And payback can be a bitch."

I don't like the way he's looking at me. Or how he's nodding. *Devious* comes to mind and I grin.

~~~~~~

With Donnie's help, the remains are relocated between a curb and some poor sucker's front lawn. My bedroom is reorganized and the entire house is scrubbed clean.

"The fact that body parts will be collected from your yard isn't going to go over big with Vincent and Sherman," Donnie warns, posing in a cop stance in my foyer, "considering your recent history and all. But the discovery of what we dumped on someone else's property should clear you."

"Should?"

He clicks his tongue. "Christ. I'll ask Rachel to be your alibi."

"Yeah," I scrub my beard, "that should work." I nod, wondering why I didn't think of that in the first place. "I appreciate your help, Don. And Rachel's."

"You better." He smirks. "Your phone call caught me in the middle of—"

I lift a hand. "Spare me." I shake my head. "I don't need to know what goes on between you and my therapist."

He pats me on the shoulder and belts out a laugh.

I shut the door and follow him down the walkway where we wait for the troops Donnie called to arrive at my house.

"And the anonymous tipoff. Do you think it worked? Think it was found by now?" I cock my head and watch him carefully.

He rests a hand on my shoulder. "Don't worry. It's all good." His eyes are glued to my head. "Hmm. You've got some head of hair there. Never noticed it before."

"Yeah. Well. Guess I was just another mutt for Jenny to groom." I shrug.

~~~

Bailey Way is lined with police cars, ambulances, rescue workers. My house is searched. I'm questioned by Detective Vincent, drilled actually, while Detective Sherman takes notes.

Hands in pockets, I stand in the front yard in predawn, watching uniformed dudes scramble, when Sherman zeroes in on me. "Looks like the work of the psycho who's been dropping bodies at the campgrounds." Sherman drags a hand down his face. "Leaving his mark. But those killings have been confined to the forests, never seen anything like this in a residential area. Is he changing his MO? Is he trying to tell us something?" Squinting, he seems to be searching for answers. "When did you happen upon the remains..." his eyes cut into mine, while his arm gestures to the wooded area bordering my yard.

"Uh," I tug on my ear, "about..."

"Right before I called you, Ed," Donnie strides over and immediately cuts in, "when a neighbor's dog started barking its head off. That's when Jack called me, and I called you."

Sherman isn't taking notes, he's scowling, shaking his head. From the look on his face, the wheels in his head are spinning.

"Yep. I do believe Angel's Bend has its first serial killer," Donnie nods at him. Moving in time, they swing their heads toward a circle of first responders still milling around, talking and pointing. "Looks like the action around here's escalating."

"Certainly seems that way." Sherman's head rocks like a pendulum. "We have two crime scenes tonight, about a mile apart," he says, disbelieving. "The rest of this body could be south of here. Forensics will let us know if it's a match."

"Two crime scenes?" Donnie cocks his head, acting surprised. "How so?"

"Anonymous caller tipped us off," Sherman replies, his head still rocking. "Crime scene guys are collecting remains from someone else's yard as we speak."

"That so ..." Donnie plucks a toothpick from a pocket, casually shoves it between his lips and starts to chew.

"Why do you think someone would hang body parts on your premises?" Sherman slips his pad from his pocket and studies me. He repeatedly clicks his ballpoint pen, annoying the shit out of me.

"Why were remains found on someone else's property tonight?" My lips pull tight, as my arms lift in the air, fall with a slap to my sides. "Like I told Detective Vincent when he questioned me," my hands dig deep into my pockets, "it's anyone's guess."

"Things have been wild since that first incident. Pieces of bodies found all over the place. A growing list of missing persons," Sherman says solemnly. "The night we found you with that dead girl ... that's when all hell broke loose."

I shrug, then grow irritated. "You think things have been wild for *you*?"

"We'll get to the bottom of it," he assures, craning his neck in Vincent's direction. "Forensics will go over the remains. ID the victim, or victims. Guess we'll be scratching a name or two off that list."

"Or adding," lifting a brow, I reply, quickly correcting, "but hopefully not."

"Still can't figure why ..." Ed scowls, "I can understand discarding bodies in back alleys, out on the trails, but ... out in the open in a residential area?" He scratches his scalp with the tip of his pen.

Setup, is what I want to scream.

Galloway wants me off the streets, or just wants to make my life more miserable than it already is. I'm not about to stoop to his level, or fall for his tricks. I'm going to use my brain — hunt him like the animal he is. Trap him. Kill him. Solo. For Jenny. Doing it the right way. Wearing a uniform.

By the time the coroner arrives and crime scene photos are taken, dawn is coloring the cloudless sky. The air is filled with birdsong. I glance around and feel my heart break. Who could have imagined a place like Angel's Bend would be faced with such horror?

Tracking An Animal

*J*enny visits me every night in dream. Her essence has been keeping me grounded. I wonder if my stability could also have something to do with the silver I've been wearing, twenty-four-seven, since the morning I woke up with the cross lying on my chest.

Whether Jenny is in my head or not, doesn't matter. At least I have her for a full eight hours when I sleep, which is more than many couples are able to share.

I'm working as a clerk at Fish and Game, where I begin each day by circling the building, exercising my legs ... and scenting. Checking for Galloway's Ninja.

My first order of business on day one was to pull up Cage Galloway's personnel records. The information he provided is limited, but the things in his file checked out. His employment history is consistently connected to the great outdoors. He did migrate to Angel's Bend from Buffalo. Prior to that, he resided in Tennessee. I was also able to place him in Washington State and Canada, which is where the trail ends, or begins. It's anyone's guess. One thing for sure, the murder rate, and number of missing persons reported, increased in the towns where he resided. The numbers declined when he moved on. Galloway didn't hang around in one place too long.

This seems to be the current case. Once Galloway caught wind of me working Forestry, with two strong legs, he dropped out of sight: Mine. The remains of the girl in the alley on Foster Road have yet to be recovered, so technically she's listed as a missing person. But I know better, and being unable to prove it is eating me alive.

I'm still not satisfied, so I light up the computer screen again when McCabe is out to lunch and start punching keys, scrolling over pages. My research takes me to Cage Galloway in Canada again. The paid site I'm on offers more information. This Galloway worked for the conservation department. Okay, it's him. He relocates to Washington State where he takes a job as mortician apprentice in the Normandy Funeral Home, the only indoor job he ever held, as far as I can tell. That took place fifty-two years ago. What the fuck?

It can't be the same guy. Not only is there a major age gap between him and the Angel's Bend Galloway, but after the funeral home, that Galloway must leave the country, because there's not a trace of him until a Galloway pops up in Tennessee, two years ago.

I don't have any other dates prior to those listed on Galloway's New York State employment records, which are recent. I'm scratching my head, trying to figure out if the old Galloway was a relative. But I can't find a damn other thing on either one of them. Too strange.

"Cage is packing up and heading out for a few days, Jack," McCabe informs as he drops the receiver of his phone into its base. He doesn't appear rattled, but there's an uneasy edge to his voice. "He's concerned about some unusual occurrences. Wants to check out the sectors east of Hosner."

He turns to me with a frown. "With the reports of disturbances around the lake, and those grisly murders," he drops his face into his hands; when he comes up for air, he's pale, "headless bodies, disemboweled torsos, limbs torn off. It's like some lunatic is feeding bodies through a meat grinder. I've seen photos. What a mess. Especially that one out on Wild Berry ..." He slaps a palm over his mouth. "I'm sorry, Jack. I didn't mean to bring it up ..."

"I know. It's okay." I grit my teeth. "It was big news. I have to get used to people talking about it."

It's obvious McCabe regrets opening the subject of Jenny's murder. He dives back into his monologue. "I'd say this town is filling up with unusual occurrences, alright. And having to temporarily suspend camping isn't going over very well our council, not to mention campers." He shakes his head, gathers his cheek. "They should only know. They wouldn't come within a thousand miles of here. Local goings on are being kept quiet, did you know that? We should be national news, but money talks, or doesn't, you know what I mean?"

"I have no idea what you're talking about."

"The missing girl is Pete Cavanaugh's daughter."

"Running for public office Cavanaugh?"

He nods.

"No shit." My eyes bulge not only because I've seen her around town, but because I've witnessed her untimely, not to mention grisly, death. "What is she, fifteen? What the hell was she doing out alone at that hour of night?"

He shoots me a curious eye, and I'm wondering if I'm divulging too much information. *Exactly how much did the local news let out?* His expression says he's about to ask, "And you know this because?" So I cover by guessing. Hey, I was a kid once. I blurt out the first trick that comes into mind. "I heard she snuck out of the house."

"Yup. To meet her boyfriend at the park."

Wheel Wolf

"Kids." I shake my head, my stomach twisting because I remember my early days with Jenny. Even at fifteen, I would never have left any girl alone like that, especially at night. "Back alleys ... What's wrong with a Saturday matinee at Lowes?"

"I hear you, Jack. This generation is out of control." He scratches the side of his neck until it's clawed pink. "The Johnson boy was interrogated, did you know that?"

"A suspect?" Of course, I'm all ears. "I'm assuming he's her boyfriend." I carefully choose my words. "Did he have something to do with her *disappearance*?"

"Doubtful, but he was questioned. He broke down bad. Said they had a fight. He walked off and left her there. Claims he went right home because she broke up with him. His parents confirm he came in all upset around midnight."

My tongue clucks. "Leaving her alone in the park, though. What a scumbag."

"I'll feel a lot better when that unit gets down here from Ludlow. Starts patrolling the entire area. Maybe we'll find out what the hell's going on out there." He draws a breath and grumbles, "Budget cuts. Maybe now the state will realize we're responsible for a damn big forestland, and we simply don't have enough help."

"Yeah. It'll be great to get some more rangers down here." When he turns back to his desk, I roll my eyes. My half-hearted statement is bullshit. I don't want rangers flooding the forest. Not only will they be disturbing innocent wildlife, but they'll spook Galloway when they try to flush out the nonexistent animal they believe responsible for the attacks. I'd like to save everyone the trouble, try to convince McCabe that Galloway is their wild animal. McCabe would probably set me up for mandatory counseling. "When will the extra troops arrive?"

"Pff. Not for a week." He sighs, shoving his chair from his desk. He walks to his wall map and studies it.

"Hmm. My place is east of Hosner," I remark, hoping I'm Galloway's next target. Being on my own turf would make it easier. Especially since I've set out a dozen traps.

"Galloway's talking about heading into the high country." McCabe is irritated. He's being put out. "Not areas directly surrounding the town, which is puzzling, as that's where the action seems to be happening."

I can't help but to throw more fuel on the fire. "So he sets his own rules, huh?"

McCabe's face prunes. "Don't get me started."

"That's cool." I hold up both hands. I could give a shit if Galloway is pissing McCabe off by running the show. If Galloway wasn't what he is, I'd pat him on the back. But I'm not in a congratulatory state of mind. My thoughts are taking other directions. He's heading for the hills? I don't think so. There's no way Galloway is hiking his way out of this one. Traveling to no-man's land where I doubt our small force of rangers ever venture more than once each season. I've got to get to him first.

"Galloway's signing out for a few days, huh?" This is my perfect opportunity to sniff around his house, shadow him. I know what Galloway's interest is, and it's not forest preservation. This I would love to shove down McCabe's throat. This I cannot, because I'd implicate myself as well.

After work, covered with leathers, I hop on my bike, tucking my cross inside my jacket. The home address Galloway listed on his paperwork takes me to the secluded shack on the outskirts of town. The one I've been watching on a nightly basis for the past week. The place where Galloway never showed. So this is my chance to find out what's inside. Find out why he listed it as his residence if he doesn't live here.

I enter through a broken side window, finding nothing unusual for an uninhabited shack. That's right. The place is deserted. No furnishings, kitchen items, clothing. The shack doesn't even have electricity or running water. I'm not sure it would even show up on the tax assessor's records. I make a mental note to check.

I'm wracking my brain, trying to figure out where Galloway has been keeping himself. Then it dawns on me. If he's working deep in the forest, he's living there as well.

~~~~~~

Early the next morning, I call in sick to work and hop on my bike. McCabe bitches, "Now I'm down two men." I remind him he should have held the ranger job for me. "I wouldn't have called in sick if the sky was falling," I reply with a mocking tone in my voice. "But a desk job is really not my thing." That's when he offers me the forest ranger position I was originally hired for, and I refuse it. "Thanks but no thanks, McCabe. I have other plans." As soon as my business is finished here, I'm gone. But this I don't mention yet.

The sun beats down, but the wind cools as I ride. I know these woodlands inside out. If Galloway is here, I'm the one who's going to track him down.

After canvassing every inch of the sectors east of Hosner Lake, I stop for a break. Munch on a granola bar and uncap a bottled water. I scratch my head. Swipe off perspiration. I've found no trace of human inhabitation, other than ashes, as the campgrounds have been cordoned off with roadblocks and large green signs: No Admittance. Campgrounds Closed Until Further Notice.

After crisscrossing the southern portion I believe Galloway may be inhabiting, my next move is to head north. I have to admit, Galloway has me stumped. No one in their right mind would shack up in the northern territory. The terrain is rocky and desolate, well-stocked with black bear and other wildlife that mankind has driven deep into the woodlands. Even though black bear aren't normally hostile, now and then you can run into a rogue with a sore asshole, who'll surprise you ... if you surprise him.

Mountain lions are a different story. Rare, but there. If you encounter a two-fifty stray, you better keep your distance and start praying. Especially if he believes you're about to poach his next meal, or worse yet, wants *you* for chow.

The northern sectors are rough to navigate on foot, and by wheel. Runoff from the mountains floods streams and tributaries, as well as the tip of Hosner Lake and smaller bodies of water. The valleys easily flood, forming dangerous swampland you don't want to trek through.

Rangers often disappear in the forest for days. So Galloway's absence wouldn't be all that unusual, if McCabe had scheduled it.

I've packed enough stuff to last at least a week. I plan on camping out for as long as it takes to bring Jenny's killer to justice. My kind of justice.

I park the Yamaha off a trail and set out on foot, using the bike as base camp. I'm not a quarter mile in when I pick up a scent, and spot the tracks. I keep moving, testing the air, my boots trampling a path covered with leaves where I crack my way through rows of saplings.

This is where I stumble upon tatters of clothing caught on thickets of brush. Dried blood streaks the fabric that ripples gruesomely in a steady breeze. My mind flashes a sick thought: multicolor, girly print flags. Christ. Has he been carrying victims through here? Could he have dumped the missing girl's remains in this forest?

I run a finger under a sliver of fabric. The blood has made what was soft, stiff. Is this part of a shirt? Shorts maybe? A skirt? As hard as I try, I can't recall how the girl on Foster Road was dressed that night. But her wounds have left a vivid impression. The side of her throat was shredded, strips of skin fluttering with the beats of her heart that was pumping her life from her body.

Wheel Wolf

When I lift my head, draw deep breaths, the rancid odor intensifies. I could swear the air is tainted with the same smell as it was the night I encountered Galloway. So I keep walking against the wind. I'm ready to head back for my bike, because the scent is leading me into rugged woodlands, treacherous, possibly requiring a quick getaway should I encounter combative wildlife. Sure I'm concerned the engine will alert Galloway, but on the other hand, I have no idea of how far I'll be hiking. Besides, all my supplies are strapped to the Yamaha.

So I double back, pick up the bike, and proceed to follow the trail, practically at an idle, until something catches my eye. An old ranger watchtower in what was once a clearing but is now overgrown with saplings and brush. Interesting. I park the bike and start nosing around. It's his place. The scent is so strong, I could puke. There's no one around. Nothing but birds, high in trees.

The Shack

Someone has attempted to construct a cabin from the remains of the tower, which has been knocked off its stilts, timbers nailed together haphazardly. Does it resemble a kid's fort? Nah. More like a poorly engineered alpine hideout.

If not for the odor, and wisps of smoke curling from a slapdash chimney planted at the pitch of the unstable roof, I'd never believe anyone or anything would call this home. As I circle the structure I sniff the rags covering what had been windows, picking up a different scent on each piece of cloth. Perfume. Fear. The victims' clothing torn and used as curtains? Sonofabitch. A pelt drapes what appears to be the door. Yeah, that scent is very familiar. Foster Road alley flashes through my mind ... again.

After peering through the glassless windows, I'm pretty sure the place is deserted. I slip inside, stepping carefully so the floorboards don't creak. They don't creak. I'm not walking on floorboards. My boots are sinking into soil. I'm standing close to the door, holding the pelt open for light as my eyes sweep the perimeter. Then my pulse picks up, because I notice charred bones grilling on smoldering embers in a makeshift fireplace. Human bones? Christ.

The place reeks of animal and rotting food. Urine and feces. My sensitive nose detects the raw, metallic fragrance of blood. This is like a cellar of the damned. I'm waiting for the guy wearing someone else's stitched-up face to come at me with a chainsaw.

My stomach is in my throat, from the atmosphere, and tension. It's been a hell of a ride, but I'm close. The nightmare could all end today. Part of it, anyway.

There is no interior light, other than waning sun trying to make its way through trees and the rags on the windows, when the luster of the spokes of a narrow wheel catches my gaze. It looks like it came off a wheelchair. I find it odd that the relatively new chrome wheel is propped into a corner of this crumbling shack. I lift it, twirl it, examine it, and when I lay the mud-caked wheel back down, I detect labored breathing. Mine is labored, but this is different. I draw a quick breath and hold it, listening. My instinct is to spin, but I carefully turn.

Maybe it's because I was beginning to relax, believing I was alone. Or that I've been so caught up in my discovery, I've foolishly neglected to inspect every corner of the dank interior where something could easily hide. Dumb move, Jack. I feel the heat of bright beady eyes before I am able to see them. Hear the anxious pant as something big and furry brushes past me, nearly knocking me off my feet.

Did I almost lose my balance to a wolf? Blood drains from my limbs.

This one looks natural. Grey. Big. At least two-hundred pounds of muscle. It flashes by so fast, the only thing I can accurately confirm is the shimmering tail as the animal bolts around the pelt and sweeps through the door. The scent it broadcasts is one I've never smelled before.

In two strides I'm following it through the opening, planting my boots on solid ground, ready to confront it. But the wolf has disappeared. I freeze, listen, slowly turn to face the snap of twigs, crackle of brush, the receding wail. Holy fuck. My heart is still pounding. So ... a wolf is living here? What's with the wheel? Shit. Someone tried to set me up by leaving grooves made by a wheelchair at the scenes of the animal mutilations. Could this be the wheel that was used?

Okay, I tell myself. Relax. You flushed the wolf out. If anything else was here, it would have attacked you by now. Get your ass back inside, check out the rest of the place. Evidence. You need to find something to connect Galloway, because in your gut, you know he's been here. Maybe he hasn't killed anyone here, but has dragged victims through the forest, dead, maybe clinging to life, only to be slaughtered, devoured. The thought makes me shiver.

My heart hasn't yet returned to a normal rhythm. In my wildest dreams I never expected to encounter a natural wolf. My mind's reeling. Is this what has been attacking cattle? Tearing humans apart?

Wolf is not what I encountered that night. That's for sure. What I wrestled was half-man, half-beast, enormous, and outrageously strong. The entire scenario is mind-blowing.

After another cautious walk around the shack, scenting the air, I slip back inside to continue my search. There isn't much to see. Frying pans blackened with age and flame. A few filthy ceramic plates crawling with insects. Plastic cups, crushed and lying on the ground.

There has to be more here than what meets the eye. Where would Galloway hide his personal items? I start tossing things aside, kicking my way from wall to wall. He has to be camping out here. Because a wolf can't light a fire. A wolf doesn't cook his own meals, use plates and cups. I spot an ax in a corner. Freshly cut firewood, not yet cured. This is not adding up. A vagrant, a squatter? I'm trying to determine this when a weak shaft of sunlight flickers across the room, reminding me to check my watch. I don't have much time. With what little light is left, I continue to sift through the unsavory contents.

With the firm tip of my boot, I nudge a pyramid of stacked firewood and it scatters. Beneath the musty stench, where the owner would never expect anyone to look, I uncover a backpack. A bit worn, but in decent enough shape to have been recently used. My chest tightens, followed by my stomach.

I set the faded backpack down on two weathered planks, balancing on stacks of cement blocks, serving as a table. My hands are shaking as I jerk the zipper, unable to open the pack fast enough, yet afraid to know what's inside. Body parts?

I hesitate, then one hand slips through the opening, fishes around, grips something smooth with an expensive feel to it. I yank and out comes a pinstriped arm, then the entire, neatly folded dress suit. The same suit Galloway wore at Jenny's funeral. No other garments or incidentals.

Working for the state has its benefits, one of which, a uniform service. You don't need clothes. The guy knows what he's doing. Moving around. Traveling light. Leaving no tracks. Well, none the authorities can find. Who the fuck is he? Why the fuck was he at Jenny's funeral? Better yet, why the fuck did he target her? What is he doing here in Angel's Bend? Why did I leave my shotgun strapped to the Yamaha?

Blood singing in my ears might be the reason I don't hear the footsteps. But I do catch the vacillating shadow as it engulfs me.

At the depth of his voice, I spin. The suit slips from my fingers. I step back and drop into a fighting stance.

A big hand has drawn the pelt aside, and sonofabitch, Cage Galloway is crouching in the doorway. Edging into the shack. Wearing an obnoxious smirk, obviously thrilled to have startled me.

January Valentine

There he stands, the guy of a million designs. Suave at the cemetery, where I figured he was a new doctor in town. Sharply dressed ranger when I ran into him in McCabe's office. Right now, he looks like a woodsman off the cover of a fairytale book.

His plaid shirt is rolled to the elbow, open at the neck, and tucked under a frayed leather belt. His jeans aren't trim, they're kind of baggy and cuffed. My eyes drop to his feet, covered by bulky work boots, making him appear as someone working the rails, or traveling in box cars.

I can't pull my eyes from his barrel chest. The thick coating of hair bristling through the button-down opening where the fabric strains.

When he bellows, my eyes snap up to meet his. "Well, if it isn't the clerk from Fish and Game." His grin widens. "Smells good in here. What's cooking, guy?" He gestures to the bones on the smoldering fire.

It's not only his size that's intimidating. It's the fact that his massive frame is blocking the doorway. My eyes shift as inconspicuously as possible, checking for the nearest exit should I need one. Fuck ... Am I gonna need one. Small windows are all I find. I think of Jenny, and panic skyrockets into conviction, and I realize why I'm not carrying a weapon. Because a gunshot is too easy for Jenny's murderer. I plan on tearing him to bits with my bare hands and teeth.

Realigning my stare, I snarl. "What are you doing here, Galloway?"

"I'm a ranger, remember?" He yanks off the folded uniform draping his shoulder, holds it out in offering, then let's it drop to the dirt floor. Grinds the heel of his boot into the trousers, as though he's extinguishing a cigarette. Then he dusts his palms off.

"I take that as a sign of your resignation?" After antagonizing him, I haul in a breath.

Wheel Wolf

"What do you think? And what are *you* doing here is the question I'd like to ask." His grin exposes big teeth that are no longer Colgate white. He takes a few steps toward me and we circle each other, scenting, snarling. We're close enough to brush shoulders; I take a step back. My chest begins to burn beneath the cross. Reminding me this is the end of the road, for one of us.

"You've been fucking with my life. My head. What do you want from me?" I want to bark, but my voice cracks. "You killed Jenny. The only woman I ever loved. You took everything from me. Even my job. Why?"

"You took everything from me, Bailey. Layla was mine. The best thing that ever happened to me. She was with me longer than you've been breathing on this earth. I taught her how to survive." He looks wistful, then his expression breaks with a demonic smile. "Given the right circumstances, chicks can be brutal. I couldn't get the wild out of that girl." He shakes his head and my ears pound with his explosion of laughter. "She was wild when I took her off the streets of Washington, even wilder when I gave her my blood ... my gift." When he growls *gift,* the timbers surrounding us rattle.

I'm wondering if the shack will collapse as he continues his tirade. "Layla was mine until the day you slaughtered her." His growl is like thunder.

"We saw you at the lake that night. Something about you excited her. She wanted you. So I hated you. I warned her, tried to stop her, but nothing could control that girl — especially when she was wolf. She loved being wolf. Wanted no part of human other than to eat it." When he nods, I notice his face is changing. His eyes are no longer bright blue; they look bloody. "Layla was true wolf. One of a kind. You destroyed my mate. All that grooming ..."

By now, I'm freaking out. Not only because some werewolf chick had her eye on me, but because my skin is tingling and burning. My bones are cracking and splitting, producing agonizing pain. My head is pounding. My eyes are crossing. My jaw is stretching. I'm salivating.

Galloway is also transforming. His eyes are raging slits. His jaw is elongating, sprouting teeth and fangs twice the size of those cutting into my tongue.

"Your girl jumped me, Galloway. She wanted to eat me. I had nothing to do with it. I don't even fucking remember ..."

"Maybe yes. Maybe no. The fact of the matter is," he moves so close, I'm breathing his foul, exhaled breath, "you decapitated my eternity ... Jack ..."

With one swipe, he rips the chain from my neck. Flings my cross to the floor with such fury, a serrated edge digs into the dirt and the cross stands upright. "Ended her life with your silver neck gear." His massive shoulders shrug. "You killed mine. I killed yours. I could kill you with one blow, but I'd rather see you struggle through an eternity of suffering. We're even. So fuck off. You go your way, I'll go mine. No one will be the wiser."

"I'll be the wiser," I snarl. "You know damn well only one of us is walking out of here." My eyes are stinging. Watering.

He swipes the cross with the sole of his boot. "For your information, silver has no affect on me. But this fucking thing cut Layla's head off." He shakes his head. "Have fun looking for a mate. You'll have to bite her to make her stay with you."

"Your bitch was the serial killer." I laugh not because what I've just said strikes me as humorous, but because the two of them had everyone fooled. "And you took her place here in Angel's Bend, after you took everything from me. Jenny. My job. My sanity." I drag my hands through my thickening hair as I let the transformation engulf me. "It's ending right here. Right now." I let out a low growl. Thrust my chest. Shake my clawed fists with fury.

Galloway's laugh resounds. "You have no idea what you're

dealing with. You were just bitten, Jack. Some of us were born this way."

I rear, I roar, and the timbers heave. "What the fuck are you talking about?"

"You'll never be like me, but I'm not going to kill you. I'm going to make you suffer. You can't get away from me. I'll be one step behind you everywhere you go. Your needs will grow. And I'll be there setting you up every day ... every night. Making your eternity miserable, without peace, without your bitch."

As my tendons stretch and twist, I bellow. "Go fuck yourself, Galloway. Your eternity is about to end."

"Since you're not going to take me up on my generous offer ... Take a few more breaths, Bailey. Taste the air I'm about to rip from your throat. But first, let me paint you a picture you can take to your grave." Legs spread wide, he squares his shoulders. Lifts his chin. "My woman was something else, but I have to tell you, your girl was special. I almost took her for my own, but ..." His black top lip snags a fang. "I knew she wouldn't go for it. She had a pair of delicious lungs on her, though, that's for sure. Your little girl was sweet, tasted just like honey. I'm still savoring the aftertaste."

His fat, charcoal tongue circles his mouth. "And was she feisty. Stood her ground until the very end. I want you to know this, Jack. How brave she was. She stuck her little hand down my throat and stabbed me," his voice booms as he pulls Jenny's crystal from a pocket, dangles it for me to see. "She jammed this thing into my gizzards."

Galloway's chest inflates. His lumberjack shirt pops every button and rips apart. His eyes are neon yellow and bloodshot. What's left of his clothing is torn from his body by his claws.

Everything slams me at once. The night, the phone call, Galloway's horrific howls. *Jenny's tormented screams.*

The heartbreaking story he sardonically relays infuriates me.

A jolt of adrenaline shoots through my body, blows my brain apart. I'm shuddering, exploding. The incredible pressure building inside me is forcing my eyeballs from their sockets, rupturing my innards, extruding my lower jaw.

The pain is so excruciating, I want to roll on the floor, crunch into a ball, cradle my blowtorch stomach. Monstrous fangs rip through my gums like steel through foam, and I feel like a million bucks ... I'm about to settle into my new self.

I hear the leather of my jacket tear, then it's in pieces on the ground. My chest is able to fully expand. I suck in a massive amount of air, shriek with rage, and lunge for him with extended claws.

We battle like rams, butting chests instead of horns. I propel myself into a somersault, angling my body so one foot hits his jaw, the other aiming for his balls.

Like lightning, he snatches my ankles and I'm doing a split, crashing onto the makeshift table, splitting the wood in half. I grab a splintered plank in each hand and hurl them like spears. One whizzes past his head, the other slams into his hand. He snaps the thick piece of wood over a knee and lets it drop. Jerks his chin and grins.

I do a roundhouse kick that should take anything down, but he deflects my battering ram body. When I crash into the wall, the timbers shudder. At the sound of his voice, I spring to my feet. "It's right here, soldier. Come and get it." Galloway's clothing has been replaced by fur. He stands on two hind legs, the muscles of his back so enormous, he looks like he's crouching. But he's not. He's growling, drooling. Jenny's crystal dangles from his outstretched claws. "This little bitch put up one hell of a fight in my gut."

He's painted a picture all right. He's sickened me. Enraged me. Torn my heart from my chest. I'm growling so ferociously, my throat is about to tear open and bleed. I leap at him, watching in horror as with a jerk of his arm, Jenny's crystal takes flight. Like a glittering missile, it flies through the air in the direction of what's left of the fire, the bones.

"No!" In midair I spin, stretching my hairy arms out before me. The crystal falls, but not into the coals. Into the palm of my hand. The blood pumping through my veins is boiling. I'm holding something dear to Jenny. I'm indestructible.

Galloway lets out an ear-shattering howl. Lunges for me. By now we're both wolf, but he's different. He's huge, with the strength of a dozen athletes. I'm buff, but he tosses me around like I'm weightless, the same as he did in the alley.

The crystal falls to the ground. This approach isn't working. He's too powerful. I'm tasting blood ... mine. He lifts me in a bear hug, hurls me across the room. Sweeps me off the floor and throws me down again. My head hits the stones surrounding the sizzling remnants of fire.

The impact of brain against skull is disabling. I'm seeing two Galloways, trying to figure out which one is real. His face lowers: this one is real. We're snout to snout. His blood-trimmed eyes are inches from mine, his black pupils contracting. As his yellow teeth gnash, he showers me with putrid breath that smells like empty, rotting stomach. Am I about to fill that cavity inside him?

Watching his lips pull back is mesmerizing. Feeling his pellets of drool hit my face is enlightening ... If I don't move, he's gonna eat me.

In my peripheral, a laser-like sparkle grabs my attention. While Galloway pounds my head into dirt, I stretch and claw, finally snagging the chain, and my fingers close around the crystal sword.

My head is in Galloway's clawed hands. He could easily snap my neck if he wanted to, but he's forcing the back of my head onto the coals. I taste the odor of singed hair. Mine. Everything on me is frozen: eyes, mind, limbs, crystal in fist. *The crystal.* Whatever is pumping through my veins can't be blood. It's bubbling lava. My body recharges. My arm shoots into the air as though suspended on a cable, and with the sudden surge of energy, my hand is like a triphammer. I'm not willing this to happen. Something has taken over my being. The crystal is rammed into Galloway's one eye, and he's staring at me with the other, as if in a total state of disbelief.

His hold loosens, his body jerks. He leaps to his feet and wails, and when he yanks, his eye pops out with the tip of the crystal. *Olive on toothpick* reanimates my stupefied mind.

I jump to my feet, ready my claws, but Galloway is already charging, smoke trickling from his ears, blood from the socket of his eye. I'm not sure how it's happened, but I'm on his shoulders in an airplane spin, then slammed onto the floor, again and again. He's going to pound me to death if I don't do something fast.

I'm getting the shit kicked out me, gasping for breath, scrambling to think my way out of this, when I land on something solid. That's when I start pleading. Let me touch you. Please don't burn my fingers.

Chest heaving, Galloway crouches in the center of the shack, his shriek filled with rage. His one-eyed stare tells me this is the end of the road. He springs, claws extended, and is gliding through the air. Snarling. Howling his ugly, rearing head off. He's pissed. Playtime is over. I'm about to be dinner.

My fingers grip the edge of smooth, cold metal. "Jenny ... this one's for you, baby." I snap my wrist, pitching the serrated cross through the air like a chakram.

Jenny's cross flows like liquid silver. Before Galloway has a chance to pounce, the gleaming blade lodges in his throat. Blood spurts. His red eye bulges with shock. He lets out a gurgling howl. When he falls face first, the impact of his body drives the cross straight through what's left of his neck. The crunch of bone is nauseating ... in a good way. Galloway has managed to sever his own head from his body.

It takes less than a moment for me to snatch the crystal sword from the ground, shake off the eyeball. When I spin to face Galloway, he is no longer a werewolf. I'm crouching where he just crouched, my jaw dropping not only saliva, but disbelief.

I've always been under the impression that when a werewolf is killed, it reverts back to a human. Not in Galloway's case. He is in no way a man. What's lying on the ground, not more than two steps from my feet, is the massive body of a grey wolf, blood pulsing from its torn neck with the help of its failing heart. Fluid seeps from the wolf's severed head which lies in grotesqueness near its body.

By now, I'm back to me. Naked and shivering, I fall to my knees, recover the bloody cross, wipe it clean with the remnants of Galloway's plaid shirt. I reattach the broken link, clip the braided chain around my neck. Lay the cross flat against my chest. It feels good. Soft and smooth, like Jenny. I can't fit the chain holding the crystal around my head. After bringing it to my lips, I loop it around the cross chain in a tight knot. My two lucky charms are meant to hang together. I'll never remove them.

I drag my ass into a corner, panting, cradling my head, hugging my knees, rocking back and forth. Now that Galloway is dead, the immensity of it all is hitting me. Holy shit. If not for Jenny's cross, I would be dead right now. That's what I wanted to be all along. Now I'm not so sure.

The sight of the wolf, and its odor, is lethal. I'm in total disbelief of what's just gone down. Tears are rolling down my cheeks, because since her passing, Jenny has never been so close to me as she is right now. And her death has been avenged.

A sob tears from my throat. "If you can hear me, Jen, it's done. You can rest now, baby. Rest in peace."

I'm not sure of how much time has passed, but the wolf has

bled out completely. I heave a sigh of relief. I've been struggling with bizarre thoughts, worrying some kind of black magic might kick in, turn the gory remains back into Galloway: alive, hateful, powerful, murderous.

My eyes keep jerking in the direction of the carcass, but I've pulled myself together enough to start thinking. Maybe not rationally, but at least my brain is off autopilot, and firing normal signals again. Find some clothes and get the fuck out of here, Jack.

I've got jeans and shirts in the pack on my bike. But for some reason, I start crawling on all fours, trying to piece together my leather pants, and I'm sobbing again. What the fuck is wrong with me? That's when I feel the heat of their stare.

"Shit!" I reel, falling back onto my butt. "Holy Christ, you almost gave me a heart attack."

Rachel strolls through the door, my clothes slung over her arm. "Get dressed, Jack. Before the police arrive." She flings a pair of jeans at me, along with a t-shirt. "Make sure you get every last remnant of your shredded leathers out of here."

Donnie is still standing in the doorway, mouth agape. His jacket is open, his hand resting on his shoulder holstered .45.

When I lift my head it starts to spin, so I drop it back down. Stare at the floor while talking to Rachel. "Where did you get my clothes?"

She drops to her knees beside me. Lays a hand on my shoulder. "From your bike. You okay?"

"Yeah." I manage to meet her gaze. "How did you know I was here?" I don't know why, but I'm whispering. My throat is so parched I can barely swallow.

Her eyes twinkle. "Don't you know who I am by now?" I'm waiting for her to confess she *is* the vampire I initially thought she was, or maybe an angel. Although with her attitude, I'd find that one hard to believe. I shoot her a dumb look.

Wheel Wolf

Her eyes narrow and drill. "Come on, Jack. You know what I am." She winks and squeezes my arm. The scent of amber floods my nose. "Let's get the hell out of here. I'm starting to get bad vibes."

"Great. I don't even want to go there. Things are crazy enough right now." I pull the shirt over my head, slipping the cross and crystal over the front. I brush strands of hair from my eyes. "You think anyone would ever believe this, Rachel?"

"You said it."

"What?"

"Believe. You're a believer, Jack Bailey."

"What the hell happened in here?" Donnie asks, his voice echoing as he steps inside and looks around. "This is some vile shit, Jack. Did you kill that wolf? There's a fine for that."

When Rachel shoots him the eye, he takes a step back. Starts rubbing his neck. "Not if it was in self-defense, I guess."

"It was," Rachel confirms. How does she know? Why do I have a gut feeling there were more than one pair of eyes watching over me?

As I slip into my jeans, I recount the events. Rachel is expressionless, but keeps nodding. Like she's in agreement, of what I have no clue. Donnie on the other hand, keeps repeating, "I don't fucking believe this. It's not possible."

"Believe," Rachel addresses Donnie, but her eyes sink into mine. *I'm believing*, mine are shooting back.

We step into dusk and my lungs fill with fresh air. A full moon is idling behind a break in the trees. It will be high soon. I will be too. After this experience, I'll be buying rounds at the Evening Sun until closing time.

The headlights of a ranger's all terrain cut through the forest. The green ATV coasts down the trail, coming to a creeping halt before us.

"Hey Vince," Donnie says, leaving Rachel and me standing

near my bike.

"I got your message. What's going down?" Vincent grasps his hand.

Donnie shrugs his head toward the shack, which is illuminated only by headlights. "You're going to want to bring in Crime Scene and spotlights."

"Fill me in. What's inside?" Vincent's face is strained. I figure he's expecting to be informed we've discovered the bodies of the missing girls, and the hikers that Galloway and his mate had been picking off.

"No human remains. Just a decapitated wolf inside." Donnie's got one hand in a pocket, gesturing with the other. He's chewing on a toothpick. "You'll also find the wheel off a wheelchair, which could be linked to the grooves imprinting the ground at those animal mutilations. It's caked with mud. There's some torn clothing and boots inside, too. Leave it all for forensics."

Since his arrival, Vincent has been dividing his glances between Donnie and me. He surprises me by calling out my name, striding to my side and sticking out his hand. "How are you doing, Jack? Good tracking. Nice bike." He points to Galloway's Ninja, ironically parked not too far from my Yamaha, only no one knows it's Galloway's, because he's not here. And there's no way I'm about to tell them the dead wolf is Cage Galloway. "Yours?"

"That one's mine." I hitch my head. "The VMAX."

"Even nicer." Vincent cocks his head. "Who owns the Ninja?"

I look him straight in the eye and shake my head. "I have no idea."

"Was it here when you arrived?" he asks.

"Not that I recall."

He folds his lips, rocks his head, hands shoved in pockets, takes a walk around the bike.

Ed has been conducting his own investigation with a flashlight. When he exits the shack, he's carrying a rectangular pouch. Its brown leather is scarred and cracking. "I found this under some debris. I doubt anyone has been living in there, but someone's been stashing stuff."

"Hold onto it. Crime Scene will comb through it all. We'll impound the bike and run the plate." Vincent's head bobs like a bobble head doll. "We'll find out who owns the Ninja and what they've been up to."

I know who owned it. I check out the expression on Rachel's face. Her sly grin confirms her agreement.

"No signs of the victims though, which is baffling," Ed says, rubbing a palm over his hair which is now buzzed like Vincent's. "Just looking at this place," he shakes his head, "I had a strong feeling we were going to find something."

"Check a couple miles east of here, in daylight. There's a thicket filled with scraps of clothing. Looks like a lunatic tried to decorate the forest for ..."

"Don't say it, Jack," Rachel warns. "Don't bring religion into this."

"Sure." I roll my eyes, which due to the glare of headlights, are sensitive.

Vincent is piecing things together. "Whoever set up shop ..." His brows fold, his eyes scan. He's acting as though he's solving the case singlehandedly. "Owned that wolf, and the bike. Possibly fled the shack when Jack arrived, because his wolf slaughtered some locals."

"Jack knows better," I mumble. So do Donnie and Rachel now.

Vincent turns to Ed. "Keep everyone out. Preserve the scene." Then he slams a palm on my shoulder. "I have to be honest Jack. I really thought you had a connection to that girl on 44, until ..."

Vincent's cell phone rings, so Ed steps in to narrate. "The identity of the girl who died at the scene of your accident was withheld pending notification of next of kin, but there wasn't any. And since no one claimed the body, it went to the state and was buried in a small town in Tennessee called Trinket."

I squint at him. "Why did you bury her in Tennessee if you didn't know who she was?"

"Give me a minute." He takes a notepad from his pocket and starts flipping pages. "When we ran her prints through the missing persons database, they belonged to a young girl named Layla — no last name mind you — who popped up as a robbery homicide suspect in an unsolved case ... in Tennessee." He scrunches his mouth, lifts his brows. "How about them apples?"

The wheels in my head are spinning as I nod. "No shit." Of course. Galloway's old stomping grounds. My stare falls on the moldy pouch in Ed's hand, then back to his eyes. I'm freaking out. I need to know what else Galloway was hiding. "Let's tear into that pouch." I stick out a hand.

Ed takes a step back and cradles the pouch. "We can't. It's evidence. I have to bag it."

Donnie and I exchange glances, then my gaze falls on Rachel whose eyes are like two laser beams trying to examine the hidden contents.

"Let me hold onto this," Donnie says to Ed as he reaches for the pouch. "I think I heard your partner calling you."

Ed's head swings around, then he shoves the pouch at Donnie and merges into a gathering of his peers.

Donnie and I turn our backs on the investigators. Of course, Rachel's head is between us, peering over our shoulders. She has one arm on Donnie, her other on me. When we unsnap the pouch, we find a packet of folded newspaper clippings, tattered and yellow with age. When we unfold them, a name tag slides out and falls to the ground. Scrambling for it, Donnie and I bump heads, but my fingers grip it first.

My mind's spinning, struggling to work coherently. My fingers tighten on the cardboard tag like I'm trying to pick up vibes. "Cage Galloway ... Normandy Funeral Home."

"Let me see that." Donnie examines Galloway's nametag, much like I did.

My gut is on fire as I unravel the newspapers. First headline: *Lucy Normandy, fifteen-year-old daughter of Funeral Director and owner of Normandy Funeral home is reported missing.* Next Headline: *Coroner's office discovers Funeral Director and Wife sealed in caskets alive.* Talk about macabre. This is too sick to be real. What kind of maniac would do this?

Now I'm thinking about the old Galloway I stumbled across on the computer, and my skin wants to creep off my body. He kidnapped her, locked her parents in coffins ... alive, and he and the girl disappeared?

"Holy shit," I mumble to Rachel, who's now pressed against my side. "I found a Galloway working at Normandy Funeral home ... fifty-two years ago." I remember staring at the computer in confusion then, as I'm staring at the newspapers now. Then it all comes together.

Donnie pales and rests his hand on my arm. "I never mentioned this before, but the prints on the Layla girl who was found lying next to your bike were a match to a girl named Lucy Normandy who went missing from Washington State. I figured it was a fuck up." He rubs the back of his neck. "Two girls with the same prints born more than fifty years apart is an impossibility."

"So, besides being a serial killer, Layla from Tennessee was Lucy Normandy, fifteen-year-old renegade daughter of the owners of the funeral home?" My temples pound. I blow out a, "Phew."

"No way," Donnie gasps and runs his hands over his face. "No way," he repeats as if trying to convince himself. "Are you telling me these two have been murdering their way from one state to another?"

We begin another round of silent staring. I have a feeling we're all experiencing similar emotions.

The news clippings are balling deeper inside my fist. "It adds up. Galloway and Layla go on a cross-country killing spree and land in Tennessee. Layla kills her boss, then robs him. So she and Galloway flee Trinket to relocate in Buffalo. And we all know what happens next." The puzzling factor though is, everyone thought Layla was a kid, not a senior citizen. How the hell?

"Let's have a look at these." Rachel plucks the clippings from my hands. "He was a collector, I see. Many are. Look at all of these articles describing animal mutilations, missing women, murders." Her lips gather. She clicks her tongue and mumbles, "This is some itinerary. Over the years he toured remote parts of England, France, and Germany. Even visited Ukraine." Her eyes pierce mine.

"You know I'm not easily shocked, Jack, but ..." She shakes her head. "This is one for the group." She lifts a brow. "The deaths are bad enough, but ... how much infection he spread is anyone's guess. Kind of makes you want to check out your neighbors when they return from a European vacation."

I drag my hands through my hair and let out a sigh. "Or a stop at Phantom Lake." My voice falls along with my stomach. I shake my head. "No one in his right mind would ever believe this story."

Rachel lets out a wicked chuckle and hitches her head toward Vincent. "Which is why I always say, leave the investigating to the investigators, and the mystery to the believers." She yanks Donnie's arm, tweaks his chin. "Right, big guy?" She pulls him close and whispers, "You're gonna solve my case later ..."

When Donnie shoots me a hopeless look, I doubt he realizes I can hone in on flies dropping shit, so Rachel's whisper is no secret to my ears. Yeah, I know you're hopeless, bro, my smirk says, and you're about to get laid. I watch them for minute and actually experience something resembling warmth. They're a good match. I should tell Donnie I'm happy for him. I'm still too raw.

A wink will have to suffice for now.

Notepad in hand, Ed approaches. Before he reaches us, he sings out, "We ran the Ninja plate. There's an APB out for a Cage Galloway."

Yeah, he's about ten feet away from us, decapitated on the floor of the shack. I slap my palm on the seat of the Ninja. "Think you'll find him?"

"We'll pick him up. He couldn't have gotten too far," Ed replies. His confidence amazes me.

"You might never know who Galloway really is ... was." I'm dying to lay the cards on the table. Would Ed believe me? I doubt it.

"We'll find out all about Galloway. There's plenty of DNA inside that shack." Ed talks while scribbling on his notepad.

"Check the wolf's. See if it matches what's on the bike." The minute I mention wolf, his eyes snap up and he stares at me like I'm high. "Hey maybe he took the wolf riding." I shrug.

Vincent saunters toward us, and while the detectives talk official business, Rachel and I start talking physical therapy.

She runs a finger over my cheek. "Your face is cut and bruised. You took a hell of a beating. How are your legs?"

"My legs are fine. I'm about ready to duck out of here. Leave the crime scene to the pros."

"Maybe you should check into rehab, just for the night. Let a doctor take a look at you, then I'll give you a massage."

"I just took a beating." I smirk. "I don't need another."

After they take my statement, and the dust has settled, I'm credited with heroism for leading the cops to the killer, *his wolf*, and his lair.

Cleared of absolutely everything, the hero me goes flying down 44, talking to wind. "One down, two to go." How do I know there are two scumbags who killed my parents? I know this because I've developed a sixth sense. How will I find them? I tap my shoulder. I'm now a firm believer in the hereafter, and have a gut feeling there's an angel nearby.

Maybe Jenny did have magic flowing through her veins. Her kisses sure as hell knocked me off my feet. If I could, I'd show the cross and crystal to Heinrich Rudéa. Maybe they *are* enchanted amulets that for some reason found their way to Jenny. Strange how things happen.

Who knows? *Stranger* things have happened. But this whole wolf thing is fucking ridiculous. Instead of the werewolf turning into a man, werewolf Galloway just turned back into a huge grey wolf. The entire opposite of what mythology or legend or folklore, shit I forget, but ... he was a fucking natural wolf.

This would mean Cage Galloway was born a wolf who somehow acquired the ability to transform into a man. That's a hell of a switch and something Dr. Heinrich Rudéa might find of significance. When all is said and done, I'm going to look the old guy up. Why do I have a feeling I'll find him alive and kicking? Pawing maybe.

As I gas the Yamaha, getting ready to split, I'm still in a state of shock over what went down.

Fifty-two years ago, Cage Galloway found himself a mate. Fifteen year old Lucy Normandy. They were perfect for each other. We know Lucy Normandy, or Layla, was a sixty-seven year old teenager when she died. There's no way of knowing how old Cage Galloway was or what wolf pack he originated from.

All that remains of Cage Galloway is a backpack, a pouch of tattered evidence, pinstriped suit, boots, and a motorcycle.

Wheel Wolf

Jack

*M*y next order of business is to track down the scumbags who murdered my parents, human or not, it doesn't matter. Either way I'm covered, because I'm both. I'll strangle them with my bare hands, or gut them with my claws.

Before leaving town, I stop by Shadow Lane Rehab. I can't split without saying a final goodbye to Rachel. She played a big part in my recovery, both physical and emotional.

A few taps and Rachel cracks open the door of her room. "Jack! You're just in time." Her grin is lopsided.

"For what?" Sniffing the room, my eyes narrow.

"Come to a gathering before you leave, Jack," she invites, pulling me through the doorway. Her eyes are pink-tinged slits. The room smells recently sprayed by a variety of fragrances. The aroma of weed and incense swirling in the air hits me first, followed by the sweetness of mango. My nose twitches. Sure enough, there's a sliced mango sitting on the table, beside it an amber pipe. "Some of my friends should be arriving soon. Donnie will be here too." She winks.

"No thanks. I've developed social anxiety." My eyes wash

over the room. Everything is black: carpet, drapes, scarves covering lampshades. Even the picture frames holding her certificates are black. But the walls are dead white. A variety of dreamcatchers: braided, feathered, beaded, hang from the ceiling, along with bamboo chimes. A polished ebony shelf holds statues and crystals. Rosary beads dangle from pottery praying hands.

"Always full of excuses." She rolls her eyes and shakes her head. After closing the door, she leans against the dark stained wood. "Sit for a while?" She motions to a comfortable looking sofa stacked with cushions.

My head shakes an automatic "No," and my shoulder tucks against the wall beside her. "What can I tell you." I shrug. "Maybe if I come back this way. Who knows ..." I reach into the pocket of my jeans. "Close your eyes and hold out your hands." When she does, I flip her my set of house keys. "Take good care of the spread. You can haunt it for as long as you like."

Her eyelids lift and she smiles. "I'll watch over it for you until it's sold." The way she holds the keys gives the impression she's trying to pick up vibes. "Are you sure you don't want to join us before you leave? We've got a diverse circle going on. You're not an outsider. We don't judge. We just are."

I level one brow and lift the other. "Nah. I'm heading down to the Keys."

She nods. I know she reads me well. "Thanks for the use of your house. I could use some wooded serenity. When you get back, we'll pick up from where we left off. Your roots are here. Remember that."

"I'll try." Holding back tears, my eyes burn.

She runs her hand down the side of my face. "I'm gonna miss you, Jack. Keep in touch."

"I'll tweet you. What's your tag?" I cock my head.

"@GypsyWoman_1950. Yours?"

"@WheelWolf_2050."

Wheel Wolf

Rachel throws her arms around me and whispers, "Don't be a stranger."

Deeply inhaling her amber fragrance, I draw back and smirk. "Can I be any stranger?" My nose twitches. "Can you?"

"That's one of the things I like most about you, Jack. Throughout this entire ordeal, you never lost your sense of humor."

"Sarcasm," I chuckle.

"Sarcasm is a way of hiding." Her gaze is intense. "Keep an open mind. You know what I'm talking about, right?"

"Sure I know what you're talking about. Freedom."

Freedom ... That's my new name. Take me as I am or go fuck yourself. I avenged Jenny's death. Now I'm on my way down to Florida. Traveling back roads at night on my bike, full furred, because that's who I am. Jack Bailey. Wheel Wolf.

Jenny

I've been hanging around my house, waiting for Jack to make his decision. I'm upstairs in my room, having one last look around. Everything is just as I left it, pink robe flung across the bed, fuzzy slippers ... one kicked here, the other there. My embroidered jewelry box is in its usual spot on my dresser, glass makeup tray, too. Dusty with eye shadow.

Nothing's been touched. I can't imagine how difficult it is for my folks to be in here. But I don't want my room locked up like a tomb, or turned into a shrine. I'm happy they'll be moving soon. Getting on with their lives. Hopefully in a lively city. I won't let sadness overcome me, we'll be together in time. This is a happy night.

I pause at the doorway, taking a final peek. There's the bedspread Jack and I fooled around on. If only it could talk. My eyes fall on my nightstand, the gum wrappers he left the night of the accident. Hindsight is twenty-twenty. Don't go there, Jenny. No sadness. Life as you knew it is over.

If I had cheeks they'd be warm, tears they would fall. But I don't so I'm heading down the stairs to say my goodbyes. Mom first. She's sitting in the kitchen, hands folded under her chin, elbows on the tabletop. She's staring over a cup of delicious smelling raspberry tea, from the look in her eyes, not seeing anything.

It's funny, the things you miss, like tea. Your nice soft bed. Hugs.

"Mom ... drink your tea before it gets cold. I hope you added honey. It will relax you. Make you sleep better." I let out a sigh, which I know she can't hear. Pause in the doorway, and what she does next surprises me. She pushes her chair out, goes to the pantry and reaches for the jar of honey. I smile. Blow her a kiss and whisper. "I love you, Mom ... Bye."

Wavering in the archway of the living room, I find Dad sacked out on the sofa, mouth open, snoring. I giggle. Dobie is rolled up beside him. Before I even step into the room, Dobie's ears shoot up. He sniffs the air. "Yes, pup. It's me. Take good care of Daddy, okay?" Dobie lets out the tiniest yelp, along with a sleepy yawn. His fat tongue hangs out of his mouth and sweeps his nose. "I'd drop a goody onto that tongue, Dobe, but I'm afraid we're all out." I shake my head. After another yawn, he drags a sloppy lick up the side of Dad's face, lays his head down and burrows closer. "That's a good pup."

I'm on my way through the kitchen door when I spot the whiteboard. Why not give it a try? I scribble a note: Buy Dobie goodies. Love you. J.

No crumbling, Jennifer. You've got a shoulder to ride on, a guy to keep on the straight and narrow.

I hang outside, waiting for Jack to lock up his house. Yup. It's on the market too. Smart move, babe.

Jack is all packed and ready to go. To say packed is an overstatement, because he's carrying only a small duffle he slings over a shoulder. He's dressed in tight leather pants, all muscular and hairy. Wait a second ... no shirt? Not even a jacket?

I want to touch him so bad. It's killing me. Killing me ... Pretty funny, Jenny. I'm laughing. I wonder if Jack hears me. I tangle my fingers in his long dark hair and pull. He stops dead in his tracks and jerks around. Licks a finger and sticks it into the air, like he's testing the direction of the wind.

"It's me!" I call out at the top of my lungs, if I had lungs, that is.

I hang on his shoulder, tug on his ear. No response. I nibble on it. Nothing. But when I reach a hand in front of him, gathering a fistful of delicious chest hair, he whirls around with a questioning expression, but stares right through me.

"Someday we're going to make eye contact." I rub his nose with mine.

I hop on the back of Jack's new bike. A glossy black and chrome Yamaha. Now that's what I call a beast. A beautiful beast. Just like my Jack. I give his mop of hair another tug, breathing in his woody scent. "Strap on your helmet, big boy," I whisper into his ear, which he immediately tugs.

"Yeah, Jack. I'm the itch in your ear." I wrap my arms around his waist. Lay my cheek against his muscular back. "When are you gonna open up those big yellow eyes, Jack Bailey. I'm right here behind you."

I love nights like this. Full moon, gentle breeze, millions of stars cluttering the endless sky.

Jack lights up the bike, and my hair blows wild in the wind as we accelerate. That's one good thing about being a ghost. No helmet needed when riding.

When Jack shouts, "Farewell Bailey Road" I giggle. He thinks he's talking to the night air.

Just before we whiz past the green road sign, our headlight flashes over the fluorescent white letters: *Leaving Angel's Bend*.

"Slow down, Jack." Hugging him tighter, I call through the wind, "It's behind us now."

Dying is the hardest part.

Being dead isn't all that bad. I'm light and airy. Can go wherever I want ... whenever. But I hang around Jack. I'll never leave Jack. He's mine. Forever.

Wheel Wolf

Acknowledgements

To my biggest fan, supporter, helper, proofreader, partner in crime, everything rolled into one very beautiful daughter – inside and out – Phaedra. :-) Her insight and creativity can be found on many of the pages of this book ... and elsewhere. I love you, Phae!

First and foremost, I have to thank my three kids, Cindy, Tom, and Phaedra, who came up with the title *Wheel Wolf* and urged me to write the book. I'll tell you how it all came to be.

After publishing *Beautiful Experiment* in June of this year, I was twenty thousand words into book two of the trilogy, and for some odd reason I just wasn't feeling it. Not that it isn't a fabulous series, but I think I was all "teened out", if that's possible. :D I needed an adult break, and since my first love is horror. Well, there you go!

During our 2013 Fourth of July pool party, I shared my predicament with the kids. The end result: three weeks later *Wheel Wolf* was a completed manuscript of over eighty thousand words. The story poured forth like my favorite drink, diet Pepsi over ice. This just goes to show you: write from the heart. Oh, and listen to your kids ;-)

January Valentine

Two special friends helped with the framework of *Wheel Wolf*. A big thank you to Steve Vera who looked at my cover and loved it, but immediately said: Blood Moon! And voila, a big red moon appeared. Without the tech support of Benedetto Scaffidi-Fonti, I wouldn't have known one end of a motorcycle from the other. Thank you, Ben, for the crash course!

I've never had a *street team*, but I do believe heaven had a hand in bringing three of the most fantastic ladies in the world into my life. Shellie Hedge, Mary Lowery, Tanya Conaway, I cannot thank you enough for your hard work with the launch of Wheel Wolf. A debt of gratitude also goes out to the participants of the astounding Event who helped Wheel Wolf climb even higher on Amazon's list of Bestselling Werewolves & Shifters, Horror, Paranormal and Suspense. A big shout out to Joe Hawkshaw & Kimberly Mayberry, two awesome fans who keep the momentum going for myself and others. You guys rock.

Thank you to the beta readers of my first draft of *Wheel Wolf*, Laura Young and Shellie Hedge, and to my good friend and talented author, Cynthia Lucas, for getting the word out and for her all around awesomeness. xo

A very special thank you to another wonderful writer and good friend, Vic Fortezza, for including my books in his traveling book shop.

Kudos to the amazing artist Vin Hill for creating the front and back covers of my dreams. Yup, I dreamed them and Vin created them.

There are many other wonderful people who have supported and encouraged my efforts as a writer, indie book publisher, and blogtalkradio host, too many to name. But to all my family, friends, acquaintances, readers and fans. Thank you for my the bottom of my heart for your generosity and inspiration.

About The Author

I'm Victoria (January) Valentine, a New York writer and indie book publisher. I've been writing for most of my life in one form or another: poetry, short stories, song lyrics, children's books, adult novels. *Wheel Wolf* is my fifth novel.

My favorite genres to read and write are horror, thrillers, and contemporary romance. Besides being inspired by my family, I owe a shout out to Robert C. Wilson, author of *Crooked Tree*, and Robert McCammon, author of *They Thirst* and other fabulous books. The moment I read their novels, I knew I wanted to write horror.

Besides writing and publishing for others, I blog and when time permits, I host Away With Words on Blogtalkradio on Wednesdays @ 6:00 PM EST USA, where I pimp indie and traditionally published authors and their amazing books and careers. Our gabfests are a blast. You're invited to join us!

Thank you for reading *Wheel Wolf*. A writer would be nowhere without the support of readers and fans. I treasure each and every one of you, and I would love to hear from you!

Indie publishing is not always easy, but it's a blessing. Dear readers ... Thank you from the bottom of my heart for supporting me and my efforts. I hope this book is as thrilling for you as writing it has been for me.